Wolves of Cold Creek

Rebel's

Tail of

Revenge

Brittany Putzer

To those forced to become their own heroes.

Trigger Warning

Rebel's Revenge is a wolf-shifter romance and contains scenes that may be upsetting for some readers. The content includes triggers such as (but not limited to): on-page child sexual assault, attempted suicide while pregnant, sexual assault, torture, murder, death, profanity, violence, graphic sexual activities, demanding alpha men, needy headstrong women, witchcraft, and guardian angels. If any of these items are upsetting to you, please do not read this book.

CONTENTS

Part 1: The Beginning

Freddy

Big Bad Wolf

Present

I tug at my restraints and the cold steel bites into my flesh, reminding me that it's been a long time since I've seen the light of day. I spit a wad of blood onto the floor. Hell, I'd even settle for a functioning lightbulb. But these pricks want to break me: mind, body, and soul. *Let them fucking try*. They want me to grovel at their feet, but I'll never kneel.

The consuming darkness presses in on me, promising a sweet escape. My eyelids grow heavy. *Fuck*. Even my brain has its own damn heartbeat. Blackness edges towards the corners of my vision. I shake my head, shoving the darkness aside. *Don't fall asleep, Freddy!*

But the haunting memories of my past claw their way through my consciousness against my will.

Past

"Hey, buddy." Dad ruffles my hair as he walks by. Then he pulls out the chair next to my mom and rubs his palms together. "This looks amazing, sweetie."

Mom waves off his compliment as usual but color kisses her cheeks. "It's just a pot roast, Rick."

"The meat is so tender it practically melts on the tip of my tongue." He purrs before winking at her. After eating a few more forkfuls, he pivots to me. "How was your day, little man?"

I take my time chewing my roasted potato. I don't want to ruin his cheerfulness with my overriding anger, but I hate that we moved *here* and joined the Fangs' pack. For one thing: there're no kids to play with and it's always cold. I hate being cold. I could fix it by shifting to fur when we walk to the park. But, no, Dad said it would draw too much attention.

"My day was fine," I grumble at my plate.

My father watches me carefully, assessing not only my words but my body language. "Hm." He pats his lips with his napkin. "Freddy, I know you're still adjusting to Carson City with Uncle Spike, but…"

My temper flares and I toss my fork across the room. "He's *not* my uncle! And it's his fault we left our home!"

Mom sighs before grabbing my utensil and handing it to me. She strokes my hair, tugging the shaggy locks out of my eyes. Then she places a kiss on the top of my head. "Honey. We are the only family Spike has left. He needs us right now."

"He's lost his mind," I mutter.

It's the truth. Spike's *brother* attacked an alpha. Then, with his dying breath, he demanded that Spike seek revenge. But instead of going after his brother's murderer, Spike ran away. Dragging my family with him. Lucky us. Now the loser is attempting to assemble

4

his own pack.

"Hey," Dad whispers. "Spike is our leader. Show more respect than that."

There's no arguing with him, so I nod before pushing my dinner around on my plate. Dad's love for his friend clouds his judgement. Carson City is a cesspool of drug dealers, pimps, and hit men. At least that's what mom says. Where we will fall into one of those categories is still unknown. I scratch my nose. Maybe being a pimp would be cool. They're always surrounded by pretty ladies.

The front door slams open, and my throat closes up as Spike drags a beaten human past the threshold, not even bothering to acknowledge us. My potato inches its way from my stomach to my mouth. Once Spike is around the corner, my neck snaps towards my mother. Surely, she won't make me stay here after *this*. But she's staring at my father.

Dad clears his throat and stands. "Don't worry. I'm sure it's just a misunderstanding. I'll check it out." He presses his lips to hers. "I'll be back soon."

"You should take some food to Spike. He looks like he's going to pass out from exhaustion." Mom busies herself as she slaps a piece of steaming meat and a pile of potatoes on a plate and hands it to Dad.

"That's very thoughtful." His hand lingers on hers before he takes the offered dinner. "I'm sure our alpha will appreciate it." Then he strides towards the carnage before looking back. "It might be a little bit. Don't wait up for me."

I don't know why he bothers to warn us. Dad is always up late. Why can't he just tell Spike no? Shouldn't Dad prioritize Mom and me instead?

"Goodnight," Dad throws over his shoulder as he disappears around the corner.

"You should finish your dinner, Freddy." Mom rubs my arm.

Muffled screams echo in the distance. Mom's eyes grow wide, but she swallows her thoughts and turns on the radio to drown out the noise. I stab a carrot and wonder what that mystery man did wrong…

"How about some homemade ice cream for dessert?" Mom kisses my cheek. "Then we can read a story before bed."

My mood perks up. My mom always knows how to make me feel better.

"You can't just hurt people."

"We have to establish our dominance, Willow. Otherwise, we won't last long here."

"You're going to piss off the wrong human and that's all it'll take for the Guardians to step in and punish us."

"They won't do that."

"Are you willing to risk *my* life or your son's?"

"You worry too much."

"Someone has to, Rick. Because you are letting Spike think *for* you and you're not worrying enough."

Even though their voices are hushed, my wolf hearing picks up every word. I frown as I clutch the sheet to my chin. I've never heard Mom so mad. Dad must have done something bad.

"I have it all under control. I promise. Now, can we please go to bed?"

"Don't you dare make promises you can't keep. You can't see the future, Rick. Stop pretending you can."

"No, because that's your job, right, *witch*?" he snarls.

Mom gasps, and the room sizzles with tension. I hold my breath. He's never called her that like it's a bad thing.

Dad curses to himself. "I'm sorry. I'm just tired of fighting with you."

"Don't use that as an excuse, husband," she sneers, venom lacing her threat. "You're tired? *You*? I gave up everything to be with you. My friends, my family, and everyone I love on the reservation."

"You're my mate," Dad replies. "Where I go, you go."

"I am your mate. But don't you think for one minute that if you put our pup in any unnecessary danger, I won't return to them."

My heart skips a beat. Why would she say that? I know Mom misses her home. Plus, her sister is nice. Aunt Debbie always bakes me peanut butter and chocolate chip cookies and shows me the magic tricks she can do. Well, not *tricks*. She and Mom come from a long line of powerful spellcasters. And every now and then, a witch is blessed with shifter abilities too. I guess it's based on a legend of an ancestor falling in love with a shifter and running off together. Either way, Mom can shift and has extra abilities. Nothing cool like flying or disappearing. But she can slow or speed up time. That's how she can cook so much food at once and clean the house super-fast. It's pretty awesome. Aunt Debbie says they can even make potions with the right items. I asked her if I'd be able to do that one day too, but she said only *girls* get the gift.

"Are you questioning my abilities to protect my pack?" Dad pulls me back to the issue at hand.

"What pack?" Mom hisses. "There's us, one other family, and Spike."

"It's a start."

"I'm not arguing about this again. I came here with you so you can help your best friend heal over the loss of his brother, not watch as you hurt innocent people for him."

"They weren't innocent! They raped and killed…"

"Then it's the police's job to put them behind bars."

"You don't understand."

"Obviously," Mom huffs.

"Hey. I'm going to make this right. You'll see."

"Well, until then, you can sleep with Freddy."

Mom's normally light footsteps stomp towards their bed. The silence swallows the oxygen in the space. My mattress creaks and Dad sighs.

"You shouldn't eavesdrop, Fredrick."

I sit up and tilt my head at his defeated expression. "Why are you guys fighting? I thought you loved each other."

He chuckles and pats my knee. "You can argue and still love someone."

I won't mention that they never used to fight before we moved here. Instead, I say, "I don't like it when you fight."

"Me either." Dad removes his shoes before he squeezes in next to me on the tiny bed. "Don't worry, son. I'll make everything right." He wraps an arm under my neck and pulls me into a hug. "The Fangs never give up. No matter what."

A yawn escapes my mouth as I burrow into him, believing every word. He's my dad, my hero.

"How much longer do I need to keep my eyes covered?" Mom

asks, a smile brightening her face.

Dad squeezes her hand as he tugs her forward. "A little longer, love." He presses a kiss to her wrist.

We've been walking for over an hour. My feet hurt and the gray clouds promise a storm is brewing. I grind my teeth. Of course, Dad couldn't buy me new shoes before our family outing. If it rains now, the holes in these soles will do nothing to protect my sore muscles.

"I hope they have ice cream where we are going," I grumble.

Dad shoots me a warning look. "Freddy, we ate before we left the compound."

"That was forever ago." I kick a pebble and it bounces against the broken sidewalk.

"Fredrick," Dad growls my full name as his last warning.

I roll my eyes and continue to follow him. Our footsteps echo down the drab streets. A rat the size of a cat scurries in the shadows towards a moldy dumpster. I huff out a snort. Why do Spike and Dad want to build a life *here*? It's filled with homeless nothings. We turn another corner and slowly the surroundings begin to morph into towering industrial buildings and skyscrapers. The pothole-etched streets curve into sleek asphalt with shiny cars adorning them.

"Where are we?" I whisper.

"It's still Carson City," Dad explains.

"It looks completely different." My eyes widen as signs flash in the distance, advertising the newest movies and accompanying salty snacks. "Are we going to the cinema?"

Dad ruffles my hair. "No hints."

Thunder rolls in the distance and lightning kisses the sky. "Will we get there *before* the rain?"

"I sure hope so." And for once, my dad looks worried as he picks

9

up his pace. He suddenly stops and holds out his arms wide. "Here we are!"

I scan the brick building with its massive billboard announcing their production of *Little Red Riding Hood*. I groan. He took us to a musical. Great.

I cover my ears as Mom squeals. She jumps up and down, her eyes twinkling with tears. "Rick!" She flings her arms around his neck. "I've always wanted to see this."

"I know, baby doll." His lips graze her neck. "Tell me you're happy."

"I am!"

He pulls away to look into her eyes. "Things may be difficult at the compound right now, but we can always leave that behind and travel into town to get away for a bit, right?"

Mom melts into him.

My nose twitches. *Oh, sweet Luna.* "Dad. Can we get some hotdogs?"

"I paid a small fortune for these tickets, buddy. I don't have enough money for all of us to have a snack."

Mom squeezes Dad's wrist, then smiles at me. "Maybe we can buy just one, for Freddy?"

I grin at her. Best mom ever. She always has my back. Dad always gives her what she wants when she uses that voice. I know magic swims in her veins, and I swear she uses it when she speaks like that.

Dad tugs out his wallet and sifts through his cash. "I have enough for one."

"That's all we need." Mom snatches it out of his hand while kissing his cheek.

We stroll towards the steaming cart. "One dog with the works," Dad instructs the vendor as mom pays. The man tops the bun off with a bit of everything, and Dad passes me my prize.

I lick my lips before wrapping them around the hot dog. Luna, this tastes like the promised land. Forget the milk and honey. I hope they have pounds of meat in the afterlife.

"Well, the show is starting soon." Dad presses an arm around my neck and mom's waist. "Shall we?"

Mom giggles in response. I peek at them. It's been a while since I've seen them this happy. I dab a napkin on my chin to wipe off the ketchup. Maybe Dad has a point. This move won't be so bad. I shove the rest of the hotdog into my mouth and toss the paper into the trash, eager to watch my hero fulfill his prophecy.

Why do they make musicals so loud and long? I was on the verge of begging my parents to leave early. When the curtains finally closed, we were the last group to exit the theater. Mom called our seats "nose-bleeders" or something like that. But her smile never faltered throughout the performance and Dad never released her hand. I could almost see them breaking out in song and dancing along with the other performers. *Gross*.

Once we make it outside, we halt at the curb.

"Oh no. It's raining." Mom's smile falls.

Raining is an understatement. It's pouring. And dad used the last of his money to buy me that hotdog. So we can't even hail a taxi.

"It's just a little water." Dad waves off her concern. "Think of it as nature's refreshing shower."

"All we need is some shampoo and soap," I grumble.

"We could shift." Mom bites her lip. "It'd be faster."

I look to Dad. He has been adamant about shredding to fur around the humans. The only time he takes his wolf form is when he's working with Spike. I shiver as I recall the bloody paw prints that usually accompany them when they return to the compound.

"Come on, honey," Mom urges. "No one will even notice. We'll change back before we get to the compound."

"Please, Dad," I add.

He sighs and rubs his face before glancing around. "Just carry your clothes in your mouth," he instructs before slipping behind an alley, sticking close to the wall and the overhang that's sheltering us from the downpour.

My heart thrums against my rib cage. I haven't shifted in so long. I miss the wind in my fur. Plus, our tuft acts as the perfect rain gear. We remain in the shadows as we gallop through the city. I love this freedom and the looks humans give us as they run out of our way. We are powerful in these forms. Rulers of their city.

A few blocks away from the compound, we find a corner to change and continue our family trip. I drag a hand through my wet hair, pulling the strands out of my face.

Dad kisses the top of Mom's head. "Did you have fun, love?"

"I did. Thank you for an amazing night."

"We'll have to do it more often. Right, son? Someone has a birthday on the horizon." He elbows my side. "Anywhere you want to go?"

Mom laughs and pats Dad's chest. "You mean to ask Freddy what he wants to eat on his big day, right?" Mom inserts before I can answer. "Your child is a bit of a foodie. If he's fed, he's happy." She winks my way. "We could get some juicy steaks for your birthday. What do you think?"

I shrug. It'd be nice to hunt in the forest and catch my meal, but

I don't want to speak those thoughts and ruin the happy bubble surrounding us. I sneak a peek at my parents. It's nice to see them acting like they used to.

"We'll have to ask if Debbie can come over for the party," Mom sings. Dad and I groan. "Hey. She's my sister and Freddy's only aunt."

"Yes, but she has a mean streak to her," Dad grumbles under his breath, but Mom quickly picks it up.

"And you don't? Don't you dare judge her after everything you've done for Spike."

Dad's face turns red with anger. And the gloves are back on for round two. *Ding, ding.*

I know Mom loves Aunt Deb, but Dad has a point. Debbie is jealous of mom's relationship with her mate, especially since Dad moved us away from their family home. She speaks her mind and I bet she'd let me hunt, instead of cowering in the Warehouse while Dad and Spike do whatever it is *they* do.

"Debbie is more than welcome to visit Freddy for his birthday in Carson City." Dad opens the Warehouse door. Once it clicks closed behind us, locking us in the large echoey building, he continues. "I just need to check with the alpha first."

Mom clenches her fists and I know she's about to dig her heels in. I grab her wrist and catch her attention. "Can we get an ice cream cake? Please?"

She meets my puppy-dog eyes and the anger melts away. Dad says it's my not-so-secret weapon. I've always been great at getting people to do what I want with that look. He also says he plans on helping me develop my talent as I get older. I can't wait for that one-on-one time with him. I mean, I know he's busy getting our pack secure, but I miss what we had before. Playing soccer in the grassy fields. Fishing in the stream…

"Of course you can have ice cream cake." Mom squeezes my

shoulder.

"Willow," Dad whispers in warning. "Get Freddy out of here."

Dread melts the once-calming environment as five shadows emerge from the corners. I square my shoulders and force the dread to morph into blood lust. I bare my teeth at the approaching group. I won't back down from these *humans*.

"Now," Dad snarls before addressing the crowd. "You don't want to do this, Cole."

The biggest man cracks his knuckles. "This is my town, mutt. You've messed with the wrong gang."

I hold back my laughter. Between our shifting abilities and Mom's magic, these men don't stand a chance. They're just lucky Dad is giving them a warning before he kills them.

Two explosive blasts echo around us. Instinctively, I cover my sensitive ears. *What was that?* I see smoke slithering towards the roof from a metal barrel. My eyes grow wide before they slowly turn to my parents.

"Rick!" Mom's scream rips through my shock as she kneels to cradle dad's head. I swallow the bile rising up my throat. Because I'm wrong. She's not cradling his head. She's cradling the place where it once was. Muscle and bone fragments decorate the floor and walls. I twist my body before I retch the contents of my stomach, unable to process what's happening. "Rick, please. You can't leave me! Rick!" Mom sobs as she rocks him. Her body twitching in shock and grief.

"Damn it, Bill." Cole flicks blood from his jacket. "The head? Really?"

"Sorry, boss." The other man shrugs.

"It makes such a fucking mess." Cole sighs before striding towards my mom. He snatches her chin. "When your alpha returns, tell him if he values his pack, he better leave Carson City." He moves his fingers to her cheek. "Because next time I visit, I won't be so nice." That same caressing palm slaps mom's head to the side, leaving an angry red handprint across her face.

"Mom." I shake myself out of my stupor and run to her side.

She whimpers but never meets my gaze. She just holds on to Dad.

"No wonder Spike let Rick do all of his grunt work. The rest of his pack is too fragile," Cole grunts, and his lackeys chuckle. "Why would he keep a worthless bitch and a scrawny brat at his side, then challenge me? Pathetic."

He shakes his head as he stalks towards the exit. He pauses to light a cigarette, illuminating his prominent chin and dark eyes. I burn those images in my memory, promising to make him pay. "Tie the bitch to the alpha's bed and rough up the kid. It'll be our last gift to Spike." Then he takes a drag and puffs the smoke out of his nostrils.

Before I can consider shifting to my beast form, a fist collides with my stomach and I'm dragged through my dad's blood by the collar of my shirt. I bite back my whimper. I won't let them have the satisfaction of hearing it. The exit clicks closed, and I know my chance of seeking revenge is gone. For now. Another hit from the brute holding me down knocks the wind out of me.

"Stop!" The sound of Mom struggling to break free echoes around the compound. "You monsters!"

Her scream fuels my fur and fangs to poke through. But rippling pain has me quickly shifting back to human form. "Mom…" I wheeze, trying to warn her as another man approaches from behind with a long piece of rope swinging from his arm.

She pivots and meets my tear-stained face. "Freddy!"

"Knock her out before she can shift!" The man pauses his assault on me to shout to his friends.

Mom closes her eyes and raises her hands. Energy sizzles around

15

us, threatening to boil our blood. She's calling upon her magical gifts. But I've never felt her reach for this much before. Even the hair on my arms vibrates in fear.

"I don't need to shift to tear you to pieces," she breathes out in a venomous hiss. I know she's the one speaking, but the voice isn't hers. Her eyes pop open and the men take a step back. Her once icy-blue irises are an eerie inky black.

"Shit." A gang member drops the rope to steady his trembling hold on his gun. "This bitch is into witchcraft!"

His trigger finger twitches and I scream. *Please, Luna, don't let him kill my mother. She's all I have left.* When his finger presses the trigger, the bullet is released, but freezes midair before bouncing off his boot.

"Preying on innocent women and children is pathetic," she snarls, exposing fangs. "Now it's my turn." Her lip twitches into a grin. "This is for murdering my mate."

Before he can blink, Mom lunges at him. He doesn't move as her canines sink into his thick neck. Terror flashes over his face as he realizes his end is near.

"Please." His screams gurgle while his hands clasp the oozing wound.

I swallow hard, unable to think straight. Even as the light leaves his eyes, Mom's chaos ensues around us.

"Mom?" My jaw falls open at the limbs littering the floor like discarded furniture, while the pints of human blood under our feet become our new carpet.

"Police! Put your hands up!"

My neck snaps towards the entrance of the compound. *Who called them?* Maybe a nervous store owner or passerby? The cops don't miss a beat as they fire their tasers at Mom. Terror grips my heart. The shock wave of multiple weapons causes her to drop to her knees with a thud.

"Mom!" I leap to her side. "Are you okay?" I shake her arm, begging her to answer me.

Her black eyes flicker as the magic disappears. Then her sky-blue eyes meet mine. She attempts to smile at me, but her body convulses, and she passes out.

"Don't worry, son. We've got you. You're safe." A cop snatches me by the waist and tugs me away from my mother's limp frame.

"Let me go!" I shout as I kick at him.

"It's okay." He passes me to someone else before checking my mom's pulse. "She's out cold. Let's get her medical attention."

More men pour in, working quickly to wrap her in linens and strap her down with silver buckles. *Where* are they taking her?

"Thank you, officers," the male voice rumbles against my ear. "She's been slowly losing her mental capabilities for months now. It's a shame it came down to this. I'd hoped she'd get better."

I snarl and bite the arm holding me back. "Let me go! She's not sick!"

A palm clamps down over my mouth with a resounding slap. "What will happen to the boy now that his parents are... unwell?"

The cop sifts through mom's purse. "We'll run her license to check who her next of kin is and go from there." The officer reaches out to me.

"Could you give me a moment with him? Maybe I can calm him down for you."

"And *who* are you exactly?"

"How silly of me." He offers the officer his free hand. "My name's Spike Fangs. The boy and his parents were living here with me until this unfortunate incident. He's like a son to me and I've aways been

17

an uncle figure in his life." His voice drips with a false pleading.

"I'll give you five minutes. Then I'm taking him to the station until we can locate a blood relative."

Paramedics rush through, checking the bodies for any signs of life. I swallow the lump in my throat as they touch my dad's wrist. Spike waits until the men in uniform are out of earshot before he glares at me. I want to scream at him for putting us in this awful situation. And remind him he's a bad, *bad* man.

"Shut the fuck up, or you'll be on the ground next to your father." Spike removes his fingers from my lips and sets me on my feet.

"You let them take her." I stab my pointer finger into his chest. "I hate you."

"Your mother tapped into too much magic and now she is no longer your mom, but a shell of herself filled with rage and murderous intentions. She would have killed you next."

"I don't believe you." My fists slam into his hard stomach.

"You don't have to believe me, boy." He grabs my shoulders with an iron grip until I meet his eyes. "What's done is *done*."

"You can't tell me what to do! I'll just shift and run away!" I threaten. "Then I'll free her!"

Spike shakes me and my teeth clank together. "The fuck you will! This is the way this is going down. You will go with the officers, settle in with your aunt, and then return to me."

"Have you lost your mind?" I sneer. "I *hate* you. I want nothing to do with your plans."

"Shut up." His alpha tone tingles down my spine. "I'm still your leader, even with your parents gone."

"My mom is not gone!"

"Mentally, she is in another world." He nods towards my dad's headless frame. "It's our job to avenge him. We will hunt down his killer and make them pay with their life and the lives of those they care about."

For a single moment, agony flashes over Spike's face and my anger falters. He loved my dad like a brother. He even cared for my mother. I swallow my pride. And if I'm going to get my revenge, I'm going to need Spike's assistance. And maybe I can convince my aunt to lend her magical powers to help me free Mom. Either way I look at the situation, I have to do what Spike wants, for now. While formulating my own agenda under his nose.

Mom and Dad moved here to be a part of the Fangs and I won't let them down. I'll grow strong and make them proud.

"I still hate you." I narrow my eyes at my self-imposed uncle.

"Every story requires a villain." He glances over at the approaching cop. "Just use that rage to help you get through the next few days." He assesses my blood-stained face. "I should have been here tonight."

That's as close to an *I'm sorry* as I'm going to get. I allow the officer to lead me to his police car. I glance over my shoulder to see Spike watching us with his hands tucked into his pockets. He dips his head as a silent promise. We *will* get our revenge and rid this city of the murderous scum lurking in the shadows.

But first…

We must grieve.

Freddy

Companion

Present

I suck in a breath as I regain consciousness, but my lungs protest from inside my bruised chest.

"See? I told you the son-of-a-bitch wasn't dead." The soldier's meaty fist slams into my cheek and my neck cracks to the side. "Aw, Freddy, where did you go, buddy?" he taunts, his nose almost touching the tip of my broken one. "Did you think you could escape us that easily after the bullshit you pulled?"

I jerk my arms forward, the chains around my wrists pulling tight. He leaps back, terror radiating off him in waves. "Pussy." I spit blood at his feet. "Those are some tough words coming from the little princess slapping around a drugged shifter in restraints."

Rage flashes in his gaze before he retracts his knuckles, then smashes them into my face. Forcing my nightmares to resurface.

Past

"He is skipping class *again*," Aunt Debbie seethes into the phone currently clutched in her hands. "*You* may not care about his education, but I'm his guardian and I say he needs to stay in school." She pinches the bridge of her nose. "Don't you dare threaten me, you pompous prick." She sighs and glances at me. "If I agree to assist you in this mission, you'll have to swear to me that you'll make him go to school *every* day." Her voice rises to the pitch only cats can hear. "Yes! It is necessary!"

I scrape my fork over my plate. It's been three months since Dad died and Mom was institutionalized. The doctors said the traumatic event fractured her mental stability, and even with treatment, they don't think she'll recover. But I don't believe them. They're only keeping her behind padded doors because of the havoc they fear she'll wreak if she's provoked.

I stare at my hands. *I miss my parents.*

Debbie watches me at her house on the reservation in Cold Creek during the boring school days, and Spike trains me in Carson City on the weekends. I'm still a member of his pack, but technically, I reside inside the Tala pack's territory. It's complicated but I'm a kid and don't have a choice in anything that goes on around me.

I don't notice that Aunt Debbie's hung up the phone until she sits back in her chair at the dinner table. She taps her nails on the wooden surface as she stares at the wall. I wish I knew what Spike asked her to do for him. It probably involves her magic.

"Are you ever going to talk to Frost about me living here with you?"

Aunt Debbie blinks out of her thoughts. "No. The Tala's alpha is too busy with his pack. He won't notice your scent. Plus, I don't want to stir trouble between him and Spike. They already have a bloody history and there's no reason to add fuel to that fire."

"Won't that get you in trouble if Frost finds out?"

She snorts. "My abilities will keep our secrets hidden from him."

I return my attention to my cold dinner. "You probably want Frost to find out I'm living here, so I'm forced from your house and gone from your life for good."

Aunt Debbie squeezes my wrist until I meet her gaze. "Don't say that. I love you, Fredrick. What happened to your parents is horrible and I won't risk something similar happening to you. I promised your mother a long time ago that I'd watch over you and I don't break my promises."

I tug my arm away. "It's Freddy, not Fredrick."

She purses her lips, then slides over a bowl of stinky peas. "Don't forget to eat your vegetables."

"I don't like them."

"Why not?"

I wrinkle my nose. "They are green and smell funny."

Aunt Debbie ignores me and scoops some onto my plate. One green terror rolls off the table and onto the floor. "They'll help you grow big and strong."

"Or they'll make me sick."

"You are not leaving this table until you eat them all." She gives me her best *try me* eyebrow raise.

"Mom wouldn't make me eat them," I snarl.

Aunt Debbie gasps as if I slapped her. Then clears her throat and pushes to her feet. "You act as if you are the only one mourning their loss," she snaps. "But I lost my only sister."

I slam my fists, sending the plate—still piled high with my green nemesis—onto the floor with a crash. "Mom's still alive! Stop acting as if she's dead."

We glare at each other, our fury identical. "Don't you think if I

23

could save her, I would? I've searched every single spell book and not one has helped her. *Not* one," she reiterates as her lip trembles. "Fredrick. She's my *sister*. I ought to be able to save her. But I can't." She swipes her wet cheeks. "So, we must move on until I can find a way to break her out of her mental prison." Aunt Debbie straightens her spine. "For now, we'll do what she would want us to do. Which is to live our lives. And that includes you going to class every day until you graduate."

Aunt Debbie said she's *tried* spells on Mom. Hope rises in my chest. My aunt *does* believe there's a chance to save Mom and she's not giving up. She's on my side.

I cross my arms over my chest and lean back in my seat. "Fine, I'll graduate. But I'm not eating the disgusting peas."

"Get off your ass. We're leaving," Spike calls down to me.

"But you *ordered* me to work on my English assignment." I glance up from my homework and sigh. "Make up your mind!" I shout, while eyeing him at the top of the stairs where his loft is located.

Yes, *his*. The master bedroom, huge bathroom, comfortable living room, and spacious kitchen. While *I* sleep downstairs in one of the few spaces with a door. I think it used to be the office. Then again, at least I have a bed. Most of the other pack members sleep on the cold concrete floor. Spike claims it's until they've earned their place in the hierarchy by proving themselves loyal followers. But I think it's because he doesn't know where to stick them or if they'll last long in the frigid winter. The Warehouse is no place to live long-term but here we are. We, as in me and a few other orphans that Spike's collected over the years since Dad died.

I roll the kink out of my shoulders. It's becoming a little easier knowing Dad isn't around. Don't get me wrong, I still miss him. But as time ticks away, the pain is less and less. I refocus my attention on the blank sheet of paper. Stupid essay. I wish it would die next. I rub my temples as a headache builds. I hate dealing with grammar. Adjectives and proper nouns can suck it.

"Don't make me tell you twice, boy." Spike stomps down the stairs, two at a time. "You can complete your schoolwork when we return."

I scramble to my feet as he snatches a few knives and some rope from our arsenal.

"Tanner, we will be back in a few hours. Make sure my dinner is ready when I return." Spike doesn't wait for the other boy to respond before he smacks the back of my head. "Get your ass moving."

I quickly lace my boots and grab my dagger. I flip it handle over blade, the silver catching the overhead light. "Where to?"

Spike nods to the exit and strides out with me on his heels. Once we are past the threshold, he grunts to the older man guarding the entrance. The pack member's rifle shines in the moonlight. I'm glad Spike finally took Aunt Debbie's advice about adding more protection around the Warehouse, especially after Cole and his goons attacked. I side-glance the man. Not that I trust *him* to keep anything out.

"I've located Cole," Spike says. I squeeze the hilt of my knife. *Yes, finally.* "He's been taking junkies' kids to the motel on 7th Street in exchange for drugs."

What does he want from them?

"My sources tell me he grabbed a little girl an hour ago."

I pick up my pace, eager to get to her before Cole can get his bloody hands on another innocent kid. I stutter a step. "Wait. You said he's *taking* kids?"

"Yes. So, you'll deal with the worthless father while I take Cole." Spike cracks his knuckles in anticipation.

I bite back the urge to demand to help him with Cole's inevitable death. I've learned you must be strategic with Spike if you want it your way. "That's a good plan."

He side-eyes me as we turn the corner. "I'm sensing a *but*. Do I want to know why?"

"Well, the kid will be scared and need to see someone a little closer to their age. Especially if Cole's already hurt her."

"I don't think Cole can handle *this* girl."

Now it's my turn to stare at him. "Why?"

"She's a shifter."

That's why he's not waiting to catch Cole *after* he's done his dirty deeds and why he's punishing the neglectful father. He wants the pup to join our ranks. *Smart.*

Raindrops kiss the tops of our heads as the motel comes into view. My nose twitches while the scent of decaying flesh stings my nostrils. I scan the dark area for its source. *Please be a rat.* When a person dies, the mess and stink linger longer. Spike pauses as he senses it too. Soon, we spot a man leaning against the peeling paint of the building.

Spike kneels and taps his finger over the figure's neck. "No pulse." He glances around. "He might be the pup's father. And if he is, she should be close by."

I frown at the body. Now the female is truly an orphan. I clench my fists. Did Cole plan to not only hurt the girl but also murder her father? Just like he killed mine. I search the man's pockets but come out empty-handed.

"Don't bother looking for anything worthwhile. He was an addict." Spike snorts. "He doesn't have anything of value, except for the pup." He strides towards the motel without a backward glance.

I yank the gold band from the dead man's ring finger and pocket it. I can pawn it later. But my heart tugs at another thought. I can gift it to the girl. I can give her *something* of her father's. No matter how big of a fuckup he might have been, I'm sure she cared for him.

Spike slams his shoulder into the closest motel room and the door explodes off its hinges.

"Shit." I jog towards the chaos to help the alpha.

"Hello, *Cole*." Spike's fangs elongate as he eyes our prey. "It's been far too long, old friend."

And there's my father's killer. Naked, dirty, and torturing an innocent girl's soul.

Before Cole can blink, fur tears through Spike's skin. His canines sink into the drug dealer's erect penis. Cole screams in agony. *Ah. Music to my ears.* And crimson splatters the walls in sweeping motions, like a canvas with a fresh splash of paint. I drag my fingers through the warm substance and lick the tangy liquid.

"Please," Cole whispers as his life force continues to seep into the dusty carpet.

His hand reaches for Spike but thumps to his side as he wheezes for breath. I watch as the light completely leaves the douchebag's eyes. "I hope you rot in hell." I spit on his face.

"Freddy!" Spike's human form snaps me to attention. *When did he change back?*

I follow his line of sight and jump onto the bed. The thin frame hiding under the covers vibrates with terror. From the fluids lingering on the sheets, it looks like we didn't arrive in time to stop Cole from hurting the girl. My heart clenches. This pup has had a rough start in life. I take a deep breath. I should be patient with her. I bite my lip. But patience isn't my strongest virtue.

What would Mom do in this situation?

"Hey. It's okay," I soothe. "We won't hurt you." I slowly pull down the blanket, revealing a set of puppy-sized, tear-stained eyes. "My name's Freddy. What's yours?"

Her lip quivers as she glances behind me towards Cole's lifeless body. "He hurt me." She swipes the snot dripping from her nose.

"If you come with us, we'll protect you." I nod to Spike, who's impatiently stomping his foot. "We'll even teach you how to fight. That way, no one can hurt you again."

She assesses my face and my heart stutters. There's something about her that just screams *home*. It's as if the universe brought us together. Maybe to ease each other's burdens in this shitty life. She stands on shaky legs, but her knees buckle, and she falls into my arms.

"I've got you," I whisper in her ear as she trembles again.

"*Carry* her, boy," Spike snaps. "It's not far." Spike pivots to the exit. "We need to leave before the police arrive."

I cradle the girl to my chest. Her bones stick out of her thin skin, and I worry I may break her. "Are you able to shift?"

"I'm not allowed to change to fur. Daddy won't let me. He says people will notice and take me away." She sniffles. "I haven't changed in a long time."

I clench my jaw. That must have been painful for the pup to mute her beast. They are a part of our souls. We need each other to be whole. "Don't worry about your dad."

"What happened to him?" She rubs her eyes and yawns.

"The drugs he loved finally brought him down."

She tenses and whimpers. "Just like Mama."

"I'm sorry. They didn't deserve you."

She wraps her arms around me. "Thank you for saving me."

I don't tell her I had no choice. That I'm not a hero. I can't. Not when she's looking at me like that. "What's your name?" I say instead.

"Angelica."

I love that name. I take in her blonde hair that acts as her own halo. It suits her. "Well, Angelica, you're one of us now, and we will look after each other from now on."

"Do we get to eat?"

"Are you hungry?"

She nuzzles her face into my neck, and I feel her cheeks heat from embarrassment. "Yes."

I tilt her chin up. "Don't worry. I'll make sure you have everything you need," I say with more confidence than I have.

"Wait!" Angelica shouts before wiggling out of my arms. The farther she walks away from me, the greater the ache in my heart grows. I miss her already. "The bad man has money." She splashes through the blood and kneels. She tugs out a wad of bills and waves it in the air triumphantly.

Pride bursts through my chest as I nod my head in approval. "You'll fit in just fine with the Fangs." I pocket the cash and then lift her back into my arms. "Let's go home."

"Is she *mute*?" Spike barks. "She hasn't spoken a single word in over a week. Not to mention, I have to shove food down her throat." He paces the loft.

Broken. That's what Angelica is. Once we settled her in the Warehouse and the adrenaline wore off, she shattered into a million pieces. She cried for three days, only stopping when she passed out. Even if her dad was a dead beat and sold her to his drug dealer, her loyalty towards him is strong. I admire that.

"She just needs time to adjust."

"Every member contributes. That's the rule. And my patience is wearing thin."

My heart clenches in my chest. What does he plan on doing with her? Surely he wouldn't kill her.

"Do you think she might thrive with another pack?" I know I am treading on thin ice with this question, but I need to know what he's thinking.

Spike's eyes lock on to mine. "And have her give them all of our secrets? No."

I wait for him to divulge his plans for the girl, but he just continues to pace.

"Let me try talking to her again. Maybe if I explain the way things work here, she'll snap out of it."

"Fine." He waves me out of the room.

I dip my chin and back out of the loft to head down the stairs. The way things are going right now, I'll be beta of the pack when I reach maturity. Rightfully so. I do most of Spike's grunt work, just like Dad did. And since I'm still considered a kid, no one suspects little old me.

When I reach the ground floor, I scan the area until I spot the golden goddess huddled in a dark corner.

"Are you hungry?" I sit beside her. "I stole some bread earlier and Spike killed a few rats."

She shakes her head. The silence is suffocating. Where's the girl who swiped a dead guy's wallet? What can break the spell strangling her spirit?

Maybe she just needs to know she can trust someone. That the world isn't all that fucked up?

"Do you want to see something cool?" When she remains stoic, I offer, "If you can't walk, can I carry you?"

I reach under her armpits. She tenses but doesn't fight me as I hold her in my arms, just like I did when I rescued her from Cole. I kick open my door and set her on my messy bed so I can rummage around the piles of odds and ends on the floor.

"Here it is." I lower myself down next to her. "Open your hand."

She bites her lip in response.

"I promise it's not a trick. If you don't like what I give you, you have my permission to punch me." I tap my cheek.

"I could never hurt you," she croaks.

"Why not?" The question just slips out. Everyone around here hurts me, one way or another. Why would she be any different?

Angelica glances at her bare feet. "Because you're special."

She must not know many people. "Just open your hand," I repeat.

Her palm trembles, but she does as I say. I plop the gift onto her soft skin and close her fingers around it. She opens her hand and tilts her head. She twirls the gold ring between her pointer and thumb. "It's too big for me to wear."

"Do you recognize it?"

She blinks at the jewelry. "No. Should I?"

Shit. Maybe I was wrong to keep it. "It was your Dad's."

She jolts and reexamines the ring. Several minutes later, tears well in her eyes and she cradles the memento to her chest. "Thank you, Freddy."

My name on her lips stirs so many emotions, but I press them down and shrug. "I'll swipe a pretty necklace so you can wear it around your neck."

31

Angelica yawns and snuggles into my ragged comforter. "Can I sleep with you? It's nicer in here."

Nothing is scarier than giving up the *one* thing you have all to yourself. But for her... with those sad blue eyes... "You can stay for the night." I push past the lump in my throat. "If you make me a promise."

"What?"

"That you'll eat and meet the other pack members."

"I don't belong here, and everyone knows it."

"Who said that?" I bristle at the thought. "We are all orphans of Carson City. The town's abandoned outcasts."

The words settle around us until Angelica tilts her head to look at me again. "I don't think we are. I think we are *rebels*."

"I like the sound of that." I smirk as a spark ignites in her eyes. "And one day, we'll rule them all."

She wrinkles her nose. "Why would we want to do that?"

"Duh. For the power and control. Then we'll never be nobodies, and they can't have the power to hurt us."

"How did they hurt you?" she whispers, almost as if she's afraid of the answer.

Fuck. I haven't told anyone in so long. The memory battles its way forward, but I punch it down.

"Long story short, the man your dad... brought you to... he was the same asshole who murdered my father and caused my mother to go into the hospital."

Angelica grabs my wrist. "I'm sorry."

"Don't be. I got my revenge. And one day, when my mom is better, we'll be together again."

"Can I live with you and your mom too?"

"If you want."

Angelica leaps onto my lap and wraps her arms around me. "I want to go wherever *you* go. Promise me you won't leave me behind. Ever."

I don't deserve her affection. I'm a nobody. "What about our alpha and our pack?"

She meets my gaze. "You are *my* pack. *You* are my alpha."

Pride fills my heart as her undiluted trust washes over me.

"One day, Freddy, we will take over and be the rebels we were forced to become."

"If we are going to do that, first we have to trick Spike into trusting us. It may be painful and feel deceitful, but as long as we are working together, it'll be worth it in the end."

"We just have to survive until then," she whispers against my heartbeat as if willing the organ to never give up or go out.

"The rebels will survive," I proclaim. "And we will get our revenge."

Angelica

Flashback

A scream rips through my throat as an inferno of pain consumes my body.

"Hurry! Before she bleeds out!"

I force myself to focus on the voice, but my vision is overcome by a blanket of darkness.

"If you don't have the money, old man, you're not getting shit."

"Please." Dad shakes as I clutch his sweaty palm. "I just need a hit."

"No cash, no product."

"Fuck, she's losing too much blood!"

"Do everything you can. If she dies, the General will have our asses!"

"Daddy?" I tremble against his chest, but he doesn't respond. I place my ear over his heart. He's sleeping, so I sneak into his bag and sift through our belongings, hoping to find a snack to curb the clawing vacancy in my stomach.

Oh, are those crackers?

I shriek as my wrist is pulled behind me, and I stumble to the cold concrete.

"Get the fuck out of there!"

I slink into myself. Don't take it to heart. Dad gets this way when he doesn't take his medicine. It'll pass.

"It's been two days since we ate. Please. I'm so hungry," I beg, even though I know it's useless when he's mad.

"Keep your paws off my stuff, you ungrateful brat."

"Her vitals are stabilizing."

"Inject her with the anti-shifting serum."

"Are you sure her body can handle it?"

"We can't have her shredding to fur. She'll maul everyone in the facility."

Another round of flames ignites under my skin. I open my mouth to scream, but the blackness of my dreams swallows my consciousness again.

"*Do you have it?*" *Dad peers around the corner as he holds out a palm.*

"*Do you have what we agreed to?*" *the stranger asks, and Dad tugs me forward.* "*And she's still innocent?*" *The man runs a knuckle across my jawline.*

"*Yes, yes. Now give me what you promised.*"

"*Half now and half after I get my fill.*"

I watch as a tiny baggie is tossed in my father's direction. He inspects the contents before turning to me. "*Angelica, you're going with my friend.*"

My eyes turn to saucers as I warm my dad's side. "*But you told me not to talk to strangers.*"

He shoves me away. "*I also told you to do as you're told.*"

The other man kneels in front of me and smiles. "*Are you hungry?*" *He pulls out the biggest roll of money I've ever seen.* "*If you spend some time with me, I'll buy you dinner.*"

Fear tingles my spine but the ache in my belly is stronger. "*Can I eat anything I want?*"

He runs a hand through my blonde hair until it catches on a knot. "*What is it you desire, beautiful?*"

Saliva pools in my mouth as I imagine a buffet of goodies. "*Ice cream!*" *I shake my head, knowing that won't fill me up or last very long.* "*No, I want cheeseburgers!*"

"*What if I told you, you could have both? Would that make you happy?*" *He grins as he holds out his palm.* "*And I promise I'll bring you back to your dad after we're done.*"

"*Can we eat before?*" *I clutch my growling abdomen.*

"*Sorry, sweets, that's not the deal. So, what'll it be?*"

My fingers wrap around his large hand. "*Okay.*"

He leads me to a small hotel room. It smells like pee, but it's better than our tent on the corner of the street. The door clicks closed, and the man pivots in my direction while waving a hand over the length of my body. "Take off your clothes."

"But…"

"Either you follow my instructions the first time, or I'll have to punish you. Do you understand me?"

"Punish me? How?"

He sits on the bed and pats his thighs. Before I can scurry off, he snatches my wrist and lays me face down across his lap. Then he tugs off my pants and slaps my butt. I scream and kick wildly. He hits me again. "The more you resist me, the harder I'm going to spank you."

I whimper while doing my best to remain still.

"That's my good girl." His fingers separate my thighs, and he tickles my private area. The feeling is strange. I have to resist the urge to squirm, so he doesn't hit me again. "Has anyone touched you here before?"

I shake my head, too scared to voice my reply.

"I want you to take off your clothes and shower. Make sure you clean everywhere. Then lie on the bed. Do you understand me?"

I leap off the man's lap and dash into the bathroom. It's been a while since I washed myself, and it takes a few attempts to turn on the shower. But soon the steam rises and I stand under the spraying water. I take my time massaging my scalp with the floral shampoo and then the white bar of soap. When I get out of the shower, I'm surprised to see the man leaning on the bathroom counter watching my every move. I ignore his gaze and return to the bed like he instructed. When my head hits the lumpy pillow, he enters the room again.

His dark shadow looms over my petite frame. "Remember what

I told you? You will listen or you will be punished. Now close your eyes, beautiful."

I do as I'm told. There's a ruffling sound and then the mattress dips with the added weight.

"Spread your legs."

Once again, I comply until something cold taps my thigh. My eyes shoot open, and I watch as the stranger sniffs me. I squeeze my eyes closed, so he doesn't hit me. Then I hear slurping sounds coming from near my stomach.

"You like when I do that, don't you?" His finger tickles my opening, and I press my legs together involuntarily. "Do you want another spanking?"

Alarm bells are going off inside my head. I whimper, trying to put distance between us.

He slides his body over mine, and this time, he rubs his peeing stick over the same spot he licked. I squirm, attempting to get away from his heaviness. "Relax, beautiful," he soothes. "It'll only take a few minutes, then I'll buy you dinner." He pushes inside me, and the skin between my thighs rips apart.

"Stop!"

He inches farther, splitting me in two.

"It hurts!"

I'd rather go hungry than endure this.

The man grunts. "It was worth every ounce I gave him." He slides out, then slams in again. "You're so fucking tight."

Tears moisten my cheeks as his thrusts grow wild.

Why did Daddy do this? I thought I was his special girl.

Then banging in the background catches the man off guard.

"It's fucking occupied! Find another room!" the man screams over his shoulder, but never pauses his movements.

With an earth-shattering boom, the door splinters off its hinges and the man is thrown to the floor. I curl myself into a ball, not sure what monster is approaching next. Howling from the corner of the room brings my attention to the ongoing battle. A wolf tears off the man's stick. Screams of agony vibrate around the room as blood splatters the walls. Suddenly, the furry creature morphs into human form.

He pivots to me while swiping the crimson from his lips. "What's your name?"

I hide under the dusty sheets and cover my ears. Please let this be a nightmare. I need to wake up.

"Freddy!" the wolfman shouts.

The bed dips, and a finger pokes at my back. "Hey. It's okay. We won't hurt you." The blanket is slowly tugged away from my face, revealing a set of warm eyes. "My name's Freddy. What's yours?"

My lip quivers as I look at the corpse on the floor. "He hurt me."

"If you come with us, we will protect you." He nods to the guy waiting for us at the exit. "We'll even teach you how to fight. That way, no one can ever hurt you again."

His words soothe me, and I go to stand but the pain causes me to crumble.

"I've got you."

"Carry her, boy. It's not far." The other man pivots on his heel before walking out the door. "We need to leave before the police arrive."

Freddy holds me to his chest. "Are you able to shift?"

"I'm not allowed to change to fur. Daddy won't let me. He says people will notice and take me away." I sniffle. "I haven't changed

in a long time."

The boy clenches his jaw. "Don't worry about your dad."

"What happened to him?"

"The drugs he loved finally brought him down."

"Just like Mama."

"I'm sorry. They didn't deserve you."

I wrap my arms around the boy. "Thank you for saving me."

He brushes off my gratitude and asks, "What's your name?"

"Angelica."

He assesses my matted hair, then stares into my eyes. "Well, Angelica, you're one of us now, and we will look after each other from now on."

"Do we get to eat?"

"Are you hungry?"

I burrow my face into his neck. "Yes."

"Don't worry. I'll make sure you have everything you need."

"Wait!" I shout, wiggling from his hold and onto my feet. He arches a brow. "The bad man has money." I splash through the blood, making my way towards the man's pants. I tug out the wad of paper bills.

Freddy grins. "You'll fit in just fine with the Fangs."

Angelica

Gone

It's been decades since I've thought about my parents and what happened to them. But even now, the pain is still there and the haunting memories slide over my cheeks.

"Easy," a male voice warns me.

I brush my tears away, clearing my vision. My blood runs cold. *No.*

"Where am I?"

"Drink this." A straw scratches my dry lips. "It's water."

My nose twitches as the scent of rubbing alcohol stings my senses, and I glance around the pale-gray room with a single barred window. *Am I in jail?* I massage my scalp, in an attempt to focus, but my brain is too foggy. *Was I arrested?*

"Where the fuck am I?"

"Don't cause a scene, okay?" The male looks around before

returning his glare to me. "I'm not your enemy. I'm just doing what I'm told."

I narrow my eyes at him. He appears younger than I am and is dressed in a pristine white lab coat. His name tag informs me that he's a doctor. Though I am not sure what kind.

"Do you prey on innocent women for fun or is that a part of your job description too?"

He purses his lips. "I'm trying to help you."

"Help? Help!" I spit in his face. "Fuck you. You've locked me in a cage!"

The metal door slams open and two armed guards stride over.

"No. Please," the doctor pleads. "I startled her. Don't hurt her."

The asshats tase me, until I'm involuntarily drooling at their boots. One of the guards snatches my chin and grins. "You belong to us now." Then he points to a black dot on the ceiling. "And we're watching your every move."

"You're going to hurt the child!" The doctor shoves the two men aside.

Shit. They can't know that I'm pregnant. I didn't even tell my mate yet.

"Once that thing's removed, she's ours," the guard sneers.

"Well, until then, she's in my care and all punishments need *my* authorization." The doctor puffs out his chest.

The two guards share a look and laugh, before the taller of the pair slams my would-be protector against the wall by his neck. "The General hired you to take care of the patients *medically*, but don't forget your place, Doc." He releases his grip and the two guards pivot out of the room.

The doctor coughs and rubs his collar. "Well, they're charming."

"How do you know I'm pregnant?" I demand once I can feel my lips again.

"The General has been keeping tabs on your whereabouts. The moment you left the health clinic in Carson City, he knew you were with child."

"That makes no sense. Why would he do that?"

The General was the official helping Spike, my alpha. But I never attended their meetings and the human male never looked twice in my direction whenever we happened to be in the same room together.

The doctor side-glances the camera before responding. "He wants you to aid his canine army."

Is that what my alpha and mate were discussing before I got shot earlier today at our compound? My fingertips dance over my wound.

"Don't worry. The child is healthy, and your injury is healing."

Images of blood and gore flash through my hazy memory. "Where's my family?"

The man offers me the straw again. This time, I suck the cool liquid and allow it to soothe my throat. "I'm sorry to be the one to tell you this, but they are gone."

"What do you mean *gone*?"

The Fangs are ruthless and rule Carson City. They wouldn't crumble under an attack.

"The General said there were no survivors after the raid on the Warehouse."

The pieces slowly click into place. *The General set us up.* He lent us a bunch of crooked men to help us fight the Tala pack, and in the end, one of his soldiers shot me.

I bare my teeth. "Are you sure? No other injured shifters were brought in?"

"I'm afraid not."

His words sink into my soul as images of Freddy flash through my head. The love of my life. This can't be happening. We were going to rule the fur world together…

My sanity snaps, and I grab anything within my reach and toss it against the wall. I call upon my wolf, but no fur breaks through my skin. Then again, I don't need her. I rip the pillows and blankets, and claw the fluff from the mattress.

"Calm down!" The man attempts to reason with me.

But it's too late.

I've lost *everything*.

My man. My wolf. And now my freedom. If I can't have that, I don't want to live.

I wrap a strip of fabric around my throat. The doctor leaps for me, but I kick him into the wall. He grunts and his body slides to the floor. If my family is gone, there's no reason to be here.

I pull the sheet until no oxygen can reach my brain. Then I succumb to my peaceful end.

Why does heaven have to be so damn bright?

My lids twitch before I peel them open. My new living arrangements consist of white walls, no windows, and a padded door. *I'm not dead.* I try to sit up and stop short. My legs and arms are chained to the bed. *I'm still the General's prisoner.* I tug until bruises form and panic sets in.

"Let me out!" My words echo all around me while the eerie quiet gnaws on my nerves.

What am I going to do? Freddy always told me what to do next. He was the planner. The alpha in my life. The glue that held my broken pieces together and fought the demons that plagued my consciousness. But my mighty king has fallen at the hands of the General.

Even his name stirs bile and rage inside my soul. That fucker is going down, and I'm taking control of my life. I'll claw and bite my way through if I must.

But for now, I'll play the obedient bitch.

The air ices over before the door to my prison creaks open. "There she is. Welcome to the Shifter Defense Unit." The devil himself strides in. "How are you feeling?" He tilts his head. "I heard you made quite the mess in the room I gave you." He tsks his tongue. "And here I thought we could be friends."

I grind my jaw and swallow down the nasty retort about where he could shove that *friendship*. "The news of my pack threw me through a loop. Surely you understand that." I nod towards his wedding ring. "We are loyal to the ones we love."

"You're very observant, mutt."

"But you knew that already, didn't you?" I snap. "Because that night at the Warehouse, you sent your soldiers to kidnap me."

"Did I?" He drags out the last syllable.

I recall the armored lackeys he sent into our home under the false pretense of protecting us from the Tala pack. When I questioned them further, I knew they were on a mission of their own.

The only question is… was it *behind* their boss's back or *with* his approval?

We stare each other down. Two strong-willed individuals trying to one up the other. I'll allow him to win this battle.

47

"I guess it doesn't matter how I ended up here," I grind out. "The important question is now that you have me, what do you want with me?"

"It's simple really." His palm warms my thigh and trails to my stomach. "You'll lie here for the rest of your life." Sweat prickles over my neck. "You'll deliver pup after pup, until your body gives out or one of your children kills you during the birthing process."

Fuck. That wasn't the answer I expected. I bite my lip. *But maybe I can sway his choice.*

"Isn't that a waste of my talents?" I purr. "I'm far more beneficial as a spy."

His laughter sends chills down my spine. "You don't have a fucking choice, *pet*. You are mine to command." His fingers slip under the covers and to the entrance of my core. "Whatever I want, I'll fucking take."

There has to be a folder with my name on it informing the General what happened to me in my past, and now he's using it as a scare tactic to keep me in line. So I change the subject before he can continue to demonstrate that he's in charge. "What are you going to do with my child?"

"It belongs to the government, and it'll serve its purpose when needed." He stands and examines my scowl. "Don't pout. Maybe I'll leash you and assign you to a handler *after* you give birth a few times."

My jaw ticks. I'm no one's plaything. If I'm going to survive, I need to think like a warrior.

A man in a white coat clears his throat as he enters the room. "Sorry to interrupt, sir. But it's time for her medicine."

The General slaps the man on the shoulder. "Take good care of them. They are extra special to me." He winks my way, then leaves as quickly as he appeared.

"Fucking prick." The doctor's white coat flutters behind him as he approaches my bed. He dangles a few pills in my face. "He raised your blood pressure. This will help stabilize it."

That *voice*.

"Were you here when they brought me in?"

"Yes."

He's been by my side since the beginning. Which means he'll be my first target in getting the upper hand. I'll work my charm until he's eating out of my paws.

"What's your name?"

He arches a brow. "Are you going to swallow these pills, or will I have to inject the medication into your system?"

My gaze never leaves his as my tongue slips out. He sets the pills in my mouth and retrieves a glass of water. He then guides the straw to my lips, and I take a healthy swig. "Are you happy now?"

He taps on the machines attached to me before pressing a finger to his cheek. "I'll be happier once your vitals return to a normal range. That serum might also be contributing to this."

"What *serum*?"

He looks over his shoulder. "The one that keeps you from shifting."

"How long does it last?"

"They are still testing it, so I'm not sure." He checks the IV in my hand. "But a pregnant shifter's metabolic rate should burn the chemicals off faster than a normal wolf."

"How will you know when it's out of my system?"

"We can read it in your bloodwork."

This technology he's speaking about is advanced. How long was I passed out for?

"If the poison wasn't utilized on me, I'd congratulate the genius who thought of it," I blurt. "Because it's brilliant."

His jaw ticks. "It's toxic to your kind."

"That's funny coming from the same guy standing over a woman who's chained to a bed against her will."

"I have no say in what they do to you or the others," he snarls.

"We always have a choice."

"Not when the General is threatening your family," he hisses so low I almost don't hear it. My ears perk up. So, the good doctor isn't fond of his boss. *Interesting.* "I'm sorry."

"Well, as long as I follow his orders and deliver a few pups, I'm off the hook. Who is he threatening?"

The doctor looks at the camera in the corner of the sterile room, then back to me. "My siblings. They are both in Basic Training right now, hoping to pass and get into the military."

"That's rough." And I mean it. No one should be forced to do anything against their will, especially when their loved ones are being dangled in front of them.

"Do you have any sisters or brothers?" he asks.

I chew on his question. Is he trying to collect more intel or generally curious? "No. It's just me."

"That must be lonely."

"It wasn't, until they murdered my pack," I whisper to myself.

Warmth spreads over my elbow. I look down and see his hand brushing over my arm. "Hey, you aren't *alone* right now."

Our eyes meet for a second, and then he jogs out of the room. Before I can question his sanity, he returns with a familiar machine. One that I became acquainted with at the free women's health clinic in Carson City.

"May I?" He points to the blanket. I roll my eyes but nod. He lifts the sheet to expose my stomach and dribbles lube on my skin. Then he rolls a Doppler across my tiny bump. "Do you hear that?"

"No."

He turns a dial until a thumping sound echoes around the room. "It's your child's heartbeat." The beautiful serenade brings tears to my eyes. "See? You'll never be alone because you'll have your child."

"Until the General steals it and impregnates me again."

"It's better than the alternative," the doctor says, and I snarl. "He's bleeding his other subjects, attempting to use their blood to power his current army."

"That's disgusting."

"Before that, they were literally *dissecting* shifters to develop the anti-shifting serum."

All those poor wolves... I wish I could claw this IV out of my arm.

"They usually survive, but from what the others have said, it's an extremely painful experience."

Is he trying to ease my discomfort by lying to me? How can you cut something up, only to have it walk away afterwards? My stomach churns. It's impossible. Right? I change the topic before I throw up the pills he gave me.

"Are the other physicians at this facility here against their wills too?"

The man uses a warm cloth to wipe the ooze from my belly. "No."

"Then why are you?"

"Because the General needed an OB/GYN quickly." He nods to my stomach.

"So I'm the reason your family is being threatened."

There go my intentions of luring him into trusting me.

He stares at me for a long minute before shaking his head as if making his mind up. "The *General* is responsible for this mess."

He's right. And that same monster of a man isn't treating me like a living creature. He's drastically diminished my functionality. No longer am I a powerful wolf, just a womb for his twisted breeding program. And to the doctor, I am the key to his family's survival.

The door slams against the wall, and another guard shoves his way inside the room. "Enough of the socializing," he orders as he grabs the doctor's elbow. "The General wants your report on the female *now*."

The doctor tugs his arm free and straightens his back. "All you had to do was ask me nicely, and I would have met you at his office."

The guard walks into the hallway, clearly amused with himself if the laughter that follows him is anything to go by. "You have exactly five seconds to get your scrawny ass to the boss or I'm going to see how many bullets that pretty little mouth of yours can hold."

Once they leave me to my silence again, my head swims with everything I've learned. I'm in deep shit *without* a shovel to work my way out. *Fuck.* I bite my quivering lip, interrupting the worthless stream of tears. I need action. I need to protect my pup.

I send a silent promise to my child. "Somehow, I'll get you out of this place."

Angelica

False Hope

"**Y**ou wanted to get a message to the boss?" The guard crosses his arms over his chest. "What is it?"

"He can't keep her like this." The doctor pins the man with a glare. "It's been months. The catheter is causing recurring urinary tract infections and she runs a huge risk of blood clots."

"It's *your* job to keep everything clean." The guard rolls his eyes and pivots on his boot.

"She'll go into preterm labor if we don't apply preventative measures," the doctor shouts at the guard's back. The door slams shut, leaving us alone again. "They're fucking animals."

"Funny, because they call shifters the animals." I smirk as he injects another dose of antibiotics into my IV.

It's been an eternity since I've stretched my limbs. My gaze flicks down as the doc scribbles notes on his tablet. He's been my only companion. He answers my questions and looks at me as though

I'm a person worth seeing. The one man who's fighting for me and not treating me like an incubator. He even apologizes when he has to prick me with a needle and attempts to be as gentle as possible.

The door beeps before the locks click. And the General saunters in, with his hands in his pockets. He pats my thigh as a greeting but doesn't bother looking at me. "David, what seems to be the problem?"

Well, now I have a *first* name. David. I chew on each syllable and smirk at the man in the white lab coat. He ignores me as he throws a glare at his boss. "Do you even read the daily reports I send you?"

The General shrugs before leaning against the wall. "I'm here now. Tell me, what're the complications?"

"Where should I start?" David racks his hair with a hand. "She needs to be able to move."

"Why?"

David tugs on my discolored wrists. "This is why."

"Does she need arms to pop out a child?"

"She'll need them to hold the infant and breastfeed."

The General waves a dismissive hand. "We'll acquire formula."

"Shifters have completely different biological makeups! You can't simply purchase their milk over the counter. Each pup has specific demands that only their mother can provide."

David's lying out of his ass. Yes, pups need shifter milk. But with supplementation, they've been known to do just fine on human formula.

I hold my breath and wait to see if the General takes the bait…

"You can press the pup to her teat," he grunts.

"I'm a doctor. Not a milkmaid."

The General takes a threatening step forward, a dark expression morphing his features. "You're whatever I say you are."

David holds up his palms in a placating gesture. "You asked me to deliver a *healthy* child. I'm only telling you how to accomplish that objective."

"And if you do well, you'll have a whole facility at your command." The General slaps the doc's shoulder, and the air is sucked out of the room.

Fuck. I'm not the only one getting the shit end of this deal.

"You said after this, I was *free* to go home," David stutters out.

"Think of this as a promotion, soldier."

"But I'm not a soldier. I'm a physician."

Once again, the General waves off David's concern. "I'll allow the bitch to have supervised movements." He strides over to me and snatches my chin in a bruising hold. "If you act up, I'll leash you again, understood?"

He's not the only one to gain intel from lurking in the shadows. From what I've learned, the General rewards loyalty, something I'll need to fake in order to stay under his radar. "I understand. Can I offer any more assistance to the cause?"

His brows rise. "You want to *help*? Why?" He tugs a thumb behind him. "Has the good doctor convinced you to play nice?"

"I want to be here for my child. Even if that means sacrificing my freedom."

The General narrows his eyes at me, attempting to read my blank stare. "I'll consider your proposal." Then he pivots towards the exit. "But you know, your child will have a mission of their own to accomplish. If it's a female, it'll be part of the breeding program. And if it's a male, it'll become a soldier."

None of those options sound ideal. I bite my tongue to keep

myself from speaking my mind. "I understand."

He pauses at the door. "And *if* I allow you to be a part of the child's life, it'll only be temporary, until they are able to fulfill their purpose."

I swallow the scream of rage and bile rising in my throat. "That makes sense."

"And what service will you provide my army?"

I finally give the man an honest smile. "I'll make it rain crimson." I don't clarify whose blood it will be.

He grins his approval. "That's my girl. I look forward to you making good on that promise."

"Me too, General. Me too."

"Take it easy and don't try to move too fast," David instructs, as the bindings are removed from my arms and legs. Sharp pricks of pain shoot through my useless appendages. "The sensation will return soon." He then massages the cold skin in question.

"Why are you looking at me like that?" I snip at the frown he's been sporting.

"Are you really going to *kill* for him?" he whispers.

I snort. He has no room to judge me. Not when he's part of the team holding a woman against her will so she can produce a litter of soldiers to be groomed into killing machines. "I'd do *anything* for my child. Just like you'll do anything for your family."

"I draw the line at *murder*."

"Well, we are two very different people." I sit up and roll my stiff neck. "My pack survived in Carson City by lending our unique abilities to the same scum *pretending* to rule the decaying city. Before that, my father sold me to his drug dealer so he could have a hit. I'm just doing what I was raised to do."

"You told me we always have a choice," David snaps. "Maybe you should follow your own advice."

"And maybe you should focus on doing your damn job," I growl. "We are just pawns in the same game, and we both need to play our parts to live another day." I swing my legs over the side of the bed, eager to gain some form of freedom. Even if it's just standing.

David offers me a shoulder to lean on. I glare but he scoots closer as he rolls his eyes at me. "Just because we are pawns doesn't mean we can't help each other move across the board."

I take my first wobbly step, then another. Even though it's not much activity, sweat rolls off my cheek.

David sets me on the bed. "You're making good progress."

"You're a horrible liar."

He smirks. "Try to use the bathroom every few hours to retrain your brain to utilize those muscles again." He types into his tablet. "I'm requesting some food for you too," he says, and my mouth waters. I've only been allowed IV fluids and protein shakes that taste like chalk. "Stay out of trouble and we might even be able to get you a rare-cooked steak."

"Don't you dare tease me like that." I swipe the drool off my chin before aiming an accusatory finger in David's direction.

He squeezes my wrist until I meet his mocha-colored eyes. Now, I want a hot fudge sundae with extra whip and a healthy serving of nuts. "Don't lose your fire, Angelica," he whispers before striding out.

My heart sings to hear my name again.

Not pet.

Not animal.

Not bitch.

I rub my belly, enjoying the feel of the bump. *What a mess I'm in.* I crawl back into the bed as tears burn my eyes. I turn onto my side, curl into the fetal position, and hold the shape of my child for the first time. "Mommy will always love you."

After I regain the use of my limbs, I make the best of my captivity. I stretch and try to exercise. It's hard at first, but after a few weeks, I'm able to do the basics with ease. I don't think I've ever been in this kind of shape. Even the soldiers are having a hard time ignoring my muscled frame. They ogle and drool at my redefined curves.

"Time to check your vitals," the good doctor commands.

I pause my marching in place and sit on the bed. I offer my arm and wait for his usual *papa wolf* dialogue.

"Your heart rate is elevated."

"I was doing cardio. Of course it's elevated."

"More so than normal, even with exercise." He taps on his screen. "And your blood pressure is elevated too. I'm going to order some more bloodwork to double-check your levels."

"You just did them." I rub my fingertips over the uprisen skin on my arm.

"And I'll do them as often as needed. Stop arguing with me."

"Is everything okay?" I arch a brow. "You seem snippier than normal."

David side-glances the camera before whispering, "They want to transfer you."

"Why?"

"You're getting closer to your delivery date, and they want a more secure location."

"We aren't secure here?"

He shrugs. "That's not my field of expertise."

Does this mean the General wants to train me for something else? Or maybe he just plans to dump my body once the child is born.

"Your heart rate just spiked," David blurts. "Angelica, what are you thinking about?"

Should I tell him that as the baby's arrival nears, I'm edging closer and closer to a full-blown panic attack?

I don't have a chance to respond before we are interrupted by my scheduled delivery of gruel. "Eat up, bitch." The bowl dances on the table and food sloshes over the ceramic side. "Be a good doggie and lick up every drop. It's the General's orders." The guard crosses his arms over his broad chest and leans against the door.

"Are you seriously going to sit there and watch me eat?"

His silence is my answer. *Fine.* I lift the spoon to my nose and sniff. *Are they trying to poison me?*

I cringe and push the bowl aside. "I'm not hungry."

The guard stomps to my side, snatches the back of my neck, and shoves my mouth into the clumpy liquid. "Just eat the damn thing, so I can leave."

I growl into the bowl, but do as I'm told. I lap it up, like the dog he thinks I am, until the container is squeaky clean. "There. It's gone. Now go run and tell your master like a good little boy," I purr.

"You forgot some, dog." The guard points to the droplets still marking the table after he slammed the bowl down.

"Is this really necessary?" David steps to my aid. "She ate it like you asked."

"Shut up." The guard reaches for his baton. "Or you're next."

I use my tongue to tease at the splatters of food.

"Yeah. That's more like it." The guard fists my hair and the jab of his erection against my back tells me I'm making my point.

Yeah, that's right, you sick fuck. I've got power over you too.

"Do you like the taste of white cream, bitch?"

I shake my rear against his thickening bulge. "Yes, I do."

He tugs me to his chest. "I can't wait until you're on the menu again. I'm going to split your pussy in two while you scream."

My vision blurs, and I sway against him.

"It's time for a little nap. Don't fight it." The guard gropes my chest and hums in my ear. I can only whimper my panic as I begin to lose consciousness. "You're not so tough now, are you?" His manic laughter is distorted. "The mighty she-wolf is nothing more than a clawless kitten."

"What's going on?" David's voice rings out in the hazy fog. "Angelica, are you…"

Peace. Quiet and numb. I'm content to stay wrapped in this velvety darkness forever. Even my wolf is purring. *Yes, I like this.*

Suddenly, movement in my stomach gives me pause. Then I remember… my child is in danger.

I fight every nerve in my body, begging each limb to react. But

I'm trapped in this drugged emptiness.

"This is going to hurt," a wavering voice warns. "I'm sorry."

What does that mean?

Searing pain burns up my arm, but my scream is silent as my body throbs in agony.

"Angelica, can you move?"

Is that David's voice? I beg my eyes to function and a sliver of light filters through a tiny slit. *Are those trees?* My ears twitch. *Do I hear birds?*

"Easy. The drug is still active. It'll be some time before the effects wear off."

"Safe?" I squeak past my useless lips.

"I removed your tracker to throw them off our trail. But we can't stay in one place for too long. Rest for now, and when you wake up, we'll head north."

There are so many questions buzzing around my mind. But sleep sucks me in before I can throttle the man in the white coat.

My eyes snap open, and I search the surrounding forest until my gaze falls on the good doctor. "What did you do?"

He pivots from the moldy log he's resting on. "I rescued you."

"No, you didn't! I was finally gaining some freedom and now you've put me in more danger!"

"No. What I did was risk *my* family's lives to save you and your child."

His words wash over me and my warring emotions rise to the surface. I lift a questioning brow. "Why would you do that?"

"Because they weren't ever going to train you to be a soldier. They planned to lock you away to be raped and bred for the rest of your life."

"And why should you care what happens to me?"

David runs a hand through his hair. "I keep asking myself that. You're a shifter, an animal. The first chance you get, you'll kill me." Then he kneels at my side. "But hearing what they wanted to do to you, even while you were lying there unconscious..." He brings my knuckles to his lips. "I may be an idiot, but I've chosen my side and it's with you." He leans his forehead on my wrist. "And I'll protect you for as long as I can. Because you're special."

I snort. "You mean I'm fucked up in the head."

He snatches my chin. "I've seen what the General has planned for your kind and they won't survive without you. You have a fire burning inside you, Angelica. The shifters need you to lead them against him."

My heart skips a beat. He has so much faith in me. I don't deserve it. "I'm not a leader."

"Then you'll *learn* to be one or you can abandon your kind in their time of need. It's your choice." He releases my chin and rubs his face. "A colleague told me about a former medical facility nearby. That's where we're going. It has medical supplies and it'll be an adequate place to birth your child."

A thousand questions rush through my brain as my fingertips dance over my abdomen. "Where is it, exactly?"

"I have the coordinates." David tugs a compass from his pocket. "It's a few days away."

"How do I know I can trust you or that the General isn't testing my loyalties?"

"You don't." We stare at each other for a long moment, as though we're each considering our options. There aren't many to choose from. David clears his throat and cradles my arm. "I was lucky to find your tracker so quickly. I'm glad the wound is healing well with no signs of infection."

I stare at my bandage under his grip. "Why would they put a tracker in me? I was locked in their facility."

"The General isn't very trusting." David rubs at his own wound. "I only knew about the devices because I eavesdropped on a group of guards as they were talking in the break room."

I guess I'm not the only one gathering information. "And how did we get here?"

"Once you were unconscious, they loaded you into an idling van. I demanded that they take me too, so I could monitor the pup. Then, after we'd been on the road for a while, they stopped for gas." David swallows as he stares at his hands. "That's when I attacked them."

I smirk. "What did you do to them? Talk until they passed out."

David itches his elbow and that's when I notice the dried blood.

Oh shit. He actually hurt them. Has the doctor really abandoned his kind and switched sides?

He clears his throat again. "Are you hungry?" He rummages through his pockets and passes me an energy bar. "They had a few of these in the vehicle."

I bite into the grainy texture and fight the urge to spit it out. "Did you find anything else?"

"I didn't grab much because I wasn't sure what was being tracked. Don't give me that look. This is my first time and I was paranoid."

Oh man. We're in trouble.

"You didn't take their guns?"

"The only weapon I took was this." David waves a hunting knife in my direction. "Like I said, I was paranoid. I've never done anything like this before."

Fuck me. I'm stuck in the middle of the woods with a man child who has no idea how to survive in the *middle of the woods*. "Have you ever watched any kind of survival shows?"

"No, I was mostly into medical stuff, like *House* and *Grey's Anatomy.*"

My jaw drops. Those aren't even real hospital shows. "Damn it." We couldn't be any more different. Thunder vibrates the ground. *Great.* Another sign pointing to us having bad luck. "We need to find shelter before we get struck by lightning," I grumble at the darkening sky.

I manage to use the tree bark to rise to my feet. If we get caught in a storm, we'll be dead before they can capture us. David leads the way, taking us farther into the thick foliage. The drugs they gave me cause my limbs to be clumsy and numb. I trip over twigs and scrape my knee against a boulder that "leaped" into my path.

David collects me into his arms without even a grunt at my additional pregnancy weight.

I squeal at the sudden jolt of movement and wrap my arms around his neck to keep from dropping onto the hard ground. "What the hell are you doing? Set me down! I'm perfectly fine walking on my own."

"Let me help, or we'll never find shelter before it rains." He narrows his eyes at my bloody knee. "We need to move faster than your current snail's crawl."

I take this opportunity to really look at the doctor. There's not a gray hair to be seen. No tattoos or scars. Even his hands, now resting on my thighs, are smooth and free of callouses. "How old are you?"

"Why do you need to know?"

"Do you even know how old I am?"

"Of course, I do. You're thirty-four."

Silence envelops us. Why won't he tell me his age? But I know how to get information. Step one: mess with his ego.

"Well, you look like you're a damn *child*."

"What? I'm a doctor!"

"The General must have snagged you from medical school." I continue to toy with him.

"I was in my residency!" David grumbles. "And what does age have to do with anything?"

"I'm guessing you're at least ten years *younger* than me."

I win!

"Don't be ridiculous. I'm not *that* young." I arch a brow and he rolls his eyes. "If you must know, I'm twenty-eight."

I pinch his cheek. "Aw, you're still a baby."

"Ouch!" He shakes me off. "Don't make me drop you, old lady."

"What? I'm not…"

A flash of lightning causes me to shriek and tighten my hold around David's neck. When did I become terrified of storms? *Probably when your existence became a series of natural disasters.*

"Look. There's a cave." David points into the distance.

I twist and see a tiny hole shrouded by bushes. "Let's hope it's bigger on the inside." David's chest shakes and I raise a brow. "What's so funny?"

He shakes his head and purses his lips. "Nothing."

"Tell me." I nudge my shoulder into his neck.

He releases a breath. "You said *let's hope it's bigger on the inside.* So I was going to respond with… *that's what he said.* But then I remembered you just called me a baby and would think that the comeback was immature. Plus, it would just be another thing to pick on me about later."

I blink at his boyish grin. Here we are, in some Luna-forsaken place about to get drenched in rain, and he's making *jokes*?

The moment takes me by surprise, and I burst into laughter. Belly-rolling, side-splitting laughter. David joins in until we reach our destination, and he sets me on my feet.

"Let me check it out first." He lowers himself onto all fours and crawls into the opening. I cackle as he curses and grumbles at the insects hidden in the nooks and crannies.

I guess the good doctor was no boy scout.

"Did a roach finish you off, David?" I tap my foot. "If it did, ask it to leave behind those coordinates, please."

David reemerges and shucks off the dead leaves with a shudder. "I feel like there's something crawling on my back."

"You're such a baby," I grumble as I twist him around. "There's nothing…" I swipe a hairy spider off his shoulder. "…there."

"Are you sure?"

I spy the insect as it scurries into the brush. "Trust me. There's nothing on your back." *Not anymore anyway.*

"Thanks for checking." David shivers involuntarily at the thought. "Other than the bugs and rats, the cave is safe. Should we grab some wood to start a fire before the rain drenches everything?"

Why didn't I think of that? It'd be nice to have the extra warmth, but what if the General is on our heels?

A misty wind chills my bones and climbs up my spine. I'll take my chances. We collect twigs, moss, and stones. Then we manage to squeeze into the damp cavern. The icy rock takes my breath away, causing my teeth to chatter.

I settle the kindling in a circle and scrape the rocks' rough edges together. After a few failed attempts, a spark flashes and ignites the moss. Soon, a fire's smoldering in the center of the space. I rub my palms over the warmth. It's not a massive bonfire, but it'll do for the night. A bolt of lightning strikes outside of the cave. Then the heavens release their watery bounty.

"Thank Luna, we made it here in time." I lean against the wall and yawn.

"Whose *Luna*?"

I take my eyes away from the entrance and watch as David tosses small twigs into the flames to feed our only heat source. His cheeks are rosy and his hair is a mess. But he looks happier than I've ever seen him.

"Luna's our deity."

"So your god is female?" He arches a brow.

"Why? Do you think a *woman* can't be all-powerful?" I cross my arms over my chest.

His grin warms my toes. "Oh, I *know* they can be."

For a moment, I forget we are running for our lives in an unknown forest, trapped in a small space with a storm raging outside. It's just me and a friend camping.

David clears his throat and refocuses on the fire. "So, she watches over you?"

I bite my lip at his blush while wondering what he's thinking about in that head of his. "Yes. She even blesses us with Guardians to protect us."

"Like guardian angels?"

69

"Something like that. But they walk the earth and are blessed with powers."

"Do you mean like healing abilities?"

"From what I've heard, their powers are more elemental in nature, like lightning and fire."

"Have you ever seen one?"

"Nope."

"Then how do you know they exist?"

I bump my shoulder against David's. "Faith."

"Yeah, right. Look where that faith has gotten you."

Shit. A punch to my gut would have hurt less.

"Hey, I had a great life, until the General fucked things up."

"Did you?"

That tone. It sounds like the good doctor has been digging up my past behind my back and believes it gives him permission to judge me.

"What have you heard?" I growl.

"Forget it. I shouldn't have said anything." He feigns a yawn. "I'm tired. Let's just get some sleep." He closes his eyes, dismissing my glare.

"No. Tell. Me."

"Just that your so-called husband was too power hungry for his own good."

I bristle at the thought. Freddy worked hard to keep our pack safe. "He was on his way to ruling the city with me as his queen. Until we were attacked by a rival pack and the General had me shot and kidnapped."

The doc shakes his head at me. "When are you going to stop protecting that cheating bastard?"

My eyes widen. My mate was using a female from another family to gather intel. *But how does David know this? Does that mean the General knows more than he's letting on?*

"Excuse me?" I screech my icy warning.

"They said he was having an affair with a female from a rival pack. How is that *loyalty*?"

"He was using her for information!"

"Whatever. You don't need to have sex with someone to do that."

"Don't *whatever* me! You're too *young* to understand that sometimes we are forced to do things to survive." My lip quivers. "Did they also tell you that I fucked soldiers while I was married too?"

No one is perfect. I'll never pretend to be.

David's jaw ticks. "That's different."

"Why? Because I have a vagina?" I clench my fist, ready to beat the shit out of this know-it-all doctor. He has no fucking clue what it's like growing up with a ruthless alpha. What it's like to be ruled by someone like Spike. Always being forced to be the ditzy blonde spy, so he can continue to sit pretty on his decaying throne.

"No. Because it's not *your* fault. A *real* man would have protected his spouse, kept her from having to go to such extremes! Freddy should have told you that you were worth *more* than any information. That your body was his *temple* to worship. Not force you to do things you didn't want to do and call it *getting intel*."

I turn away from David's heated accusations. He's *wrong*. Freddy was a great man. Everything we did was for our future.

I rub my chilled arms. "Well, at least he wasn't a worthless *human*," I snarl at the wall. Lightning flashes, attempting to break through our blanket of silence.

"Get some sleep," David snips. "I'll take the first watch."

I bite my tongue to keep from reminding him that *he* was the one who said he was tired. Instead, I curl into a ball. The sound of the pattering rain and crackling fire is no comfort. Tears wet my cheeks as I remember the man I lost. He'd be so disappointed in what I've become. I cradle my child as sobs shake my frame. David has a point. Luna has forsaken my family. Leaving us to fend for ourselves. Again. Warmth covers my back before an arm drapes over my side and rubs my chilled skin.

Luna may have taken my pack, but she's also given me a second chance for a better life. Even if he only has two legs. Something pokes me in the back and I smirk.

Okay, maybe three legs.

I twist and meet David's searching gaze. "For a human, you're not as worthless as I thought," I whisper.

"I know." He grins.

"You do?"

"I saved you, didn't I?"

I peek around our tiny hiding spot. "You call this saving?"

He tugs me to his chest. "A simple *thank you* will suffice."

"You're an idiot," I hum against his beating heart.

Angelica

Virgin

"What do you mean you don't know how to hunt?"

We've been walking since dawn, trying to put as much distance as we can between us and the van David ditched. We were in such a hurry we didn't eat, and now I'm beyond starving.

"I'm a *doctor*. When would I have had spare time to prance around the woods and kill innocent animals?"

I rub my temples. I'd love to remind him that those *innocent* animals are our only food source. There's no supermarket in the middle of the Luna-forsaken woods. "Just give me the knife and I'll murder Bambi."

This man is hopeless when it comes to providing any real food. If I don't get iron in me soon, lethargy will set in.

"Whoa!" David's shout echoes around us, scaring off a flock of nesting birds. "Look at your arm!"

I follow his line of sight and my heart leaps. "Fur!" I rub the soft warmth. "I've missed you."

"The serum must be wearing off." David scratches his own scruff and I wonder if he's jealous.

I frown when only patches of pelt spring up. "Do you remember when my last injection was?"

"The guards administered it, not me. Shouldn't you remember?"

"The days run together. I had no concept of how much time had passed." I rub my stomach. "Too bad the fur is the only thing making an appearance. I'd love my claws and fangs right about now."

"Do you think it's your body's response to being cold?"

"Well, I'm starving. So if that were the case, it would let me hunt too."

"Don't worry. I'll get us something to eat." David puffs out his chest.

I arch a brow at the confidence that wasn't there a minute ago. "It's *not* like going through a drive-through window. It takes time, patience, and planning."

He strides farther into the forest. *Is he ignoring me?*

After a few minutes of silence, I open my mouth but quickly close it when David ushers us into another cave. I groan but follow him inside. I swipe away cobwebs, then settle onto the cold floor, glad to be off my aching feet.

"You're not an experienced hunter," I continue to remind him as I massage a knot in my arch. "There's no way you can get us food."

"Ye of little faith. I'll be back soon." He squeezes my wrist.

"I have more experience than you do," I repeat. "If anyone is leaving to grab a carcass, it's me."

"No, you're going to rest here."

"But what if you get hurt?" The words slip out and surprise even me. *Am I starting to have feelings for this man? As more than a friend?* "You know, because you are a pain in the ass and won't share the coordinates with me."

David searches my gaze before brushing a thumb over my chin. "You listen to me, Angelica. You and this child…" He rests a palm on my stomach. "…are the most important things right now. If something happens to me, you leave and *never* look back. You run as far and as fast as you can."

It should be easy enough to agree to. He's only a human after all. Right? But my heart clenches at the thought of him not traveling by my side, even if he is a pestering know-it-all.

David watches my lips, and just when I think he's going to dip his head and press his mouth to mine, he turns around and exits the cave.

I don't know what surprises me more. That I thought he was going to make a move. Or… the fact that I'm disappointed that he didn't follow through.

Four hours later, I'm going stir crazy. Although more fur is poking through my skin, nothing else is making an appearance. I stick close to the shelter and collect a few things to build a fire. It won't last long, but it'll warm me up after all this muggy air drenched my only pair of clothes. I stir the embers, wishing the rain hadn't saturated the forest floor last night. I hope David can find more kindling, or we're going to freeze when the sun sets.

For the hundredth time, I glance at the entrance of our temporary home.

Where is he? We shouldn't be in one spot too long. We need to be on the move and forget the food. *Should I leave and never look back, like he suggested?*

The child inside me kicks. It's right. I can't *not* eat. The little pup is growing and needs me to provide them with sustenance.

I soothe the unborn child. "He'll be back. You'll see." My stomach growls in protest next. "And he better have food, or I'm going to eat him."

I recall his thick bulge digging into my back last night and lick my lips. I'd love to suck him dry and eat that protein. The thought sends goose bumps rising over my arms. I shake my head. Between my pregnancy hormones and my wolf instincts returning, I'm losing control.

My neck snaps as footsteps approach. A twig cracks and I bare my teeth, ready for a fight. My nose twitches and I let out a breath at the familiar scent. "Where did you go? China?"

When David pushes inside the cave, I bite my lip to hold back a laugh. Poor guy is covered head to toe in mud. Or at least I hope it's mud and not animal shit.

"Did you do a little mud wrestling along the way?"

He ignores my jab at his appearance. "I found some dry sticks in another cave," he grumbles as he pokes at the fire.

I inch closer as the embers roar to life. "What about food?"

David reaches into his pocket and hands me six eggs. "That's the best I could do." I blink at them, then at the dry kindling at his feet. A bird's nest. "With your wolf abilities returning, you should be able to eat them raw without any consequences."

I fight the urge to gag. *Gross.* "What will you eat?"

"I'll be fine. I'm not even hungry," he says, and I frown at his pale face. He's shivering and dehydrated. My fingers tug at his wet shirt. "What are you doing?"

"You need to dry off or you'll get sick."

He shimmies out of his shirt, and I lay it on the warmer side of the cave.

"Now for your pants." I point to his khakis.

"What?" His voice squeaks.

"Aw, don't get shy on me now." I smirk. "We're both adults. I'll keep my paws to myself."

David clears his throat and straightens his spine. "You're right." But his pink cheeks tell me otherwise. At least he's getting some color back. He tosses his pants by his shirt. He's been hiding a lot from me, including a six-pack. How does a doctor have time to go to a gym? My imagination is playing tricks on me, because I swear his dick just twitched under his boxers, trying to say hi.

"Did you find water?" I aim to change the topic.

"Yes. There's a clean stream not too far from here." He points to his pants. "I filled an empty water bottle if you're thirsty."

I scramble to pull out the plastic jug and chug its contents. *Damn, it feels heavenly going down my dry throat.* I crack the eggs and greedily slurp the yolks. It's like swallowing gummy worms. And they do little to satisfy my hunger.

"You were right." He sighs.

I settle in by the fire. "I know. I'm always right." When he chuckles, I continue, "What was I right about this time?"

"I have little experience with life because I've spent most of my time in school or at the library studying. Plus, I hardly had any friends."

When did I say all of that? Either way, I'll take the credit for being right any day.

I pick a piece of shell out of my teeth. "Were there any serious girlfriends in college?" I ask, and David shakes his head. "How about boyfriends?"

"No."

The innocent twinkle in his gaze causes me to blink. "Wait. Are you telling me you're a *virgin*?"

His red face confirms it. "Is it that obvious?"

Is that why he's latched on to me? He's lacked proper... *companions*?

"Do you want to fix that?"

"*Fix* it? Just because I've never had sex doesn't mean I'm *broken*."

I grin at the anger burning in his statement. It stokes my own fire. My fingers glide over his thigh, then under his waistband. His cock springs to life.

"You're definitely not *broken*."

He hisses at my caress but doesn't shy away.

"Do you want to know what I imagined earlier?" I ask, and when David's heated gaze meets mine again, I take it as a sign to continue. "Popping your thick cock into my mouth." The appendage in question weeps. "Has anyone done that to you?"

He swallows and shakes his head.

"Pity. It's an amazing feeling." I tilt my head. "But you know how great an orgasm can feel, right?"

David nods.

"How about you show me how you jerk off?" I move his hand in place of mine. He strangles his width from shaft to tip. "Let me give you some more mental stimulation, big boy." I peel off my clothes, and his tempo increases. "You like that, don't you?" I massage my chest, tweaking my nipples. He licks his lips. "Do you want *this*?" I tease his bottom lip with my stiff peak.

His growl cuts through the air before he presses my back against the stone as his body dominates mine. He places urgent kisses over my neck, making his way down to my plump breasts. I dip my head back and moan as he worships every inch of my body. A tingling sensation surprises me before liquid seeps from my nipples.

"What the heck?"

He pulls back long enough to answer my question. "It's normal for breastmilk to release when your nipples are stimulated." He lowers his head and suckles, and I cry out at the overpowering sensations.

"Fuck." I tug his hair as pressure builds in my core and becomes unbearable. "David."

"Tell me what you need, Angelica. I'll do anything for you."

I spread my legs, eager to play doctor with him. "Explore everything I'm offering you."

His tongue glides over every inch of my body, pausing now and then to gauge my pleasure, until he's located all my panty-melting spots. When he circles my swollen bits, my breathing hitches.

"Right there," I beg as my legs quake. "Please, I need you right there."

David drags his teeth over my clit, and I scream as my climax rips through my body. This man is relentless as he slips a finger inside me, testing the tight channel. "You're perfect."

I grab his wrist, forcing his finger in and out. "Less talking, more doing."

"How many can you take?" He nips my ear while he inserts two more. "Can I make you come like this?"

I hum softly at the fullness, thrusting my hips with his motions.

"What if I pinch down?" His curiosity fuels my desire. He tugs at my throbbing clit and I see stars as I explode again.

81

The things he's doing to me take my breath away. Once my orgasmic convulsing ceases, David holds himself over me, teasing my entrance with his stiff tip.

He palms my face. "God, you're so beautiful. I love hearing you say my name like that."

I lean into his touch. "If you want me to do it again, fuck me rough, pretty boy."

Hesitation flickers over his face for a second as he tests the honesty in my words. I grin before bringing my palm across his face. The red mark jolts him from his stupor and he gives me what I'm begging for. He slams into me, eliciting an amazing pain between my legs. I moan and claw his back.

"Are you okay?" His arms ripple as he holds back his release.

"Yes." I clutch his ass, my nails slicing into his skin. "Now move faster." His thrusts are weak but quicker than before. "I know you can do better than that. I'm not going to break."

An animalistic groan tears from his throat before his hips bruise mine, and I'm riding another wave of mindless pleasure. "You feel amazing," he grunts out. "I'm going to come, but I don't want you disappointed with how long I last."

"Sweetheart, I've had three orgasms. You deserve one too." I pinch his nipples, throwing him over the edge as he howls his hot release. I milk every drop from his cock until he collapses next to me and tugs me to his chest.

Once our breathing steadies, he kisses my neck and strokes my arm. "How'd I do?"

"Do you want it on a scale of one to ten?"

His chest vibrates with laughter. "Sure."

"Three."

"What?"

I twist around to meet his frown. "Don't worry. We have plenty of time to improve that score." I snatch his member to fondle it. He closes his eyes and moans. "Are you ready to take notes?" I collect him in my mouth and tease his sensitive tip.

"Shit," he hisses. "Can you fit my whole cock in your mouth?"

I swirl my tongue over his thickness until he's back to his full size. Then I suck until I'm gagging, and his balls are tapping my chin.

"Damn." His hands wind through my hair and he guides my actions. "I'm going to come fast and hard," he warns huskily. "So if you don't want to swallow…" Before he can finish that thought, his seed spurts free and coats my throat.

I gulp down every drop and grin at his satisfied expression. A smart-ass retort is on the tip of my tongue when he hugs me to his chest and kisses me deeply. Our juices mingle in our mouths. Then he disengages, and his lips dance over my forehead.

"This has been the best day of my life," he whispers. "Thank you."

His words shock me. I rub the scab from where he removed my tracker. "This won't last. You know that, right?"

"Can't we just enjoy the moment and *pretend* it can?"

"David. We come from two very different worlds, and soon my wolf will crave the company of other shifters."

"We can create our own pack." He massages my baby bump. "We can raise the child, forget our pasts, and look forward to a brighter future together."

I snuggle into his embrace at the lovely images his words paint in my imagination. They give me hope that this darkness surrounding my life won't last forever. That maybe David can be the light I've been missing.

Angelica

Fur Suit

"**H**oly shit!"

Why is David shouting? Are we under attack? I assess the cave until my gaze falls on his alarmed expression, which is hyperfocused *on me*.

"You're huge!"

"What do you mean?" I spit out, but no words leave my mouth.

That's when I notice what's going on. My claws click over the stone floor as I prance around with four slender paws and a warm fur coat. Damn, it feels good to be in my beast form again.

"Wow." David's voice is full of awe as he runs his hands over my frame. "This is *unbelievable*. I can even feel your growing abdomen."

His fingertips trigger the rumbling of my stomach and remind me of how hungry I am. *"Breakfast time."* Drool slips over my tongue as I step into the early morning light. My nose twitches in the cool air. *"There's a bunch of rabbits nearby."*

"Can you please shift to two feet so we can talk?"

Oh, right. David can't hear my wolf thoughts.

Realization hits me. I don't *need* David anymore. I could run and not even bother to look back...

I take a step towards freedom but my paws freeze, begging me to reconsider. I don't know where we are, or how close we are to a pack or the city. Plus, I'm going to need the doctor's medical experience to deliver my pup.

I snort at the obstacles in my path. I finally get an ounce of independence, and I can't even enjoy it. I tilt my head to the side as a rabbit gallops into the shadows created by a gathering of shrubs. I lick my lips. Being able to shift means I can hunt, and we can travel faster.

We.

That's right. The good doctor is still waiting for me to speak to him. I morph into a naked woman and smirk as I watch David's jaw hit the floor. "What do you want to talk about?"

He shakes his head. "I know you want to hunt, but we should travel while the weather is on our side."

"But we haven't eaten anything yet and we won't make it very far if we're constantly running on fumes."

David collects my hands in his. "The General has many men at his disposal. Even beasts who can survive without food or water for longer periods of time than we can." He kisses my knuckles. "We need to keep traveling towards the medical facility."

I swallow the bile rising up my throat at the possibility of hybrid beasts chasing us. My wolf whimpers, agreeing with the good doctor. We should move towards safety.

"Then let's go," I grumble. "We can travel until dark and find another cave to rest in." We collect the few items we own and head into the woods. "Do you think they'll be able to track my human or my wolf scent easier?"

David shrugs. "I assume you have a similar smell in both forms."

"Good." I shred to paws again and crouch down to urge him onto my furry back.

"I don't think this is a great idea, Angelica." He glances at my protruding belly, but when I nuzzle him, he slides on top. "This feels weird," he gripes. "Tell me if I'm too heavy or if I become a burden."

David must not have observed shifters in action. I'll show him how capable we are. My claws sink into the earth. I stretch my muscles, then bullet through the tree line. *Luna, this is what I need.* Branches whip around us, but nothing scrapes my ankles as I navigate the maze of obstacles. The beast in me hums with contentment. Traveling this way is more exhausting but so much faster.

David tugs out his compass and points towards our intended path. We pause only to drink. Then we pick up the pace again until nightfall. We hunt for a hidden cave but end up settling under a grove of trees, their branches offering us a canopy of cover.

David slips off my back and strokes my paw as fur slips to skin. "How are you feeling?"

"Like I could eat a whole deer and sleep for a week."

His arms engulf my waist as he scoops me up and settles us against a sturdy tree. "You didn't have to carry me. I could have walked or jogged beside you."

"A simple thank you would suffice." I smirk as I bury my face in his chest.

"*Thank you.*" He kisses my forehead. "For everything."

We gaze up at the stars. They shimmer and dance in the night sky as the insects serenade the forest. David's steady heartbeat against my ear adds to the melody around us. It's so beautiful, and I realize I'm the happiest I've been in a long time. I'm protected, loved, and cherished. All by a human man. A grin spreads over my face. I can't believe I traded in a ruthless shifter for someone with two feet. I sigh and think back to my husband.

It was different with Freddy. Yes, I was loved by him. But cherished or protected? Not really. Plus, he commanded me to spread my legs to aid in our rise to power. Of course, I never objected, because I didn't know any better.

I bite my lip. My mate would also sleep around and claim it was for the cause. He even got close to a female from a rival pack. *Skylar.* She wrapped him around her perfectly primped paw. He said it was the other way around, but I know better. Then, when I tried to confront him about it, he barked and pushed me away.

I snuggle into David, and he traces lazy circles over my bare shoulder. But the doctor is different. I can see a future with him. Where I'm not fucking around to win his praise. Because he gives it willingly.

"Tomorrow we should be about halfway to the facility." His voice tugs me out of my thoughts.

Damn. Why is it taking forever? I was hoping we were almost there.

"Well, I'm telling you right now I'm eating some meat before we travel again."

He kisses my neck and I tremble at the affection. "I'll give you all the *meat* you need." His chuckle warms my ear. "Now rest. I'll take first watch."

His words soothe me and I slip into dreamland, imagining our serene future. David, me, and our pup. And for the first time in a long time, I'm hopeful.

I stretch out like a lazy feline. There's still no indication that the General or his men are tracking our movements. Maybe our luck has finally changed.

My fingertips comb through my companion's shaggy hair. David should be watching our surroundings, but he must have fallen asleep while he kept guard. I detach his heavy arm from my chest. He looks so peaceful when he's dreaming.

I rise to my feet, careful not to wake him, and look out across the forest. There're some small rodents, mushrooms, and birds in the general area. But I don't sense anything larger. I nibble my bottom lip and my fangs elongate as I savor the thought of warm blood dripping from my canines.

If I back track to the stream, maybe I can catch an unsuspecting thirsty prey? Or at least a large bass.

The sky flashes before a boom of thunder vibrates the forest floor. The rumbling in the gray clouds causes the doctor to stir. His eyes are wide until they land on me. He lets out a breath and rubs his face. "Is everything okay, Angelica?"

Is it bad luck to speak the positive thoughts in my head aloud? I peek up at the darkening sky. Energy buzzes around me. A storm is brewing and I'm not taking any chances.

"I need to hunt before the lightning frightens the prey away. You should grab some dry wood for a fire." I glance around our leaf-covered canopy. "We won't be able to travel far at the moment, so we should search for a safer shelter. One that will protect us from the giant raindrops that are approaching."

I don't wait for him to comment on my plan, and step in the direction of the lake. Time to shift and hunt. I take a breath and roll my shoulders. *Let's do this.* A pain shoots up my side and my baby bump tightens. I bend over and gasp. *What the fuck? Am I literally starving?*

David rushes over. "What's happening?"

"It's just a cramp." I straighten my back and hold out my arms. "See? I'm fine."

His gaze wraps around my frame and he goes into doctor mode. "You probably overexerted yourself yesterday. Plus, you're dehydrated and malnourished." He runs a palm through his hair and pulls. "Damn it. This is all my fault."

"Stop whining," I grind out and his spine snaps to attention at the harshness of my tone, so I soften the blow. "Right now, our priority is to stay alive and keep walking." Lightning snakes through the sky again. "You *will* find wood and shelter," I prompt him. "And I'll meet you with food and water."

He snatches my elbow. "Tell me the truth. Are you sure you're feeling up to it?"

I would love to snarl and remind him that I don't have any other options *but* to keep moving. I mean, I'm glad we haven't run into any of the General's soldiers. But this storm could put us behind and allow them to catch up.

"I'm fine."

My words wash over him, but instead of letting me go, David tugs me to his chest. He crushes his lips to mine and his tongue demands entrance. *Luna, I love his passion.* My toes curl at the hot mess building between my legs. I moan and lean into him, demanding more. He massages my tongue with his until my knees grow weak.

He breaks our embrace and meets my glare. "I had to do that, in case I don't see you again."

I search his dark eyes. He's scared of losing me.

I cup his cheeks and rub my nose against his. "Stop being a pussy."

He chuckles but holds me tighter. "If I die or if I'm captured… run and never look back." His hand strokes my back. "Do not risk your child's safety for *my* well-being."

I look away from his demanding gaze. Fuck *him*. Why does he get to make that call? It's my life. My choice.

He snatches my chin. "Tell me you understand, Angelica."

I blink at his forceful tone, and my center clenches with desire. *There's* that alpha I know exists. But he should know me by now. I don't follow orders blindly.

"*I'll* make that call if it comes down to that and not a moment before. But it won't happen." I demand it into existence. "We are going to make it to that compound and live happily ever after. I won't deter from our objective, and neither should you."

Even as the words surround us it dawns on me that I lied. That is *not* our future. Because I will be seeking my revenge. One way or another, the General will pay for killing my pack and leashing me as his personal womb.

Will David understand? Will he shudder at the waves of crimson flowing from my soul?

I shake my head, trying to rid myself of the dread swarming in my mind. We will worry about tomorrow another day. Not now.

"I'll see you soon." He encourages me forward with a slap to my ass. "Get a move on before the rain comes."

I wink at the doctor's playful antics. Wishing we had more time so I can fuck some of this tension out of my body. Then I morph into my wolf form and conquer the forest floor in search of our next meal.

An hour later, I pad through the small cave entrance that smells like David.

"That's a great haul." He nods towards the rabbits dangling from my jowls.

I drop my kills at his feet, then shake off the droplets decorating my fur. Of course, it started sprinkling while I was hunting. I begrudgingly shift from my warm pelt to two legs.

I shiver, then rub my hands vigorously over the fire. "I was lucky to have located them. They were feasting on a patch of hidden clovers in the field."

He holds one of the rabbits by the hind leg and examines it as if it's one of his patients. "How should we remove the fur?" He aims his knife at its nose. "From top to bottom?"

I rest my hand on his and guide his blade. "You start the incision at their feet." He glides through the tuft before I add, "All the meat and organs are edible."

"Did you eat a lot of rabbits in your pack?"

"The Fangs lived in the city, which meant we mostly ate human cuisine. I was a huge fan of supreme pizza and cheeseburgers." I smirk as I tug at the white fur. "But we did hunt occasionally, and when we did, we'd use everything from the animal. Nothing went to waste."

"Not even the bones?" David cringes at the thought.

"*Not even the bones*. You can boil them to make a broth."

"Surely there's nothing you can do with the ears?" He smirks, like he's caught me in a lie.

"They make for a good snack." I grin, showing off my fangs.

David wrinkles his nose and turns towards the fire. He hands me some long twigs. "We can make kabobs." He stabs some berries and mushrooms, then reaches for pieces of rabbit meat. "We can always hold on to the bones and try to make a broth another time."

"That sounds delicious." I settle in the corner of our tiny shelter and rest while David cooks. Although there's more head space in this cavern, the surface area is small. I cringe as a cramp racks my body.

Shit. I bite my lip and stare at David's back, hoping he won't notice. I don't want him to play doctor with me—at least not until I've eaten my fill of those rabbits.

"Does this look ready to eat?" He moves the meat under my nose.

I don't bother checking it before I sink my fangs into its flesh. *Luna, this is amazing.* The fat drips over my chin.

"Yes, perfect," I mumble through bites.

"Cheers." We clank the sticks together before munching away.

I pause on my third kabob. "Why did you choose to be an OB?"

David freezes with his food an inch from his mouth. "Because of my mother." He lowers his skewer and sighs at his feet. "But it's a long story."

"You don't have to tell me." I keep my tone soothing.

David gives me a lopsided grin. "It's just not something I normally like to talk about." He stares at the stone walls and his eyes take on a glazed look. "My mom died while giving birth to my little brother."

"I'm so sorry."

"I wanted to learn everything I could so I might save lives and honor her memory."

"That's very sweet."

He scoffs and waves a hand around. "But it didn't do me any good, did it?"

I place his palm on my belly. "It did. You saved *us*."

"What if he kills Lauren and Brad for what I've done?" David whispers as his thumb strokes my stomach. "My brother and sister mean the world to me."

"We won't let that happen," I tell him. "Once we settle in at the compound, we'll build an army and rescue them. They can join our group. And together, we'll bring down the General."

"What if they don't want to fight for our cause?"

"Then at least they'll *have* a choice."

His lip twitches. "You're amazing, you know that?"

"Yes, I do."

We share a laugh, then nibble on our breakfast, both lost in our thoughts. It won't be easy. But I know with his medical skills and my leadership abilities, we can bring peace to our world.

"Are you sure you don't want the last one?" I ask, and David smirks.

"Just eat it before I change my mind."

I devour the remaining grub and lean into him. The rain drips in the forest and lulls me into a content trance.

"I was surprised when you came back to me."

His words wrap around my heart and squeeze the breath from my lungs. I wish I could lie and say the thought never crossed my mind, because it did. "You have the coordinates, remember?" When David doesn't respond, I bump his shoulder. "Who else is going to deliver this child?"

He wraps his arm around me. "I can't wait for you to meet my brother and sister. They're going to love you and your sense of humor."

"Is that before or after you explain I'm a shifter and that I stole your virginity?"

His chuckle warms my neck. "We'll just keep that information to ourselves."

I lean my head on his shoulder. "You really love them, don't you?"

"It's hard not to love them. I mean, Brad is a hard-headed brute with a soft spot for children and Lauren is a spoiled brat but a genius with computers and technology."

"Then why did you set me free?" I vomit the words and instantly regret them.

"Because that's what they would have wanted me to do. They joined the military to *fight* for our country and protect those in danger."

"I hope they're safe." I trace a circle over David's bicep and resist the urge to say: *unlike my pack brothers and sisters*.

"Me too." He kisses the top of my head. "Angelica?"

"Yes?"

"I'm sorry for all that you and your family have suffered through. You deserve so much more than *this*."

I drag my finger through the dirt, creating a wolf's head as memories claw their way into my head. "Things have always been tough for me, and this is just the icing on the shit cake I call *my* life."

David tips my chin and brushes my lips with his. "I hope to change all that for you and give you a new life filled with happiness."

That's the sweetest thing anyone has ever said to me. My hormones go berserk, and I pounce onto his lap as I deepen the kiss. I devour his mouth, begging for another taste. My palm rubs his erection and

I swallow his guttural groan as he thrusts into my hand.

I envy David's innocence and simple past.

The emotion is so strong that I find myself wishing that I could break him in the most beautiful way possible, so that he can understand what I've been through. I tug at the fabric separating us until we are both naked. Once his length is free, I spear myself and ride his dick without mercy. His thickness soothes my devious reflections. I clutch his wrists and place them on my breasts. He squeezes, then tweaks the nipples to hard peaks.

"Do you like that?" he purrs huskily before sucking one into his mouth.

"Yes," I moan while throwing my head back.

I shiver and goose bumps riddle my frame. Everything is more sensitive with this pregnancy. Even my orgasms have reached new heights. My thighs quiver as I scream my release and see stars. David follows shortly after, and I listen as his heart beats rapidly.

He strokes my sweaty hair. "I love you."

The admission jump-starts my brain and the electricity shocks my limbs, energizing them so that I can leap off his cock. "What?"

No one has ever said that to me. Not my father. Not even my mate. I shake my head. I must not have heard him right. A human cannot love a damaged shifter like me.

"I know our situation is *complicated*, but I wanted you to know how I felt."

"Stop!" I hold up my hands to protect my soul. "*This*…" I gesture between us. "…is not love. You are just pussy whipped. That's all. Because I'm the first woman you've ever slept with."

David straightens his spine. "You can't tell *me* who to love." He clenches his fists. "I'm not some ignorant child!"

"I can and will when you're telling me you love *me*! I'm not lovable, David. I'm the monster your parents warned you about. The Big Bad Wolf that…" I clutch my side as pain shoots through me.

It was all fun and games until the L-word was thrown into the mix. I mean, I do care for David. But love?

"Angelica." David rushes over. "Take a breath and have a seat." He's in doctor mode again. "Tell me where the pain is."

I plop onto the cold stone floor, which shocks my muscles. That's when I notice the blood slithering down my thighs. I peek over and see the same crimson color painting David's dick.

Our eyes meet and we know we're out of time.

Angelica

Sacrifices

"Why didn't you tell me you were still cramping?" David demands.

"Because it didn't hurt like *this*."

"I'm going to check your cervix." He gently separates my knees. "This isn't going to feel good," he warns before shoving a finger inside me. "Shit. You're dilated."

I grit my teeth through another breath-taking pain. In the time I spent with my pack family, no females birthed any pups. Other than the tiny informational pamphlets I snatched at the health clinic, I'm clueless about the whole event.

Fuck. Why didn't I ask more questions? Probably because I was so shocked that my birth control failed me.

"Can you walk? We need to move to the facility."

My eyes snap to David's worried expression. "Is the baby coming

"Take it easy, Angelica. Dilation just means your body is preparing itself. It does not mean it's happening *today*."

I take a deep breath. *I can do this. No, I have to do this.*

I look at the crimson decorating his fingertips. "Why am I bleeding? Is the baby all right?"

"It's spotting from intercourse. It's nothing to worry about. Most pregnant women experience it in their last trimester."

"Thank Luna." I wipe the anxious thoughts from my forehead. I haven't even officially become a mother. How will I keep my cool when the pup arrives?

"No sex for a while. I don't want to encourage the infant to descend any earlier than it should." He kisses the top of my head. "I won't let anything happen to you or the baby."

We huddle by the edge of the dying flames. Tears kiss my cheeks as the logs crack and pop. Everything is happening too fast. What if we don't make it to the compound and I give birth in the middle of the fucking woods?

I clench my fist. *Get a grip. Women have been doing this for centuries.* I nuzzle David's chest. At least I have a professional baby catcher with me.

Once the fire is completely extinguished, we trudge through the forest. The humidity is suffocating. I cross my arms over my chest and glare at the morning fog, already missing my fur. David thought it would be safer if I remained in my human form while we travel. Apparently, canines have a different birthing process and he wants to be able to assist as much as possible when the time comes.

The thought of shoving a watermelon-sized object out of an apple-sized hole causes me to shudder. As if sensing my distress, David dances his fingertips over my knuckles before our hands clasp together. *I can do this,* I repeat to myself for the hundredth time. The sun shimmers through the hazy atmosphere and begins to burn off the lingering mist. We walk in a comfortable silence, enjoying the quiet of the morning for nearly an hour.

"Have you thought of any names?" David questions me.

I smirk. "Do you mean to ask if I am naming the child after you?"

"You have to admit *Dave* does have a nice ring to it."

"Unless it's a *girl.*"

"Then you can name her Davina."

"You're ridiculous."

"Maybe you should name it after yourself?"

"Why the hell would I want to do that? Angelica is a horrible name and carries a lot of bad luck." I kick an ant hill, enjoying their frantic movements.

"How about Angel?"

I scrunch up my nose. "For a girl?"

"Not just for a girl. It's a unisex name."

"It sounds girly to me."

David kisses my wrist. "Name it whatever you want."

"How about *Baby*?"

He snorts. "Please don't do that."

"You're no fun."

He checks his compass and then glances at a tiny slip of paper.

"What's wrong, David?"

"Nothing," he fibs before increasing his pace.

After a few more hours, my feet develop sores and I desperately need water. "I should shift to search for food."

"We've talked about this."

"It'll be super quick." I rub my swollen ankle. "Plus, my wolf has pads on her toes."

"This isn't a good idea. But if you really need to..."

"I'll be back soon." I don't wait for him to object. I shred to fur and bullet through the foliage.

My nose twitches, guiding me to the closest watering hole. My claws dig into the dirt before I leap over fallen logs. *This is so much better!* My tongue hangs to the side, and the wind whips through my matted fur. Even my pregnant belly doesn't stop me from enjoying my freedom.

This is the good life.

The birds cower in their nests, protecting their offspring. And bees hunker in their hives, guarding their trove of sweet honey. I skid to a stop while ice freezes my limbs. My ears rotate, listening for anything out of the ordinary. *Something is wrong. It's quiet. Too quiet.*

That's when I spot it. A bush not quite like the others. It's out of place and slightly discolored. *Am I seeing things? Could it be...*

I swallow down my fear and gallop as fast as I can towards David.

"That was fast. We will lose sunlight soon... Angelica? You're drenched in sweat. Are you okay?"

My human feet wobble as I warn, "*They're* here."

"How do you know that?" David visibly pales. "Did they see you?"

"I don't know. I only saw their tent."

"Fuck." He drags a hand through his hair. "Have they been tracking us this whole time?"

"That doesn't matter right now. What we need to do is knock them off our trail. We can either hide until they give up and leave, or run as fast and as far as we can for as long as we can," I tell him. "I vote for the latter."

"You're in no condition to run at full speed with me on your back."

I stab a finger into his chest. "I *won't* go back there! I can't," I whisper the last word as my lip quivers.

"Are there any packs nearby? Someone who can aid us?"

"I haven't recognized any other canine scents. I could howl but it'll also grab the attention of the *General's* men."

"Are you sure it's his men?" David rubs my arms, attempting to cool my panic and get me to focus.

"I didn't stay long enough to find out. Either way, there're humans nearby and I'm not sure if they're friendly."

He shakes his head and curses under his breath. "You're right. We should keep moving. Stick to the shadows. But you can't shift to a wolf. That's my compromise. Don't give me that look. You know we can hide more easily when you're a smaller human."

I side-glance the direction of the river. "Would it be safer to swim and not leave our scent or footprints?"

"Wasn't that where they were stationed? By the water's edge?"

The pieces click into place, and I bite my lip. "They know we'd need to hydrate eventually, so they are blocking the only water source."

"Don't lose hope. We can find berries and large leaves holding rain water." David guides me in the opposite direction. "We can do this."

I squeeze his hand like a lifeline and recite his mantra to myself. *We can do this.*

Hours go by as we trek on with no mercy. Neither of us wants to return to our prison. I snort at the idea. The General isn't naïve. He won't trust us again. We'll be chained in a dark cell for the rest of our miserable existences.

I swallow my suffocating panic and grit my teeth. I'd kill myself before I'd let that jackass get his hands on me. I'll slit my own throat or drown myself in the river. *Anything* to preserve my sense of freedom.

Maybe it was just a group of innocent hunters or campers?

My legs burn as we keep our back-breaking pace. How much longer can we keep this up? Shouldn't we be closer by now? I lift my chin. *Stop being such a pussy. Suck it up and...*

My toe stumbles into a boulder. But before my face collides with the forest floor, David's arm wraps around my waist.

"I got you." He steadies me.

"Thanks," I mutter as his warmth seeps into my tired bones.

"Maybe we should stop for the day."

"No."

"Angelica, we are exhausted and hungry. If we continue like this, we'll injure and immobilize ourselves."

"Fine. But we are only *resting* for a few hours. Then we're getting back on the trail."

David brushes his sweaty hair off his forehead. "That's a good compromise." He scans the forest floor. "There's a clearing over there." He gestures to the side. "And if my eyes aren't deceiving me, it also looks like there's a creek. But it could be a mirage." He licks his cracked lips.

I squint in that direction. A glimmer in the distance causes hope to rise in my chest. *There's water!* That means there's fish and possibly ducks. Heck, I'd even eat a frog at this point. "Let's go."

Our steps are motivated by the prospect of cold crisp water and a warm dinner. As we get closer, I almost jump for joy at the sight.

"We can sleep under the roots of those trees." David points out the thicket before tugging me towards it. I rest my palm on its thick bark. I've never seen these before. They are massive and their spidery roots spread across the space. David removes his grimy shirt and lays it on the dirt. "Here. You rest, and I'll attempt to locate food."

Will this man ever learn? I don't like taking commands or playing the part of the damsel in distress. I morph into my fur suit. We are far enough to keep my scent from carrying with the breeze. Besides, my wolf moves so much faster than my human skin. I pad to the water's edge and greedily slurp the cold liquid.

"We shouldn't build a fire with the possibility of other people nearby. The smoke could give away our location," David instructs. "So why don't you eat whatever you can, and I'll eat when we can find berries or something?"

I wish I could offer advice on edible plants, fruits, and vegetables. Maybe he can eat raw fish. I mean, that's what sushi is, right?

I stare at my matted fur on the water's surface and cringe. When was the last time I showered? I paw at my reflection, and the ripples erase the haunting image of the starving, dirty canine. Maybe this is who I am now that I'm free of a pack and mate?

A glimmer of silver catches my attention before I leap into the frigid creek. My fangs sink into my first catch, and I triumphantly prance to David's feet to drop my flopping prey. I repeat this process until the scaled creatures hide deeper in the stream. *Cowards.*

"That's my girl," the doctor praises while scratching behind my ear. "Let's feast."

My coat shakes side to side, throwing droplets off my fur. I yawn and I swear my jaw clicks from the power of it. At this point, I can't tell if I'm more tired or hungry. And these constant cramps and walking on sore feet are irritating me.

David doesn't even wait for me as he tears into his food like a starving man. I smirk. Maybe there's a predator lingering beneath that polished surface after all. Blood slithers down his chin and his eyes meet mine.

"What?" he mumbles with his mouth full.

I shrug and shred through the scales too. I won't admit how grateful I am that he risked his life to save mine. Or that I owe him so much. Nope. Not when I have more pressing matters. The warm meat soothes my weary soul and hope rises in my heart. We survived another day. And the more of those we have under our belts, the more confident I get about the life we'll share together.

Once our bellies are full, we lick our fingers clean. Damn, it's been too long. I steal a glance at David. He looks satisfied too. I just pray he doesn't get food poisoning from the raw meat. We can't afford to have him get sick. I snuggle into the crook of his arm, ignoring his need to shower.

"Thank you for being a good provider." David kisses the tip of my nose. "When we get settled, I'll make you a hearty stew with fresh biscuits to dip in the broth."

"That sounds amazing."

"Brad and Lauren say it's the only thing I know how to cook." He chuckles as he watches the full moon.

Say not *said.* He's hoping the General hasn't killed them for his disloyalty. I bite my lip and attempt to lighten the mood. "Yeah, well, you hold up your part and deliver this baby and I'll continue to hunt for meat."

"Deal," he whispers.

The stars glitter to the melody of the forest while the earth tilts on its axis, creating an ethereal kaleidoscope. A yawn slips past my lips as my lids become heavy.

Where the fuck am I? I'm surrounded by a suffocating blackness while the sound of claws scraping metal echoes in the distance. I hold my ears as the screech of ripping metal conquers my senses. Sparks sizzle and pop, illuminating an approaching beast. Its eyes smolder as it curls its talons, beckoning me to join it. I shake my head, begging the creature to leave. A howl rips through my silent plea. I clutch my stomach. I must protect my child. A deep, guttural snarl vibrates my mental prison before the creature lunges forward and slices through my body.

"Fuck." I jolt awake.

"Easy, Angelica." A male voice soothes as he wipes at my brow. "Just breathe."

I thrash and scream.

"Hey." He shakes my shoulders, forcing me to focus on his face. He's not the monster of my nightmare. He's David. *My* David.

Before I can relax into his hold, another scream rips through my throat. What I thought was a weapon cutting into me is actually contractions squeezing the oxygen out of my lungs.

"I don't think we are going to make it to the facility." David shuffles around my feet. "This isn't an ideal location to give birth, but we can do it."

"No."

"We don't have a choice." He inspects the space between my thighs. "I can see the baby's head."

"What?" I shove him away. "Not here. Not now. We had a plan."

"You have to push."

"Are you *listening* to me? I said no!" I lean against the tree and moan through another ripple of agony. This pain is mind-numbing.

"Snap out of it!" David slaps his palms against my cheeks. "Angelica. You will lose this child if you don't *listen* to me."

"What?" It's hard to comprehend anything past the burning sensation.

"The baby is turning *blue*. We have to be quick, or you'll have a birth and a funeral on the same day."

I'm already failing as a mother. Of fucking course. "What's happening to the baby?"

"The umbilical cord must be wrapped around its neck," he explains, and my lip quivers. "Hey! Don't give up! Fight for them! Focus. We can do this. *Together*."

I nod and follow David's instructions. I crouch and use my palms to shove my belly bump downwards, while David crams his fingers into my vagina and pulls.

"That's good. Very good. Just a few more strong pushes."

A shit-ton of pressure slips past my legs, then I flop on the ground, attempting to catch my breath.

"Come on, little *girl*."

The moon blurs in my vision, and I send a silent prayer to Luna to give me the strength to save my…

"Wait... Did you say little *girl*?"

David doesn't answer me as he rubs the newborn, concentrating on getting it to take its first breath. Silence surrounds us and time seems to stand still.

No. I did what he said. My baby can't die. I crawl to David as he cradles the blue lump. Tears slip past my chin as I claw my way to my new family. *Please, Luna.* I continue to beg before I reach out a hand to brush the baby's soft cheek.

"Don't leave me. You're all I have left of your daddy." I lean my forehead on theirs as images of Freddy flash in my head. I couldn't save him, but I'll do whatever I can to protect our daughter. "Don't be scared. Mommy is here."

The tiny frame wiggles.

"Keep speaking to her. She's listening," David urges.

"Sweetheart?" I massage her cold limbs, forcing the blood to flow. "I'll never leave your side."

How could I abandon her? This petite pup would be defenseless just like I was. My tears plop on the child's nose. The same nose that looks almost identical to her father's. And those ears. I trail my fingertip over the little lobe. They are like mine. Perfect in every way.

A low squeak pushes past her lips. Then my daughter bellows a healthy screech and color gradually returns to her tiny body. My gaze meets David's as we cuddle our miracle. She defied all odds. Through kidnapping, abuse, and near starvation, her heart is still beating. I rest my ear against her chest to confirm the steady rhythm.

"Welcome to the world." David kisses her tiny hand. "Angelica, you should try to nurse her. It'll soothe her and keep her quiet." He nods to the darkness. "We don't need any extra attention."

My nipple teases the child's trembling lip. Then she latches on and suckles.

"She's a natural." David props my back against a tree as he helps deliver the rest of the afterbirth.

I ignore his movements as my child's warmth seeps into mine. "Praise Luna," I whisper in her ear. "We'll make an unstoppable team, little one."

"All things considered, everything looks good. Rest and we'll move towards the compound at first light. We'll need more water to keep you hydrated. Otherwise, your milk will dry up."

I watch David pace, making lists in his head as he plans our next adventure. He's the sweetest.

"Stop worrying for five seconds and *sit* with us."

He pauses his steps and offers me a smile. "You're right." He snuggles at my side and runs a finger over the baby's brow. "She's beautiful."

"And perfect."

"Have you decided what you are going to name her?"

"Considering all the work I just did, I say *Angel*."

"All the work *you* did?"

"Fine. All the work *we* did." I pat his hand. "Are you happy now, Mr. Sensitive?"

"Yes." He leans his head on mine. "And Angel is an amazing name. She'll be strong and courageous, just like her mother. Although her role model raises the bar pretty high. Your shoes are some big ones to fill."

"Thank you."

I gaze into the night sky and bite my lip as I think about the pup's father. I hope he and the rest of our pack are raining blessings down on us. I sigh. I wonder if another fur family will take us in. Because to survive on our own will be near impossible.

Maybe one that is close to Carson City where the Fangs resided? Maybe Robert's pack? *Any* pack will do, except for the Talas. They can rot in hell for all I care.

Or, if I decide to form my own pack, she'll be high ranking and reign one day. Exactly what her father would have wanted for his offspring. No matter where we are, Angel'll be loved, cared for, and most importantly have *power* to do what she wishes.

I brush my lips over her cheek. She's my world now. Whatever path she chooses for herself, I'll be there to support her.

Angelica

Mama Wolf

Angel's sobs wake me from my nap. I reach out to quiet her. But my hand hits air. *Where the fuck is she?*

"Take her to the van."

Who the fuck? My eyes snap open. I grind my teeth together as I push to my feet, but I'm weak and I sway. This frame won't do shit against the man stealing my child. I call upon my wolf and fur rips through my pores. My snarl vibrates the pebbles resting under my large paws.

"Don't move!" Guns lift from their holsters and aim at my head.

A grin breaks over my face. I was hoping they'd choose to go down with a fight. Before they can blink, I lunge at their throats. My fangs rip through soft tissue and crack bone as I snap the fuckers into two pieces. Their screams of agony fuel my rage. No one will harm my pup. Soon, my paws splash in crimson as I stand on my new tower of body parts. Blood drips from my chin.

Who's next?

The thug dares to clutch my screaming bundle as he shouts his worthless threat. "Stop! Or I'll…" Sweat pours over his face as his eyes grow wide. "No! Stay right there," he shouts as he pisses his pants. He backpedals, tripping over a stump.

"NO!" I yelp as he throws his hands out to save himself. *Shit!*

Time slows. Angel wails as the soldier releases her and her tiny body drifts towards the hard ground. My nose dives down while my body twists. The wind is knocked from my lungs as she lands on my sensitive gut. Once Angel realizes she's safe, she snuggles into my fur while her lips search for a teat. I sigh with relief and lick her elbow.

That was too close. But they're all dead. I just need to find David and start moving away from this area. I morph into two feet and hold Angel to my chest.

"Don't worry, little one. We're safe," I remind her. "David?" I hiss. Where could he be? *Shit!* I spot his crumbled frame only five feet away. My heart skips as I kneel at his side. "Please don't be dead." I stare at his chest, waiting for it to rise with a breath. He coughs and blood-tinged spittle drops to his chin. "David, can you stand?"

"Go," he wheezes. "Take Angel. Leave me." It takes too much effort for him to speak.

Damn it. I won't lose him!

"Get the fuck up right now!"

He moans but does his best to rise. "Happy?" He leans on a tree for support. He'll need help walking.

"Give me your shirt." I tug it off him before he can complain, then I make a tiny pouch to cradle my daughter to my chest. "Here. Lean on me so we can get to the compound."

He steps forward but freezes. "What did you do?" David's eyes are wide as he takes in the carnage surrounding us. Then he frowns at a set of boot prints heading away from the slaughter. "Did you let one escape?"

My heart clenches. *No. I thought I killed them all.*

"If one slipped past me, it's only because I just popped out a child. I'm beyond exhausted, so if I killed all but one, don't you dare give me shit for it."

David swipes at his bloody brow. "I'm sorry. But…"

I know he's going to demand that I double-check, but we need to move. "No fucking *buts*! Let's just leave it at *you're sorry*."

David locks eyes with me and silently begs me to reconsider. One guy with a gun can ruin everything we've worked so hard to achieve.

My jaw ticks. I know what needs to be done to ensure our safe travels. "Fine."

David lowers himself back to the dirt and holds out his arms. "You can hunt him faster without Angel."

I blink at my baby girl, then at my injured friend. Can I trust him with the only thing in my life that matters? "If something happens to her…"

"I'll kill *myself*," he declares with a raised chin. "Her life means more to me than my own. You know that." I consider my options before David presses, "We are running out of time."

I cradle the soft bundle and kiss her forehead. "I'll be right back." Then I hand her to the doctor with a warning glare. "Don't make me regret this."

He smirks and opens his mouth, likely to shoot off some smart-ass retort but winces when his fat lip cracks and blood seeps out.

The quicker I leave, the sooner I can return.

Fur splits my pores and I bullet after an unfamiliar scent, already tasting its life force on my tongue. Once I'm on his heels, the soldier turns and screams, picking up his pace. My ears pin back to my skull before I soar over a fallen log with my talons stretched towards their target. The fucker's wide eyes are the last thing I see before my teeth tear out his jugular. I wait till his heart stutters to a stop, and sniff the air. When my canine senses don't detect any more troops, I trot back to my family, eager to leave this area and start our new life.

"See? She's in one piece." David lifts the infant to my outstretched arms.

I rub noses with her and breathe in her scent. "I'm sorry I doubted you."

David pulls himself off the leaf-littered ground, his limbs shaking with the effort. "I'm sorry I couldn't protect you better." He winces as he holds his side. "You should just leave me behind." He offers me his weapon. Then he flips it so the hilt shines in the early morning sun. "This is a multi-tool. It has a compass…" He twists a hidden knob at the bottom of the handle to tug out a tiny folded piece of paper from its depths. "And the map is inside. You can get to the compound on your own."

I bite my quivering lip. This can't be our goodbye. "So you expect me to do *everything?*"

He blinks at the bark in my tone. "Uh. No? But I'll just slow you…"

"Good. Now quit yapping and let's move before we lose light."

David's tired, bruised eyes meet mine. He nods at my resolve before tucking the blade away.

We lean on each other and demand our trembling limbs to keep walking. Just one more step for one more second. Because once we quit moving, we'll drop dead from exhaustion.

We only make it a few feet before the hairs on my arms stand on end. I tense. *No. How could I have missed his scent?*

"David?" I whisper.

"Yes?"

"You need to take her and run."

"What?"

But it's too late…

"Give me the child, Angelica," the masculine voice demands from behind us.

I pivot to face him head-on while clutching my pup tight. "I'm surprised you took time out of your busy schedule to come here *yourself*," I snarl.

"For you, I'd travel to the ends of the earth." He bows mockingly before he straightens his spine and lands me with a cocky grin. "I admire your tenacity. But as you can see, you've clearly lost this battle. Now hand over *my* pup."

"Fuck you!" I sneer.

His gaze lingers over the various body parts strewn about. "You've been a naughty girl." His toe taps an arm that was ripped from its owner's shoulder. Instead of the rage I assumed would flash over his features, he almost looks impressed.

"They were stealing *my* child!" Fur threatens to poke through my skin. "Leave us be, or you'll be lying next to them."

"No, I don't think so." He snaps his fingers.

David grunts in agony. I was so focused on the General I didn't see a group of soldiers slip behind me to grab him.

"David!" I can't shift to protect him and hold the baby at the same time. *Fuck.*

He coughs as he rises to his knees. He ignores my plea as he addresses the General. "Angelica was forced to come with me. She didn't leave of her own free will. *I* took her. She tried to return, but I wouldn't allow her."

A gun cocks before its cold metal is pressed into David's forehead. "You made the wrong call."

Once the attention is off me and Angel, David leans into the barrel. "I would do it all over again if I had the choice."

"Such wasted chivalry. Don't you realize it doesn't matter how it happened? You've fulfilled your purpose. No matter how the events transpired, you delivered a shifter child to *me*." He nods towards Angel. "Now, your services are no longer required." The General's villainous grin clenches my heart. "Goodbye."

"Wait!" I shout before I can think better of it. "What about the *other* females you plan to breed?" My eyes dart from the doctor to the gun. "He's an asset to your objectives."

"I have no room for *traitors*." The General doesn't even bother to glance my way.

Fuck. He's going to murder my friend, and there's nothing I can say or do about it. I won't let his sacrifice be in vain. I step away from the brewing chaos. David's last gift to me and Angel can be to distract the soldiers so I can make a run for it.

The General's gaze never leaves David's as he addresses me again. "I wouldn't do that, if I were you."

Fuck him. I may be outnumbered, but I'm not helpless.

"Why not? I can shift and kill anyone who gets in my way."

"True, but you'll be *hunted* like animals until we get what we want."

His threat slams into my chest. The truth vibrates through my soul. If it were just me, I'd survive and gladly accept my punishment rather than be caged. But—I nuzzle the bundle in my arms—I can't do that with a crying newborn. Remaining hidden with an infant would be impossible.

Tears stream down my chin and onto Angel's tiny face.

"I know you love your child, so do what's right and what will keep her *safe*." Our enemy's voice is surprisingly soothing. "Give her to me. That's what a good mother would do."

Or would it be failing her and offering her up on a silver platter for his vicious methods?

"What will happen to her?"

"She'll be taken care of. More so than she would be stumbling through the woods, always looking over her shoulder, waiting for us to locate her. And trust me, we will find her. And I won't be as *charming* when we meet next time. Who knows? Maybe I'll trap her and torture her for the wasted time I spent searching." He grinds his teeth as I clutch my child closer to my chest. "Give her to me willingly, and she'll have everything she needs. Refuse my generous offer, and you'll both bleed out at my feet. Either way, *dog,* my patience is wearing thin."

My brain hurts. I'm so tired and my body aches. Maybe death isn't a bad choice. I bite my lip. But it's not just my life on the line. It's my innocent child's too.

"If I…" My words shake and I take a breath. "If I agree, I want to remain by her side."

His manic laughter shakes the leaves at our feet. "Do you really think you are in any position to negotiate? First, you slaughter my men and now you're asking *me* for a favor. You're delusional, just like your alpha *and* your former mate," he sneers.

I ignore the sting in my heart at the mention of Spike and Freddy. They made their choices based on protecting themselves and revenge. I'm doing this out of love for my offspring. If the General takes Angel, I need to make sure she's not mistreated. At least until I find a way to escape with her. But if I'm dead, there's nothing I can do to protect her.

"Yes, I'm serious. It's the only way I'll go with you without a fight."

"Why would you think I'd consider your proposal?"

Value. I need to remind him that he can't do this without my help. He wants purpose for everything, so I'll give him that.

I lift and drop my shoulder, like I don't have a care in the world. "You just said it. I murdered your men, in mere seconds. Even after just giving birth. Imagine what I can do to those who oppose you."

My wolf snarls a warning at me, urging me not to cross the line. Reminding me that we shouldn't trust him. In turn, I remind *her* that we will have our revenge. But first, we must keep Angel safe and rebuild our strength.

The General's wheels are turning. He sizes me up, then pivots towards the destruction surrounding us. "After she's *weaned,* you will be required to give her up for training."

He's giving my request a second thought. I should be grateful, right? I mean, he's not going to slice my throat open immediately. Or harm my daughter… at least not until she's no longer breastfeeding. My heart stutters. But how long is that? Months? A year? What's his definition of weaned?

He taps his foot impatiently. "Decide now. Take my offer or leave it."

"I want to be able to visit her daily," I plead. "I'll do whatever you need. I just want to make sure she's taken care of."

He narrows his eyes at me. "You may have yearly visits, if you both fulfill your duties."

"That's too long of a wait!"

"You'll take the deal or die. It's simple as that." He turns the weapon on me. "Choose quickly."

I squeeze my lids and cradle the reason I'm *not* ripping him to

120

shreds. *Think clearly, Angelica.* The General must be stalling for time or I'd already be dead. Maybe he doesn't have backup? If he had additional troops, more would be rushing to his side. He *needs* me to comply, so he doesn't return to his superiors with a massive body count *and* nothing to show for it.

"I'll go with you willingly and be leashed to kill your enemies, *if* you allow me to visit with my child weekly." I kiss Angel's forehead as I seal our fate. "That's my final offer." My wolf eyes morph to meet his gaze, driving my point across. He either agrees or I'm splitting fur and leaving. "I encourage you to accept."

His lip twitches. Then he shrugs as he returns his gun to its holster. "I think I can work with those terms."

I sag with relief. It's not perfect, but at least I'll have more time to plot his demise and our escape.

"*Before* I agree, let me hold the child." He steps towards me. "Let's see if she's worth the trouble."

I squeeze Angel to my chest. Anything but that.

"I *need* her, remember? I have no reason to cause her any harm." His fingertip grazes my arm. "*Prove* that you can obey me, or I may decide you are both not worth my time." He kicks a detached head at our feet. "And I'll add you to the body count."

My brain screams *no*. But my choices are limited. I'm too weak to fight him head-on. He holds his arms out and my lip quivers as I give in to the monster and hand him my precious bundle.

He grins as he cradles her. "She's so innocent." Angel snuggles into the crook of his arm. "Yet they grow up into bloodthirsty beasts."

"You don't need to have *fur* to be a piece of shit."

He meets my eyes. "If you want to return with us, you need to prove your loyalty."

My heart skips a beat. "*If?*" I stutter. "I handed you my daughter.

Isn't that enough!" I scream, dislodging a flock of birds from their perch in a nearby tree.

"There's no reason for hysterics. *If* I allow you to join my team, you'll learn to control yourself." The General passes me a dagger. He's testing me. Damn it all to hell, because it takes every ounce of my willpower not to slice his throat right here, right now. I meet the General's calculating stare, and he urges me to comply. "Since the doctor stole you from my facility, *you* will punish him."

My gaze locks on to my friend lying on the ground. *Shit*. I test the weight of the metal and realize it's David's knife, the one holding the coordinates to our salvation. I glare at the General. The cunning bastard wants me to kill David with his own weapon.

"You just murdered an entire squad. What's one more?"

David meets my gaze and gives me a small nod. My heart drops to my stomach.

"No, I can't." I don't know if I'm replying to him or the General. Either way, it's the truth. I've only killed in self-defense.

"That's your only option." The General shrugs. "Prove yourself, Angelica, or die beside him."

The adrenaline is gone as dread consumes me. My knees quake and give out. David has been my friend through all of these nightmares. He rescued me from captivity. This man chose me over his safety and at the cost of protecting his own family. Warmth creeps up my leg and I glance to the bruised hand resting on my thigh.

"Do it for *her*," David wheezes. "I'm as good as dead anyway. Whether it be at your hands or theirs." He guides my wrist to his neck, the blade now resting just under his chin. "It's okay."

"It shouldn't be this complicated. The doctor stole you from the transport, took your freedom, and now he deserves to pay the price," the General coos. "Just as your alpha deserved the same fate for his sins against your pack."

Images of Fangs and our final battle together slam into my memories. But this is different. Isn't it? We were orphans... nobodies. David is someone's son, brother, and—I look at Angel as she nestles into the General's warmth—someone's savior.

"There has to be another way to prove myself."

"Do it or I'm leaving with the child and *without* you."

This is too much for my brain to process. Sticks dig into my legs, and I welcome the pain. *Fuck.* I tug at my matted hair. *What do I do?*

David clutches my wrists. "You will do this." His forehead taps mine and he whispers, "I love you and nothing will ever change that."

The cold metal burns my palm. "I don't... I don't want to do this to you," I whimper.

"I know. But you'll have a chance to save the world with this little sacrifice."

I'm trading one horror for another. There is no *saving,* just prolonging my agony. But I owe it to my pup to watch over her. Who knows what the General is planning next?

"I'm so sorry." My heart splinters as I raise the weapon. "I really wanted to have that happily ever after," I whisper. "You, me, and Angel."

David's lip quivers until he stiffens it. "There's no reason to be sorry. You and Angel will get that one day. I know it."

I line the edge against his carotid artery. He'll die quick and painlessly. I take a breath. "Good bye..."

"Not there," the General interrupts. "I want him to suffer. I want to witness the doctor struggle to take his last *agonizing* breath." A vein in his neck sticks out and I know I'm out of time.

If I'm to survive, I must play the part perfectly.

I force myself to meet my master's fury and begin my new hell. "*Where* do you want me to do it, sir?"

His grin touches his ears. "Carve into his abdomen and drag out his entrails." The General leans in to get a front-row seat to the massacre as he strokes my cheek. "Get it over with so we can leave and feed the child."

We. Fuck, it boils my blood. There's a raging inferno about to erupt. He can take that *we* and shove it!

I grind my molars. "As you wish."

I give David my full attention. I burn his dark gaze into my memory, never forgetting the kindness he's demonstrated towards me. The way he loved me and Angel, even in his final hours. As I stare into his eyes, so many emotions pass between us. I mentally thank him for everything. I thank him for helping me when he hardly knew me. I thank him for saving us. I thank him for keeping me sane. I thank him for showing me how love is supposed to be.

Then I press my lips against his *one last time.*

He returns my kiss, before whispering into my ear. To the General, it appears to be a sweet goodbye. But in reality, it's my future safe haven. The *coordinates* to the abandoned facility. "Make them pay for what they've done," David grinds out so that everyone can hear him.

I can only nod. Even now, moments before his execution, he's only thinking of me. It's my turn to do the same. "I'll make sure your family is safe."

I don't say goodbye. I simply *can't.*

I line up the tip and slam down until the hilt hits his belly button. His lids squeeze shut as he grunts, attempting to hold back his agony. Blood swirls over my fingertips. I twist the metal and tug the silver blade across his pale skin, creating a straight line. His anguished screams rip past his lips and vibrate the trees around us. Instinctively, David reaches over to staunch the flow of blood, and his hands pale as they clutch his gaping wound.

"Make it stop!" he shrieks.

His plea slices through my heart. My hold on the weapon falters. *What am I doing?*

I swallow down my last ounce of courage and finish the job. David releases a guttural wail before he rolls onto his side. My wrists shake as I reach inside my friend and complete the task. His intestines are warm as I heave them inch by inch at the General's boots. David gurgles incoherently. And then he stills, his once beautiful eyes directed skyward. Blank and unblinking.

This is what I've become for my daughter.

"Let the animals feast on his remains." The General kicks David's lifeless corpse. "Come, pet. It's time to leave."

Drenched in crimson, with my sanity shattered, I place the dagger on David's chest and whisper the last promise I'll ever make to him. "They'll suffer for these injustices. I'll make it rain red."

Part 2: The Rebels Rise

Angelica

Collar

Present

I *killed* David.

I killed *David.*

My brain repeats this over and over again as the military vehicle weaves in and out of the city traffic. I stare at the sleeping bundle in my arms. I hope it was worth it.

I miss him, with his bossy attitude and charming smile.

I cringe as the memory fades and his life force coating my skin screams back at me. No matter what he meant to me, in the end, I slaughtered him. Not just that, but I tortured him.

I swallow the bile burning my throat. I'll worry about the consequences later. I lean into my seat and my heavy lids close as exhaustion finally sweeps me under.

"Wake up!" the General demands as he ushers me out of the car and towards my new prison. He holds open the front door and I squeeze Angel tight as I cross the threshold of the tiny cottage.

Why am I not at a facility? Where're all the guards?

"Give me the child while you shower." My captor doesn't wait for me to answer before he pries my daughter out of my arms.

I open my mouth to protest but bite it back. If he had wanted to hurt her, he would have done so already. I take a minute to assess the man in front of me. Although he's an asshole, the little girl in his arms seems to have stolen his cold, dead heart. He whispers in her ear and tickles her chin.

Am I delusional right now?

He meets my searching gaze and narrows his. A silent warning passes between us before I scurry towards the bathroom. The room isn't hard to locate in the tiny one-bedroom home. The white tiles scream as I drag my grime over them. That's all I am right now, caked-on blood and mud. Nothing more.

I force myself under the cascading water. My discretions swirling together before slipping past the drain with the last of David's life.

My palm shakes as I stare at my hands. The doctor is gone because of me. I lower myself to the floor and sob into my knees as the memories choke me. He trusted me. Broke me out. Delivered Angel. And how did I repay his generosity? With his own knife to the gut while he begged for it all to end.

"Stop crying. You did what you had to survive."

I ignore the harsh voice and shake my head.

"A soldier knows when he's been outgunned."

"But I'm *not* a soldier."

"You are now," the General growls. "Now clean yourself up."

I can't muster the strength. When did I last eat or drink? Between the mental and physical exertion, my body is shutting down.

"For fuck's sake." He slips into the shower fully clothed as if I'm not even here. He grabs the bar of soap and viscously scrubs it over my exposed skin. The creamy bubbles morph to an inky black sludge.

Why is he in here with me? Is this more mental warfare?

My head shoots up. "Where's Angel?"

"Resting in her bassinet." For being the spawn of Satan, his caresses are tender.

"Why do you hate us?" The words slip past my cracked lips before I can stop them.

"Who said that I hated you?" The General takes his time stroking my engorged breasts, rubbing his thumb over my nipple as he goes. "Your kind is an abomination, a disease," he says as if he's reporting the weather. His fingertips graze my collarbone before wrapping around my neck. "Your kind must be eradicated *or* enslaved." My pulse quickens as my oxygen trickles past his hold. "So, what do you choose, pet?" When I don't answer, he releases my neck to tug my wet hair until I meet his gaze. "What will it be? Enslavement or eradication?"

"I choose my *daughter*. So whatever action will keep her by my side, that's my choice," I sneer, my fangs elongating as I spit the words in his face.

"There's that fire." The General's husky tone vibrates the steam-filled air. "The moment I met you at the Warehouse, I knew I had to have *you* on my team." He licks his lips, his gaze far off as he whispers, "You remind me of her."

"Who?"

He shakes his head, as if clearing his thoughts. "Finish washing so you can feed the child." He squirts shampoo into my palm to drive his point across. "I have a physician on his way to perform a physical exam on you to make sure you're not damaged."

I massage my scalp as he watches. Then I do the same with the floral conditioner. The whole time, I imagine myself cutting off his dick and shoving it down his fucking throat.

Of course, I'll be written up as fucking damaged. He made me this way.

"What if I am broken?"

"Then you will wean the pup and be put down."

My heart races. "But you said…"

"That was under specific conditions. You can't expect me to leash an animal if they are unable to perform their intended duties."

I stand under the shower stream, feeling a little more like myself than I did a moment ago. Once I've rinsed, the General shuts off the faucet and glides a soft towel across my skin.

"For now, I'll be your handler." He guides me to the sink with his palm on the small of my back. Before I can protest, he clinks a metal choker around my neck. "You will protect me with your life and attack on my command. Any funny business and I will electrocute you and watch you drool into the carpet."

I scratch at the weight of my collar, watching as he passes me a thin hospital gown.

"You will nurse the child, then rest because tomorrow starts your new life."

I stare at my reflection in the mirror. Even with my flabby postpartum belly, I'm boney. My cheekbones stick out, and there're black circles under my eyes. I blink and curse. All of that running from the General was for nothing. Was he tracking us the entire time? Just waiting until I gave birth before interfering? The cold steel hugging my neck chills my bones.

REBEL'S TAIL OF REVENGE

It doesn't matter because this is my life now.

"Every *good* girl deserves a pretty collar." The General's knuckle traces my arm, causing goose bumps to rise along my skin.

Funny. I used to think humans were the shifters' enemy. But it's not the human species as a whole. It's their corrupt government that's the problem.

I claw at the metal necklace and glare at my captor. "And what do *bad* girls deserve?"

"Go ahead and test me to find out for yourself. But I promise you, mutt, you won't like the outcome for you *or* your daughter."

Angelica

Mission Ready

After days of being probed and scanned, the truth is uncovered. I am damaged. Not only mentally, but physically too. But that's old news to me.

"She's unfit for the breeding program." The doctor adjusts his thick glasses. "And her psychological evaluations suggest that she's unable to perform under the pressures of your other program."

The General runs a thumb over his stubble. "What are you suggesting we do with her?"

I cross my arms over my chest and bite my tongue. *Yes, let's talk about her as if she's not sitting in the damn room.*

"At this time, we deny her request to aid our efforts. But when her offspring is of age, we can use it in her place."

I leap from my seat. "What did you *say*?"

The man takes a step away from me. "That's just my medical

opinion."

"How about I show you just how capable I am?" My growl vibrates the walls. "I might be damaged, but I can still follow orders and kill on command." I side-eye the General, and his dark smirk is the only encouragement I need.

The doctor swipes his sweaty forehead. "With proper training, technically, the patient could…"

I shove him into his mahogany desk. "The patient has a fucking *name*. Stop treating me like the shit stuck to the bottom of your shoe."

"Sorry. *Angelica*…" the doctor squeaks. "…might prove to be effective in other ways, with proper training of course."

His hands are shaking and he's about to piss his pants. There's no way I'm letting this pompous know-it-all judge me and decide my fate. Or that of my kid.

"Useful in what way?" The General arches a brow.

"She has street smarts and knows the art of seduction. Both could be useful additions to your arsenal if she's kept on a tight leash."

I narrow my eyes. I'm not going to fuck anyone for information again.

The General unfolds his long legs and rises from his chair. "What am I going to do with you?" His fingertips dance over my cheek. "Pity. It looks like I'll have to put a bullet between your eyes and call it a lost cause."

He can't do this. Not after how far I've come. The things I've done…

"I'm *not* worthless." I stab my chin towards my captor.

"The doctor says otherwise, and unfortunately, he must sign off on all my soldiers. It's protocol." His metal weapon hisses as it's freed from its holster. "I did have high hopes for you. I really did."

The safety's click echoes around the office.

My daughter's life flashes before me. The missed birthdays. The family barbecues. The many men I'd kill because they broke her fragile heart.

I crumble at the General's feet from the weight of the loss. "I'm not *worthless*. Let me prove my loyalty."

The icy barrel presses against my temple. The chill causes me to suck in my last lungful of oxygen and pray to Luna to watch over my baby girl when I'm gone.

"Do *not* make another mess in *my* office." The doctor's brevity returns. "Take the bitch outside and do it properly."

The General's jaw ticks. His dark eyes slowly shift from me to the man in front of us. "What did you say to me?"

A glacial chill slithers to my toes. *Oh, shit.* Someone doesn't like being told what to do.

Clearly, the doctor doesn't take the hint. "The last time you put down a shifter that failed its exam, there was brain matter all over my paperwork and it took me days to clean it up."

The General returns his weapon to its holster while clicking the safety back on. "Oh, my apologies. I'll be more careful with how I handle my business from now on." He strokes my hair until his palm rests under my chin. "I'll also be more careful with whom I trust to work on my team." He takes a step away from my prone form before plucking an invisible piece of lent from his uniform. "And I think I'll start today." He lowers himself onto his leather seat and crosses one leg over the other, then leans back.

The tension sizzles around the tiny area as his words sink in.

The man in the white coat clears his throat. "I think that is very wise. You wouldn't want to sully your record of providing the best troops for the shifter unit."

"Was there ever any doubt in my abilities?" The words slice the air as sharp as a well-honed dagger.

"Never," the doctor stutters.

"So, if I were to believe that Angelica is an exceptional candidate, you'd heed my opinion and sign off on her paperwork?"

My ears perk up as I glance in the General's direction.

He ignores me and waves his hand to my folder. "Well?"

"I…" The doctor's gaze bounces from me to the General.

"Angelica, it seems that the doctor can't make up his mind. This is your chance to convince him of your *qualifications*."

I stand to my full height and brush my hair off my shoulder. "What did you have in mind, boss?" I grin at the sweating lump of man meat cowering in front of us. "Should I demonstrate my knife skills or maybe my hand-to-hand combat?"

"No need," the doctor squeaks. He snatches a pen with a shaky wrist and scribbles over the papers. "I have complete confidence in your judgement, General," he says as he hands over the folder.

"Are you sure?" the General taunts. "I've seen her gut a lover and unwind his intestines without thinking twice."

I swallow down the bile as the memories of executing David swarm my vision. I force my back to remain straight. *I can't show weakness.*

"Yes, I've given her a clean bill of health and I've released her for duty."

"Excellent." The General lazily unfolds his legs again and stands. "Always a pleasure to work with you." And with a flick of his wrist, he motions me to his side.

I follow at his heels and let the information sink in. I press my fingertips against my barren stomach. I'll never feel a child kick or somersault inside me again. That fact hurts more than I ever imagined it would.

We turn the corner and enter an abandoned hallway. I almost ram my forehead into the General's back when he stops suddenly.

"Dr. Carter knows too much," he whispers so low I think I'm hearing things until he adds, "If he squeals to my superiors, my judgement will be questioned." The General taps his watch and adjusts the collar of his shirt. "He is taking his lunch break now. Make sure he doesn't return to the building. Then meet me out front. If you can manage that without being detected, I'll agree to train you."

I nod and pivot, sticking to the shadows as I stalk my prey's pungent scent outside. If this is what it'll take to keep my pup safe, I'll do it. I cross my arms over my chest and lean on a shady oak tree. "Hello, Doc."

Dr. Carter's spine snaps to attention and his fear taints the cool, crisp breeze.

"You know, we have something in common."

He swallows hard and raises his hands in a pitiful display of self-defense.

I curl my lip into a sneer. "It seems we are both *unfit* for duty."

He doesn't have time to scream before I pounce.

When the job is done, I slide into the SUV and shut the door. The General's gaze sweeps across my frame. I suppress a smirk. There's not even a drop of evidence visible. He won't find a hair out of place. This isn't my first or *last* murder. He dips his chin in silent approval before the vehicle pulls away from the crime scene.

"Make sure Angelica has her identification card expedited. We'll also accelerate her basic training and advanced shifter training," he says as our driver merges onto the highway.

"Yes, sir."

The trees blur into a concrete forest. Smog builds from the tall skyscrapers. This isn't Carson City. *Fuck. How far away are we from my home?* My heart splinters. *Now I'm an orphan with no home in sight, only prisons and cages.*

Oh, the things we give up for the sake of our children. To protect them. I side-eye the man beside me. To keep them away from the monsters lurking in the shadows. One day. He'll pay. As if sensing his imminent downfall, the General glances up from his phone. I lift my chin and he arches a brow in challenge.

Let the fun begin.

His door opens, the cheerful sun slaps me in the face, and I break our silent standoff to shield my melting eyes. General:1, me: 0.

"Follow, pet," the asshole demands as he exits the SUV.

At least he didn't slap his leg and whistle while calling, "Here, girl." Although I wouldn't have minded a tasty treat when I obeyed. I'm famished. Especially after killing the doctor in my beast form.

Instead of verbalizing as much, I bite my tongue and follow him. I squint at the suburban home looming in the distance. *What is this place?* I look over my shoulder and my jaw falls open. We are in the middle of a neighborhood. The General lifts a hand in greeting as a woman jogs behind a stroller.

"Morning, Levi," she sings.

"How's the family doing, Jill?"

"Caleb is teething, so everyone has to suffer." She laughs. "How's Jake?"

"He's doing well. Thank you."

"That's great. You must be proud."

"Yes, I am."

"Well, I won't keep you." She nods and picks up her pace again.

"I'll see you tonight at the FRG meeting."

Does this woman not realize who this man is? What does FRG stand for? Freaks Rage Group? Fuckers Repent Gathering?

"Looking forward to it." He waits until the chipper woman passes. Then he rolls his eyes and mutters to his secretary, "I hate those meetings."

"They always have decent coffee and cake." The kid shrugs. "Plus, it keeps up with appearances, especially with Jake…"

The General cuts his secretary a glare and the kid snaps his lips closed. "You are dismissed. Be here before the meeting." The General pivots to the front door and swings it open without another word.

I fight the urge to scratch my head and mutter, *"What the fuck?"*

"Pet." The darkness of the home beckons me forward.

I suck in a breath, straighten my back, and enter my new hell. I stumble. *Why are there beige walls with paintings of far-off places with lush grasses? Oh shit. Is that a fully stocked bar?* My mouth waters at the prospect of a stiff drink. Even if I have to lap it up on all fours. My weary soul needs a strong whiskey or bourbon.

"Welcome, miss," a honey-laced voice announces herself. "My name's Julia."

I blink at the woman's pressed outfit and gelled hair. Her attire is immaculate. Then I glance down at my black pants and shirt and feel like a disheveled pig.

"Hi?" I peek over at the General, unsure how he wants me to interact with the newcomer.

Big mistake. His Dark Lordship is cradling Angel. My pulse spikes. Is he going to hurt her? Did I do something wrong?

"Julia is a trained pediatric nurse and an essential member of the shifter program. She will be assisting with the pup's care until we transfer the child to one of our training facilities."

I swallow down my growing terror. "When will Angel be transferred?"

"I've been informed that pups need their mother's milk to grow adequately and be most effective to our cause." He hands the newborn to Julia. "So once the pup is weaned, she'll be transferred."

My hands shake at my side. I want to grab my daughter and run. "May I hold her?"

The General ignores my request and addresses the nurse instead. "Julia, show my pet to her new cage and explain what's to be expected of her." He strides to the bar and uncorks an amber liquid, dismissing us.

"Right this way." Julia glides towards an open bedroom. It's plain with no pictures or decorations. It screams *temporary* lodging, but there's no cage or shackles. A single twin bed in one corner and a crib in the other stare back at me. Julia nods to a wooden rocking chair in the center of the room. "Please have a seat."

I hold back my shock when she *invites* me to sit. When was the last time someone asked rather than demanded I do something? I lower myself into the uncomfortable chair. Julia smiles at Angel before rewarding me with the bundle of joy. I force down my blubbering as my sweet little girl blinks at me. *She's perfect.*

I kiss her temple and press her to my chest. "I missed you, little one."

"Let me close this to give you some privacy." Julia strides over to the open doorway and pulls it shut. She pivots to us and nods to my shirt. "It's time to feed her."

I guess I'm not getting privacy from *her*. I grumble but remove the barrier and rest the pup at my engorged breast. The newborn latches on and eagerly suckles. I lean into the tall back of my chair and rock. My eyes drift closed, and I can almost imagine us in the woods with David. His finger tracing soothing circles over Angel's cheek and his face lowering to kiss the top of my head.

"Men like the General are ambitious, which makes them cautious when it comes to *someone* new." Julia tugs me out of my brief escape from reality as she leans against the wall, watching me. "He doesn't trust easily."

It takes me a second to catch on to her meaning, but I meet her inquisitive stare. "Well, I'm not a *new* toy," I snap. "Unfortunately, I've known him for years. The General stalked my pack, then destroyed everything I loved. Only to *generously* let me live."

"Is the pup the offspring of a strong sire?"

My lip quivers at the mental image of my mate. Was Freddy strong? *Yes.* Stupid? Abso-fucking-lutely.

"Her father was the strongest alpha in Cold Creek."

"That explains why the General has taken a special interest in her." The nurse scratches her nose and lowers her voice. "And you're planning to stay by her side?"

Her question throws me off. "Why? Did you expect me to just shoot my child out of my vagina and abandon her?" I snarl. "I'll never leave her. Never," I hiss for emphasis. "No matter what that monster puts *me* through."

"And you also understand that you've offered yourself and your abilities to a dangerous man who has obtained his status through torture and murder?"

"I can take care of myself," I whisper to my pup. "But she can't."

A small smile plays on the nurse's lips. I must have answered correctly. "You realize the General will continue to refer to you as his pet," she presses with a hint of amusement.

"Isn't he just a big *sweetheart*?" I growl.

"I like your spirit." She pushes off the wall with a sigh. "You'll have to be careful. He'll knock that sarcasm right out of you."

"Yeah." I stroke Angel's arm. "I picked up on that."

Laughter brightens the room as we share a rare moment of understanding. Julia busies herself, pointing out the diapers and other infant care items. I let out a breath and my shoulders sag into the chair. In another world or maybe even another life, we could have been friends, but as things stand, I'll have to kill her when I escape with my daughter.

The pup's suckles get slower the more milk she consumes. Then they stop altogether. Her mouth remains open in an O-shape, and she drifts into a milk-drunk slumber.

"She's beautiful," Julia coos.

"Thank you."

The nurse nods, then readies the crib. "Would you like to lay her down?"

I hold my daughter tighter. "Give me five more minutes."

"Five more minutes, then you'll have to let her go or you'll risk both our necks."

I rub my nose on Angel's forehead and kiss her cheek, soaking up every second of our time together.

Three months later...

Whoever categorized this as *basic* training should be shot. My training is from dusk to dawn, or until I pass the fuck out. The General is ruthless. He's always demanding I push myself more, and on top of that, he's a complete asshole, taking pleasure in my suffering.

The only brightness to my shit-filled days is my daughter. Angel is growing like a weed, and I enjoy all the time I have cuddling with her. It's during these moments that I forget the hell I live, and I suffocate her with my motherly snuggles.

In the darkness of the night, I recite the tales of our people, ones I learned from Spike while sitting around the campfire with the stars twinkling above our pack. I also explain who her father was and how we met that dark day so many years ago. I remind her of what her brave bonus dad David sacrificed for us so we could live another day together. And as I gently lay the sleeping girl in her crib, I don't stop the sobs that rack my frame.

In that lonely dimness, I release the pent-up exhaustion, pain, and tremendous loss so it doesn't continue to etch away at my compassion and love. Because that trapped *poison* constantly churns my insides, battling to win over my humanity and twist me into the devil yanking on my leash. But I won't give the General *this* victory. He may hold my restraint, but I'll never surrender my sanity.

Angel's cries break me from my dark thoughts.

"Shhh. I've got you, little one," I coo as I pull her from her crib. I lower myself onto the rocking chair and wipe her tears. "It's okay. Mommy is here." She latches on and eagerly drinks her fill. "Did I tell you your daddy hates peas?" A yawn cracks my jaw. "He won't touch them." My eyes fight to stay open. "Can't even smell them without gagging."

I jolt awake, as the bedroom light is turned on and smacks me in the face. I squint at the clock. It's only three in the morning. Angel buries her face into my chest, begging for another snack.

"We leave in ten minutes," the General snips. "Pump what you have, and the nurse will supplement with formula as needed."

I kiss my daughter's forehead and whisper, "I love you," before handing her over to the nurse. We nod at one another in understanding. She'll take care of my infant, and if not, I'll tear her head from her shoulders. Consequences be damned.

"Good luck," Julia says under her breath as she lays Angel down to change her diaper.

I snatch the automatic breast pump and shove it in my bra as I pull out my issued black tactical pants and tank top. As I tug the shirt over my head, careful not to dislodge the pump in my bra, I pause to rub the scar on my arm. The same area where David cut out my tracker. My eyes mist at the lost life I should have had with him.

But there's no crying over spilled blood.

Not now. Not ever.

I lace up my boots and shove my weapons into their holsters. Even though my claws are sharper, the General prefers that I blend in with the team. Plus, he enjoys the shock on his enemies' faces when he releases his beast from her leash.

I set the expressed milk down by Julia as she tickles Angelica's chubby knees. *Luna, help me.* My baby girl is growing so fast. I know my time with her is fleeting, and soon we'll be ripped apart. I clutch my chest at the ache.

"Shit," I curse at my wristwatch. I'm out of time. I run down the hall and stand at attention by the front door with seconds to spare.

The General stomps forward and assesses my attire before nodding his approval. "An experiment has escaped, and we are on a time crunch before the authorities can hunt him down."

My eyes snap towards the keyrings hanging on the wall. "What vehicle do you require for transport?"

"None of those. We're being retrieved by the team."

The *team* is a bunch of spoiled, high-ranking military jerks. Yes, they know their way around weapons, but they hate me. The feeling is mutual.

A horn blares from outside, and I swing open the door, bowing my head as I wait for my master to exit. Acid coats the back of my throat as I force out the, "As you wish, sir."

We've been driving for hours. Our bodies jolt as the high-performance tires tackle another fallen log in its path. The climate is changing from a chilly breeze to an icy blizzard with snow-covered foliage beyond what the eyes can see.

"We are almost there, General," one of the men announces as he taps on his laptop.

"When we arrive, you are to strip and shift," the General demands.

The others smirk in my direction. I'm the only shifter, so they know *who* he's talking to. They get to remain warm and toasty, while I'm naked and miserable. Well, joke's on them. Thick fur is much better than their thin skin. The vehicle jerks to a halt and I peel off my outfit, leaving my weapons behind.

"Act like professionals," the General growls to the group.

My attention is redirected to the soldier leering at my heavy breasts. The subordinate pivots and finds his boots more fascinating. I snort. *Wow. Times have changed.* My old alpha used my body *sexually* to obtain intel from our enemies. Now my new one uses my brute strength to kill first and ask questions later.

"Who's the target?" I question my handler.

The General slides over his tablet, and a picture of a scarred shifter with dark eyes stares back at me from the screen. "Experiment 217. He's killed a handful of soldiers, so use caution." He then passes me a piece of shredded fabric. "Here's his scent."

I pinch the grimy garment between my fingertips. "Do you want him dead or alive?"

"His betrayal is inexcusable. If he's not dead when you retrieve him, he will be when I get my hands on him."

"I understand." But I really don't. Any caged shifter in that position would have run for his freedom. It's our natural instinct.

"It's imperative that he doesn't end up in the *wrong* hands. If the authorities find him, they may shut down our experiments."

David's words slam into my chest and remind me how the scientists would drain the blood and even cut tissue cells off shifters, as they attempted to replicate their capabilities. Experiment 217 must be one of their test subjects. My finger glides over my target's disfigured frame. I should snap his neck and put him out of his misery *and* out of the General's grasp.

"Is there a problem, pet?" The General's icy tone straightens my spine.

"No, sir." I open the door, and the cold air takes our breath away.

"Rendezvous in three hours."

I've been dragging my paws through ice and snow for two and a half hours. *Fuck me.* I shake the powdery flakes from my pelt. *Why can't I catch a glimpse of a paw print, fur, anything? Did the team give us the wrong coordinates?* Either way, the General won't like my report when I come back empty-handed. My wolf grimaces as I pivot towards our rendezvous point, not looking forward to explaining the situation.

An icy breeze tickles my snout and I pause. I squint into the darkening horizon. Is that a cabin with smoke bellowing from its chimney?

I bullet towards it, throwing white fluff in my wake. Please let this be *something*. Once I reach my destination, I skid to a halt, dusting the side of the home with tiny silver crystals of snow. I crouch and lick the surrounding area. There are two shifters nearby.

Hmm, a musky, woodsy taste just like the scent left on the fabric the General handed me. Experiment 217 is close.

I arch my neck to see into the cabin's window and blink past the blinding light filtering out of the glass pane. Once my eyes adjust, the scene before me steals my breath. The experiment is in human form and has a female bent at the hips while he rage fucks her from behind. Is this consensual? Scratches mar the woman's dark frame and tears wet her cheeks.

Did he break out just to have a one-night stand?

Pain wraps an invisible hand over my neck and squeezes. I wince and fall to the ground as my collar ignites another sharp zap. *Fuck. There's no time to help the woman.* The General's reminding me of our scheduled meet-up, and if I'm not back soon, I'll be a fried kabob. I peek one more time to make sure my spasm didn't catch the humping beast's attention. *Nope.* He's still grunting as he takes advantage of the girl.

Haunting memories of Cole raping me as a child threaten to take over my thoughts. But I snap the lid shut on that, leap into a snow drift, and gallop back to the SUV to return to my master.

"Why are you late?" The General's thumb dances over the zapper's remote. "Report."

I rub my scorched neck. "I found Experiment 217."

His brow shoots up. "And you let him get away?"

"No. You did," I snap. My knees fail me and I crumble to the snow as his trigger finger taps my torture device. "He's at a cabin," I wheeze out. "Let me take you to him."

The pain stops and the General glares at me. "What was he doing? Did he see you?"

"No, he didn't see me. He was mating with another shifter."

My master's eyes sparkle with that bit of information. "Was his partner a female?"

Well, this is getting awkward.

"Yes, it was a female."

It's like Christmas morning for the sick bastard. He's practically salivating at the gift I've dropped into his lap. "Prepare to move out," he barks at the team. The soldiers gear up, only mildly grumbling about freezing their asses off. The General throws a jacket to me. "You too, pet."

"You don't want me in fur?"

"No. I don't want him to know we have a shifter at our disposal. It may scare him into hiding again." The General rubs his stubble. "We could wait a few hours before collecting our prize." A sinister grin creeps over his features. "I would *love* to add another pup to our program." He watches me. "Wouldn't Angel benefit from having a playmate?"

I grind my jaw. "Whatever you want, sir."

I don't wish this life on anyone. Human or shifter.

A few hours later, I clutch my jacket as the wind picks up. *Stupid cold.* I silently signal to the log cabin on top of a hill. The team approaches slowly with their weapons raised. They do a quick assessment of the outside perimeter.

"Doesn't look like anyone is... Oh, shit," a soldier stutters.

We peek around the corner to see blood decorating the cabin walls. My eyes widen. *Did he kill the woman?*

I kneel by the closest splatter, brushing my finger across it before tasting the sample. "This is from another male."

"The fireplace is still warm. They can't be far." The General gestures for his team to follow him. "Let's move out."

We are shoved into the blistering snow again. The temperatures are dropping, it's getting dark, and my boobs are begging to be emptied. But I clamp my mouth shut, knowing damn well who's in charge. After a few hours of playing flashlight tag in the dark, the team's morale plummets.

"Fuck!" The General kicks a tree. "Where did they go?"

"Do you want me to shift, sir?"

He assesses the storm brewing in the clouds and shakes his head. "We'll reconvene in the morning after the weather clears." He glances out towards the team again. "Johnson!"

"Yes, General?"

"Keep close to the cabin. If the local authorities show up, wave your badge and keep them from looking too hard into our whereabouts. The rest of you, return to base."

We pick up the pace, eager to get back to the vehicle and out of the cold. My mind drifts to the dark-skinned stranger. I hope she's okay. I scratch under my collar. If only I could find a way to help her.

"Was the female shifter in heat?" The General taps a finger on his tablet, making notes for his report.

"I'm not sure," I answer honestly.

"We assumed the bitches could be sniffed out," one of the General's lackeys chimes in while elbowing his buddy. "Just like a peach *ripe* for the picking." They share a laugh.

"The *males* can detect the scent, not the females." I roll my eyes skyward. "We track our cycles, but we don't go around sniffing for pussy. It's not like a roasting chicken with the little tabs in the breast that poke out when it's hot and ready."

The men blink and then burst into laughter again. "That's the most I've heard the bitch speak."

Assholes. I've been helping them for months, and yet I get no respect. I'm always the bitch, mutt, or pet to them.

"Enough," The General barks. "Load up, before I decide to leave you behind with Johnson."

We leap into the warm vehicle, and I melt into the toasty leather. The driver drops off the others at the facility. Then the General spends some time speaking with the scientists behind closed doors. I sit like a loyal pooch, straining to hear their conversation. But it's just muffled voices. I rub my forehead, unable to get the woman out of my thoughts.

Did she know who that man was? How long will he let her live?

"Follow, pet," the General orders as he strides out of the office, and I tread at his heel.

The car ride home is silent, and tension radiates from my captor. I bet his superiors aren't happy with his report. I don't blame them. This kind of escape is unheard of. I smirk to myself. Well, except for when David got me out. Is the General's chain of command becoming impatient with him? I cringe at the realization. What will happen to me and Angel if he's pulled off the shifter program?

Fuck, it's all so complicated.

Angelica

Run Away

*O*nce we pull into the driveway, I rush to open the front door. I bow my head as the General brushes past me without a word.

"Welcome back, sir," Julia greets.

He grunts and stomps towards the bar.

The nurse and I share a look that says we *better not get on his bad side.* Then she passes me my daughter. "She was perfect, as usual, and took her naps without a fuss."

I bury my face into my baby girl's stomach, and she giggles while tugging at my hair. *Luna, I've missed her.* No matter how my day goes, she always makes it better.

The front door opens and a female in uniform enters. She pauses when she sees us, and her brows knit together.

"Report," the General snarls over his crystal decanter.

She scurries over to him and hands him a folder. He flips through it, only to slam it on the table. He sips his amber liquid in deep thought.

I share another glance with Julia. *Something's wrong.* I hold Angel closer, praying whatever it is won't rip her from my arms.

"That's all. You are dismissed," he commands the female soldier.

"Are you sure you don't want me to stay?" She pouts, disappointment written all over her pretty face.

I sniff the air and her arousal is obvious. *Well, well, well. Does the General have a play toy?*

"May I be excused to feed Angel?" I cut into their stare-off.

The other woman looks down her nose at me like I'm an insect buzzing around her mouthwatering meal.

"Don't make me dismiss you again." The General waves her out the front door. When it shuts behind her, he holds his hands out to Angel. I bite my lip, hating the helpless feeling in the pit of my stomach as I pass my daughter to him. "Have you been a good girl?" He rubs noses with hers. She squeals and smacks his cheek. Then he pins the nurse with a glare. "She looks pale."

Julia swallows. "It's just past her bedtime, sir."

He returns his attention to Angel. "How will you grow into a warrior and rain terror down on our enemies if you don't sleep?"

"She was also a little gassy today. I think the formula hurts her stomach," Julia tells me.

The General massages the infant's belly. "Do you need to be fed?" He cradles her to his chest, then hands her back to me. "Feed her." He scowls. "Then you need to pump every few hours tonight to give Julia enough supply for tomorrow," he says, striding off without another word before locking himself in his office.

The nurse releases her breath. "That man is a ticking time bomb," she whispers.

I take Angel to the nursery but pause at the picture frames littering the walls. I've lived here for months now, and I never asked. "Is this the General's home?"

"Yes," Julia answers.

I blink at a photo of him, a woman, and a little boy. "Where's his family?"

"That information is classified." She nods towards my room, clearly dismissing my inquiry. "The General asked me to return first thing in the morning to watch over Angel." She ushers us into the bedroom. "Hopefully, you both can get a few hours of sleep." Then she leaves the door cracked open as she exits.

I huff, dropping myself into the rocking chair and tugging off my shirt. Angel nuzzles my nipple and suckles greedily. I sigh as pressure eases from my chest. "How was your day, little one?" When she doesn't respond, I tell her all about my day and she listens intently, until her eyes grow too heavy. Then she becomes milk drunk and her mouth hangs open on a contented sigh. I kiss her puffy cheeks. "Sleep well, sweetheart."

I lay her down. Then I stare at my uneven chest size. Why does Angel always favor the right side? Exhaustion floods my brain and all I want to do is curl into bed, but I won't be able to rest until I pump the other engorged breast.

I tug open the drawers in the nursery but I can't find my pump. A crash from the living room causes me to withdraw the weapon from the sheath on my thigh. I dash into the dimly-lit space with my weapon at the ready.

"I told you to go home," the General growls.

"But I know you didn't mean it." The female soldier from earlier purrs.

"I did."

"Why? Because your pet is here?" she hisses, stepping into his

157

personal space.

Bad idea.

My training kicks in and I shred my clothes and morph to fur. I warm his side and snarl. She sidesteps and gasps while the General strokes my hackles. "My *pet* is obedient, loyal, and powerful."

"After everything we've been through, you are really going to choose a shifter over me?"

I step towards her, warning her to back down.

"What the fuck are you going to do? You are *leashed,* bitch. Nothing more than government *property.*" She slams her boot into my face. The force causes me to stumble. "See? And I bet you can't even take a shit without permission."

"Enough!" the General roars.

Knowing I can't attack unless commanded or the General's life is in immediate danger, I shake my ears, to ease the sting of her blow. My master kneels to inspect the bump forming below my eye. The woman growls before lunging at us. I push past his inspection and dig my claws into her shoulders, pinning her to the soft carpet.

"Get her off me!"

The General tilts his head at her and places his hands behind his back. "You are a disappointment, soldier."

She visibly pales. "What?"

"There's no room for disloyalty on my team." He pours himself a hefty serving of whiskey from the bar and throws it back. "Take her in the woods and make it look like an accident." He turns his back to us and dispenses another drink.

"No! You can't do this!"

His thunderous footsteps break through her panicked screech, and the General pushes me aside to grab the woman. "I *can't?*"

Rage fuels his unspoken threat. "Trust me. I'm capable of many unspeakable things."

Angel starts wailing from the nursery. The General's jaw ticks. Then he swipes out a hand and slaps the woman, knocking her unconscious.

He rubs his temples. "I'll tend to the child. You do what I asked."

I morph into two feet and quickly toss the limp body over a shoulder.

"Wait." He curses under his breath. "You feed Angel and I'll deal with... *that*." His words are slurring and his mind is slower. He's going to need to sleep this off soon.

I drop the woman to the floor with a thud. "As you wish." Before he can change his mind, I rush to my pup. "It's okay. Mommy's here." I cradle her. "Everything is fine." She locates my swollen breast, and I hum as the pressure is once again released. "Eat all you want." I smooth her hair. "You're safe."

After thirty minutes, Angel is fast asleep in her crib. Being a mom is exhausting. I feel like it's not even my body anymore. I'm just a milking cow. *When does it get easier?*

I pivot and squeak. *How did I not notice his scent?*

The General's large frame is blocking my only exit. "How is she?" he asks.

"She's fine. She was just startled." I take in his blood-splattered clothes and his half-buttoned shirt with chest hair sprouting from the top. Odd. Normally, he keeps his kills clean.

He swirls the amber liquid clutched in his hand and the ice cubes clink against the glass. He usually limits himself to one nightcap. Whatever is going on... it has him spooked. "Experiment 217's hatred for me runs deep. I've kept him chained in a cage for years."

I swallow, thanking my lucky stars my daughter and I currently share a different fate.

The General brushes past me and kisses Angel's chubby hand. "If he finds us, he won't hesitate to destroy the child."

"Thank you for protecting her."

Because what else can I say?

His drunken gaze dances over my naked frame. His tongue darts across his lips. A cold dread creeps up my neck as he beckons me to follow him. Then he strides back to his bottle and pours another drink. "You look like her."

He's said this before. I can't help my curiosity. "Like who, sir?"

His chin juts towards a picture. "My wife." We do have similar facial features. "She was a spitfire, just like you."

What can I say to that? I could demand that he go to bed to sleep the liquor off, but I know hell will freeze over before that happens. "I'm sorry, sir."

"Sorry? Sorry!" He stalks towards me. "Your kind *stole* her from me!" He chucks his cup, and I yelp as glass shatters around us. "The shifters will regret the day they broke up my family." The corded muscles of his arms trap me to the wall.

My brain is in overdrive. He's my boss. The fate of my daughter's life is in his hands. One wrong move and it's game over.

"I understand why you feel that way." I swallow the knot in my throat and meet his gaze. "But just like humans, not all shifters are the same." I leave out the part where most of the shifters I've known probably would have kidnapped a human if the price were right.

He rubs his nose down my neck and inhales my scent. A growl rumbles deep in his throat. "Do you know how long I've wanted to fuck you into submission?" He palms my sex, and I gasp. "You're everything I love and *hate*, Angelica."

"Please don't do this."

His chuckle is dark and dripping with promises of pain. "Say it again. But this time…" He clutches my jaw. "Look me in the eye when you beg."

It always comes down to this. Men using my body as a weapon or as punishment. My lip quivers as my strong façade splinters. How do I get myself into these situations? I've been a good girl. Served my alpha. Yet here I am, once again begging someone to view me as more than a sex toy.

"*Please* don't do this."

The General slams his mouth onto mine, swallowing my plea like the sweetest honey. I try to take a step back, but I'm still trapped against the wall and his arms. His tongue swipes my lips, begging for entrance but I won't budge. The slap across my already-bruised cheek echoes around the room. I cry out as the pain sears my skin like a branding iron. My wolf claws at my surface, urging me to rip him to shreds.

"You will *not* refuse what is owed to me. I spared your life. Brought you into my home. And now I'm going to claim your pussy and own *every* part of you, pet."

I grit my teeth as my wolf barks in protest. My knee connects with the General's testicles. He releases a satisfying whoosh of air before he groans and falls to his side. Before he can catch his breath, I dash to my room.

I'm about to slam the door when his warning snarl gives me pause. "That was a fatal mistake, pet. But I may be willing to overlook it." He peels himself off the floor and brushes a hand over a wrinkle in his clothes. "You will return to me on your knees and beg for my forgiveness." When I don't immediately move to do his bidding, he adds, "*Before* I decide to electrocute you and put your collar on your daughter instead."

Angel stirs in her crib, releasing a soft coo in her sleep. And my eyes flick in her direction.

Would he really do that to her?

Angelica

On Your Knees

"**W**hat's it going to be, pet?" the General taunts.

I could shift and shred him limb from limb. Right here. Right now. And end his tyranny. There'd be no witnesses. I could take Angel and run.

Fur tickles my arm. Angel turns in the crib, then sucks on her tiny thumb. But last time we ran, how far did we get before the General was on us again?

Fuck. My wolf cowers. She won't put her pup in danger. Angel needs to be stronger for us to be able to survive on our own.

My master snaps his fingers, gaining my attention. A sinister grin darkens his face as he points at his feet. I clench my fists. What I wouldn't give to punch his lights out…

"That's right. Be my good girl and come." His zipper slides down and his erection groans against the fabric of his briefs.

I imagine a hundred different ways to destroy him. Including chomping off his pencil dick and choking him with his own nut sack.

"Get on your knees where you belong, pet."

I glare into the darkness of his soul as I do his bidding. I crawl to him like a loyal pooch. Before I can rest on my heels, he tugs my hair back until my neck screams for relief.

"You are going to suck my dick until my cum coats your throat."

Sick fuck. I turn my lips up into a snarl and open my mouth to toss my hatred in his face, but he thrusts his rod past my teeth. Shock riddles my frame as his thickness jabs at my tonsils. I cough, trying to remove the blockage from my windpipe.

His nails dig into my scalp. "You've been a naughty girl, Angelica. I warned you to behave. Now, take your punishment like a good whore."

Do this for your daughter's safety. Give him the best blow job of his fucking life. Then demolish him when he least expects it.

Well, if I'm doing this, it'll have to be believable. He wants a *whore*, so I give him one. I swirl my tongue over his length before nipping his weeping tip.

He groans out, "Fuck. Yes."

His demanding thrusts become more violent. I massage his ass, scratching him as I knead his cheeks. A guttural sound escapes his lips. I cup his balls, and just before he bursts, I give them a tight squeeze. He roars, and the pleasure causes him to stumble to his knees. Then I rise to my feet.

That's right, *General.* Look who's *bowing* to whom?

I swipe a hand over my chin and battle the urge to spit his fluids on him. Men like the one in front of me deserve to be put behind bars and gang raped. Not only does he condone experiments on other living beings, but he's forcing them to pleasure him. He's just like all the other lowlifes I was ordered to spy on. Always taking what he wants no matter the effect it has on others.

His eyes snap to mine. And for a second, I question whether I spoke my feelings out loud. He growls, the sound vibrating off the living room walls before he grabs my thighs. I scream as I stumble, trying to put distance between us. His hold only tightens, and my back meets the wall again. Like a starved madman, the General devours my pussy, greedily inserting his tongue as he laps at my neglected center.

Luna be damned. How long has it been?

His teeth graze my clit and my traitorous hips buck. He weaves his villainous sex magic, using his fingers to plunge into my warmth. The delicious pressure forces my eyes to roll back.

All too sudden the pleasure is gone, leaving cold emptiness at my throbbing core. The devil's claws scrape over my thighs as he bites and sucks all the way up my frame before he clamps down on the sensitive spot behind my ear.

"Oh, Luna!" I wheeze out as my knees shake.

If I were in wolf form, I'd be a puddle of goo on the ground, and he'd be fucking me from behind.

"That's right, pet." His thumb forces my chin up. My breathing comes out in quick, hot huffs. "You may pretend to hate what I do to you, but secretly you're begging for it."

I clench my traitorous thighs together, but there's no hiding the wetness. "You're wrong. I hate everything you do to me."

The General grabs my waist and twirls me around. I get a glimpse of the beige paint before he crushes my cheek against the unforgiving wall. His chest warms my back as he chuckles in my ear. "Is that so?" His knee separates my legs. "Because I think you love it, Angelica."

I suck in a breath and wait for him to force himself inside me.

"You're mine." He bites the tender spot again, and I whimper. Then he twists my body around and growls, "Say it."

He's fucking lost his mind. This madness goes far beyond the alcohol flooding his system. Whatever he read in the reports must have been soul-crushing.

Deal with that later. Focus on the now, Angelica.

I have a sex-crazed general waiting for me to comply. My mind replaces his face with my fallen mate's features, then David's. A slow grin lifts my heated cheeks. "You're right. I'm all yours."

The General's sanity snaps, and we tumble to the carpet as he removes the rest of his clothes. He snatches my ankles and throws them over his shoulders. Then his warm mouth is on my throbbing core again. I gasp and throw my head back. Ecstasy floods my mind as I allow desire to mingle with my hatred.

At the brink of my climax, he pulls away long enough to growl, "You will scream my name when I let you come." His thumb grazes my clit and my back arches.

"Yes, *General*."

"My *real* name."

My eyes flutter, unsure if I heard him correctly. He's never told me his first name. He slaps my pussy, drawing my attention back to my desperate need for a release.

"My name is Levi. And you will use it when you come."

I nod my understanding before dragging my fingertips through his hair and then to my pulsing bits. "I'm so close."

He devours my drenched center, until my voice goes hoarse from screaming and I collapse from my orgasm. When my euphoria settles, I'm on the floor with the General's arm draped over my frame and his chest resting against my back. He teases my slickness with his cock and I open wide for him.

"That's my good girl." He rubs his tip around my juices and moans. "From now on, you'll take me *whenever* I ask." His teeth dig into my neck at the same time he slams into me. I whimper at the delicious pain. "*This* dick will be the only one permitted inside your pussy. I don't share." His hips move teasingly slow. "Fuck, you're so tight." He flicks my clit and stars erupt behind my eyes. "Do you want *this*?"

"Yes," I moan, but his thrusts are just skimming where I need the pressure. "Faster."

His member fills me to the hilt, and I groan. "Did Freddy ever claim your tight ass?" His thumb grazes my other hole in question before dipping inside.

My eyes snap open at the mention of my lost mate. I grind my jaw. How dare he bring him up now. This bastard will pay in blood. A slap against my ass reminds me he's waiting for an answer.

"My *husband* claimed me in every possible way."

A snarl erupts from his throat before the General's rage fuels his thrusts. I grit my teeth to contain my agony. He's right. I do love rough sex. But I also had a child, and it's been months since anything's been inside me. His balls slap against me as he rides me like a bull. Hopefully, he only lasts eight seconds.

With a final grunt, he pours himself into me as his seed claims my womb. Then he tugs his dick out, dripping our juices over my sweaty body while marking me as his. He grabs a handful of my hair and pulls me until I meet his gaze. "Your *dead* partner won't be fucking anyone anymore. I made sure of that," the General spits out. "Now, I'm all you have left, pet. You are *mine*. Mind..." He pokes my forehead. "And body." He warms my pussy. He releases me with a parting sneer, his wet dick swaying between his legs like a victory flag. "Your breasts are leaking. Pump, then suck me off." He doesn't look back as he closes his bedroom door.

I glare towards his shadow. Sure, he can take my body as often as he wants. But he'll never get into my head. I'm not even trying and I'm already gaining all the intel I need to escape.

I'm going to burn your world down, *Levi*.

"Dad?"

My head shoots up at the sound of the young man's voice. I side-eye the General... Levi... whatever the fuck his name is.

"Shit." He throws the covers off our naked bodies. "Shift and act like a loyal bitch," he snarls over his shoulder as he tugs on his clothes. Then he throws open his bedroom door and slips out. "Jake? Shouldn't you be on base?"

I trot to my owner's side and sit at his heel. I cock my furry head at the other man in the room. He's in his twenties. I sniff the air around him. And he likes cheeseburgers and onion rings.

"When did *you* get a dog?" Jake grins as he kneels and strokes my shoulders. "You hate animals of any kind."

"I asked you a question," the General barks. "Answer me."

Jake sighs and meets his father head-on. "Don't you remember? It's Christmas vacation and we get leave. Or did you forget about me as per usual?"

"Watch your tone." The General pokes a finger at the kid's chest. "I have a full schedule, and I don't have time to manage yours on top of it."

"Has mom called?" Jake ignores his father and snatches up a handful of candy from a crystal container. There's a hint of mischief sparkling in his gaze, and I know whatever comes next involves a fresh wave of anger.

The General's eyes bulge out and his face turns red. "You've been in contact with her?"

I tilt my head. *So this wife of his is still around. Interesting.*

"She's my mother and it's my holiday break," the kid replies with a shrug. "But since we aren't allowed cell phones in the barracks, I thought maybe she'd call here."

The General slams his open palms against his son's chest until the kid's back hits the wall. "You will not speak to that traitor!"

"She left *you,* Dad. Not me," Jake snarls.

The General's ringtone blares from his bedroom. He tears his gaze from his son and towards the hallway. "We aren't done talking about this."

"I look forward to our next argument," Jake taunts.

The older man's jaw ticks before he stomps to his bedroom and slams the door shut. Pictures on the walls dance but stay in place. They must have practice. Jake pops his sweet treats into his mouth before striding towards the kitchen.

Shit. Do I stay by my master or follow the kid to the food? Pretending to be a dog is hard work.

I pad to the bedroom and press my ear to the door. I hear bits and pieces of work-related conversation before I decide to retreat. If the General thinks I'm snooping, he'll whack my nose with a newspaper. I trot towards the kid, my sharp claws clicking on the tiled floor. His head pops up from the open fridge.

He assesses me much like his father does, trying to figure out if I'm worthy of his attention. Then he waves a wedge of cheese in my direction. "Do you want this?"

My furry butt plops onto the cold floor and I hold back a wince after last night's activities. I wag my tail. *'Cause why not, right?* He tosses the piece in the air, and I catch it mid-flight.

169

"Wow. That's impressive."

Of course, I am.

He assembles a sandwich and takes a bite, peeking over at his dad's room as he chews. "I'm surprised the old man remembers to feed you. He's a horrible provider." Jake snorts before digging his teeth into the bread again. "Dad hardly remembered to take care of me after mom left." He munches thoughtfully. "Well, she didn't leave necessarily."

I rub my forehead on his pants to encourage his slip of the tongue. The kid blinks, as if just now remembering my existence, then reaches out a hand to massage my ears.

"Don't take his shit. Dad can be a controlling, self-absorbed dick."

Don't I know it. I lean into Jake's touch.

The house phone chimes and the boy leaps to answer it before the second ring. "Mom?" He releases a breath. "I miss you too... No, as usual, his work phone is glued to his ear." Jake chuckles, then rubs the bridge of his nose. "I'm fine. Really." There's a long pause. "If it keeps him out of your territory, then it's worth it... Yes, I do need to *protect* you! He's a fucking monster. You haven't seen the things I have, Ma." His shoulders shudder. "You know I can't tell you. Just trust me, giving up my degree is worth keeping you and the others safe." More chatter. He slams his palm on the counter. "Stop. We don't have much time to talk before he realizes who's on the phone. How're the pups?... Yeah? I bet they're getting big."

What the fuck? Territory. Pups. It sounds like she's a shifter. *Did the General's wife leave him and join a pack? Or was she part of the breeding program until my master realized a human and a shifter won't produce a pup?* My mind is going a million miles a second at the possibilities.

"Now. Where were we?" the General snarls as he exits his room and marches towards us.

"Love you, bye." Jake hangs up and pivots, just in time to lock eyes with his father. "We were discussing my attitude."

"No." The General steps up until the two are almost nose-to-nose. "We were talking about your loyalty."

"Isn't it enough that I gave up my life to do what you wanted me to do?"

"You will not speak to Elizabeth while you are staying in my home, or you'll give me no choice but to test that loyalty. Maybe on that old college fling of yours? What was her name again? Lilac?"

Jake's eyes flare. "Leave her out of this."

"Oh, that's right. *Lily*."

Jake pales and swallows. "How... how do you know her name?"

The General shrugs. "I found some old letters between you two."

"You went through my *personal* belongings?"

The General ignores the tantrum. "Do we understand each other? You will *not* speak to Elizabeth, and I'll leave your little girl toy alone."

"She's my mother." Jake's jaw clenches with the last bit of fight in him. "Please, for once in my life, show some compassion."

The General fists the kid's shirt and tugs him closer. "You are a grown-ass man. Start acting like one. She's *gone*. Forever. The sooner you accept that, the better you can focus on what's in front of you. Like your training and next duty station."

Their stare-off is impressive, but Jake is no match for his heartless father. "Yes, sir."

"Good." He releases his hold on the kid's shirt. "Now clean up. We're going out to dinner with some top brass."

Jake strides off, his shoulders slumped. Once he's hidden in his bedroom, the General narrows his eyes at me next. "If I find out you're sticking that wet nose where it doesn't belong, you'll disappear next," he growls. "Do you understand?"

I nod, fluffy ears flopping. I already have as much intel as I can gather right now. And depending on how long Jake is home, I can have him eating out of my paws while he feeds me juicier bits.

"You will not be alone with him again. You'll be by my side or locked in the room with your child, quietly taking care of her. Because if I'm forced to explain why there's an infant in the house, you'll be childless."

I cower at his feet and offer my belly. For a second, I forgot Angel was here. I glance at her closed door. I bet the nurse is huddled up, doing her best to keep my baby girl entertained.

"I'm ready." Jake reenters the room, anger still radiating from his frame.

"I need to lock the dog in her kennel, so she doesn't get into trouble while we're gone." The General snatches my collar and tugs me away before throwing over his shoulder, "Meet me in the car."

Jake grumbles as he stomps out the door.

As soon as it slams shut, the General snarls at me, "Shift."

I do as I'm told and morph to two legs. Then, in three quick strides, he has me pinned against the wall with his hips. His warm breathing dangerously close to mine.

"Stay the fuck away from Jake and forget he exists," the General hisses, and I can only nod my understanding. "I won't warn you again, pet." He strokes a knuckle over my full breasts before tugging on a sensitive nipple. Pain and pleasure shoot to my core before he lowers his mouth and sucks at my peak. I gasp as he finds enjoyment in making me squirm. Finally, he lifts his head and swipes his tongue over his lips. "Don't fuck up. I'd hate to ruin all the fun we're having together."

Sure, I'll play nice. But when I'm away from this shithole, I'm going to go after the *only* thing his cold heart cares about. The same thing he's been dangling over my head.

His child.

The next morning, I'm sitting next to the General in his work vehicle. He's bright-eyed and tail*less* as he reads over the latest report. I don't comment on the fact that his son's scent wasn't in the home when I woke up. I bet he forced the kid to return to the barracks to keep me from prying. *Smart move.*

"Currently, law enforcement is still investigating the scene at the cabin." The General swipes up a document as he peruses it. "There's a rumor floating around that a shifter's body was located in a cave a few miles north."

We'll be in deep shit and placed under a microscope if it's Experiment 217. I bite my lip. Still, I'm hoping the body doesn't belong to the female. She's innocent in all of this.

"Only one?" I question.

The General taps through the program on his tablet and his brows rise. "No. There were two."

I fight the urge to strangle him. I hate it when he only feeds me bits of information.

"It's also been reported that the female shifter in question is related to a high-ranking shifter."

High-ranking?

"Do you mean to say that she's related to an alpha?"

"No, a creature calling itself a *Guardian.*"

I hope he's wrong.

"What are they exactly?"

"Luna's protectors. They're rumored to have special abilities, along the lines of *superpowers*."

The General scratches his chin. "That could be useful to our team."

"Or extremely damaging, considering they are supposed to keep *peace* between shifters and humans. And I doubt they'll consider what you are doing as peaceful." I mutter the last part under my breath as I stare out the car window. This could be my chance at freedom. If only I could have a conversation with the Guardian.

"You're right," the General sighs. I blink my disbelief. He ignores my obvious shock and barks at his assistant. "There's no new information in our system. Call the onsite team and get me an up-to-date status report."

There's a quick pause, followed by a muffled conversation, before the other man hangs up the phone and says, "Johnson is in place, keeping the situation under control until we arrive, General."

"We're here," the driver informs us as he parks the car.

The General meets my gaze. "Shift and report back within the hour. Do *not* engage or be seen."

I slip out of the car and shiver before morphing into beast mode. It's freezing. I shake the white powder from my fur coat. I sniff out the decaying body and slink into the shadows of the cave. Disappointment radiates through me when there's no sign of the Guardian. There goes my possible escape route.

"She was found on top of it?" a male questions.

"Yes, pretty much *frozen* to his corpse."

"Was she his lover?"

"She was pretty bruised up. I doubt she was with him willingly. Maybe she was a hostage?"

"How'd he die?"

"The man's skull was bashed in. The cause of death appears to be a direct blow to his frontal lobe." I hear some shuffling of feet and then he continues. "Probably a boulder that became dislodged during the snow storm and fell on the guy. The wind gusts last night were pretty impressive."

"Well, the other possibility could be that the girl was assaulted one too many times and finally had enough."

They share a moment of silence, as they both appear to consider that option. And I have to admit I'd be in awe and a bit jealous if the woman did murder her captor.

"Let's bag the body and scout the area for further evidence. Then we'll follow up with the woman at the hospital."

I slip out of the cave and gallop through the woods, doing my best to create odd trails for the authorities to track to nowhere as well as to get a bit more exercise. By the time I'm back at the rendezvous point, I have two minutes to spare.

"Report," the devil bites out before I can tug my clothes back on. Through chattering teeth, I tell him everything I learned. He makes a few phone calls. Then tosses his phone onto his lap and drags his hands through his hair. "Our orders are to stand down." He grinds his jaw. "It's time to regroup."

I know that look. We're fucked. How fucked is yet to be determined. They must not trust us with recovering the victim or maybe it's that they don't want us on this case. Either way, a moody general means punishment for his team. Though that doesn't stop me from passing out as we drive through the rough terrain. Between the stinging cold and the lack of sleep from our sexcapades last night, I'm exhausted.

The sudden stop of the vehicle causes my body to jerk awake. The adrenaline kicks in as I take in the deserted wooded area surrounding us. "Where are we?" I rub the sleep from my eyes.

"Give us a moment," the General orders the others. Once they leave, he pivots to me. His gaze eats up every inch of my frame before crushing me. "My superiors have ordered that I assign you a new handler."

Icy cold creeps up my spine. Words fail me as terror grips my heart.

"Your services to me are no longer required. You are dismissed." He nods to my door. "Do yourself a favor and don't make a scene."

Don't make a *scene*? Don't *make* a motherfucking scene! He trained, terrorized, and then fucked me, only to discard me like trash. Volcanic rage boils beneath my skin. But I bite my tongue, a metallic taste burning my throat.

Keep calm. You need to think clearly and get answers.

"What about my daughter?"

"I am a man of my word. She'll be with you until she's weaned. Then I'll decide what program to place her in." For once, I see regret etched in his features. He loves that little girl.

"She'll miss you," I push out as I glide my fingers over his thigh.

He smacks my false affections away. "I'll visit Angel often and make sure she is being treated well." *At least he's giving me that.* He lifts his chin and the door opens to a brute of a man grinning at me. The General passes the stranger my collar remote. "You have a new handler. Obey him as you have me, and you'll remain by your pup's side."

No. No. No. This can't be happening.

I swallow my terror. "And will I get to visit her weekly after she is weaned?" My eyes beg him to reward me for my sacrifices. That he offer a fragment of sympathy for her sake.

"I will continue to track your progress, and as long as you perform adequately, I'll consider rewarding you for your good behavior."

I stare into his gaze with equal intensity, mentally reminding him I *know* about his recent murder, as well as about his wife and his son. He's not the only formidable force with a hand of cards at play. He *will* let me see my pup and she will be taken care of… or else.

His eyes spark with fury but also understanding. I think, in his own fucked-up way, he does care for me. I offer him a parting smile and bow my head.

"She's all yours, Captain," the General addresses the other man.

"Let's go, bitch." Mr. Muscles tugs me by my collar. The momentum causes me to lose my balance and my chin collides with the rough forest floor.

Blood pools in my mouth. *Great. I traded one monster for another.*

My former so-called team wastes no time in escaping this hellhole, and the SUV's tires squeal in their wake, throwing dust into my eyes. I cough and shake my head. Why did I think this would end any differently? Before I can stand, the Captain clutches a fistful of my hair and drags me forward. Rocks and twigs cut into my knees, and I scream in agony.

Who knew the General was the more civil one in his chain of command?

The captain throws me through a metal door while singing, "Welcome to your new cage."

Then the exit is sealed shut, along with my fate.

Angelica

Great Escape

A lifetime ago, I traded the plush carpet and soft bed covers at the General's for a mattress on the concrete floor to sleep on and a bucket in the corner to shit in.

"Who the fuck do you think you're talking to like that?"

My body slams into the wall, and my teeth slice into my tongue on impact. After four *years* of torment at the hands of the Captain and his goons, *this* new recruit doesn't fucking scare me. I've had enough of their bullshit. My manic laughter echoes around my prison, and blood pools in my mouth before sliding down my chin.

"Kid, I'm your worst fucking nightmare."

"You?" His steel gaze trails along my filthy, naked body before he laughs in my face.

This man child is fresh from basic training, and his superiors are testing his interrogation skills on me. I snort. *Good luck, pretty boy.* I've been chained up and raped, had every bone in my body broken but I've never given their trainees anything more than a crooked middle finger. *That's right.* I've been *promoted* from field work to *this*.

I drag a nail over the kid's corded arm. "If you let the beast out of her cage, she may become your loyal bitch."

"They were right when they warned me that you were fucking insane. You should be put out of your fucking misery."

We've been at it for hours. When will this peon give up and cut his losses? I bite back my growl as I glance at his watch. I should be with Angel right now.

"Where's my daughter?" I lean into him. "Tell me and I'll spare your life," I purr into his ear.

"Spare me? Look around! You're behind bars with venom in your veins to keep you leashed. You'll never see the light of day again."

"So that's a no?" I bat my lashes, my adrenaline surging to life.

"That's a *hell* no."

"Pity. I liked you." I flip the switch and wildly slash at the clean-cut, boyish face that's keeping me from seeing my little girl.

He screams, lifting his arms to protect himself. While he's entertained by the blood leaking out of his body, I snatch his key card and use it to bolt through the door, quickly slamming it shut on its new occupant.

"You fucking whore! Let me out!"

I tug on my ear as a grin spreads across my lips. "What was that? Oh! You want me to leave you here so I can visit with my daughter? Aw! You're a sweetie!"

I stare down the dark hallway. If they won't *tell* me where she is, I'll locate her myself. My feet patter against the cobblestone corridor that's lined with doors leading to the other prisoners. Each room holds a female or child shifter. They keep us separated, so we can't communicate, but little do they know, while the guards are napping, we converse through the drafty walls. The assholes may control our bodies but never our minds. We've slowly been formulating our great escape, and once all the pieces fall into place, we'll bring this place down brick by brick.

"Angel?" I call out to the shadows.

The echoes of my own feet are unnerving. I increase my pace. This facility may be understaffed, but I know I'm running out of time.

"She's near the end of the hallway," a female whispers under the crack of her door.

"Thank you, Sylvia," I reply before I jog in that direction while I continue to hiss out my daughter's name.

The guards like to play cruel jokes on us, switching our rooms around every few days, so we don't know where our pups or friends are being held.

"Mom?" a voice squeaks.

My heart clenches at her angelic tone. I swipe the soldier's stolen key card against the reader. Hopefully, he at least has clearance to open the doors. I'm rewarded with a ding, accompanied by a green light before I'm greeted by a twig of a girl.

She rushes forward to wrap her arms around me. "Mommy, you're bleeding again."

I collect her against my chest. "I'm fine, sweetheart. How are you?"

"I want to leave." She buries her face into my neck. I hold her tight and breathe in her scent.

"I know, little one." I peek over her shoulder and spot a tiny pink rose on her bed. "Did the General bring that to you?"

"Yes. He always brings me a flower and a snack when he visits."

181

I grit my teeth as her voice spills over with admiration. That ass doesn't deserve my daughter's affection. I swallow back my negativity. "What treat did he bring you?"

"Something called a Twinkie."

I stroke her hair. "Did you like it?"

"It was too sweet, and it had a weird shape."

"Maybe you should ask him to bring you a juicy steak next time."

Boots pound down the halls as my captors near. *Fuck. We're out of time.*

"Hands up! Now!"

I kiss Angel's forehead and give her tiny body one more tight hug before placing her on the hard floor again. "Go to sleep, baby."

Her lip trembles. "But, Mommy…"

"Go," I order with an alpha tone that I've gained during my time here.

Her toes patter over the floor. Then she dives under her thin sheet. Before I can say goodnight, a baton strikes the back of my head, causing black spots to overtake my vision. I fall to my knees, and Angel whimpers from under her false protection.

"Was it worth it, bitch?" my steel-eyed friend snarls.

The soldiers tug me through the corridor with the occasional grunt.

"You know what? You actually look better with those stripes." I nod to the gashes on his cheeks—the ones delivered by yours truly. "You look like a tiger."

"Fuck you." He back hands me across the face before strapping me down onto the *no-no* chair in our interrogation room. Then he steps aside, waiting for his next orders.

Smoke bellows from the dark recesses of the room as a poisonous fog rolls through the air. Then the real *monster* steps into the dim light. "Angelica." His fangs slip out as he smiles. "My favorite pet."

"Aw. Do you say that to all the shifters?" I tilt my head at the Captain, my golden locks draping over one shoulder.

"Oh, now. Come on, sweetheart. You know I only have eyes for you." He takes a drag of his plump cigar, the orange embers lighting up his face. "Why are you so mischievous?"

"If he'd let me see my daughter, none of this would have happened." I nod to the recruit still leering at me.

My handler tugs on the other man's chin and *tsks* at my nail art. "Go get that cleaned up, soldier."

"What about *her*?" The kid glares at me. I pucker my lips and pretend to send him a kiss. He snarls and steps towards me while flicking his wrist to extend his blade. "You fucking cunt."

"Don't worry about the fleabag," the Captain barks. "Now go."

The soldier crosses his arms over his chest. "I want to hear her scream first."

Bad idea.

The Captain pivots on a boot before jabbing the recruit in the chest with a sharp finger. "You'll do whatever I fucking tell you to do. Now leave us," he roars, and everyone scurries out. Then he turns a sinister smile back towards me. "Now, baby, it's just the two of us." He glides his finger down my bruised cheek. "Your child's purpose is different from yours. She'll be a soldier when she's old enough. And if her genes are anything like her mother's, we'll win every battle." He wraps his thick hand around my neck. "Remind me… what is *your* job?"

"To protect and love my daughter."

"Wrong. It's to be *obedient* and follow my commands. And I ordered you to break in the newbie." He squeezes my windpipe. "I

183

never gave you permission to bark out demands like you outrank my soldiers. Don't make me move the child to another facility to prove my authority."

"You wouldn't," I wheeze past my hand necklace.

"We've known each other for years. Surely, you know what I'm capable of." He unclasps my throat, and his laughter bounces off the dark walls as I suck in air. "Now, tell me, why did you cut up James?"

"He wouldn't let me see my kid," I hiss past my sore vocal cords. "And the deal was that I get to see her once a week. It's been a week, and he said no."

The Captain picks up his lit cigar and sucks on the tip, then releases the smoke so that it billows around my face. "What am I going to do with you?"

"You could start by following through with what the General promised me when he transferred me to you."

The Captain and the General don't see eye to eye. From what I've heard, the man in front of me runs the show around here, but he's constantly being bullied by the General's team whenever they check in. He's on a tight leash with his superior and he hates it.

He smothers his burning cigar on the inside of my wrist. "Fuck that piece of shit."

Searing pain ignites my arm. I bite my cheek to contain my scream as my eyes water, while the scent of melting flesh stings my nose.

"What a disappointment." The Captain methodically unbuttons his uniform shirt before hanging it on a hook. "I was really hoping to hear that ear-splitting scream of yours." He presses his lips to the side of my head. "Just like the *old* days."

"Fuck!" I can't stop the automatic waterworks that fall over my cheek as misery snaps me back to the present.

"Oh, sweet music."

My fingers tremble. Blood drips as it coats the arm of the chair I'm still strapped to. The shithead is beginning to yank my nails off with pliers.

"One down, nine more to go."

I pinch my eyes closed and bite my lip to keep from screaming.

"Don't be like that, baby girl," he coos as he tugs off the second nail.

Stars dance in my vision. When I release a howl, he crashes his mouth to mine to swallow the sound. He devours me until I bite into his tongue. Then he pulls back and cackles.

He dips his fingers into the crimson staining his chin and wipes it over my forehead. "Yes, you're my favorite bitch. I look forward to the day you're of no use to the cause. Because I'll leash you *my* way. Then I'll have more time with you, begging for mercy."

Tiger Face opens the door.

"What the fuck have I said about interrupting me when I'm working?" the Captain barks.

"Sorry, sir. The General is on the phone. He said it's urgent."

The Captain clenches his jaw shut as he pivots towards me again. "Sorry, sweets. This shouldn't take long." He pats my head like a dog. Then he grabs his shirt from the hook. He strides out with the kid in tow, and I strain to eavesdrop on their conversation.

"They recruited Freddy from the old Carson City pack to hunt more shifters but…"

At the mention of my mate, my body jolts. Freddy's still *alive*? No. Everyone died in the attack. I even saw pictures of the aftermath tucked in a folder in the General's study. Why would the team leave loose ends? Unless they were desperate… But once they get everything they need, they'll dispose of him. Just like the General did with me.

But why hasn't my mate come for me?

The thick blood drops from my broken fingers. The dripping sound is oddly therapeutic and heals some of the jagged pieces of my heart.

Fuck waiting on a male to rescue me. My new life starts right here, right fucking now.

The girl who was sold and raped so her father could get a quick hit, the same girl who found her Luna-chosen mate only to be ripped apart from him, the girl who was treated like an incubator then forced to have her child's safety dangled over her head... Well, that girl is gone.

My tale's painfully unfinished but now's the time to begin a new chapter. My limbs tremble as my new persona clicks into position. The woman who is going to step out of the shadows and learn to be her own damn hero.

Using the fresh blood from my wounds as a lubricant, I wiggle my wrists until my arms are free from their restraints. Next, I undo my leg straps and stand. I sway a bit and quickly grab the edge of the table. I swallow a shriek as pain jolts from my injured nail beds. I side-glance my exit. In their rush to run to answer their master's call, the idiots left the hallway unguarded.

Suckers. I jam my uninjured fingers into the folds between my legs. *That's right, assholes. You forgot to get this back.* I remove the key card I snatched from my tiger-striped friend and a grin spreads over my face.

It's time to gain my freedom or die trying.

I tap the key card against its metal counterparts as I dash past the other prisoner's doors. The occupants poke their heads out, and I place my finger over my lips and wave them towards the exit. Hope sparks in their eyes as they join my side. This is what we've been secretly training for every night.

The only good thing about living at this facility, and not with the

General, is we don't have tracking collars around our necks because they don't consider us flight risks. Most of the females were already pregnant upon arrival or accompanied by young children, which meant the soldiers had everything they needed to leash us.

Again, their mistake. But we are injected with anti-shifting serums daily, so we can't access our inner beasts. *Not yet anyway.*

Angel rubs the sleep from her eyes. "Is it time to leave, Mommy?"

I collect her in my arms. "Yes, baby, and we have to move fast. Hold on to my neck and close your eyes."

I lead the group to the end of the corridor. "Stay close." I glance over a shoulder while taking in my ragged pack. "Our priority is the children." I nod to the mothers clutching their pups. "If one of us goes down, watch our little ones as you would your own."

"Don't worry, Angelica. I'll hold them off as long as possible to give you more time to reach safety," a woman behind me declares through a clenched jaw. My heart goes out to her. Her newborn son passed away a few nights ago, and now she has no reason to make it to our promised land. Her new priority is to join her son by Luna's side. "Remember to take the river until the end, like we've talked about, and you'll be free."

Between our small group, we've heard bits and pieces from the soldiers who've come and go. So we have an idea of where it's safer to travel, but nothing's definitive. Our objective is to get as far away as possible.

I clutch the woman's wrist. We've developed strong friendships that have blossomed from our misery in this hellhole. And I appreciate the sacrifice she's making so we can escape. "Give them hell."

"Will do. And make sure the entire Shifter Defense Unit pays for what they've done, Angelica."

"You know I will." I take a deep breath and steady my panicked heart.

This is it. I straighten my shoulders, make sure Angel is holding tight, scan the key card, and dash past the exit. Alarms blare and men shout orders. But we don't pause as we run for as long as our legs allow us. Soon gunshots ring through the air, accompanied by the sound of bodies dropping. Still, I don't stop. We all agreed there're no victories without sacrifices.

I squeeze Angel. *She* is what matters. My nose twitches at a cool, crisp scent. "We made it," I whisper to my girl.

"But, Mommy, they're still coming."

I turn, and terror rises in my throat when I spot a group of four-wheelers on our heels. *Where did those come from?*

"Don't let them get away!" my handler hollers over the roar of the engine.

Bullets continue to shower our group, and one penetrates the shifter's head in front of me, creating a bloody rainbow in the clear blue sky.

"Jump in the river! *Now!*"

We cradle our children, suck in a deep breath, and take the icy plunge.

"No!" my handler snarls as he slams on the brake at the water's edge, then pivots the vehicle in an attempt to trail the bank.

His shouts drift along the wind and become quieter with every minute as the river embraces us. My legs ache from the physical exertion, so I allow the current to carry us farther into the forest. I glance at the exhausted bunch around me. Most of them are bleeding from bullet grazes while a few bodies float face down.

"Angelica! Sammy!" a female cries.

I pivot in time to see a baby boy slipping out of his mother's hold as she passes out from blood loss. I paddle as quickly as I can and press him to my chest. "Shh," I soothe his cries. "I got you, Sammy." But the combined weight of the two pups wears on my frail back. "Angel, can you swim?"

Her doe eyes meet mine, and I know I'm fucked. I double-check the others. They're all carrying a child or two and struggling just as much as I am. I clutch the pups. *I can do this.* There's no other choice. I can't fail them. Hours pass and I question if we'll make it to a sandy bank before nightfall.

"Brian!" A little boy drifts from his tired mother's hands. The current propels him forward, and I maneuver my body so he bounces into my back, stopping his watery joy ride. His mom grabs him and kisses his cheek. "Thank you, Angelica."

"Mommy. I'm tired." Angel yawns.

"Don't worry, honey. We're almost there." I look up as darkness swallows the light and realize I have no idea where the fuck we are anymore. We figured if we drifted with the current, we'd eventually get somewhere safe. *Were we wrong?*

I yawn for the hundredth time as I attempt to keep my mouth above the water and the kids from drowning. My eyes flutter from exhaustion or blood loss—I'm not certain which. All I know is that the velvety darkness beckons my weary soul and I have no choice but to obey.

"Help!" A shriek slaps me to attention.

Fuck! Where are the kids? I scan the water's surface and panic rises as the pitch-black conditions reflect back at me. "Angel?"

"Mom!" Her voice is garbled, as if she's dipping under the surface.

Her scream of terror echoes from the left, and I paddle that way. "Keep talking, baby."

Silence.

"Angel? Angel!" I frantically wave through the river. *There!* I snatch a wrist and tug. I hear her sputter and gulp for air. "Are you okay?"

"Where's Sammy?" she asks as she grips on to my neck.

My heart clenches. There's no way the other pup made it. I… *killed* him.

Damn me. I wanted this escape. No, I begged Luna for it. But now that it's happening…

"I'm sure one of the other women grabbed him," I lie as I stroke her wet hair.

I bite my trembling lip. Did I make the right choice or have I doomed us all?

Something brushes over my toes. Sand! I can finally stand. I stomp out of the river on shaky legs and crash to the rocky shore while cradling my daughter to my chest. The sun peeks over the skyline, illuminating the world. Orange and red hues beckon us to celebrate our freedom.

"Mommy, what's that?" Angel points to the globe on the horizon.

I smirk. I forgot these kids haven't seen the outside world yet. I stroke her cheek. "It's the sun."

"It's beautiful."

I hold her tight. "Yes, it is and it'll warm us up."

Our misfit pack huddles together to witness the first sunrise of our new life.

Whatever serum they were giving us to ward off our shifting abilities is stronger than I thought. Because we are still on two feet. What I wouldn't give to be in fur right now. I side-glance my little girl. I can't wait to see her shift too. The independence it gives you is addictive.

"My feet hurt," Angel cries as her toe finds another jagged rock.

"I know, baby." I swipe at my brow. "Just a little farther."

"You said that hours ago."

I wish we had shoes for the children. I cringe at their red skin. Or at least some sunblock. Our first hour of freedom was an amazing learning experience. The kids gawked at the green grass, tall trees, and scurrying insects. But now, it's gotten old, and everyone is complaining.

I bite my lip. I hope I didn't memorize the wrong coordinates all those years ago. Or maybe David made a mistake? It was a very chaotic time. Anything could have happened.

"Angelica! Over here!" my friend shouts from a grove of oak trees.

I skid to a stop and my mouth hangs open.

"We found it," I whisper as my gratitude leaks down my cheek.

"It's a pile of rubble," my second-in-command grunts in response.

"Looks can be deceiving." I pat her back. "Gather everyone together. I've got a surprise."

The woman raises her brow but does what she's told.

Once the pack is standing by the dilapidated building, I nod. "I know this looks bleak on the outside..."

"There're no windows or doors," someone interrupts.

"We'll freeze to death, especially without fur," another grumbles.

"We'll get our fur back soon. Just be patient. Now stay close and follow me." Angel warms my side as I continue to try to motivate the group. "It used to be a medical complex that fell into ruin. It's been abandoned for a long time."

"Oh, is it like our own castle?" Angel grins up at me.

I run my hand down her face. I've told her all about fairy tales to keep her imagination alive and her hope from burning out. She always loved the story of *Cinderella* with her prince and castle. "Yes, baby. A castle for us to grow strong and train in."

The gray clouds burst, and rain pelts our naked bodies. Lightning snakes through the sky. I kick the overgrown weeds, desperate to find a hidden entrance, tunnel... anything! It has to be here. I didn't risk everything for nothing. I look around the forest again but it's all the same. Dead leaves, vines, and broken concrete.

Luna please! Exhaustion conquers me and I drop to my knees and crawl on the ground. *You've fucked up my life enough. Please just give this to me!*

"Can I help too, Mommy?" Angel lowers herself to the mud beside me.

"Of course, little one."

The rest of the pack weaves through the dense foliage. My fingertips graze metal and I pause. I frantically heave the vines encasing the hidden door. Then I tug it open. The strong odors of mold and mildew assault my nostrils but the unknown is more welcoming than the wind and rain.

"Wait here. Let me check that it's safe," I shout to the group over the raging storm.

I leap down the hole. My feet thud and dust scatters along with rats the size of adult cats. I pat the cold walls, praying for a switch. *Bingo!* I flick it on and hold my breath. Lights buzz, then flicker before eliciting a steady stream of brilliance. I lean my wet forehead on the wall. *Maybe Luna is finally gracing us with some luck.*

"Come on down, everyone." I help the others past the entrance before gesturing around the room. "What do you think?"

"Angelica, this is amazing!" My beta's voice is full of wonder.

"Thanks, Sylvia." I pat her blood-crusted shoulder and sigh.

"We'll be here for a few days. The river won't tell them where we went, and the rain will cover our tracks and diminish our scent. They're human. They'll give up quickly."

I don't bring up the *hybrid* shifters my handler mentioned. Although I've never seen proof (unless you count Experiment 217), I'll take every precaution if it means we can keep our freedom. At least until we get our abilities back. Then it's fucking game on.

"We should scout the area for supplies," Sylvia suggests. "Most of the pack is injured and dehydrated."

"Great idea. Have someone sit with the children, while we check the pathways." I take inventory of my pack. We lost a lot of women and children. I swallow the lump in my throat at the thought of the little boy who slipped from my arms. I pray he survived. And if he did, his tale would be fascinating to hear.

"Let's hear it for our alpha!" Sylvia hollers.

The collective applause is a sweet melody that breeds confidence in every cell of my body. We will ravage the world and take what is owed to us. We'll fuck up their lives as they know it and remind them we are bloodthirsty animals who won't be leashed.

"Rebels through and through!" I fist the air.

"Rebels until the day we die!" the group cheers in reply.

I breathe in their optimism and allow it to shape my certainty. We'll etch out our own future. One where we are our own masters.

New Start

*W*e stick to the shadows of the forest, the leaves cushioning our paws and silencing our movements. Our furry ears pivot to each thump of the heavy boot steps.

After years of tender love and care, our facility is fully operational and our mission to free shifters is in full swing.

"They're getting closer. Steady. Wait for my signal."

My hackles rise as I taste their stench. These assholes ruined our lives, and now payback is being served with fangs and claws.

Once the soldiers emerge from the compound to greet a group of newcomers, we lower ourselves into the overgrown vegetation.

"Wait until they're in range."

My pack listens to every word I send through our wolf link. Drool dripping from their canines and into the soil at our paws.

A naked male is thrown into the leaves. The air is knocked out of his lungs and his face scrapes over twigs and rocks. He groans and moves to stand but the soldiers aim their handguns.

"If you aren't going to fuck the bitch in heat." They each load a bullet into their chambers in warning. "You can join your brother, six feet under the ground."

The shifter's agony vibrates through the air. I snarl. No one should be forced to rape another being.

"What was that?" The soldiers take their eyes off their prisoner and focus on the tree line.

"Now!"

Claws rip through the earth as we launch from the shadows and pounce onto our enemies. We snap their necks, spilling their blood at the kneeling male's feet. Shock registers over his dark face before he joins in the fun. We tear the soldiers limb from limb. Bone splinters under my bite, and muscles rip as I shake my muzzle from side to side. Their screams of agony fuel my adrenaline. When silence fills the space, I shift to two legs and take in our destruction.

"Thank you for rescuing me." The prisoner bows, stealing my attention. "How can I repay you?"

"The choice is yours. You can either join our pack and help us fight, or return to your family."

"They took my mate, and she's my world. I have to find her, but they stole my shifting powers."

The General's been getting ballsy with his anti-shifting serum dosages. Some of the shifters we rescued weeks ago still can't call on their beast forms, while others get it back in hours.

"Your shifting abilities should return within a few days." I clasp my hand around his arm to help him stand. "I'm Angelica. What's your name?"

"I'm Rodney." He glances around the forest. "Do you know where they're keeping the others?"

"The soldiers move them around whenever the females go into heat."

His jaw ticks. "Then I'll join your ranks until my wife is free."

This is how mates should act. His devotion warms my heart, but I clear my throat before my emotions can take over. "Stay as long as you like, Rodney. Just be prepared to fight. We're freeing every shifter we can. And when you aren't in the field, you'll be assisting with the essentials to keep the rebel pack safe and fed."

"Angelica." Sylvia waves me over. "We've cleared the compound."

I scan the tiny group of rescued shifters at her side, all in different stages of undress and cleanliness.

"Where are the children?" I question the shivering adults. Their only response is an ominous silence.

"Our intel was either not accurate or they've moved the kids to another facility." My beta taps notes on her tablet. "Either way, there was no sign of young ones inside."

Rodney furrows his brows. "What are they doing to the pups?"

"The soldiers force the kids to serve at their beck and call," I explain. "They are treated just as *well* as the adult shifters and are subjected to rape and many other unspeakable brutalities."

This is the fourth compound we've attacked, and it never ceases to amaze me how many shifters they shove into these small spaces. They have a limited number of guards though, so that's helpful. But I know our luck is running out as reports of our attacks become more widespread.

"Here are the maps we found inside." Sylvia unravels a piece of paper. "See here? If we travel a few days, we can hit this facility next."

Days. I'm not sure how long my aching muscles can handle that.

"Let's gather around, everyone." I wait for my warriors to join

197

my side. "Squads two and three will return to base with the freed shifters to keep them safe. The others will follow me to the next assignment."

The group nods their understanding before preparing for the long trek back home.

Once my soldiers are quiet again, I gesture towards the dead soldiers sprawled out on the ground. "Destroy the evidence. We leave in an hour."

I stride into the compound to take one last look inside before we torch it. *How long will this go on?* I rub my blood-caked face. They're like fucking roaches, unstoppable. I glance into the interrogation room. My fingers ache from the memories of that monster peeling back my nails.

We can't give up. I clench my fist, to ease the trembling. They can't continue these injustices.

"Are you sure you don't want to return home and let me take the lead on this mission?"

I pivot and take in the crimson-covered beta. She's lost everything. Her mate. Her children. And it's molded her into a fierce and bloodthirsty beast. Even more so than I am.

She bows at my silence. "I'm sorry if I offended you, but you instructed me to remind you that *Angel* is your priority."

Her words wash over me. Images of my blonde-haired girl pull me from my devastating past. I've been away from my growing pup for too long. I run my hands through my short hair. "You're right, Sylvia. This is taking longer than I anticipated. I mean, *fuck*," I admit quietly as I tug at my roots. "Will our children be forced to continue this war when we're gone?"

She scans the little office, the pictures and documents that litter our surroundings a testimony to their brutality. They torture and experiment on our kind. And for what? So they can attempt to harness our Luna-given powers? At what cost?

"We will do what we must and fight until everyone is free." Her fingers wrap around mine. "Then we'll remind the little shits who we are."

A weak smile tugs at the corners of my mouth before I squeeze her hand in understanding. We'll have each other's backs no matter what. "Make sure you stick to the shadows, stay together, and cover your tracks. If you do not return, I'll send a search party. And if you're captured…"

"I won't hesitate to kill myself or the others before they can extract any information."

Our gazes lock for a minute as we let our emotions broadcast between us. She's my sister in every way but blood. Our love is stronger than even my mate's, because we've been through hell and back. If I lost her, I'd lose myself in the process.

I tug Sylvia into a tight hug. "Safe travels."

"Same to you." She squeezes back.

We separate and part ways. I trudge in the direction of the shifters returning home, knowing the mission is in her capable paws.

Freddy

Misjudged

Decades have passed since Angelica and I declared ourselves *rebels*. Luna, how I wish I could go back to those simpler days like when we found out we were mates and fucked every hour for a week. Yeah, I'd revisit those steamy moments. I still dream about her plump breasts and the way they bounced as she rode my cock. My fingers digging into her ample hips, marking her as mine. Her screams of ecstasy as her release squeezes my own out of my lungs.

Damn, I miss her. I can still taste her glistening pussy on my greedy tongue. Sweet like honey with a hint of salt. The most delectable cocktail. What I wouldn't give to *live* between her thick, juicy thighs again. Or grip her golden locks as her warm mouth glides over my throbbing cock.

A kick pounds on my kidney. Agony jolts me from my mental escape. My entire being is consumed by misery again. I spit blood at their boots. But I won't give them the satisfaction of hearing me howl. These fucking soldiers. The same bastards who Spike assisted, so they'd help us get on top of the food chain in Carson

City.

Damn it. They tricked us, and now they are killing us off to cover their tracks.

My ribs scream after another battering is targeted at my chest. When will death cradle my broken soul?

"Well, look what I found at the pound."

A cruel voice jars me from my torture. I snarl, refusing to meet his holier-than-thou stare. Another jab slams into my bleeding lips.

"Wake the fuck up."

I force my eyes open and glare at the assholes using me as their personal punching bag, while my hands are tied behind my back. A bunch of pussies.

"I'd be hiding if I were you," I warn. "The Guardian is hunting you down as we speak."

Although, as of late, they've been silent. *Could it be a consequence of my aunt's spells? Are they working too well to hide my sins?* Sins like stealing shifters from the packs of Cold Creek to keep Skylar Canis safe. *But that's a story I'm not reliving right now.* It's complicated, a full-length novel about *her* happily ever after, while I fucking rot.

The General cackles, bringing my attention to his freshly shaven face. "How could your pitiful Guardian be tracking me? *You* don't even know who I am or what I'm doing."

"He read my memories, dickhead." I smirk but fight the urge to cringe as the scabbed-over cut breaks open on my lip. "So he saw everything I saw."

I don't mention that I'm not entirely sure what information the big blue idiot was privy to. We may all be screwed if my aunt's spells really did the trick. But like fuck will I admit that. Let the stooge sweat it out.

"Oh, poor dog." He sighs. "You put way too much faith in your false heroes."

I hate that smug look. I tug on my restraints, causing him to take a step back. *Good. Fear me, you feeble human.*

To someone on the outside looking in, it may seem like I betrayed the shifters, but it was the only way to save my unborn child from monsters like *him*.

"I brought you the wolves you required. Plus a bonus female in heat! It was *your* fault they escaped your poorly-guarded facility!"

The vein in his neck protrudes and pulses. "That little setback has ruined *years* of research, and you are going to help rectify your mistake!" He pokes a finger into my bruised chest.

So that's why he's here. To grovel for help. After his actions caused Angelica and the rest of our pack to die, I'm done playing his little errand boy.

Now it's my turn to laugh. No matter how painful it is, it's worth witnessing that pitiful scowl on his face. "I'm not helping you do *shit*! Do what you want with me. I'm no one's bitch." Spittle slinks down my chin. Blood taints the liquid and drips between us. I've given him too much. Never again.

He grinds his jaw, pivoting on his boot before he waves a hand in the air. "I don't have time for his bullshit. I want his death to be painful—drag it out for *days*."

"It'll be our pleasure, boss." His men grin before resuming their torture with new vigor. My vision darkens again, and I welcome the escape like an old friend.

"His vitals are stable."

"Good. Keep me posted. I need to check on Azure."

"Is the serum working?"

"We'll know soon."

Where am I? My eyes slowly open. The room spins around me. *Shit! Am I at the General's breeding facility?*

"Easy." A hand presses against my shoulder.

I scan the woman at my bedside. "Bridgett?"

She smirks as she busies herself with all the equipment around me. "You're lucky I found you when I did. The soldiers buried you *alive.*"

That's fucked up, even for the General.

Bridgett brushes the hair off my forehead. "Why?"

I swat her hand away. "Why what, exactly?" I bark. "I've done a lot of shit. Ya gotta be more specific."

She swallows. "Why did you steal my packmates and bring them to that man? I thought we were…"

After Angelica died, I was so lost. I fucked anything within reach to keep my mind from dwelling on how much I missed my mate.

"Were what?" I sneer. "*Fuck* buddies? Friends?" I roll my eyes. "You were a distraction, a means to relieve some bent-up frustration."

"Stop." She narrows her eyes. "You can act like the big bad wolf all you want, but I see who you really are."

"Oh, really? Enlighten me then."

"Everything you've done has been to help others."

"Really?" I draw out.

"When you were in Carson City, you were helping Spike or

Angelica. Then, when you joined the Tala pack, it was Sky."

"Think what you want." I nestle into the pillow. "Why did you bring me here anyway?"

"I'm a nurse. It's my *job* to care for injured people. No matter how big of an asshole they are," she grinds out before she pricks me with the end of a syringe.

"Hey!"

"Oh, I'm sorry. Did that little *prick* hurt you?" She bats her lashes. "I'll have to be more careful next time."

I look around the windowless white room. "Where am I?"

"The hospital." Bridgett doesn't meet my eyes, and I know she's hiding something.

"If I'm at the hospital, where's the doctor?"

"You'll see her soon."

Her smirk twists my stomach. Did I trade one monster for another?

"Who's my doctor?"

"You'll see soon enough, Freddy," she purrs my name as she saunters towards the only door in the room. "Sleep well, fuck buddy."

My brain swims with fog. My head is heavy. *Son of a bitch. She drugged me.*

A slap echoes around the room a few seconds before the sting burns my cheek. A delayed reaction.

"Shit." I force myself to focus.

"Hello, Fredrick," an icy feminine voice answers. "I'm glad to see you haven't lost your spunk after all the bullshit you put my children through."

A cold chill caresses my spine. Nothing is scarier than a mother scorned. "Hello, Celeste. How's your litter of pups doing?"

"Wow. Impressive. Even with all that scheming you've done to my pack, you remembered *my* name. I'm truly honored." Her death glare says differently. I *feel* the flames of hell burning behind her eyes.

"Come on, Celeste. If you really hated me so much, then why are you caring for my injuries? Why not just let me become worm food?" I show her my best puppy-dog eyes to drive my words home. She's not a murderer. She's everyone's pretty savior. Trained in the art of healing.

She pours clear liquid over my open wound, and my body is engulfed by a blinding pain. A scream rips through my throat, and tears sting my eyes.

"Why would I let the worms *ruin* all of my fun?" She swipes a cloth over my bruised ribs, and I arch my back. "Oh, dear. Is that painful? How about this?" Her pointer finger jabs at my side, where stitches hold my skin together, and stars trickle over my vision.

"What do you want from me?" I seethe through clenched teeth.

She leans forward, letting our eyes meet. "I want you to feel the agony you inflicted on my children. You sexually assaulted Skylar for years before you impregnated her. Then, after she lost her pup, you tried to run away from the chaos you caused."

"I was mourning the loss of *my* child..."

"No!" The venom in that one word cuts me off. "You don't get to play the victim. You are in *my* domain, little boy. I'm the alpha and your life is in *my* hands." A scalpel grazes my neck, skimming over my Adam's apple. "On top of hurting my Skylar, you also went after Sable," Celeste growls out as she continues to list my sins. "You attacked my baby boy and brought him to that horrible facility."

"I never attacked him."

"You told those brutes where they could abduct him!" she roars. "We searched for him for months! *Months*! We wrote his name on a headstone, for Luna's sake! And you just *watched* from the shadows like the snake you are."

I won't argue with her. But to be fair, Sable and his mate shouldn't have been in that territory when the soldiers drove by in search of nomadic shifters.

"Then, as if that's not enough, you stole Maya from us!"

I also won't point out that when I carried Maya to that same facility, I dragged her bloody dress through the foliage so the pack could sniff out her location and bring down the bastards who were holding her and her mate captive. But what-the-fuck-ever. Tomato, *tamato*.

My alpha warned me all those years ago that *every story needs a motherfucking villain*. I'm happy to play the big bad wolf in this tale.

What the packs of Cold Creek don't realize is that the General is the real villain in this series of unfortunate events. If I didn't distract him from the packs, by giving him the locations of lesser wolves, he would have brought the war to every fur family in the area. Whether Celeste wants to admit it or not, I kept the human dictator on a tight leash. But now that he's loose to do what he wants, who knows what he will accomplish?

I'm not sure I'm living this shitty life the way you're supposed to. Hell, I'm sure Celeste isn't the only one ready to carve me up for my indiscretions. But someone has to make the hard choices... the heart-wrenching sacrifices... and be willing to suffer for the greater good. And there's no going back for me. I accept my cage. Saving most of the wolves of Cold Creek is worth the price I paid. I won't be welcomed with open paws after everything that's happened, not even if my acts of so-called *treason* buy the shifters more time to prepare in the end.

And unfortunately, the war is not over. It's barely begun. But that's not what the sheltered doctor wants to hear.

"What do you expect from me?" I tilt my aching head. "To say that I'm sorry? Well, I won't. Everything I did was for a purpose: to survive."

"What a horrible excuse to hurt innocent people." She steps back, as if she's finally seeing me for the monster I am.

"Keep telling yourself that," I taunt. "But chew on this: when was the last time you had to do something truly awful to live another day? You've had everything handed to you on a silver spoon."

"You're not the only one with an ugly past," she whispers. "Maya was stolen from her parents and…"

"She robbed stores and hurt people to survive in Carson City too! But did anyone torture *her* for her actions? No, of course not."

I won't waste my breath and point out that I am the way I am because of the many injustices that have surfaced in my life too. Including the deaths of my father, pack, and mate. Death's shadow is constantly nipping at my furry heels, destroying everyone I've ever cared about while chipping away my last remaining thread of sanity.

"*You* stole Maya from Frost and Raven." Celeste's accusation pulls me back to the hospital room.

"Wrong again." I let the words echo around us. "I *assisted* Spike when he took her so he wouldn't kill me for disobeying a direct order."

Her spine becomes rigid.

"Ah. You remember Spike well, don't you? The same brute *your alpha* permitted to live tormented me my entire life." I shake my head. "Did you know Spike forced me to suck his dick because he found out I was sneaking around in your territory with Skylar?"

Celeste gasps.

"And instead of giving him details about your precious family, I *chose* to get on my knees and suck the bastard dry."

She removes the burning liquid from my broken body and sets it on the side table. Fury blazes through her eyes. She opens her mouth to speak but then she pivots to exit.

A drama queen, just like her daughter. The door clicks closed and I huff out an annoyed breath. *Great.* I'm locked in again.

I stare up at the ceiling. She can play the good guy all she wants. But she's holding me against my will until Luna knows when. What *hero* does that?

At least I've never pretended to be perfect. And I never will.

Freddy

Pack Laws

I have no idea how long I've been locked in this hospital prison. That said, this unplanned *vacation* has given me ample opportunities to strategize what I'm going to do when I break out. My wounds are mostly healed, and they've allowed me to walk and use the small toilet in the corner, but that's where my freedom ends. They'll fuck up eventually. Leave the door unlocked, forget to give me a dose of anti-shifting serum, something...

I clench my jaw as I lift my body into another push up. *Damn, my chest is still tender.* I bet that serum is hindering my naturally-quick healing abilities too. I wonder how Celeste got hold of the experimental drug? I thought only the General had it.

My arms quake as I hold my stance in the up position. *Is she working for him?*

I stand on shaky legs and wipe my face with my thin hospital gown. I hate these flimsy things. I rub at my exposed cheeks. They're breezy and my ass is always freezing.

A loud commotion spills in from outside my door. I tiptoe towards the wall and jump at the sudden thud.

"No!" Bridgett yells.

"You better move your skanky ass away from that fucking door."

Is that Carly? I know it's a pussy move, but I press my ear to the wall.

"How dare you come here and disrespect me!"

"Oh, that's sweet coming from the medical professional who's clearly up to some shady shit."

Yup, that's her. But what is Sky's best friend doing here? I smirk as I cross the room to lean against the bed with my arms crossed, expecting her to barge through the door at any second. She's a pest, but she's loyal. If she's here, Skylar must be in trouble, and she needs me.

"You need to leave before I call security!" Bridgett barks.

"Yes, why don't we call security?" Then I hear a familiar repeated clicking sound, and I can only assume Carly is tapping her heel on the floor. "I'm sure the hospital staff would love to know about this hidden area *and* that you are holding a wanted fugitive behind that door."

I'm a fugitive now? I shrug. Another tick to add to my bad boy resume.

"I don't know what you are talking about. This is Celeste's personal laboratory."

"So, you're *not* hiding Freddy behind this door?" There's another knock and then Carly yells out, "Hey, jackass! It's me. Tell Bridgett to fuck off so I can properly beat the ever-loving shit out of you."

I chuckle. It's been forever since I had a good laugh. I've missed my little play toy. "Only in your dreams, sweetheart. But go ahead and try."

"Stop! I won't let you in there. Celeste gave me strict instructions…"

"Well, she's not here, is she?" Carly's voice is more like a shriek by this point.

My ears perk up. *Did something happen to the doctor?*

"She's not scheduled to work until…"

"She won't be coming in."

Shit, if she's dead, what's that mean for me? Will I be left to rot here?

"Why wouldn't she be returning?" Bridgett's tone is nearing panic.

There's a long pause before Carly whispers, "Not out here. Let me see the prick and I'll explain everything."

"He's not chained."

"So?"

"You're just a human. He could kill you."

I can't help my grin. I'd love to dig my claws into her flesh. It's been too long since I've had a decent kill.

"Then it'll be one less problem for you, right?"

"Fine. It's your funeral," Bridgett snarls as she fiddles with the lock. "Why is the entire Tala pack a pain in my ass?"

The door swings open and I offer the girls an exaggerated bow. "So kind of you to visit my prison cell. Did you miss me that much?"

Carly's anger radiates off her chest as she stomps towards me. I know what's coming, but I don't dare stop it. *I live for this kind of pain.* The resounding crack echoes around us as she leaves her handprint on my cheek.

"That's for Sky," she hisses before slapping the other side. "That's for me." She glares. "And this is for…"

I snatch her leg as it zeros in on my balls. She fumbles and falls on her back onto my bed. I slam my body on top of hers and breathe in her floral scent. "If you wanted to fuck me, all you had to do was ask. No need for all the foreplay, baby."

Bridgett tugs on my shoulder. "Enough!"

I wrap my hand around Carly's neck. "Tell me what you came to say, before I decide to make you my personal chew toy."

"Freddy!" Bridgett snarls, fur already poking through her skin. "Don't make me chain you up."

I release my hold on the golden goddess and step back with my hands up. "She's the one sending me mixed signals."

Carly coughs. "You haven't changed a damn bit."

"Neither have you." I smirk. "You're *still* doing Sky's bitch work. Tell me… are you still playing *second* best to all of her boyfriends too?"

Her lip curls. "Fuck you. I'm now married to Sky." She wiggles her finger and the light shimmers across a wedding band.

I sniff the air again and hum. "You snagged yourself a *Guardian* too. Or should I say shagged him?"

"That's none of your concern," she snips.

"No. Fucking. Way." I throw my head back and laugh. "*Sky* is Azure's mate. You're still in second place. Do they keep you as a pet? Fuck you out of pity?"

Her leash snaps and she lunges right into my waiting arms. She tries to claw my face, but I hold her hands to her sides.

I sigh and feign boredom. "I can do this all day. Trust me. I've been bored to tears."

Bridgett dangles a set of handcuffs in front of me. "Let her go."

"She attacked me," I remind her calmly. "Maybe you should put the cuffs on Carly." I push the blonde towards the nurse while offering them a wink. "Go ahead. I'll watch."

"Prick." Carly flips me off.

"Carly. Focus. Tell me what's going on before I actually listen to the brute's suggestion."

I blow Bridgett a kiss, then watch as Carly continues to stew.

"Where is Celeste?" Bridgett demands.

"Gone."

"Dead?" I ask the obvious.

Bridgett smacks me. "Shut up. Don't even suggest that."

"Why not? She's had me locked up here for Luna knows how long," I grumble.

"She saved your life." Bridgett bristles. "You owe her for not letting you suffocate in that hole."

"She should have turned him over to the *proper* authorities," Carly sneers. "To be put down like the dog he is."

"You can't be serious. You know he escaped them twice already." Bridgett rolls her eyes. "Either way, he's here now, and Celeste isn't. So before I lose my patience, tell me what the fuck is going on. What are you doing here?"

Carly points a finger at me. "I'm here because *he* knows where she is."

I blink, unsure I heard her correctly. "Excuse me? Haven't you been listening? I've been *locked up.*"

Carly glances between me and Bridgett. "Unless you two are working together."

215

"Have you lost your fucking marbles? If I were free, why the fuck would I be in this dump?" I hold out my arms for emphasis.

"Wait. Are you saying Celeste is missing?" Bridgett cuts in.

I tap a finger on my forearm. *If she's gone, I bet I can convince Bridgett to release me...*

"Not missing, *taken*," Carly sneers. "By his pack."

This chick is bonkers. "Bridgett, you might need to institutionalize her."

Bridgett glances at me, then back to Carly. She's considering her options.

I lean against the wall and rub the bridge of my nose. "Fine. I'll play along. What happened when my imaginary pack stole the good doctor?"

"You tell me. Your *mate* stole her in the dead of night."

That's fucking it. My patience snaps and my temper thrums. It only takes two steps before I have the blonde woman against the wall.

"Freddy!" Bridgett tugs at my arm. I pivot and back hand her across the face. Her head slams into the bed post before she crumbles to the floor.

Then I return my attention to the filthy liar in front of me. Her pulse quickens under my fingers as she realizes her buffer is out cold. I take a deep breath and will myself to not kill the tiny human. At least not until I get my answers.

"I know you are a cold *bitch*," I snarl into her ear. "But mentioning my *dead* wife is a little too much, even for you."

"She's not dead," Carly wheezes.

The hospital told me she was gone. They gave me her belongings. I signed the fucking paperwork, marked her soul on the tree of life,

216

and have been grieving her loss for years. "What do you have to gain from *torturing* me with this little game of yours?"

"It's not a fucking game."

"If it isn't, why not ask your precious husband to help you? Doesn't he have powers? Surely, he can locate his mother-in-law." I squeeze Carly's throat and relish the way she squirms. "Why come to me?"

Her hand shakes as she shoves her phone into my face. I narrow my eyes on her, then to the picture she's pulled up on her screen.

Shit. Fuck. Damn it.

I drop Carly to the floor and clench her phone in my hands. I sit on the edge of the bed as I stare at the ghost from my past. I stroke my thumb over her high cheekbones and piercing gaze. "Where was this taken?"

"It's from the security footage, at the Wolves' Den."

"Take me to her."

Carly rubs at her neck. "I can't." Then she holds up her hands to stop my next attack. "That's why I came here." She curls her lip with the last word. "I was hoping you'd know where they were hiding out. But obviously you're out of the loop too."

Realization slams into my gut. *Why didn't Angelica find me? This doesn't make any sense.*

Unless she thinks you're dead.

I slam my fist on the table. *Alive. She's alive.* I run for the door, but Carly tugs on my arm.

"I can help."

"You have two seconds to release me before I rip you to shreds."

"Listen. Azure is injured and can't help me get Celeste back. And Sky is safe by his bedside. We need to be quick and efficient."

She waves her phone in my direction again. "I know where we can begin our search." She clutches the device to her chest when I move to grab it. "*Together*. If you help me, you'll find your wife and you can be as evil as you want."

"Why isn't your wife's precious Tala pack going after the doctor?"

Carly nibbles her bottom lip. "They don't know she's gone."

"You better start making sense, human."

She presses play on her phone. I lean in and frown. Celeste willingly walked into the woods with Angelica. Not bound or thrown over a shoulder. I scratch my chin. Celeste helped build the restaurant. She would have known where the cameras were placed. Which means she wanted Carly to know who she left with.

"How did you know I was here?" I demand. "I doubt they broadcasted that information willingly."

"I overheard Celeste asking Bridgett to keep watch over you while she took a few days off for a last-minute conference."

I tug on Carly's ear. "Wow, *Grandma,* what big ears you have."

She smacks my wrist away. "The packs are already on edge, with the General's facilities being raided and finding out he was experimenting on pups. I didn't want to worry them. Or worse, have them thinking Celeste is involved with the bad guys."

"Raided?" I shake my head. "Wait. Did they capture the General?"

Carly nods.

"Where is he now?" I clench my fists. "I want to end his life for everything he's done."

"Well, get in line, big boy." She crosses her arms over her chest. "And shouldn't you be more concerned about locating your wife?"

I can't tell Carly how terrified I am to find out why Angelica has abandoned me. "I don't know where she is, *but* you know where he is."

"You're not even going to try to sniff her out?" She arches a manicured brow.

"Even my superior wolf senses have their limitations, human."

"What if I could narrow down the general area of her location?" She smirks at my disbelief. "Celeste dropped her cell phone, and her tracker is still live."

I step towards her, until her back hits the wall. "What makes you think I won't just leave you behind and get to the good doctor myself? Maybe pay her back for locking me up."

"Because you'd be going out there blind. You pissed off the only ally you may have had." Carly peeks over my shoulder and grins.

What the fuck is she smiling at?

A guttural growl sounds from behind me. Fuck. Carly was blabbering long enough to give *Bridgett* time to come to and shift. I lift my hands in the air in mock surrender before her fangs tear my head from my shoulders.

"Whoa there, beasty. I underestimated you. I won't make the same mistake twice."

"Don't make promises you can't keep." Carly brushes past me to stand beside the wolf. "Can we trust him, or should we leave him locked up? I mean, he's already admitted to not knowing where his mate is and we have enough information to go looking for her on our own."

I narrow my eyes. "You wouldn't dare."

"See? There you go again, underestimating *me*." She tsks her tongue.

Bridgett morphs into two feet and returns my scowl. "If we let him go, there will be some stipulations."

"Like what?" I bark. "I already can't shift!"

The two women share a look, then a grin. *Fuck me. Whatever they're thinking, I'm already sure I won't like it one bit.*

"Stop bitching!" Carly sneers.

"Then pick up the fucking pace. You're slowing us down," I bark as I scratch at the metal collar they slapped around my neck. *Yup.* The condition they had for me joining their little search party was to wear *this*.

The General had a shit-ton of them in the facilities they shut down, including a handy remote that sends jolts of electricity through me if I put a paw out of place. *Barbaric.* But I'm also curious about how I can get my hands on some to use for myself. I'd love to gift these beauties to some corrupt politicians and military officials.

"You knew I was human when you begged us to come." Carly smacks a mosquito on her arm. "So shut the fuck up about it." She sucks in a breath to continue her bitching but side-eyes Bridgett when the other woman groans. "What? You agree with him?"

Bridgett rolls her eyes at my smirk. *Of course she does.* "Not exactly. But when I thought we'd be trekking through the woods, I kind of figured we'd drive as far as we could, then shift to paws once the anti-shifting serum wore off." She holds up a palm. "I can easily hold you on my back. You wouldn't have to use Freddy."

I'd love to give her the ride of her life. Maybe I'd toss Carly into a tree. *Whoops.* Little brat has been complaining the whole trip. At least ten times an hour. I guess she's not very outdoorsy. Come to think of it, neither is Sky.

"Freddy can't shift with the collar on, and I don't trust him without one." Carly shoots me a glare.

"We haven't tried that theory yet," Bridgett interjects. "He may not lose his head." She jabs an elbow into my chest. "Do you want to try it out, tough guy?"

"Fuck that," I snarl. "I finally get my mate back and you're trying to kill me before I get to see her? Aren't you supposed to be the good guys?"

"I don't care who I have to be, as long as my family is together again." Carly waves off my protests. "The collar stays on. Oh! Bridgett! We could gallop through the forest and Freddy can attempt to keep up on two feet."

I might be able to run fast, but not as quick as a wolf. I don't bother explaining the obvious. The sun glowers in the trees, warning us that half the day is already gone. Bridgett wipes the sweat from her brow and notices the same problem as she glances at her tracking app. Carly needs to either trust me and let us pick up the pace or we'll never make it before nightfall.

I stretch out my back. I've missed the forest. I breathe in the pine scent, sprinkled with rodent musk, and my mouth waters. I can finally hunt again. *Luna, that's what I want.* Warm blood dripping off my chin and the feel of the prey's final heartbeats pumping under my paws. My nose twitches and my neck snaps to the grove of oak trees lingering in our path.

"Stop," I whisper.

Bridgett freezes as she realizes what we've done. But the human is oblivious.

"What are you going on about?" Carly snaps.

Bridgett hands Carly the tracker and backpack with our supplies. "It'll take longer to go around their territory, which means we'll never reach Celeste."

The blonde blinks at the other woman like she's lost her mind. "Where are you going?"

"I'll keep them from searching for you two." Bridgett's eyes snap to mine. "Don't make me regret this," she sneers. "Keep Carly safe, or you'll have the entire Tala pack at your balls." She presses a button, and my necklace drops to the floor. Bridgett snatches it up and shoves it in Carly's bag. "You can put it back on him if you need to."

Carly shakes her head. "Have you lost your...?" A trio of howls vibrates deep in our bones. They know someone's invaded their property. I shred to fur and growl at Carly to jump on my back. She's pale and can't peel her gaze off Bridgett. "But what about you?"

"You have to leave now." Bridgett lifts Carly in the air until the human is resting between my shoulder blades. "I'll make my way to my pack when I can." She swallows but I can taste the unspoken word... *if* these shifters don't punish her for crossing over without permission.

It's rare, but with the General's men and stolen shifters, it's not unlikely. The only thing Bridgett has going for her is that she's not mated. They may fuck her amongst each other until she's no longer fun and then discard her.

"Dr. Canis is your priority. Bring her home safe, Carly. I'll see her again at work on Monday morning." Bridgett's lip trembles, but she shifts and gallops into the enemy's territory.

I don't wait to hear the males pounce on her. I hightail it out of there, stopping to smell the marks they've clawed and pissed on in the forest. If Carly had just let us shift earlier, we wouldn't be in this mess. We would have noticed the border.

But whatever. I'm a free man now. My tongue hangs out as the wind caresses my body.

"We need to travel along the river!" Carly yells in my ear.

I snap at the air, wishing I could explain that wolves have great *hearing* and shouting is just going to piss me off even more than having her sit on me like I'm a fucking Clydesdale. I grind my jaw.

She could have an *accident*. Then I'd take this journey on my own with her tracking device as my guide. I mean, once we get to my mate, the safety deal is off the table anyway.

Drool pools in my mouth. Maybe Carly will be my first kill since gaining my freedom? Who cares if Sky and Azure are at my neck? It's not like I'm their bestie right now. *Fuck them and their perfect lives.* They wouldn't know hardship if it bit them on the ass. I'll let Carly hitch a ride until we find Celeste. Then I'll present the girl as a gift to my wife and let my mate decide the other woman's fate.

Who knows? Angelica may be too busy sucking me dry to give a shit about the others. I know I'm eager to bury my face between her legs and give her sweet pussy a proper welcoming.

I stick close to the water's edge, sniffing for other markers from shifters or humans. But it's bare. No-man's-land. My sides heave and I slow to a trot. Even though I've been working out in the hospital room, I'm not as fit as I used to be. I skid to a halt. Carly shrieks as she flies over my head and plops ass-first into the tall grass.

"What the fuck!" she screams as she rubs her bruised cheeks.

I ignore her outburst and walk towards the crisp liquid and lap it up. It's refreshing and instantly refuels my beast's soul. My eyes scan the horizon. *There's nothing here.* Carly drinks beside me and keeps a healthy distance from my dripping muzzle.

"Celeste's phone is really close," she huffs out, as if she's been the one running. I stretch my travel-worn limbs, then nudge her to get back on before we lose daylight. She narrows her eyes at me. "Next time, stop more carefully so I don't land on my ass." I arch a furry brow at her command, then she clenches her jaw and growls out, "Please."

I roll my eyes as she settles between my shoulder blades. She grips two fistfuls of hair, like it's a fucking seat belt that will help her stay in place. A twinge of pain shoots through my neck, and I snarl a warning.

"Big fucking baby pup," she complains, but loosens her clenched fingers.

I leap over a fallen tree, talons scoring the dirt under my paws. The breeze tosses my mane, and I pick up the pace.

"The trail ends here." Carly's raised voice causes me to shake my head, smacking her in the face with my ear. "Ouch!" She slaps me. "I was just letting you know…"

I brake abruptly, and she falls forward again. Only this time, she lands on her back, not her ass. As promised.

I could stare at her gaping, pained expression all day. Mouth open in an O-shape, cheeks rosy, and eyes wide. But we have work to do. I morph to two legs and snatch the device from her clumsy hands. Sure enough, the dot is blinking, notifying us that the phone should be right *here*.

I search the foliage. A rabbit hops from a clover patch, weeds dangling from its mouth. A butterfly flutters from flower to flower unhurriedly. But there are no buildings or packs in sight for miles.

"Are you sure this app is reliable?" I smack the side of Carly's phone. "I think your fat ass crushed it when you fell."

She groans as she rises to her feet. "I didn't *fall*." She snatches the device from my grasp. "You dropped me." She brushes the dirt off her pants. "Oh, and before I forget… you're an asshole and I hope you rot in hell."

"Are you sure I dropped you?" I cross my corded arms over my broad, naked chest. "Because from where I was standing, it looked like you literally *flew* off my back. Was the tiny human pretending to have wings?"

"That's it," she snarls and stomps towards me.

Aw, a kitten with teeny-tiny claws.

A crunch echoes from under her shoes. "Shit." She kneels and brushes the dead leaves away. "It's the phone." Carly shimmies the cracked device out of the wet mud. "Great, and now it's broken."

"Well, this was a fucking waste of time." I tug a hand through my hair.

Carly twirls in a circle, like the good doctor is just going to pop out of a tree or something. "Celeste has to be here somewhere."

"Well, clearly she's not."

"Stop whining and shift so you can sniff her out."

"I'm not a fucking bloodhound!"

"Where are you going?" Carly shouts at my back as I stride towards the tall brush.

"Home. I'm done with incompetent humans fucking around with me."

"But what about Celeste and Angelica?"

I pivot, directing my glare at the blonde girl who doesn't seem to know when it's in her best interest to keep her mouth shut. "If they were here, don't you think they would have shown up by now?"

"So you're going to give up on your mate?"

"No," I snarl. "I'm going to go back home, get a good night's rest, without being drugged by a nutcase of a doctor, and then I'll search for my wife." I'm exhausted, starving, and I must be on the verge of becoming delirious because I'm actually considering *not* killing Carly. Instead, I'm going to leave her fate in the hands of whatever wild animals are lurking in these woods.

That'll teach her to not run her mouth.

I shred to fur and step away from the crazy blonde. She snatches my fluffy tail and tugs at the sensitive hair. "Give me *five* more minutes. Just five. I swear they're here. I feel it." She taps her heart. "If I'm wrong, I'll leave it alone and you can go crawl back into that hole of yours and I won't tell anyone where you are."

I pause to consider her words. Oh, right. *That's* why I wanted to kill her. She knows too much.

"What do you have to lose? You already have to start at the bottom, right? Because the General destroyed your pack, your home, and essentially your life. If this works, you'll get your mate back and you can start a new life together."

Damn, she has a point. Plus, if I leave, where would my new home be? Carson City?

Fuck me, I'm stuck with her.

I snort in her face, leaving a line of thick snot on her cheeks. The sooner I prove I'm right and she's wrong, the better. I nuzzle the dirt, sniffing for any hints of shifters in the area.

Carly swipes the mucus off. "You're fucking disgusting." But she watches me like a hawk and follows at my wolf's heels.

I claw at a tree trunk and my nose twitches. *Is that fur snagged in the bark?* My ears prick as shadows emerge in the distance. Their movements soundless.

"Who's that?" Carly asks as she tracks my gaze. "Are they friendly?" At my silence, she pokes my chest. "Why won't you talk to me."

I don't waste my breath to remind her that it's safer for me to remain in beast form.

"You are trespassing on private property," a female voice carries through the air. "Turn back now and no harm will come to you."

"We can't," Carly hollers back in reply.

"Why not?" The figure has yet to come into full view.

Carly bites her lip, then clears her throat. "I've sprained my ankle and I won't be able to make it home before nightfall. Please, if you could just give us shelter for the night, we'll be on our way home at first light."

Finally, the approaching group steps into our path. *Interesting*. A mix of *humans* and shifters. All of them equipped with military armor and dark weapons at the ready.

A female lifts her chin at Carly. The same female, judging by the voice. "You do not look injured."

Carly shrugs. "I'm hiding my pain, so I don't look weak."

A soft chuckle rolls from the other female's throat. "*No*. You are not weak, but you are a liar." She lifts a hand, signaling her group to surround us.

My hackles rise and I expose my canines. There's no way I'm going down without a fight. Especially not at the hands of this group of nobodies.

Carly raises her palms in a placating gesture. "Stop. I'm unarmed."

The woman snorts. "You're not unarmed, girl. You have a sharp tongue, and some may even say that it cuts deeper than steel."

I bite back my laughter. Carly is exactly like that. She has a sharp tongue all right. But the girl is sure as hell lacking in the brain department.

"You don't know me." Carly bristles.

"I know you're a human traveling with a male shifter. I also saw you fly over his shoulders and berate him like he's your personal lap dog."

I growl in response. *I'm no one's lap dog.*

"And yet you just *stood* there and watched like a bunch of perves!" Carly snarls. "Who are you people anyway?"

"See? Stronger than steel." The woman smirks. "And because of that, I'm intrigued, so I'll grant you ten seconds to explain who you are and why you are here."

The sound of bullets being chambered echoes around us.

Carly waves Celeste's shattered phone around. "I've tracked my mother-in-law here. This is her phone." She cringes at the broken screen. "Or it was before I stepped on it," she mumbles under her breath. "And I demand you take me to her. Now."

"Why should we?"

Carly taps her own device and shoves it in the air, displaying the picture of Celeste and my mate. "Because I know Angelica took Celeste, and I'm not leaving until I get her back."

Silence thickens the air as the group chews over her words.

"And I'm willing to trade Angelica's mate..." She waves at me. "...for my mother-in-law."

Trade me? Like I'm a fucking pair of shoes.

Carly's lip trembles. "Please. She's the only mother I have. I can't lose her." She squares her shoulders. "If you don't take me to her right this minute, I'll bring the Guardians here to get her instead."

This gets the group mumbling.

"That's right. I'm married to Azure, and he'll come for me with lightning blazing. So, what's it going to be? Are you going to bring me to her, or am I going to call my husband to bring the heat?" Her finger dances over the contact list on her phone. "Better hurry and make up your minds or my thumb might just slip and dial."

This woman is the real beast, and she doesn't even have fangs or fur to back up her empty threats. But will they smell her lies?

For one: Carly assumes that Celeste is here. Two: Azure is injured, and he won't be coming to her rescue anytime soon.

"If we bring you closer, you must be willing to forfeit your lives as our leader sees fit." The woman arches a brow. "Do we have a deal?"

"And you say my tongue is the weapon." Carly sighs. "Yes, we agree."

I shoot Carly a glare, reminding her that she doesn't speak on *my* behalf. But she, of course, ignores me while we are herded farther into the woodlands. I can't help the hope as it rises in my chest. The warriors never denied that Angelica was here. Which means every step I take is one step closer to reconnecting with my mate.

Angelica

Intruder

My fingertips massage my dirt-crusted scalp, creating wonderful floral-scented suds. I lean my head back and let the scalding water rinse the day down the drain.

Who knew that taking down a corrupt government and freeing shifters would take up so much of your time?

I moan as the cascading tendrils of liquid melt the knots from my stiff shoulders just as a lover would. A shiver runs along my spine as my finger grazes my sex.

How long has it been since an orgasm ripped through my body?

A knock fractures my five minutes of peace. "Angelica, sorry to bother you, but we have a situation."

It's always *something*. "What is it?"

"The Guardians have been spotted in the Cold Creek area."

I push my scowl past the shower curtain. "And this information couldn't have waited until I was dressed?" Of course, it's unusual for multiple Guardians to be near, but I only needed a few more minutes to chase my release.

"Yes, but I thought you'd want to know that they are also freeing prisoners. We've received multiple reports saying as much," she clarifies before I can ask.

Fuck. I trust the reports. Especially if they're from one of the loyal spies I've positioned in the forests. They are mostly rescued shifters, who don't want to join our pack because they would rather fend for themselves. The only thing I require is that they provide information when I ask for it.

"Send more eyes and ears into the area. Have them report on what Luna's super beasts are up to." I grind my molars at another thought. "The Guardians should have been helping from the very *beginning*. This is *our* operation now and I won't have them fucking it up. Or worse, taking credit for our hard work."

"As you wish." My packmate scurries out with a bow.

I turn off the water. My heated moment completely iced over. I glide the towel over my damp, scarred skin. The Guardians' involvement will either help us or bite us in the ass. I need to know what *they know* before we show our hands, because I won't risk being thrown into another prison.

I tug on a shirt and yawn. I'll have to worry about all that drama in the morning. I have more pressing matters to attend to first, preferably *before* I drop dead from exhaustion.

My eyes adjust to my dark bedroom. I smile at the lump huddled under the covers. She must have sneaked in while I was showering. *My little spy.* I climb under the cool sheets and moan as they glide over my skin. This is more comfortable than the hard, unforgiving forest ground. I rub my forehead against Angel's sleeping back and breathe in her scent. She still smells like my sweet pup.

"Mama?" She cups my cheeks in her hands, as if testing that I'm really here. "Hi."

"Hey, baby." I kiss her nose. "Go back to sleep."

She snuggles into my chest and purrs. "Did you rescue people?"

I stroke her hair as I recount our heroic tale. Every gory detail. My princess isn't afraid of violence. She thrives on it.

"Did you find Daddy too?"

"No, sweetie." I don't lie to my kid. She knows who her father is and what he's done. But that hope leaking from her tone... Damn it. She's already imagining the best-case scenario, a happily ever after with her parents.

"Is he okay?" She tugs on a loose thread in the sheet. "I hope he is."

"I'm not sure."

"Do you think he'll join us when we find him?"

My stomach tightens. In the end, I'll have to make the call regarding Freddy's future. I have two choices. I will have to slice his throat for his betrayals, or leash him until he can prove himself.

I kiss the top of Angel's head. "I love that you care so much for others, but remember to take care of yourself too and right now you don't need that extra stress. That's tomorrow's worries. Let's rest in today's peace."

"All right." She sighs. "I love you, Mommy."

"I love you more, little one."

I should really listen to my own advice. I watch until her breathing evens out. Then I too drift off to dreamland.

The security alarms blare, and I jolt. The spot where Angel was resting is cold and empty.

"Fuck. If this is a scheduled drill, I'm going to rip someone's head off." I shove a pillow on top of my head, hoping to mute the annoying beeping. I give up and snatch up my phone to call my beta.

Before I can even ask, she answers with, "Angel is safe and with the others. Two intruders have crossed into our territory at the south entrance. We are intercepting them now."

My sleep-deprived brain can't keep up as a million questions try to escape at one time. I jerk to a sitting position. "Are they soldiers?"

"No. But, as we've trained, we are taking every precaution necessary to ensure the safety of the pack."

I throw off the covers and snarl. *Who the fuck is trying to get through our defenses?* "I'm on my way."

She's right. We've trained for this type of situation a hundred times. I tug my legs through my cargo pants and sheath my daggers before sliding my gun into its holster on my thigh. I drag my fingertips through my short golden hair, not even bothering to glance in the mirror. I gave up on my appearance when I decided to fight with my fists instead of my looks.

I slip out of my room and skid to a stop at the shifter waiting for me right outside of my door. "Please. Don't hurt her."

I shake my groggy head. "Not now, Celeste." I step forward, attempting to pass her, but the other woman blocks my path. "You have five seconds to explain what the fuck you want before I throw you in a holding cell."

"I know who's here," she replies. "And it's my fault."

I grind my molars, snatching her wrist and pulling her to my side. "I knew you'd be trouble."

"Then why did you *ask* for my help?" She tugs her arm free.

234

"Don't treat me like a child. I'm your elder. You should be honored that I shared my antidote with you." She means the one that reverses the effects of the General's anti-shifting serum.

"Yeah," I snip. "I'm so *honored* that your presence has two unknown beings approaching my top-secret facility."

"I never asked them to come," the doctor retorts. "I was planning on returning home tonight, before anyone noticed I was gone."

I guide Celeste through our maze of underground tunnels. The earthy scent of packed soil burns my throat. Darkness creeps into my skin. I hate these passageways. But I want to check out our visitors from the shadows and this is the way to do it.

A shiver from beside me draws my attention. "We're almost there."

"How can you tell?" Celeste whispers, as if the darkness may hear her.

"I helped shovel out these tunnels. I can navigate them in my sleep. And every pack member is required to know them too."

The words sink in, and the doctor swallows. "And the ones who don't reside here, will they parish in an attack?"

I shrug. "Or get taken prisoner."

"That's harsh," Celeste bristles.

"No. That's war," I growl. "Do you think I was born this way? I wasn't. Harsh treatment and being forced to fight in order to survive molded me into the leader I am." My thumb caresses the scar on my arm as my memories tug me to the woods with David... followed by everything that happened between us. The good and the bad.

"We are *not* at war." Celeste's fear radiates off her skin, like a slick tar, and it's clouding her judgement.

"You can play pretend all you want. Keep your head buried in the sand. But whether you like it or not, the General started this bloody madness, and I intend to put an end to it."

We break through the musty underground. The fresh air fills my lungs, and the sun burns my eyes. I hide my footsteps as we inch closer to the trespassers.

"I know Angelica stole Celeste, and I'm not leaving until I get her back," a female blares.

This human knows me. How? I shoot Celeste a glare. "*Who* is that?"

"My daughter-in-law, Carly."

"I'll trade Angelica's mate..." Carly waves at the shifter beside her.

I misstep and nearly fall to the floor. *No. It can't be.* My nose twitches. He smells... *different.* My heart squeezes and my wolf's tail wags. Our mate. I can't believe he's here. I shake my head, warning my furry soul that we can't trust him. Not after the intel we've picked up about his whereabouts. And we can't let him near Angel. She'll get attached.

I snort. *Who am I kidding?* I'll get attached too. I mean, he's the shifter Luna created for me. My mouth waters as I remember his head between my thighs, devouring my center. He's always known exactly what I wanted and how I liked to fuck. Before drool can drip from my chin, I square my shoulders and continue to listen.

"*If* we bring you closer, you must be willing to forfeit your lives as our leader sees fit." My packmate stares down the intruders. "Do we have a deal?"

The blonde mutters something under her breath before responding, "Yes, we agree."

The trick here is I must act indifferent. Adjust my warrior face while looking detached and calm. I stomp through the thick foliage, permitting my boots to crunch over the dead leaves. The group watches my approach. My team nods their acknowledgment while keeping their weapons close.

"Mom!" The woman dashes to Celeste's side, and my packmates crouch into position. Ready to attack. I hold up a palm and they freeze, their eyes never leaving the blonde as she leaps into Celeste's waiting arms.

"What are you doing here?" The doctor wipes at the girl's tears.

I don't wait for an explanation. I stride past my mate and over to my companions. When I reach their side, I pivot to face Freddy, who's either in shock or gone mute since we last spoke. Either way, I know punching him in the face would be the opposite of keeping my cool. So I guess knocking out my husband isn't an option.

"Any weapons?" I question my beta.

"Other than some false threats? No."

"I'm offended. Surely, you've heard about all the fun I've been having while we were apart." I tilt my head. "Are you really stupid enough to think I wouldn't kill you when I saw you again?"

Freddy shakes his head, clearing his lust-filled gaze. "I was imprisoned by Celeste before showing up here. So I apologize if my only concern was finding you and *not* you attempting to cut my balls off," he snarls.

This is news to me. The doctor never mentioned Freddy.

I glance at Celeste, and she shrugs. "I was going to use him as a bargaining chip if our little trip here went south."

"I used him like that too," Carly sings proudly.

My mate snarls as talons extend from his fingertips. "I'm not your play thing."

I tsk my tongue, drawing his attention back to me. "I see you still have that temper."

"Why don't you invite me inside, and I'll remind you what I can still do *all night long?*"

I contain the moan fighting its way up my throat. We've always had this hot passion. Toxic too. We've cheated on each other. Lied to cover our deeds. It can't continue like it was. Not now, after I've given up everything to build this pack from the ground up. Not after I've sacrificed so much.

"Oh, you mean just like you fucked Skylar?" I smirk as Freddy tenses. "If I were Celeste, I would have neutered you like the mutt you are after the way you nearly tore her family a part." I nod towards the doctor. "And I'm still having a hard time understanding why you thought I'd welcome you back with open paws after you worked alongside our enemy."

"I can explain…"

"You still don't get it," I cut him off. "I don't trust you."

He sucks in a breath and hurt flashes behind his eyes. "Angelica," he pleads. "I love you more than life itself. You know me better than that. Everything I do is for a purpose…"

"Stop." My dagger hisses as I unsheathe it and aim it at his chest. "You stole your own kind, handed them over to that bloodthirsty asshole, fucked the enemy for information and got her *pregnant*, and all for your *own* agenda." I twist the blade, imagining it digging into that cold heart of his.

"When we were in Carson City, I told you everything I did and why. We are a team." He steps towards me with his palms still raised. "I did everything for our future. You are my queen. *My everything.*"

I assess the pain etched on my mate's face. After all these years, he looks the same. Except for a few new scars. Just like me. We've changed, morphed into different breeds of monsters. We aren't the same wolves who once lived in Carson City and dreamed of crowns. We've been forged into new beings, with different objectives.

"Baby. I thought you were *dead.*" It's a whisper, only meant for me to hear, dripping with so much agony my heart squeezes. "The hospital told me you died from that gunshot wound."

A burning sensation tingles along my scar. Yes, I remember being shot. It still haunts my nightmares. It was the same night the General abducted me and said my entire pack was obliterated. My lips tug down into a frown. The General must have also spread his web of lies to Freddy too. Got into his head and planted the same distrust and delusions.

Fuck. And here I thought Freddy's tale was black and white. That he left me for dead, discarded me like trash. But it seems we were both deceived. I narrow my eyes as a thought surfaces. *What if my mate is still acting as the General's ally? What if Freddy was sent here to disband the rebels?*

"Did you scan him for trackers?" I shout to Celeste.

She looks between me and Freddy. Her face pales. "I didn't consider that."

"I'd never let the General do that to me," he snarls.

"Do you honestly think *any* shifter lets that monster touch them?" I ignore the way he's glaring at me, his eyes so full of pity, and fight the urge to add: *Yes, even me.*

He takes a step forward. *Is his rage directed towards the General or at me?*

"Give me another chance. I'll do anything you want me to and prove my loyalty."

"Give me your arm."

Even with my extensive muscle building training, Freddy's massive frame shadows mine. His dark eyes lock on my narrowed stare, promising so many dirty and delicious things. The distance he leaves between our bodies is respectful, but also reminds me that he's begging me to take a bite of him. I battle the delightful shiver tingling up my spine. If we had sex right here right now, his cock would be punishing, demanding, and would own every inch of me.

Luna knows I've been a naughty girl, and I desperately need a spanking and a cock slammed down my throat.

My beta coughs before placing a device in my hand. A tiny scanner we swiped from a military compound during one of our raids. I breathe in my husband's scent and square my shoulders. This is the moment of truth.

Freddy

Trust Issues

"**D**o you honestly think *any* shifter lets that monster touch them?"

Angelica's statement bounces around in my head. The sorrow seeps through her words and I clench my fists. *The General fucking touched her.* The same man I was working with to save my unborn child was also keeping my wife behind bars. Bile rises in the back of my throat. He's more insane than I realized.

Angelica's warm palm envelops my wrist. "Are you sure there's nothing you want to admit before I do this?" she asks while she waves a scanner in the air with her free hand.

I lift my other hand and stroke her cheek as I gaze into her eyes. There are so many things I want to tell her. That I'll protect her, love her, and never leave her side again. But instead, I say, "I've nothing to hide from you."

Disbelief shines back at me. How many times do I have to remind her of that? After all of these years, shouldn't she be happier to see me?

Has she found someone else?

A growl slips out and she arches a brow. I'll rip apart the fucker who's sharing my mate's bed. *She's mine.* Every curve, scar, and slick hole. My nose twitches. No matter how hard she tries to hide it, she's aching for my dick, and I'm more than willing to grab a fistful of her long…

Shit. Where did her golden locks go? I drag my gaze over her athletic frame, all the way up to her military buzz cut. She's still beautiful. Just seemingly more lethal. My lip twitches. My queen has evolved into a badass.

"I'll do whatever I need to, to remind you that we're mates for a fucking reason. We belong together," I whisper to her.

"You'll do anything?" She bats her lashes, her naughty side peeking through. "We'll start with scanning you for trackers." She glides the scanner over my arms.

I open my mouth to say *I told you I'm clean*, but before I can blink, her knife slices into my forearm. Crimson coats my elbow before the inferno of pain shoots through me.

What the fuck? I pull away from my mate. My vision swirls and I collapse at her feet. *I'm going to die. Not at my enemy's hands, but my wife's.* I fight to stay conscious. If anyone deserves to ruin me, it's her. The fog tugs me farther down, and the last thing I see is a grin and a wink.

I gasp awake while clutching my wrist.

"Hold still, you fucking baby."

I blink at the woman next to me. "And here I thought I would burn in hell for all of eternity." I snort. "But my wife is by my side lecturing me so I must be in Luna's presence." My neck rests on a soft pillow. Wherever I am, it sure is comfortable. A lot better than wherever Celeste was keeping me.

So, yeah, it must be the afterlife.

The stinging sensation on my forehead has me second-guessing that assessment.

"You're an idiot. You aren't dead. I cut the trackers out of you, so you don't lead the military straight to our location."

I refocus on my mate. She dabs a cotton ball on my open sores. Each time it touches my skin, it stings. But no amount of pain can keep me on this bed. I leap from the mattress and tug her into my arms, exactly where she belongs, before crushing my mouth against hers. I've missed her so damn much.

Her slap across my face echoes around the room but I don't release my hold. "Get off me!"

"But we haven't seen each other in years," I mutter through the ache in my jaw. "And now you have me in a bed all alone."

"Oh, so now you care about being by my side."

"I already told you they lied to me and said you died!"

Angelica opens and closes her mouth like a fish out of water. The badass front falters, and I feel my mate returning to her old demeanor. Having her in my arms means a vital piece of my soul clicks into place. *I'm whole again.*

"Angelica." I wait for her to lift her chin and meet my gaze head-on. "If I would have *known* you were alive, I would have torn through every damn pack until I found you." I stroke her cheek. "You're even more beautiful than the day we met." My thumb sweeps over her lips. "Do you remember that day? When I wrapped you in my arms and promised to always be there for you."

Her eyes glitter with unshed tears and my heart fractures.

"Help me fill in the gaps since we were ripped apart. Starting with who the fuck did this to you."

She shrugs, but her agony shines through her nonchalance. "The General kept me as his prisoner, but I freed us in the end."

Bastard! His blood will coat my hands while his life drains from his eyes.

The door beside us swings open, and a little girl bounces inside. She skids to a stop before looking up at me. Her blue eyes glimmer as she snatches Angelica's wrist. "Who's that, Mommy?"

My heart ceases to beat while my eyes grow into saucers and almost fly out of their fucking sockets. "*Mommy?*" is all I can sputter out.

Angelica gently guides the girl towards the exit. "I'll be right out, Angel."

The little girl gives me one more glance before she saunters back through the door. I do the math in my head before I grasp Angelica's elbow. "Who's her father?"

"A lowlife coward," Angelica hisses. "Who should be thanking his lucky stars that I allowed him to stay with *my* army."

"Who the fuck are you calling a coward?" I shake my head at the millions of questions swarming my overloaded brain. "Wait… What army?"

"While you've been out fucking anything with two and four legs, I've been recruiting other shifters to *fight*."

"I've only slept with *two* people in the five years since you died! Because you *died*!" I hate that I have to keep repeating myself. "How many men have you fucked?"

The instant the words fly from my mouth, I regret every fucking syllable as jagged agony flashes across my mate's gorgeous face. She presses her palms into my chest and shoves me against the wall. "I hate you," she snarls.

She's fucking hurt. I get that. But she has to know I'd kill for her, and that no matter what, she's my queen. My reason for living.

"I don't care how long we've been a part or what's happened since we were forced to serve the General. Because, Angelica, I fucking love you and *only* you."

Her breath hitches.

"I never realized how much you meant to me until you were bleeding in my arms." My pride is thick as it bobs past the lump in my throat and I confess, "I'm *sorry*." I nuzzle her neck. "Sorry for the pain I caused you." I brush my lips over her throbbing pulse. "Please don't make me live this shitty life without you."

Angelica doesn't need me. She never has. But I pray she lets me back into her life. Whatever she decides, I'll support her choice. Even if I have to bleed out at her feet to do it.

My breath tickles her parted lips as I growl, "Kill me now and end my suffering or fuck me and make me whole again." My thumbs stroke her hips.

She releases a guttural moan, then leaps into my arms and ravages my mouth like a starving wolf lapping water. My fingertips dig into her ass cheeks as I press her body into mine. Her tongue pushes past my barriers and my heart splinters at her unspoken decision. Angelica is mine and I'm undeniably hers. No matter how stubborn and power hungry we are, we can't deny the connection between us. No matter how long we've been separated, we were created for one another to bring chaos and devastation to anybody dumb enough to move against us.

When she pulls away from our heated kiss, she assesses me and I do the same to her, noting how those swollen lips she's sporting would feel amazing around my thick erection.

"I *want* to believe your words, Freddy."

I falter as her statement cuts me to the core.

"But we've known each other long enough that I know I *can't* trust you."

I'm losing her. Again. "What do you want from me?" Fuck being the tough alpha male. I'm ready to beg her to take my cock so I can reclaim what's mine.

"I want the truth."

I shake my head, unsure I heard her correctly. I set her back on her feet. I've never lied to her. "What do you want to know?"

"Why the fuck were you working with that piece of shit and stealing shifters for his experiments?"

I stumble back from her verbal assault. The bed hits the undersides of my knees, and I fall onto my ass. *Will my mate understand the situation I was in with Skylar?*

I let out a breath. If she wants the truth, then she'll have it. "The General was threatening my *son*."

Angelica takes a step back like I slapped her. "What son?" she snarls out. Then she pinches the bridge of her nose. "What were you thinking having unprotected sex?"

"When you died…" I hold my palms out, as she storms towards me, and rephrase, "When they informed me that you had died with the rest of our family, I had nowhere to go and I was overcome by my grief. I stayed by Sky's side so I'd have the protection of the Tala pack from our enemies." I meet her impatient glare. "It's a long tale but the short version of it is that she got pregnant, and the General found out that the pup was mine and swooped in with his usual promises of death and destruction unless I helped him. But I swear on my life I only helped him to save my unborn child."

"Where is your pup now?"

Fuck, it hurts to remember what happened to him. How one minute I was looking at his tiny feet in an ultrasound picture, planning his future. Then the next… "He's dead."

A blanket of unease slices through us as we get lost in our pasts. No matter what we've done, death has always lapped at our heels, stealing innocent people all around us.

Angelica clears her throat. "How'd it happen?"

Saying it out loud might very well break me. But if this is what it takes to get my mate back, fine. I'll bare my bleeding soul to her.

"Sky lost the pup due to stress, after her brother went missing, which is basically linked to one of my many fuckups." My fingers tangle in my hair. *That's right. I failed my child.* I failed everyone around me. "You know what? Forget forgiving me. I don't deserve it. You should slice my throat and let me choke on my own failure."

Angelica snatches my chin. Her eyes scan every curve of my face before meeting my gaze. "If I let you stay here, you need to prove yourself. I mean it. One single claw out of line, and you're done." She doesn't wait for me to answer her before she tugs on my wrist. "Now follow me. I'll introduce you to my pack."

I remain at her side as we stride out into the hallway. "What about the girl from earlier?"

"Her name is Angel." Angelica shrugs. "And before you ask again, yes, she is ours. I was pregnant with her when you abandoned me in the hospital."

Even though she's taking a stab at me, it doesn't have the same sharp edge it did just a few minutes ago. This time, she's saying it to be stubborn and push my buttons. *Fine. I'll play along.* I rein in my excitement, at the chance to meet my offspring, and play my mate's game instead.

"Wow. Naming a child after yourself is a little selfish, isn't it?"

Angelica pivots and jabs a finger into my chest. "Fathers name their sons after themselves all the damn time, so why can't I name my daughter after me? Am I not good enough?"

Those embers spark behind her eyes. My cock twitches, begging me to have her dig her claws into my back and scream. I snatch a fistful of her thick ass, causing her to yelp, then press my body into hers until her back hits the wall. "I've missed that fire, baby."

Angelica melts into my heated frame. "Why are you using pet names?" She's nearly breathless as she reminds me, "You're not out of the doghouse."

I nip her neck. "What do you want me to call you, then?"

She shoves me off her. "How about master or commander?" She flicks her wrist in the air and beckons me to follow her lead. "Keep up and pay attention to where everything is, because I will not be repeating myself."

My wife surprises me at every turn. Her appearance, her attitude, and even her territory are one of a kind. This place is impressive. I blink at the massive compound. There are tunnels to the left and right, each dark corridor leading to more doors.

"This is where we sleep. The level below us is where our training area and cafeteria are located."

I crane my neck towards the ceiling. "And what's above us?"

We're interrupted by a younger shifter holding a clipboard. "Alpha, everything's on track."

Angelica flips through the pages. She silently scans the documents before nodding and passing them back to him. "Where's the Guardian now?"

"Reports claim that he's staying with the Tala pack."

Angelica arches a brow. "Why hasn't he moved on from their territory?" She stares at the wall in deep thought and whispers to no one in particular, "Maybe he's learned of our plans to attack the other facilities."

"How would you like us to proceed, alpha?"

Angelica taps her lips before looking at me. "You were staying with the Tala pack for a few years and have experience with the Guardian. What are the odds that he will leave the area quickly and not shove his nose where it doesn't belong?"

Hope rises in my chest. My mate is asking *me* for advice. "He may not leave at all." They both stare unblinking, waiting for me to continue. "Because the Guardian has a weak spot within the Tala pack."

"Bullshit." Angelica rolls her eyes. "He's an all-powerful being. What does that pack have that he can't get elsewhere?"

"It is not what but *who*."

"Do you mean he's fallen for a female?"

"Yes."

"Do you know who?"

"If I tell you, I want a guaranteed spot in your pack." It's the only leverage I have to get in her good graces.

"I'll think about it. But for now, let's proceed with the tour." She pivots and continues down the hallway, leaving the male with the clipboard behind us.

I follow her through the winding paths until we arrive at a set of double doors. Angelica smirks before pushing them open. My breath catches as I gaze upon the group of men and women. How have they remained hidden this long? It's the largest pack I've ever seen. And how do they survive without anyone fighting for dominance?

"I started collecting loyal members from inside the General's compound. Then, when the time was right, we fought our way here. Now we travel from compound to compound, liberating captive shifters. Some have had their abilities stripped from them while others have been experimented on and given super strength."

"Is that why you asked Celeste to help you? So she can cure their ailments?"

Angelica leans against the wall and sighs. "It fucking sucks that we can't help all of them. And if I'm being honest, it keeps me up at night thinking about how their lives will never be the same again." She picks at a scar on her arm. "So, yes, I brought the doctor here to aid in our research. If her serum can help just one shifter, it's a win in my book."

"How many military compounds are out there?"

She side-eyes me. "You mean your master didn't tell you?"

"The General has major trust issues."

Angelica snorts and stares out into the distance. "We aren't sure how many holding facilities there are. I want to believe Cold Creek has been the only area affected, but we haven't been able to confirm that."

"Do we know *where* the General is? If we find the old bastard and dig our claws into him, I bet he'd tell us."

A dark shadow passes over my mate's face before she growls out, "I've shared enough information with you. Now pay up. What's the Guardian after? What do they want with the Tala pack?"

"Skylar Canis."

A flash of silver is the last thing I glimpse before Angelica slams me against the wall with a knife to my neck. Silence fills the room as all eyes shoot at us. "Do you think this is a fucking joke, Freddy?" A few chairs are pushed back as shifters rise to support their leader. "If you think for one second I'm going to be tricked into bringing your *ex* here, you're sadly mistaken."

I lean into the blade, ignoring the sting of pain. "This is no trick. When I asked the Guardian about his interest in Sky while he was interrogating me at the police station, he got very protective over her. Then Carly confessed that she and Sky were married to him. She even hinted that he might be injured."

"Do you think Sky will keep him busy for a while?"

"If they are fated to be together, they are probably already shacked up."

"Good. Because we have a job to do."

"We?"

"Can I trust you?"

"Abso-fucking-lutely."

"Prove it," she hisses while moving the dagger from my throat.

My lips twitch as I take a knee and bow my head. Gasps fill the room, mixed with whispers from the onlookers. But I don't fucking care.

Angelica

Burning Desire

"Can we trust him?" Sylvia asks me as she passes a folder to Brad. I watch as David's brother, now a member of my team, takes it and passes it on while laughing with a coworker.

Funny how things end up. At one point, I never thought shifters and humans could work together, let alone fight a shared enemy. I itch the raised scar on my arm. Not a day goes by that I don't miss the brave doctor who saved my life. I'm glad I was able to locate his siblings and rescue them from the General's wrath.

Not every hero has fur and not all villains wear uniforms.

My beta clears her throat, demanding my attention. I rub the bridge of my nose. "Honestly, I don't know if we *can* trust Freddy. But he *deserves* a chance to prove himself."

Her jaw ticks. "But he worked for that prick."

I know she doesn't mean to, but her words strike a chord in my broken soul and I snarl out, "We all worked for the bastard in one way or another."

Her gaze lowers and I know memories of her own torture are replaying in her mind.

I rub her shoulder and sigh. "If Freddy proves himself, he'll be a great addition to our arsenal. But, if he doesn't..." I unsheathe my dagger and flip it blade over hilt. The fluorescent light causes it to shimmer with the warning. "I won't hesitate to help him meet his creator."

"And where is the dead man now?"

"I sent him to the mat with Daniel."

Her grin widens. "Freddy's in for a rude awakening."

Daniel is our most lethal warrior. Whenever newbies enter our ranks, I send them to him to assess their readiness in combat. If they pass his evaluation, they can join our task force. If they fail, he will write up a training regimen for them to complete before he assesses them again. We are here to save lives, not to put anyone in unnecessary danger.

Heavy footsteps have me turning to see David's sister pushing into the room. She's out of breath, and when her dark eyes meet mine, she jogs over to my side. "Angelica?"

"Easy." I pass her a bottle of water and wait for her to chug it. "What's going on?"

"We have aerial confirmation that the General's son is overseeing the next shipment of shifters."

I knew those drones would come in handy. "Where are they delivering the wolves?"

"Not far from the Pawson pack," Lauren tells me.

"Good job." I pat her back. "Let me know when he actually arrives at the facility."

There's no use in following up on this tidbit until our prize is on the radar. Plans change so quickly around here, and I wouldn't want to organize a team, only to have the military pull him out at the last minute. No. *Patience* is key.

"He's already there. That's why I ran over here." She swipes a palm over her forehead. "I knew you'd want to know right away."

"Fuck." The bastard is slimy. Every time we attempt to snatch him, he disappears. "Do we know how long he'll be there?"

"No."

"Thank you for letting me know."

Lauren nods, pivots, then walks out of the training room.

"Damn it." I tap a finger on my arm. I want to keep an eye on Freddy, but if I don't lead the extraction team and it goes to hell...

"Stop overthinking shit. Before steam starts escaping from your ears. I'll watch over the soon-to-be dead wolf," my beta groans. "You take the team to extract the General's son."

"Are you sure?"

"No. But we need to use the kid as bait. Nothing else has worked so far." She crosses her arms over her chest. "And I'll do just about anything to get my claws on the man who destroyed my life, even babysit a prickly male."

I love my beta, but she gets under people's skin with her pushy attitude. I shift my gaze to my mate and smirk. *What better way to test my husband?*

I pivot and hand Sylvia the appropriate mission folder. "The General is behind bars, inside the Carson City police department. Take a team and move fast before the federal government decides to transfer him." As soon as she nods her understanding, I continue. "When he sees we have his son, he'll finally spill all his secrets."

"Or we'll spill his blood." Sylvia's jaw ticks.

I clasp her shoulders and meet her gaze. "It's been a long time coming, my friend, and today we will finally receive our justice."

We've worked side by side for so long. It's unfathomable to think that it'll be over soon. That our rebellion will disintegrate and our team will start new, peaceful lives. Because that was always our plan. Bring down the bad guys and rise above them, so we can move on and keep our families and friends safer.

"Mommy!" Angel squeals, breaking our moment. "When can Daddy move into our room?"

The beta ruffles Angel's hair. "That's my cue to leave. I need to get ready for the mission anyway."

"Wait." Angel looks between us. "I want to go." She locks eyes with me. "You promised me that I could go on the next one."

"But…" I begin.

"Mom." She squares her shoulders. The perfect mini-me. "We don't break our word in this family."

I release my breath. *Damn her.* My beta's laughter echoes around the room. I glare at my second-in-command. *Wow. She's no help.* "Fine. Angel, you can help *Sylvia*."

That shuts up the cackling wolf. "What? You can't be serious."

"Yay! It's going to be great! Just like you've trained me!" Angel sings. "I'll get my blades!" The ball of energy becomes a blur in the background.

"Are you serious?" Sylvia huffs.

"Hey. Your mission is safer than mine." I elbow her.

"But now I have to watch over Freddy and Angel. That's not fair."

"Life isn't fair. Now quit yapping and let's get moving." I stride past her.

She snatches my wrist to stop me. "What if he runs?" She rolls her eyes at my quirked brow. "He's been trapped for so long, he might hightail it as soon as he has a taste of freedom."

I chew on her words. It'll hurt his daughter if he leaves her just moments after meeting her. Shit, it'll be painful for me too. Especially my wolf. But he's an adult. "If Freddy leaves, let him. I don't force anyone to stay."

"But what if he shares our location?"

"He may act like a dick, but he loves me and wouldn't hurt me like that or endanger his own offspring." I'm certain of that. I mean, he only worked for the General because of his pregnant girlfriend and I'm his *mate* and Angel is our daughter.

"May I make a suggestion, Angelica?" Sylvia tugs me into the hallway.

"Of course you can."

She glances around before leaning in so only I can hear her. "Fuck the brute. Leave your scent on him and remind him what he's fighting for."

Her bluntness takes my breath away. I twist to scold her but pause. *She's got a point.* It's been years since we've reconnected. I lick my lips. *Luna, help me.* Just the memory of him slamming into me makes me wet. I shake my head. "We don't have time for that right now. We need to move out immediately."

"*Make* the time. Freddy can either be an ally or an enemy." She shrugs. "I'm sure the little shit will blow his load in under five minutes anyway."

I choke on my laughter and shake my head. "I'll speak with him about the mission and see how things unfold. I make no promises of sex. Just ensure the teams are ready to go before my five minutes are up."

A small group of onlookers giggle, even as they try to appear as though they didn't overhear our inappropriate conversation. But most of them are shifters with amazing hearing while the humans elbow their furry friends, asking for details. Soon all eyes are on me as I stride towards the training room door.

I adjust my cleavage and sigh. *Freddy better make this worth it.* Because if I miss my chance to grab our enemies because he couldn't perform, I may just chop his dick off and feed it to him.

My approaching footsteps are hushed by the thuds and grunts of the training room. I peek in and smirk at the string of curse words spilling from my mate. I lean on the open doorway to examine his form. He's gotten slow in his old age.

I scratch my chin. We're only in our thirties but time hasn't been kind to either of us. With our graying hair and wrinkles, we could easily pass for forty. But who the fuck cares? Age is just a number. And we've earned every sliver of wisdom that streaks our heads.

A boom echoes around the room, drawing my attention to my long-lost husband lying flat on his back on the bright-red mat. "Again," he snarls up at Daniel.

"I think you've had enough." The instructor offers a tanned arm to help Freddy stand.

Freddy slaps it aside and jumps up. "I'll make that call," he sneers before getting into the starting position.

Daniel arches a brow but nods. They dance on their toes in a circle. Freddy throws the first punch and misses. As the teacher pivots out of the way, Freddy swipes his foot out and knocks Daniel onto his ass.

The room goes silent. It's a rare occurrence to see someone take the instructor to the mat.

"I think *you've* had enough," Freddy taunts. "Don't wanna be forced to leave scars on that pretty face."

Daniel narrows his eyes. But before he can start another round, I step out of the shadows. Freddy's nose twitches and he pivots. His heated gaze takes in my fighting leathers and the daggers resting on my thighs.

"Are you here to play, mate?" He arches a brow. "It's been a while since we've gone a round or two."

"I don't spar with newbies." I tilt my head. "Because I may break them."

"I'd be willing to test that theory." He curls his fingers in a challenge. "For old time's sake."

The way every word slips off his tongue, dripping in arrogance. That cocky grin. I wish I could say it's a turnoff. But I've always been a sucker for a man who knows what he wants and how to get it.

"Come now, Freddy," I purr. "I don't want to embarrass you in front of all your new friends."

He doesn't even look around. "*Nothing* about you could ever embarrass me, Angelica."

"Will everyone excuse us for five minutes, please?"

The other pack members gather their things before brushing past me with smirks and the occasional "get him, girl." Daniel takes his time. He slings his gym bag over his shoulder, then gives Freddy a pointed stare. He doesn't have to say the words for everyone to know what it means. *Hurt our leader and the whole pack will fuck you up.*

Freddy dips his chin in understanding and acceptance. Once the doors close behind my back, my mate pats his forehead with a towel, his gaze never leaving mine. "Not that you need or want me to say it, but I'm fucking proud of you, Angelica. You've really built up an empire here and they'd snap my neck in a second if you asked them to."

I brush off his compliment and shrug. "I'd kill for them too. Respect goes both ways."

He bows. "And what does my queen require of me?"

I watch sweat glisten past his abs and dissolve into the waistband of his gray sweatpants. I'm jealous of those droplets. They've seen more action than I have in years. I imagine their delectable trail as they slither past the barrier and over his thickness.

Freddy follows my line of sight. "You want this?" He tugs at the drawstring with a fist. "Baby, all you had to do was ask."

He shimmies out of his pants and kicks them aside, leaving himself bare except for his tented boxers. I step forward and take my time eye-fucking him. My fingertip dances over his chest, pausing at the new scars.

"The General's goons kicked the shit out of me and left me some parting *gifts*."

"And what about this?" My thumb glides over the new ink before I whisper the words, "Only when I meet death shall I have peace." My gaze snaps to his. "When did you get this?"

He brushes his lips over my knuckles. "After I lost *you*."

His words cause an emotional tornado of memories to swirl in my head. *He never forgot about me.*

His chuckle is low as he stares into my eyes. "I can't help but think that I'm still dreaming all this shit up. Because it's hard for my mind to accept that I've *found* that unattainable peace." I brush my palm over his stubble and he leans into my touch. "It's always been you. Always you."

"We've been a part for so long," I remind him.

"And not a day went by when I didn't think about you and the future that was taken from us." He drags his tongue over my neck in a slow caress. My body involuntarily presses against his. "Fuck," he groans as his erection rubs against my stomach. "Are you going to let me see that pretty pussy again? I've missed her too." He cups the apex of my thighs. "Is this for me? I feel your slick cunt through these pants." He nips my ear. "What do I need to do to get a taste of you, even if it's just a single drop of that sweet nectar?"

His words nearly make me combust. My mind is foggy with desire. *What do I want?* I rub my hips against his in an attempt to ease the pressure growing between my legs.

"If you won't use your words, mate, I'll just *take* what I want."

Memories of the many beatings I've endured flash behind my eyes. How men always take from me…

"No."

He steps back with his hands up. The hurt that darkens his features soon transforms into fury. His snarl bounces off the training room walls. "Give me their names and I'll bring their severed heads to you on a platter."

I squeeze my eyes shut, burying the trauma deep inside my soul. I don't have time to fall apart or let Freddy fight my battles. Those soldiers will suffer at *my* hands, not my mate's. Every ounce of pain they've caused me will be repaid tenfold. I'm not a simpering lamb or a damsel in distress. I am a dangerous, badass bitch.

I stride towards the exit. Freddy tugs on my wrist, and my neck snaps to him. "I never asked to be rescued. I can handle my enemies on my own."

He drops to his knees in front of me. "I know you don't need my help, but it's here if you ever want it, love. Anything you want, it's yours." He unbuttons my pants, then shoves them down to my ankles. "So tell me. What can I do for you?" His fingertips dance between my thighs.

My knees quake and my back presses against the wall. The pressure is building again. His breath tickles my skin through the thin fabric of my underwear.

"I can smell that sweet pussy. Let me have a taste."

I snatch a fistful of his hair and pull his neck back to look him in the eyes. "Eat your fill, then fuck me."

His pupils dilate and he licks his lips. Once the words flutter between us, he wastes no time. He shreds my underwear and plunges his tongue inside my heat.

"Oh, Luna!" I scream out as I grind my hips against him.

"I've missed this." He dips two fingers into my core and pumps. "You're so wet."

The vibrations from his dirty talk send shivers up my spine. It feels so good, but the pressure is unbearable. "The longer you take, the less time you'll have to get your *dick* wet."

"As long as you explode on my face, I don't care about my dick. I can choke him later. This is all about you." He applies long strokes with his masterful tongue, from one end to the other, until I'm writhing and bucking. "This pussy has always been so fucking greedy."

"Now," I demand, unable to keep my composure and not willing to beg for my release.

His teeth graze my swollen clit. The pain swirls with pleasure as I scream his name and melt into a puddle on the floor. Freddy cradles me as my body convulses with my orgasm.

"Perfection." He strokes my cheek. "You're the only one for me, Angelica." His lips brush against mine. The taste of my arousal lingering on his breath. "Is my time up, mate? Or do you want me to fuck you next?"

I can't catch my breath. That orgasm. *Damn.* I've forgotten how intense it can be between mates. We were created for each other. Plus, that filthy mouth of his. *Fuck.*

He kisses my sweaty forehead. "How about this? We get the mission done, then I can make love to you until we drift off to sleep."

Make love? Freddy has never called it that before. I bite the inside of my cheek. I need this to be fast and hard, with a side of hair pulling. My fingers rip at his boxers, until his bulge is free. I grin at the weeping tip. "Well, I'm not the only one who's wet with desire."

He fists his cock and more liquid drips out. "How do you want it?" He tilts his head. "I know I've fucked every one of your holes, but which one do you prefer now?"

So many choices.

He tugs again and groans. "Or how about I just mark you with my cum?"

I spread my legs and his heated gaze lingers on my dripping center. He releases his cock and leaps on top of me. His mouth devours mine in a frenzy of teeth and tongue. I arch my hips to meet his, my body begging for his ruthless thrusts.

"How long has it been?" he grunts to himself.

"Too long," I whimper.

He rubs his tip over my clit. "I won't be able to control myself. It may hurt." He clenches his jaw. "Just like the first time we fucked."

I don't remind him that my life is filled with so much suffering I'm immune to it. Instead, I snatch a fistful of his hair and demand, "Get on with it."

When I give him permission, his patience snaps, and he slams into me in one quick thrust. I scream at the jolt of discomfort, but he drowns it out with his kisses while his fingers tease my clit, building up my next release.

"This pussy feels like home."

His other hand tweaks my nipples to hard peaks. My eyes roll back as I ride the waves of ecstasy. I forget where I am and what's happened to me. It's just blazing pleasure as it ripples through every surface of my body until my mate and I become one again and the bond between our wolves is restored.

Freddy slams into me a few more times, then removes his thick cock and spurts ribbons of white onto my chest. The hot liquid mingles with my sweat before he uses his palm to mark his claim over my belly, then my pussy. I arch my hips as he flicks my swollen girly bits on the way down before he bends his head and presses a kiss on it. I moan and relax onto the mat.

Luna, have mercy. This is what it feels like to be completely satisfied. And yet my pulse is already quickening, begging for another round.

"You wear my cum beautifully." Freddy admires his work. "I think you should leave it here until I help you wash up tonight."

"How about I make you lick it off me?"

His lip quirks. "Is that a command?"

I glance at the clock on the wall. Fuck, we don't have time for this. Before I can answer, his warm tongue skims my ankles. I moan and let my head fall back.

"Eyes on me, mate. I want you to see that I can follow your orders."

I lean up on my elbows and do just that. He cleans every inch of my body, making sure to be very thorough *inside* my pussy. It's hot. I can't stop watching him as he worships me. Not even if I tried.

"Do you want to come again?" He doesn't wait for my answer, before he bites and kisses me until I see stars and scream my release.

Words are not wording. *Luna, the things this man does to me.* I tense at the thought. *Is Freddy my weakness or pillar of strength?*

Freddy strokes a finger over my arm. "Why do you save them? The shifters *and* humans?"

Why would he ask something like that? Does he think I'm a heartless monster? I pull away from his touch and tug on my clothes. "Because it's the right thing to do."

"I didn't mean to upset you." He passes me my pants.

Did he really offend me by asking me a question? *Fuck no.* But when he kisses me, it makes me feel things I shouldn't. Things like maybe we can have something that'll last forever. And I don't want to get my hopes up. Especially in my line of work. Then there's the whole *I don't trust him yet* part.

I button my pants and sigh at my feet. *How can I not open up to him after everything that's happened between us?*

"When I try to fix others, I don't have time to reflect on how *broken* I am. I know how stupid that sounds, but there it is."

He wraps his arms around me. Those thick biceps hide the insecurities leaking down my cheeks. "Baby, we are all broken." He strokes my hair. "But now, we can be broken together."

I wiggle into his warmth.

"I know I don't say the right words. I've never been much of a romantic," he says. I snort and he pinches my ass. "But I'll *show* you how much I love you every day in other ways."

Freddy

Paradise

Angelica's breathing remains uneven from our lovemaking session, and it's a beautiful symphony. A calm I haven't felt in years settles in my wounded soul. She squeezes me tightly, like she's afraid to let me go. I don't blame her for that lingering doubt. But I am her mate, and she doesn't love me because she wants to change me into something she can predict. She thrives under pressure and irregularity. And I'll rightfully keep her on her toes.

The door swings open and the beta arches a brow at Angelica's wet cheeks. "Is everything okay?" She glares at me. "Or should I put the mutt down?"

"Who the fuck…" I begin to snarl.

Angelica clears her throat as she covers my mouth with her palm. "Everything is fine. Are the teams ready to move out?"

I glance from the beta back to Angelica again. "There are multiple missions?"

Angelica adjusts her shirt. "Freddy, you will go with Angel and pick up the General with team one, while I move out with my team to snatch his son."

Son? Since when did the spawn of Satan procreate? I never even got a whiff of a child on the old man. My mate strides past me as if she didn't just suggest we separate after being apart for so long.

I snatch her wrist. "I'm going with you."

"No." She shakes off my grip and the word slaps me across the face. "Your job is to protect our daughter and prove yourself. Then we can *discuss* your future."

I laid my heart out at her feet and she's stomping it to bloody pulp. Her glare jabs at my chest before it drags through my flesh. I clench my fists. "Will I ever be good enough for you?" I whisper.

"I ask all of our pack members to contribute, and this is how you can help." She pats my shoulder, the gesture meant to be as condescending as it feels. "If I didn't trust you, I'd keep you away from your daughter. Think of this as your chance to get to know her better. Don't overthink it."

She doesn't even bother to give me a goodbye kiss. The queen just leaves the room, dismissing me as if I'm absolutely *nothing*. The beta winks at me, then follows at her alpha's heels.

My snarl vibrates against the training room walls. I'm alone *again*, fighting battles for others and being their muscle. I swore I wouldn't put myself into this situation again. That I'd be my own man.

I pinch the bridge of my nose, trying to hush the voices in my head. *Angelica is back in our life. We should be by her side*, my wolf insists.

I should have expected this. We may be mates, but we aren't the same shifters we used to be. Not after so many years apart. We have chemistry but is that it?

I tug at my hair and kick at the wall as my demons battle over the memories of being the bitch for Spike, then the General. Is this what Angelica wants? To punish me?

Then again, at least I have my mate and my daughter close by. I take a steadying breath and straighten my back. I'll do this mission, grab the motherfucker who ruined my life, and see how things go from there.

"What's your favorite color?" Angel skips at my side. "I like red because it's bright."

"Uh. Black?" I scratch my chin. "I've never thought about it before."

"It can't be black, Dad. Pick an actual color."

The way the title rolls off her lips still causes me to sidestep. *I'm a father.*

"We need to be quiet now." The beta rubs the girl's back. "We're getting closer."

Angel pretends to zip her lips. But I give no such promises.

"I don't like using her as bait." My gaze never leaves my daughter's tiny figure. She's the spitting image of her mother. I feel bad for us when she's a teenager. We'll be fighting boys left and right to keep them away from her.

"Angel is far more capable than you are." The beta pats Angel's shoulder. "She's a fighter, just like her mother."

The sharp bite directed at my abilities boils my blood. This is supposed to be my chance to prove my loyalty and the bitch isn't even going to give me an honest shot. "You don't know anything about me."

"I *know* you will do whatever it takes to keep your own tail safe."

Images of my ex-girlfriend's pregnant stomach float in my mind. The General's warning of enslaving my child still shakes me to my core. I brush off the beta's comment. "I don't have to explain *shit* to you. You're just jealous that I'll outrank you one day soon. Maybe I'll assign you toilet duty and make you lick the bowls clean?"

She starts to respond before dropping it with a wave of her hand. "You know, she'll never forgive you for *abandoning* her and your daughter."

This bitch. And saying that in front of my kid. My rage topples over and spews from my mouth. "Listen here, you little shit! The hospital told me she was dead!"

"They're coming," another shifter hisses from where he's crouching in the shadows in front of us.

I glare at the beta and resolve to continue this later. I duck behind the brush, eager to get a glimpse of the General. We monitor the entrance to the police station as a tinted vehicle creeps up to the curb. Shouts echo around us before a soldier leaps out and disappears inside the building.

This is it. They're going to transfer the bastard to a more secure location. Drool pools in my mouth at the thought of getting another glimpse of the man who took everything from me. I can't wait to sink my fangs into his neck.

"Shit," the beta curses, and I quickly follow her line of sight.

No. Fucking. Way. There's a group of shifters scouting the perimeter. This was supposed to be a quick grab and go. I clench my fists. But this doesn't change a thing. We can defeat them. The General is coming back with us no matter what.

"Stand down," the beta commands. "There are too many witnesses. Our orders are to return to base."

The rest of the team morphs into fur and stays in the shadows of the trees. Their bodies melt into the darkness as they travel back to the compound. Only the beta and Angel humor me. Or are they babysitting me?

"If the General is free, he'll continue to experiment on us. Can't you see? Our very existence hangs in the balance. Shifters' lives are at stake!"

The beta grinds her jaw and steps towards me. "Just stop with the act already! Everyone knows what you're doing. Trying to redeem yourself for all the fucked-up shit you've done. Stealing shifters, shacking up with someone's mate... The list keeps growing."

"Oh. Is that what I'm doing? Really? Well, please continue to enlighten me on what else I've done."

"Everything you've done to *help*..." She throws up air quotes. "...has only made matters worse. For your pack, your mate, and your daughter." Angel squeaks and tugs on the beta's arm, but the woman ignores the girl's pleas and continues, "Stop trying to be the alpha, because you'll always be the loser. It's the only thing you're actually good at."

I won't be talked to like this, especially not when revenge is so close I can taste it. The beta opens her big mouth again, but my patience is on empty and my sanity cracks. My hand snaps up and pins the beta's neck to a tree.

"Why do people keep underestimating me?" I squeeze until the female gurgles and kicks. "Don't treat me like I'm beneath you. You have no idea what I'm capable of," I snarl. "You think I'm a problem now? Just you wait. I've been dragged through hell for too long." I tilt my head and smirk. "My enemies will be drenched in crimson as they pay for the crimes they've committed against my family."

I release my hold, and the beta crumbles at my feet. She coughs as she crawls away. But before she can get too far, I kneel and pinch her chin. Fear flashes in her gaze.

"You won't attempt to stop me from seeking my vengeance. And you will not follow me. You are to return to base and tell my mate I'll return soon with a pretty present for her."

"Daddy, can I come with you?" Angel looks between me and the beta. In all the chaos, I forgot she was here. She blends into the shadows so well.

Fuck. Day one as a dad, and I'm already proving to be a superb role model. And the way she says that word. *Daddy.* It melts some ice on my heart. Especially whenever she drags out the ending. As if I've been around her all of her life and her love has no bounds.

I rub a thumb over my daughter's cheek. If something were to happen to her, I'd never forgive myself. "Not this time, sweets. I have to make an example of those who've hurt us, and it'll get messy."

"But I can help."

I smirk at her bright eyes, burning with promises of retribution. "I know you can. But I need to do this mission on my own."

"Can I go next time?"

"Let's see if Mom lets me live that long." I guide Angel towards the waiting beta. "Go back home with the pack and I'll be there soon."

Ever the rebellious child, Angel wraps her arms around me. "Please come back home."

It should feel awkward embracing my child for the first time. But for me, it's as natural as breathing. I hug her slim frame. "If I don't return, it'll be because I'm in a body bag." I meet her blue eyes. "Because now that I know you and your mother are alive, I'll bring down anyone who stands in my way to get back to you. I love ya, kid."

Angel walks a few steps before she pivots. "I'll see you soon." She waves at me before skipping off with the beta.

I return the gesture and watch until the group disappears. *How did I get so lucky?* I pivot back to the police station and my eyes grow wide. The transport vehicle's gone. *No!*

I jog around the dimly-lit area and curse when I sniff the air and come up short. I run a hand through my hair. *Fine. I'll just track the bastard.* I scan the parking lot, then glance back in the direction of the beta. I can return to Angelica with my tail between my legs or…

I scratch my stubble as the thought forms in my mind. I can find someone to aid me in my pursuit. Someone who will help prove that I'm worthy of my fur family and that I *can* contribute to my mate's mission. I lift my chin with new resolve. I need the one woman who will do anything for me, no matter what it is.

An hour later, I break through the tree line with my fangs bared and saliva dripping from my chin. The journey was long and hot, and I have no patience for the shit standing in my way. I snarl at the man blocking my path.

"Stop right there." His fingers dance towards his gun.

My nose twitches in the air. This place should really be guarded by shifters too.

I morph into two legs and shake out my mane, releasing twigs and leaves. I run my hand through my hair and sigh. "Listen. You don't have to lose your life," I say and the man blinks. "They don't pay you enough for that."

The guard quivers. Fear permeates his pores, taking over his scent. His trigger finger rattles. "Go back to where you came from, *freak*."

If he thinks I'm a freak, clearly no one explained who or what he's guarding. The man snakes his hand to his radio to call for backup.

Fuck me. I didn't want things to get messy.

I lunge forward and the guy reacts by smashing the end of his gun into my head. I waver on my feet and roll to the side.

Quick little bastard.

I leap on my toes, and before he knows I'm behind him, I snap his neck in a clean mercy kill. The human doesn't even have a chance to scream before he crumbles to the floor.

"Sorry, man." I grab his key card and wave it over the security panel. "I tried to be nice."

I weave through the sterile hospital, sticking to the shadows. They've kept her hidden for a long time, but they can't keep her locked in her cage forever. I smirk as the door emerges from the darkness.

The humans never should have messed with the wolves of Cold Creek. Beasts, freaks, whatever they want to call us. We won't stand for it any longer. It's time the shifters rose up and took back the respect we should have received long ago. And there's only one more man standing in my way.

I grin at the guard and wiggle my fingers. "Hand over the key and I'll only knock you out."

His eyes grow wide as he appears to consider his options. "Do you know what you're doing? If you unleash her…"

"I don't need a lecture," I snarl. "Just the keys, pretty boy."

"Please. I have a wife and kid."

"Then, for their sakes, I suggest you do as you're told."

He shuffles through his pocket before tossing me a ring of keys.

"Have a nice nap." I punch him, knocking him out. In two steps, I'm in front of her door and grinning like the Cheshire cat. "Did you miss me?" I ask through the barred window.

"Fredrick? I thought that was you." Her chapped lips tip into a smile. "I did miss you." She glances around. "Are you causing trouble?"

"A little mischief here and there keeps you young." The lock clicks and I swing open the door.

"Freddy. What are you doing here?"

"Mom. I need your help tracking someone down. After we're done, I promise to help you get to wherever it is you want to go."

She suffocates me with a tight hug. "I'll always be here for you."

I return her embrace and frown at the bones sticking out of her thin skin. I pull back and really look at her. Her hair is peppered gray with balding spots throughout, and her once-radiant skin is pasty. "Mom, are you all right?"

Her eyes sparkle, bright and full of love. "Nothing a good cheeseburger and a few fries can't fix." She kisses my cheek. "How about we grab a bite to eat, and you can explain what's going on?"

It's as if no time has passed.

"Sounds good."

My mother is a badass but with a heart of gold. I side-glance her. Why didn't I think of breaking her out sooner? I know the doctors said she had a mental breakdown when Dad was murdered, but maybe she's better now?

Boots thump from around the corner. *Shit.* I use my body to push my mother behind me. *Maybe we can sneak out the back door?*

"Hands up!" A group of armed guards steps into our path, the man who pleaded for his wife and kid now standing front and center. *Of fucking course.* I show one human an ounce of kindness and it fucks everything up.

"I'm sorry, Mom." I sigh and shake my head. "I just wanted to help my pack."

"There's nothing to be sorry about, baby. Now step aside and let mother through." I blink at her, but she hisses through her teeth, "Don't make me ask twice."

Her glare sends a shiver down my spine, but my need to protect her wins out. "No way."

278

She brushes past me anyway. "Gentlemen, we can be civil. Let me and my boy leave peacefully or you'll be sorry." An energy sizzles around the room. Warm and powerful as it encompasses us.

Shit. Is this coming from her?

I arch a brow, and my mother winks before addressing the men again. But their guns never waiver. "I gave you a fair warning." She sighs.

The men tense before the man in front shouts, "Fire!"

I don't have time to move or think as silver rains upon us. Regret sinks deep into my soul as my failures blanket my last moments on this earth. *I'll never hold Angelica or Angel again.*

But the pain doesn't come. I peek an eye open and see the bullets are frozen midair.

"What the fuck?" I rub my face with my knuckles. The metal casings clang onto the tile at our feet. The noise vibrates around us like the calm before the storm.

How did she use those powers? Are they unlimited?

I clear my throat. Answers can come later. We need to escape this facility and go after the General before he slithers into another hole. I raise my chin at the simpering humans, daring them to make a move. Between Mom's magic and my tenacity, we're an unstoppable team. They wanted to leash and destroy her abilities, but I'm releasing her onto the world. They better watch out because this mama has a bite that's far worse than her bark.

Mom's gaze widens on the guards. "How dare you shoot at my child."

"Willow, please understand… We can't let you leave." One of

the men steps forward with a placating gesture. "But maybe we can negotiate…"

"No. You had a chance to discuss this in a civil manner but you chose to fire on us." With a flick of her wrist, my mother watches on as the guards' necks snap to an odd angle and their bodies crash to the floor.

I swallow the bile rising in my throat. "Shit." I step away from the blood pooling at our feet. "What the hell? Did you have to kill them? We could have locked them in your cell."

"Freddy, I've had many years to imagine how I'd get my revenge and this is just the beginning."

Her eyes shine bright again. But instead of love, it's anger burning behind those blue depths. Anger over my dad's murder, her mistreatment, and now my request for aid. "I was always careful of how much magic I used. But now…" Her grin is feral and for a split second, I question if I've made the right choice by releasing her. "I'm not holding back. I'm going to make my son's enemies pay before I'm in my grave."

Maybe her loyalty can ground her? Make her see reason?

My mother waves me forward. "Your kingdom awaits, son."

She might have sold her soul to the devil in exchange for her dark powers, but she is still my mother. So I obey. We stride past the slaughter and into the flickering lights of the main lobby. No more hiding. We are making ourselves known. I aim a naughty finger at the security camera, hoping the military goons who took everything from me will watch as I conquer and crush their existence.

As our feet hit the smooth pavement, Mom takes a deep breath. The wind whips her graying hair around her angled face. "Luna, I've missed this." She peers at the moon and her eyes glisten. "I've dreamt of this moment." She squeezes my hand. "Thank you for never abandoning me."

I return the pressure. "I could never forget you."

"I knew you wouldn't." She releases my wrist and gazes into the stars. "But I know someone who has." She clenches her fists while appearing lost in thought. "I need to have a nice sit down with my sister."

My mother's words slam into my chest. She's right. Aunt Debbie never took time to check on Mom, choosing to stay behind whenever I would visit. That's fucked up but I do feel bad for my aunt. She's going to have to deal with my mother's wrath. Should I warn her?

She abandoned me too. After the Guardian arrived at the Tala pack. I grind my jaw. But Debbie does have a little girl to protect now, so she may fight back and hurt Mom.

"We can check on her soon." Mom's neck twists to meet my gaze. I shrug it off and clarify, "First, I have someone I'd like you to meet and destroy."

I lean against a dilapidated brick building and pull a cigarette from the pack I grabbed before my trip here. I rub it against my nose. It's been months since I've had a smoke. My mouth pools with saliva, begging for a taste of the sweet nicotine nestled inside the wrapper.

Mom snatches the cigarette from my lips and tsks. "You shouldn't smoke. It'll make you sick." She assesses my face. "Why do you need these things to cope? Tell me who hurt you, Fredrick?"

"Do you want the full *list* or just the top three?"

"Just one name at a time." Her palms rest on my cheeks. "Mommy is here to make them disappear."

I toss the pack of smokes to the floor and crush them with my foot. I can stop smoking, if it means having my mother's magic at our disposal. Plus, Angelica never liked the habit anyway. "Then let's not keep our enemies waiting, Mother."

We shred to fur and howl at the city skyline. We're coming for them. *All* of them.

Angelica

Triumph

"I just received word that the other team has returned," my third-in-command announces before whispering to me, "There were complications. And long story short, they were unable to retrieve the General."

How did they fuck that up?

"We'll question the team about it later. For the moment, let's focus on our mission. Because even though they failed, we will not." I motion for the first group of rebels to approach the underground military compound and place the explosives. As they work, I shudder at the thought of being buried alive. That's not the way I want to die. If I meet my end in battle, fine. But eating dirt in the pitch black? *Nope.*

They wait for my signal before hitting their detonators. The ground rumbles beneath our boots. Our goal isn't to bring down the facility, just give everyone a good scare. And just like an ant hill, when we disturb their home, the soldiers rush out, armed with piss-poor attitudes.

"Remember, do not harm the shifters or any soldiers who choose to surrender," I order my group. "Let's move out."

Half the team shifts while the rest position themselves in the trees overlooking the area. We've learned from experience that each compound has a mix of soldiers and shifters that are *forced* to serve their superiors. My aerial team has arrows tinted with a special serum that knocks out their victims until we can give them a choice to help us or return to their packs. Sadly, most of the wolves in these places have either been born and bred here and have no homes to return to. Or they've been experimented on for so long, their memories of their past are wiped clean.

The compound alarms blare in the clearing. Men scatter from all corners of the open field and the battle ensues. A howl at the entrance signals my opening to sneak in and snatch our target.

Finally. I stride through the gaping hole, swinging my dagger. I sniff the air and head towards the scent of fear. The building shutters and the power flickers. I brace a hand on the walls until it passes. Sirens continue to shriek and flash, as if they alone could deter us from completing our mission.

A gun goes off. Then a woman screams. *Fuck*. I grind my jaw and sprint forward, stepping over bodies as I go. *Damn it. There're so many fucking corridors!*

"Jake," a shaky voice squeaks. "Stop! You're better than this!"

My ears perk up and I pivot towards the sound of arguing. The hair on my neck stands on end and I turn back around to see a man headed my way.

"Where the fuck do you think you're going?" he sneers.

I don't have time to humor him or play. Lives are at stake and I've already heard two gunshots. That's two too many. The soldier doesn't have time to aim his gun before I leap into the air, my dagger slicing his neck. He crumbles, but before the full weight of his body hits the floor, I'm already gone.

I slide to a stop and grin, blood trickling off my blade. "Well, well, well. If it isn't the General's spawn."

He's not the same young man I saw at the General's house all those years ago. I drag my gaze over his blood-soaked clothes. He's morphed into a murdering prick. Like father, like son.

Jake's eyes grow wide as I stride towards him. He shoves a shifter in front of him, using the woman like a shield. "Back the fuck up." He presses his pistol to her temple.

I feign boredom as I lean on the wall and pick at my fang. "Using a defenseless woman as body armor is a dick move." I spit at his feet. "You're a pussy just like your worthless father."

"Let me leave safely and I'll release her."

Wow. He thinks he can negotiate with me.

"I've saved most of the shifters here. One life for the General's pussy-ass son's blood is well worth it." My talons extend, ready to slice his pretty face.

"Aw, did Daddy leave a nasty taste in your mouth, bitch?" Jake cackles. "He did enjoy fucking his hostages."

My breath hitches as memories constrict my airways.

"Tell me. Did he cut into your skin while he rode you? Dad loves to hear his woman scream while he slams home."

"You little…" I snap and leap at him. "How dare you!"

I slam into the hostage first, knocking Jake off balance. When he wavers, I roll the girl out of harm's way. My team should be here any minute to grab her. I just need to distract him long enough to keep *her* alive. I slam my fist into Jake's face. Bone crunches under my knuckles. And, damn, it feels good.

"Over here!" one of my pack members calls out to the girl.

I wait until she's safely out of the splatter zone and grin at Jake. "Should I cut into *your* skin?"

He sneers but doesn't throw any smart-ass comments my way.

I grip his uniform and tug him up. "Come on, pretty boy, it's time to go. You and I have lots to talk about."

I break through the smoke billowing around the compound exit and stroll out like a fucking boss. I finally have leverage on the douchebag. How fucking poetic. He used Angel to keep me on a tight leash. Now I'm using his son. Oh, how the mighty will fall.

"Report," I demand.

"We rescued four shifters plus the General's trained beasts. Unfortunately, no humans surrendered."

Of course not. They were the man's ride-or-die groupies. I nod at the females huddled by the shimmering lake. "Are they injured?"

"Minor scrapes but nothing serious. We can travel back whenever you're ready."

A twig snaps and we pivot towards the tall brush. We're not alone.

"Wolves incoming!" one of my spies announces from the top of a towering oak. My crew jumps into action and circles the wounded females in a protective barrier, armed to the fangs with weapons and itching for more blood. Two tall shadows slide to a stop at the edge of the woods.

"Announce your intentions or face the consequences." I glare at the darkness.

"We come in peace," a baritone voice rumbles. "Lily!" His eyes light up and he steps towards a hostage.

My pack stands in her way, shielding the disheveled females. *She* may know the brutes, but this is about more than just her. The other hostages have been raped and beaten. They have every fucking right to feel safe now.

"Let her go!" one of the males shouts, his muscles bunching. *I wonder if they're mates.*

The second man snatches his friend's arm. "They're only trying to protect her. They don't know who we are."

We don't have time for this. We need to leave before reinforcements arrive. I drag Jake behind me as I step forward, all eyes on us. I toss the soldier at the feet of my third-in-command. "Get him ready for transport."

Terror streaks Jake's face as he realizes there's no one coming to his rescue. "Let me go!"

That whiney voice grates on my nerves. I kneel and pinch his chin with my thumb and forefinger. "You don't get to tell me what the fuck to do." I nod towards my family. "When I'm done with your sorry ass, I'm feeding you to the wolves. These defenseless women have been abducted, abused, and raped by your men and they aren't happy about it." Snarls echo off the trees, and I lean into his ear. "I'll enjoy watching them rip you to shreds."

He swallows hard. "You all don't know who I am," he stutters. "Who my father is."

When some of the females whimper, I slap him to regain his attention. "I know exactly who your father is, you little prick." I fist his torn uniform and lift him into the air. "That fucker tortured me and stole my child from me."

"Wait, please!" a feminine voice squeaks.

"Why?" I reply but I don't take my eyes off the prick quivering in my grip.

"I need to know if he hurt my Nana." Her sorrow coats every syllable. Are they out murdering grannies now too? "Please."

I slam Jake against a tree and snarl. Spittle clings to his cheek. "Did you hurt her family?"

He swallows again, and I already know the fucking answer. But the woman deserves the truth. I shake Jake so hard his teeth clatter. "Yes!"

"How could you?" the girl sobs.

"Get him out of my sight." I toss the garbage to my waiting group.

"What about these two?" one of my packmates asks.

Excellent question. I stride towards the newcomers. "What do we have here?" I tilt my head at the broad-shouldered alpha. *Why is he so far from home?* "Now that's a face I haven't seen in a while." My gaze sweeps over their naked frames. Tall, dark, handsome, *and* members of the Tala pack. Sable and Jackson. The same men who helped bring down my old pack. "I would say it's nice to see you again, but the last time we were in a room together, you murdered my alpha." The image of Spike's mangled body on a gurney floats through my mind. I press down on the haunting scene and growl.

Sable tilts his head. "Seeing as your mate sold me to the General and marked me for dead, we're even."

I repress my cringe. Sable was one of the shifters Freddy brought to the General? Fuck. How dumb is my husband?

I brush dirt off my shoulder and shrug as the lie slips from my tongue. "I haven't seen Freddy in a long time, so you can't blame me for his life choices." I don't meet his gaze as I pick at my nails. Fine, he wants to bring up transgressions and get a rise out of me… "Last I heard, he was fucking your sister. How's that bitch doing?" I lift my eyes to his while a menacing grin decorates my face.

Take that.

Sable releases a guttural growl and leaps forward, but Jackson holds him back. "Keep Sky out of this! Freddy ruined her and I'm happy to report he's dead!"

I snort at his misplaced confidence. "Did you see Freddy's body? Because he seems to be more feline than canine with his nine lives. I seriously doubt he's six feet under." I love the sparks practically sizzling off Sable's sculpted chest. His muscles ripple with fury. He's so easy to piss off.

"We need to move out, Angelica," my packmate reminds me, stealing my fun.

I sigh and nod before assessing the two wayward wolves. "What am I going to do with you two?" I scratch my chin. "Why are you even here?"

"We came to rescue a fellow pack member," Jackson replies.

Maybe my game can continue. "And who are you?" I ask, even though I already know the answer.

"Jackson. Beta of the Tala pack." He winces as the words drip off his tongue. "Or at least I was. I disobeyed a direct order to save her."

Well, someone does have a spine after all. "Frost is a jackass. I don't think his reign will last long." I pivot back towards the hostages. I smooth my tone, showing them the compassion they need. "You have two choices, ladies. Join my cause and help others who are trapped like you were, or return to your packs. Either way, you are free to do as you please."

As soon as my team steps aside, Jackson rushes to the female's side. He picks her up, and she sobs in his neck while he buries his nose in her hair. "I'm here," he whispers.

My chest aches. The stupid romantic in me wants that kind of reunion. But my scarred heart knows that will never happen. A happily ever after is not in my tale, and the sooner that traitorous organ realizes it, the better.

"So, you're the alpha of the rebels?" Sable grunts. "*Your* pack is *murdering* humans."

I narrow my eyes at the prick. "I'm releasing shifters who were stolen from their families to be bred like animals... *and* preventing their offspring from being turned into trained weapons."

"Angelica. I get it." Sable shuffles forward, and I step back with a hiss. "They did the same thing to me. But we can't retaliate like this. We have to find peace."

How fucking dare he judge me and pretend he understands my fucked-up life. Anger burns in my throat and I release flames as I curse him. "Fuck you and your fictitious ideals of peace." My shout echoes around the forest, ringing truth throughout the wilderness. I take a breath and wave off his pleasantries. Then I pivot towards my group. "We are moving out." I stride off but pause to glare behind me. "You are *not* welcome to follow us. I'll only warn you once."

I can't afford to have them fuck everything up or endanger my child.

I scan the broken bodies littering the perimeter of the compound. This wasn't how I thought my day would play out. But we are doing the world a favor by getting rid of scum. The government thinks they've morphed us into their personal arsenal. Soon, they will discover the harsh reality of their mistake.

"Transfer our VIP guest to the interview suite," I purr as we enter our den. "Don't touch him until I arrive. I want to see the bastard squirm."

"Yes, alpha." My third-in-command drags Jake through the many tunnels towards our interrogation chamber. My chest fills with pride as our newest escapees are gently guided to their assigned rooms so they can get fresh clothes and a hot shower. They're finally safe. These shifters will never again be taken advantage of.

"Mommy!" Angel barrels into me, tears dripping past her cheeks.

"Sweetheart, what happened?" I kneel to wipe at her face. "Are you hurt?"

"Daddy's gone!"

A thousand questions fight for dominance in my head, trying to break free from my mouth. "What?" wins out.

"He got in a fight with Sylvia. She said mean things to him and he left." She sobs into my chest. "Is he going to come back?"

I lift her into my arms. "It's okay, little one." I kiss the top of her head and brush the loose strands aside. "Let's get you a cookie from the kitchen and talk about it."

I'm dead-ass tired and I have a murderer in my facility. I should deal with those issues first, but my baby girl is priority. I weave through the hallways until we arrive at the cafeteria. I push through the crowds and wave over David's sister. She quickly assesses Angel's face and knows exactly what to do. She ducks behind the counter and grabs our secret weapon. *Monster cookies.* These delicious morsels are baked to perfection with rich peanut butter, oatmeal, and semi-sweet chocolate chips.

"Here you go," Lauren sings as she strides to our table with a plate of goodies. She kneels beside Angel. "Are you all right?"

Angel shakes her head but grabs a cookie and shoves it in her mouth. Her cheeks puff out like a chipmunk.

"I'm sure Mama will make everything better." Lauren kisses my daughter's nose. "I'm gonna grab you a cup of ice-cold milk to help wash down that cookie." Then she stands, offers me an encouraging wink, and saunters off towards the fridge.

I rub Angel's knee and wait until she swallows. It only takes her a second before she animatedly retells the tale of Freddy and Sylvia's screaming match. I groan and rub my temples. I knew my beta would give him a hard time, but this is pure *jealousy. Luna help me.* It does at least sound like Freddy is planning to rejoin us but when and with what is up in the air.

"Don't worry about it. I'm sure Daddy will be back real soon." I move Angel's hair aside so she doesn't accidentally chew on it when she devours cookie number three. There's only one more on the plate, and I snatch it up so her sugar high doesn't destroy us all. I take a bite, allowing the sweetness to ease my own turmoil. I can't believe my mate bailed.

What if he gets caught and someone uncovers our location? I should put this place on lockdown and add more patrols just in case.

"I'm heading to the common room, Angel. Would you like to watch a movie with me while your mom gets some work done?" Lauren opens her arms in invitation.

I smile as the pair embraces. She's the aunt Angel will never have. My heart aches with all the loss crushing down on me, but I shake it off. Lauren is right. I need to work, and the first order of business is to question the General's son.

"I'll meet you guys in a few hours." I kiss Angel's cheek. "Behave, and I promise we'll talk more about Daddy after I have a chat with my new *friend*."

Angel barely spares me a glance before she grins at Lauren. "Can we watch *Beauty and the Beast*?"

"Again?"

"It's my favorite. I love how the beast looks like a wolf."

"Fine. But after that, we're watching *Minions*." Angel giggles as Lauren tickles her belly. "Because I love their fart guns," Lauren says.

They stride out, leaving me behind to finish my cookie and clean up. As I place the dishes in the soapy sink water, my beta enters the room. I raise my brows at her guilty expression.

"Angel already beat you to giving me the report. Not only did you *not* retrieve the General, but you pushed so hard that my mate left."

She rubs her bruised neck. "We both said things to each other that we shouldn't have."

That's a fuckin' understatement.

"Sylvia, you knew how important this mission was."

"But there were shifters escorting the General. We couldn't risk…"

I slam the sponge down and growl. "You know that's not what I meant. I just got Freddy back and this was supposed to be his test."

She crosses her arms over her chest. "One he failed spectacularly."

"Because of you. Not because of his own actions."

"He abandoned the mission and his daughter!"

"No. You abandoned the mission and let Freddy walk away." I point a soggy finger at her chest. "Do you even know where he went? Did you even think to send someone to keep an eye on him?"

"I didn't think he was *worth* the trouble."

I pinch the bridge of my nose as a headache starts to build. *What is this? Preschool?*

"We'll talk about this later, after you've taken a chill pill. Got it? We'll have a nice sit down and assess how the mission went wrong and what we can do to improve future assignments." I place the clean dishes in the rack and shoulder-check her on my way out. I pause at the frown adoring her face. "I know you meant well. But you are my beta and were personally trained by me. Your actions are supposed to reflect that. Remember that your failures are my failures."

I shake my head and continue towards the interrogation room. Hopefully, this next conversation will be more successful.

Freddy

Root Beer Floats

The first stop I make is to get my safe deposit box. Where I've hidden most of my valuable possessions. A stash of cash and the notes on what I know about the General and his operations. I tug it open and dig through the papers until I reach the bottom of the container. I'm a fucking sentimental old fool. I glide the gold band that once belonged to my wife over my pinkie. The light bounces off the jewelry and twinkles, causing a typhoon of memories to pull me under.

"I'm sorry for your loss." The nurse frowns. "These are Angelica's belongings."

I fist the plastic bag. The remnants of the years I had with my mate all equate to this. Fuck. I wish I had more time to prove my love to her. To hear her laughter ringing throughout the room.

The present blurs back into focus as my hand wipes tears from my face.

"Are you okay, son?"

I clear my throat. "Yeah. Let's go get some grub. I'm starving."

The streets of Carson City are no better than they were the last time I was here. Lined on all sides with beggars and scumbags. My lip curls, as a drug deal goes down at the corner of 6th and 9th. They don't even bat an eyelash as we brush past them. Just pocket their goods and move on to the next junkie looking for a hit.

I keep my head lowered as we stalk towards the abandoned compound that once belonged to the Fangs. Even my mom seems to pick up the pace as we pass it. Each of us consumed by the haunting memories of the day we lost the ones we loved most.

I pull open the diner's entrance and bow to my mom as she strides inside. "Here we are, the Greasy Spoon." Back in the day, we used to hate the name of our local burger place, but I don't give a shit anymore. I glance around at the booths as the scent of fried food slams into my face.

"For old times' sake." Mom waves me into the booth in the back of the restaurant.

I slide in and smirk. "If only Dad could be here, he'd order…"

"A giant root beer float and french fries." Mom's eyes shimmer as she finishes the statement.

I clutch her hand. "I'm sorry, Mom. I didn't mean to… It just slipped out."

"Don't apologize for remembering a great man." She sniffles. "I miss him every day."

"I know, Ma." I kiss her wrist. "He loved you too."

She sighs and leans back as the waitress comes over to get our order. "We'll have two cheeseburgers—rare—a large order of fries and two root beer floats."

"Anything else?" The brunette blows a bubble with her gum.

"What do you think, Freddy?" My mom's face brightens with humor. "Have you grown to enjoying peas or any other vegetable?"

I smirk and shake my head at the waitress. "That's all for now." Once she leaves, I arch a brow in my mother's direction. "I can't believe you remembered that I don't like that stuff."

"A mother never forgets."

We stare at each other, neither mentioning the fact that she's fucking lost her mind and actually did forget for a long time.

Mom lets out a breath and sets her napkin on her lap. "They come and go."

"What does?"

"The *episodes*," she says delicately.

I lean forward. "I never realized you were so powerful. What you did at the asylum was intense."

"Only because I had decades of power stored inside me. Now that most of it is extinguished, I have to be more careful." She clasps her hands together. "Magic always has a price, hence my instability." Her wrists shake. "Freddy." Her gaze flicks to mine. "I won't be this coherent forever."

I rest my palm on her trembling hands and squeeze. "We will figure this out together. The place I'm taking you to is filled with tons of nerds. I'm sure they can help us figure out a cure of some sort. Don't worry. We got this."

Her eyes water as she touches my cheek. "Your father would be so proud of the man you've become."

"I wouldn't go that far. I've made a fuck-ton of mistakes."

She opens her mouth to respond when our plates are delivered, and we slowly dig into the warm food. As per tradition, we dip our fries into the root beer floats and cheers before chomping on the sweet and salty treat.

Once our bellies are full, Mom leans back and pats her lips with a napkin. "Son, you said you made some mistakes. Tell your mother what's weighing so heavily on your shoulders."

"Can't we just let it go and pretend like everything is fine?"

Her arched brow tells me that's a *no*. So I go on to explain all about Spike, Scarlett, Sky, and most importantly, Angelica. I highlight the diabolical plans the General spun together, and her spine straightens. By the end of my tale, anger radiates from her pores and her fangs are glimmering.

"Well, it sounds like we need to pay a visit to the Carson City police station." She slides out of the booth. And I swear if I closed my eyes, I could hear my dad's laughter at her mother hen attitude. She's always been a great provider and ass kicker.

I throw cash on the table for our bill, including a decent tip.

"But the General is gone." I look up and see my mom is outside. "Ma!" I rush to catch up to her, but when I exit the Greasy Spoon, she's in fur. Galloping through traffic without a care in the world. "Fuck." I rake my hands through my hair.

Is this the craziness she was worried about? Did I spark it to life? I jog after her and pray I can get to the police department before she does.

Damn it. She's fast for an old lady.

Smoke billows in the air and I blink. "Shit."

Is that coming from the precinct? I growl and force my aching limbs to pound the concrete. I wipe the sweat inching closer to my eyes. *Please let Mom be okay.* I slide to a stop and my jaw drops. The building is an inferno of angry flames with puffs of black tendrils rising towards the heavens. I cough into my sleeve and back up. *What the fuck?*

"Mom!" On cue, a woman walks through the carnage, her hair flying behind her. Sirens blare and I glance around the parking lot.

The fire department will be on our heels soon. I pull her arm. "We have to leave." She turns to me. Her gaze is far off until it zooms in on my face. "Are you hurt?"

"I know where to find him." Even with black soot covering her small frame, my mother lights up with excitement. "Let's take down the General."

Bright lights flash all around us, and I tug her into the woods. Fuck, she lost control in there. Does she really know where the General is? I take in her smoke-singed skin and sigh. Only one way to find out. "Okay, Mom. Tell me where we can find him."

The wind whips across my thick fur as my claws tear through the dead leaves. My muscled body sprints closer to my goal. *I can almost taste his fear.* As the structure nears, I skid to a stop, throwing dust clouds into the night air. I sniff the area, then morph to two legs.

"Where is he?" I snarl into the silence. I kick the foundation of the ruined building. They gave Mom the wrong information and we're back at square one.

"We'll find him, even if I have to bring down every government building to do it."

We pivot at the sound of approaching footsteps. And I grin as a shadow emerges. *There's my beautiful mate.* That same grin quickly melts into a frown when I notice her tightened jaw. I know that look well. I'm in trouble.

"I can't *believe* you. Why would you stoop this low?" Angelica snarls at the woman standing at my side. "She's unpredictable."

I look between the two of them. "Just hear me out, Angelica..." I raise my palms while stepping in front of my mother.

"I fucking knew you were power hungry, but not *suicidal*!"

Ouch. Does she not have faith in me? Maybe her beta was speaking for the both of them when she said I was worthless.

Mom brushes past me again. "You can't talk to him like that."

The anger is simmering beneath her skin. I can't have her proving my mate right. "Mom, I'd like you to meet my mate, Angelica."

And just like that, Mom smiles ear to ear as she holds out a hand. "Welcome to our family."

Angelica's jaw ticks. "You both have lost your Luna-loving minds. Freddy, return her to the hospital where she belongs and get back to base. Your daughter thinks you've abandoned her." She pivots on a boot and stomps towards the tree line.

I side-glance my mother. *Why can't Angelica accept her help?*

"When can I meet my grandchild?" Mom questions.

Angelica freezes and her spine straightens before she spins back around. "When you are safely behind bars, then I'll consider bringing her to meet you."

"Just because you are my son's mate doesn't mean you get to…" Mom wobbles, then drops to the floor.

I kneel beside her and feel her pulse. That's when I notice the dart protruding from her arm. "What the fuck?"

"You'll thank me later." Angelica snaps her fingers and more shadows emerge from the tree line.

Is she seriously trying to hold my mother captive? After everything that's happened…

"Wait. Let's talk about this." I tug the ring from my pinkie and hold it out to her as a peace offering. "You can trust me to make the right choices."

She arches a brow but snatches it. Her eyes widen as she twirls the gold band in her hand. "I thought the General threw this out when he imprisoned me."

"The hospital gave it to me with your belongings." I swallow the lump in my throat. "That ring was your father's. What would you give to have more time with him? That's all I'm asking. Just some more time to spend with my mom and let her help us find the General."

Angelica tosses the ring at my feet, as if the metal burned her skin. "My father *sold* me for drugs," she spits while rage contorts her beautiful face. "Fuck him and fuck his cheap ring symbolizing so many broken promises."

"But you wore that ring to represent our marriage."

Her laughter vibrates off the trees. "I wore it so I'd never forget how fucked up my past was. It was a reminder to move forward."

Angelica is upset. Once she calms the fuck down, she'll want this back. I swipe the gold band from the ground and tug it over my knuckle again. I'm a patient man and I'll welcome her back with open paws. "I'll consider readmitting my mother *when* we've located the General for you."

"You've got to be joking, right? She's been in a mental hospital for decades. She doesn't even know how to function in the real world."

"Only because no one has given her the chance." I grab Angelica's hands, searching her gaze. "Please. Give her a chance to prove herself. For me. For the cause."

"She's too dangerous."

"Maybe. But maybe not. What we do know is that she's loyal."

"Oh, really? To whom?"

My lips brush Angelica's knuckles. "To our pack."

"She's a liability. What if she leaks our location?"

"We can find another one. You can't tell me you love hiding in the shadows. Scrambling for supplies… for food. Living in darkness."

That is no way to live. We should know. We did it with the Fangs in Carson City for years.

Angelica straightens her spine. "We've managed to do really well."

"But are you *thriving*?" I question. She appears to consider my words, so I push on. "We can give our daughter everything. A kingdom to rule without fear or sacrifice." I nod to the limp frame at our feet. "And Mom can help us establish our power."

"Wait. You said you were returning her *after* you found the General."

"I said I'd consider it. Just like I want you to consider what I'm saying. If Mom can control her abilities, I know she can do more for us."

Angelica shakes her head. "We have everything we need to succeed here."

"Do we?"

She takes a step away from me, shaking her head. "Freddy, you're too focused on your revenge. You aren't seeing clearly."

"And you are too focused on *hiding* that you've forgotten who the fuck you are. A queen and *my* mate."

Her mouth falls open before she stutters out, "I'm hiding? *Hiding*! I've been *clawing* my way through this shitty life. Through my failure yes, but also my many victories. And you know what? I am where I am today because of the lessons I learned along the way. And now, I have an empire at my paws!" She pinches the bridge of her nose. "I'm trying to make the world a better place by freeing our kind and showing that shifters and humans can coexist. While *you* are attempting to destroy the human race."

"Not all of them." I got along with Carly for a little while. Doesn't that count for something? But Angelica does have a point. "Humans are the weaker beings. They *need* us to rule over them."

"We need to coexist!" she repeats.

"Really? Even fucked-up monsters like the fucking General?" I snarl. "The same man who ripped apart our pack and destroyed our lives! He's human. He needs to be punished. They all do."

My mate used to do whatever it took to be ahead. No matter what.

"Freddy. You need to grow the fuck up and let your anger go so you can live out your life with your family." She sighs at my silence. "You're letting the chains of your past dictate your actions. Cut the restraints and come home with me, without your mom."

I love my wife but she's wrong. "And if I don't?"

"Then you'll be building a false, temporary kingdom without your mate *or* your daughter."

We are destined to be together. I clench my fist. Why can't she see the errors of her ways? Humans are fickle creatures. They will always try to rule over any being they see as a threat to their strength, putting our family at risk.

"I won't let you walk out of my life with my pup," I snarl, my alpha tone ringing through.

Shadows emerge from the forest and growl their displeasure. Angelica brought an army with her. They'll defend their leader at all costs. I look down at my mom's crumbled frame. She's still passed out. I can't leave her unprotected.

"Freddy. You don't have a say in what I do or do not do anymore." Angelica's bottom lip quivers. "I wish you'd change your mind before you lose everything, but it's still your choice to make."

I tug at my hair with my hands. This isn't happening. Not after everything. "It looks like I've already lost."

She turns her back to me, then strolls into the forest but stops to meet my gaze. "I'll let you spend some time with your mother before we return her to the hospital. Don't make me regret extending my generosity."

"Your false sense of security won't last long. Especially when you trust humans," I grunt.

"We'll see soon enough."

"Finally. Something we can agree on."

She waves as she walks towards her pack, not bothering to say more.

"I'll keep your location a secret," I call after, and she falters, as if just now remembering that I know where to find her. "Tell Angel I'll visit as soon as I snatch up the General."

I let the unspoken words simmer between us. If she keeps my child from me, I'll fuck up her whole operation. It'll remind her I hold some power too. I hate using Angel as a bargaining chip, but I need to see my daughter again, explain my side of the story, and get to know her better.

Angelica strides farther into the darkness. My wolf aches to draw closer to our mate. To feel her curves and fuck her into tomorrow. For a moment, I question my decision. *How can I live, knowing she's near but not by my side?*

Mom stirs at my feet, and I shake my head. I'll show my mate how wrong she is about my mother. Angelica will see to reason. Then we'll finally be a family.

Angelica

Snitch

My bony knuckles collide with the metal table. The pain radiates through my arm, removing some of the anguish incinerating my heart. *Freddy chose his mother over me.* I swipe my arm across the desk, disrupting countless files. *Why am I never good enough?* My tormented scream mingles with the question in my head as the sound echoes around my office. *I thought my mate loved me.*

What is wrong with me? Soft thuds vibrate to my left. I lift my head and watch small droplets of blood seep through the cracked skin on my hand. I suck on my wound as I remember the interactions between me and my mate a few hours ago. Not that the asshole would admit it, but *we* let our anger get the best of us.

But *damn it.* My dad's wedding band threw me into a mental tailspin. Horrible nightmares resurfaced when Freddy handed it to me. Then the jackass broke his mother out of her cage. I comb a hand through my hair with my shaky fingers and tug at the strands until a sharp sting radiates from my scalp. That woman isn't stable. Even *Spike* feared Willow. I know she's Freddy's mother, but fuck…

He could have just *visited* her, said hi, and been on his way. If we don't return her to her cell, destruction is the only thing on our horizon.

I'm overreacting.

I release my anxiety in one quick breath. *Think, Angelica. Plan your next move and keep one step ahead of your enemy.* I need to have a chat with someone who's lived with Willow. Someone who can contain the devil's abilities. I straighten my spine with finality. As much as I hate to say it, it's time I travel into rival territory.

A knock tugs me out of my revelation, and I pivot as my beta strides into my office. I know she's upset that I've been ignoring her and putting her on bathroom and kitchen duty for the mess she caused with Freddy.

"Can we talk?"

"About what, exactly?"

She leans on the doorframe. "About the false information Jake gave you."

My jaw ticks. *That fucker.* We beat the General's son senseless and he still didn't break. But what confuses me most is how Freddy *and* I both got bad intel from two different sources. Was it planned? A cover up to conceal the General's location? Or was the prick really supposed to be there?

My head aches as the stress pounds at my thin thread of sanity. "There's nothing to talk about."

"Do you want me to take a swing at him? I can pull on a few fingernails or bite off a thumb?"

"Did you clean the toilets like I asked?"

She picks at her fangs. "Yeah, but I figured you'd take me out of the doghouse eventually and let me actually *help* with more important matters."

"Toilets are *important*, Sylvia. They're a necessity." I meet her gaze. Yes, she fucked up. But so did I. And it's time we both fix the errors of our ways so we can work together to protect the future of our pack. "I might let you tag along with the small team I'm taking into the Tala territory."

She arches a brow. "Can't we just send Celeste a message to meet us at the steakhouse again?"

"No. It's time we bring the alpha in on this mission. Because when the time comes, if I can't contain Willow, she will bring down all the wolves in Cold Creek next."

"Do you think her sister will help us?"

"That's a tough one. Debbie has a daughter to protect and I don't think she'd risk everything for a sister who hasn't been around. But you never can predict these things." I brush past the beta, then pause a few feet into the hallway. "Are you just going to stand there looking like an idiot, or are you coming with me?"

A grin brightens her face before she feigns disinterest. "I don't know. I was really looking forward to scrubbing the toilets with your toothbrush."

My lip quirks and I hug the little shit. We laugh and hold each other tight.

"Angelica, I'm sorry. I took things too far with Freddy."

"We all make mistakes. It's how we learn and recover from them that matters."

"Since we are being all philosophical and shit, I'd like to remind you that you're one tough bitch and you don't *need* him."

I roll my eyes, but nod. She's right. I've been through so much and Freddy choosing his mother over me shouldn't dictate my self-worth. *I'm a badass.*

"Mommy!" Angel joins our hug. "Can I go with you too?"

I arch a brow. "Were you spying on us?"

She smirks. "Maybe."

"What am I going to do with you?" I run a hand through my daughter's golden hair.

"Take me with you?" She gives me her signature puppy-dog eyes. "I promise I'll be extra careful."

Do I trust my rival pack enough to include my offspring in this mission? I do trust Celeste to keep her alpha in line. I mean, she risked everything to help us and, while she was here, she treated Angel like one of her own pups.

I glance at Sylvia. "What do you think?"

Her eyes twinkle at the opportunity to offer her opinion again. "It has been a while since Angel played with other shifters her own age."

Our wolves gallop through the woods, soaring over fallen logs and saplings that get in our way. The breeze our four legs creates brush our fur back and cool our heated frames. It's a long trip, and it'll test our agility and endurance. I peek over at Angel. She's keeping up without a problem. Her tongue hangs out and she pants, but she doesn't complain or slow her strides.

She's one tough pup.

My nose twitches and I slow to a trot. We are getting close to the pack's boundary lines. The others follow my lead until we halt in front of a beautiful white wolf. She tilts her head before morphing into her human form.

"Welcome," Celeste greets as she strokes our fur. "I did as you asked and haven't warned Frost of your arrival. Although I'm not sure why you've asked me to do that."

A howl rips through the air and a dust cloud moves through the valley, heading straight for us. I smirk and nod. See? *Not telling them is far more entertaining.*

Celeste leans against a boulder and crosses her arms over her chest. "Frost is already in a foul mood after the stunt Jackson and Sable pulled to rescue Lily. Plus, his poor wife is in the doghouse for assisting the boys. So please try not to push his buttons."

I don't bother to shift and ask if the alpha has any idea that the good doctor helped us with the anti-shifting antidote. If I were him, I'd be damn proud. Celeste's medical research has saved countless lives.

Snarls shake the tree line as four wolves march towards us in an attack formation. I recognize Sable and Jackson. I'm guessing the other two are... I tilt my head. One is massive with a black pelt streaked in blue. The markings seem to sizzle with little bolts of electricity. *He must be the Guardian who roughed Freddy up before the General got a hold of him.* So I can only assume the last is Frost. I scan his graying fur. He's getting too old to keep up with the younger pups.

"I'm vouching for them." Celeste steps into the light with her hands up in surrender. "They've come in peace, to warn us."

Frost morphs into two legs, ignoring her and glaring at us. "Return home immediately. We don't *want* your warning."

The other shifters glance between us. *Frost's being a stubborn ass and wasting my time.*

I join him in my human state and lift my chin. "We are guests in your territory. At least have the decency to offer us water and a meal first."

Before the alpha can reply, the Guardian's rumbling voice takes over. "Is this visit about the destruction being done in Carson City and the surrounding government buildings?"

Power simmers under his skin. Shouldn't his abilities provide that answer for him? I squint and notice his skin color is sickly. Interesting. *What took down the mighty hunter?*

Jackson kneels by Angel and strokes her sweat-drenched fur. "You look exhausted."

My daughter's legs are trembling, but she's still holding her head high.

"Frost, at least allow the child some rest. She's only following her alpha's misguided lead." Jackson shoots me a glare that I ignore.

"Don't bark orders at me," Frost growls. "You're lucky I allowed you to tag along after the stunt you pulled."

Jackson throws a glance at Sable, who nods and shifts. "I agree with Jackson." He elbows Azure before Frost can snarl. "What do you think, Guardian?"

Azure scratches his chin. "I think we owe them our time, especially after they rescued a member of our pack." He bows his head. "Thank you for saving my sister. I'm in your debt."

Frost throws his hands up. "Why am I even here if my decision was going to be overridden?" He points a finger at me. "You step a toe out of line, and I'll send you home in a body bag, rebel!"

"Do you really think I want to be here? No. I'm doing this as a favor to you and your family," I snarl. "So feed us, listen to what we have to tell you, say thank you, and then *graciously* send us on our way."

Frost narrows his eyes, but Jackson steps in first. "Do you want me to carry you?" he asks Angel before pivoting to me. "If you're all right with that."

I bite my lip, my attention focused on Angel and Sylvia. Both appear sore and tired. But Angel has less experience with muscle-failure exercises. And showing that I trust the beta with my child proves I can be trusted too.

"If she's comfortable with it, I think it's a good idea." I smile at my daughter. "Honey, do you want Jackson to help you?"

Angel looks him over, then whimpers her agreement. He chuckles and gently lifts her, holding her to his chest. "Don't worry. It's not too far. Plus, Raven has been barbecuing all day so we have burgers, ribs, steaks, and all kinds of delicious sides."

Angel sighs and rests her head on the beta's broad shoulder while her fluffy tail wags with excitement.

We trudge through the Tala pack's territory. Memories rack my mind as I remember sneaking past their barriers and stealing females for Spike's fucked-up plan to get back at the group for killing his brother. I side-glance Frost and cringe at his glare. Nope, he hasn't forgotten that either.

Celeste squeezes my wrist and smiles. If the mother of one of the stolen pack members can forgive me, there's hope for the alpha too. Besides, we didn't harm the shifters we took all those years ago and they were rescued in a few hours.

My nose twitches as the delectable aroma of smoked meat greets us. I wipe the spittle from my chin. But Frost turns away from the food and into a cave. I sigh and fight a pout as we follow him. The feast will have to wait.

"Sit," the alpha commands as he plops into a leather recliner facing a set of couches.

We scatter around the open areas. I choose the sofa closest to the exit, flanked by my beta and Jackson, who's still holding Angel. I glance at her face and realize she's sleeping.

"The child shouldn't be here. Take her to your cave." Frost waves off my pup, as if she's a gnat buzzing around the room.

Before I can attack, his wife enters. "Stop acting like a brute and show some respect to our guests. The child will stay with her

315

mother." She smacks Frost's foot, which is resting on the coffee table. "What is wrong with you? Don't answer that." She pivots towards us and mercifully offers a platter of sandwiches. "I'm sorry. Don't let his rude behavior impact your opinion of the Tala pack. My name is Raven and this is my daughter, Maya."

A second woman steps forward with an armful of bottled waters. She passes one to each of us, then sits on Sable's lap. I blink as I take in her appearance and realize why she seems so familiar. I knew her as *Scarlett*, Spike's old bed buddy. She eyes me wearily, and I sip my liquid refreshment. Spike forced Freddy's aunt to do some hocus-pocus bullshit so he could keep Maya's identity hidden from her family—another attempt at revenge against his brother's murderer. But that's her tale to tell and not why I came here today.

I force down the rest of the water and clear my throat. "I know most of you don't have any reason to trust what I'm about to tell you." I nod to Frost. "But what I have to say affects the safety of all the families in Cold Creek."

The alpha snorts, and his wife shoots him a glare. Then she glances in my direction. "Is it true that your pack consists of humans and shifters?" I tilt my head at the change of topic, and Raven clarifies, "I pulled Celeste's arm a bit. Don't worry about any leaked secrets. The only information she gave me was how impressed she was that the two groups coexist in such tight quarters." She pats my leg in a motherly way. "That is beyond impressive, dear. You should be proud."

I sit a little taller, trying to put a damper on my shock. "Thank you. And, yes, it is true. When we free shifters…"

"You mean burn down government buildings and murder those who oppose you?" Frost interjects.

"Dad!" Maya huffs. "Those facilities steal shifters and force them to breed," she snarls as she squeezes her husband's hand.

Frost purses his lips, allowing me to continue.

"When we *free* the shifters, we also offer positions to the human soldiers who choose to surrender."

"Do many of them join you?" Raven leans forward, appearing to hang on my every word.

"Not many. But the ones who do are grateful." My eyes mist at the thought of David and his sacrifices. "Many of the soldiers are closer to me than my own family was." I rub the scar on my arm. "They fight just as hard as shifters and aren't afraid of dying in battle."

"It's a testimony to the rest of our kind." Raven side-glances her husband. "We should all try to get along better so we can achieve real lasting peace."

Azure's grin catches my attention. "The Tala pack is ahead of most others in Cold Creek, considering you've allowed a *human* female to marry a shifter woman and man." He puffs out his chest. "And Carly has been doing a wonderful job as liaison while convincing the human authorities that we aren't the animals the General portrayed us to be."

Celeste leans against my side and whispers, "Azure married Sky *and* Carly. The latter of whom is acting as our human liaison, traveling between territories and asking people to vote against the ill treatment of our kind in hopes of getting these compounds shutdown with less bloodshed."

Well, color me impressed. Here I thought I was the only one attempting to do good for all shifter kind.

"Can we get back on track?" Frost asks. "So we can send our guests on their way as soon as possible."

"Fine. I'll say my peace and gladly return to the woods." I offer Frost a pretty smile, fangs and all, then turn to the rest of the group. "Freddy broke his mother out of the hospital and is dead set on finding the General at all costs."

"What?" Sable roars. "You said you haven't seen your mate," he reminds me. "You lied then. Why should we believe you now?"

I shrug. "In the end, it's your call. But mark my words: If you don't take this threat seriously, it'll bite you in the ass later."

A weighted silence fills the room.

Maya glances between us and caresses her pregnant belly. "I know Freddy is a jackass, but what's up with his mother? Why is this a bad thing?"

Sable strokes her back. "Willow is a rare hybrid. She has magical abilities like Debbie, but she can shift too."

"Shit." Maya leans closer to her mate.

"I've seen Fredrick's memories," Azure chimes in. "His mother brutally murdered the group of humans who killed her husband. She was never the same after that. The magic Willow tapped into that day cost the hybrid her mind. Which in turn, forced the orphaned pup to live with his aunt and Spike." He scratches his stubble. "Why would Fredrick break her out? When I read his past, there was a hint of fear whenever he thought about her. It was clear he didn't want her freed."

Sylvia tenses next to me and I choose to ignore the fact that my beta pushed my mate over the edge, using his need to prove himself to accomplish it. Instead I say, "Freddy's thirst for vengeance against the General has consumed him." I stroke Angel's hair as she sleeps, and it calms me. "He has lost his ability to reason."

"We need to warn the humans too," Azure continues. "And the other Guardians. Hopefully, this will expedite the treaty."

"What treaty?" I question.

Azure's eyes meet mine. "One that will put an end to the experiments and imprison those who still wish to harm shifters. The Guardians have been meeting with various government officials. The process is slower than I'd like, but it's a step in the right direction."

Why the hell was I not informed about any of this? Have I

really secluded myself that much? This news is amazing. A yawn involuntarily rips through my mouth.

"You should rest, dear," Raven suggests. "We'll contact Debbie and formulate a plan to return Willow to the hospital."

"What about Freddy?" I blurt. "What will you do with him?" He may be misguided but I don't want him hurt.

"I'll revisit his memories and we can go from there as to what his punishment should be." Azure's jaw ticks but his words seem to ring true.

"And what about her?" Frost points to me. "She's murdered soldiers too. Where's her punishment? I bet the government would be in our debt if we handed her over to them."

I wish I had the strength to leap across the room and throttle him. Before I can consider that option, Angel jolts awake and scans the room with wide eyes. Once she sees me, she moves from Jackson's arms onto my lap and hides her face in my chest.

"She's risked everything to warn us. Including the confidence of her own mate and mother-in-law," Raven hisses. "Give her a little bit more respect than that."

Maya lifts her chin at her father. "And she saved Lily along with other shifters too."

"Yes, my sister is here because of you," Azure adds. "I will never be able to thank you enough for that."

Jackson and Sable both snort at the singular praise directed my way but keep their mouths shut.

"You're welcome, and you may show your gratitude by making sure my pack remains hidden and *safe* from prying eyes," I insist. "In return, I will allow this treaty to go into effect before I attack any more government facilities."

"Angelica," my beta hisses. "It's our duty to free the shifters, treaty or not. What if it never works, or they ignore the rules like the General did? All of our work and sacrifices will be wasted."

"How about we stay in contact, communicate our progress on *both* ends, and maybe act more like a team?" Raven suggests.

"I believe that's an excellent start." Azure nods.

"Now that everything is settled without me, I think it's time for you to leave," Frost sneers.

"Jackson, can you ask Lily if Angelica's team can spend the night in her old cave?" Raven questions.

"What?" Frost leaps from his chair, and Jackson guides us out the front door before the alpha can continue his toddler-sized outburst.

I stretch my hands above my head. "So, who's going to pull that stick out of *his* ass?"

"His daughter," Jackson teases, and Maya swats his arm. He laughs and pinches her cheek. "You've had to deal with him for a much shorter time. It's only fair."

"I was abducted, you ass. I didn't choose to stay away." She goes to kick his butt.

The beta dodges her and smirks. "Likely story."

Sable tucks Maya protectively into the crook of his arm. "How about we let Frost's mate deal with him? That way, we can get some amazing steaks and watch the sunset from the top of Willow Creek." He rubs his wife's baby bump.

Maya side-eyes Jackson but nuzzles into her husband. "That sounds perfect."

The two lovebirds stride off to the food-laden table, leaving us to follow Jackson. He opens a cave door and shouts, "I'm entering with known terrorists. You've been warned."

"Excuse me?" I snarl.

Before he can apologize, I'm entangled in a tight embrace. I blink at the dark-skinned woman. That's when it hits me. This is the shifter I rescued near the Pawson territory the day we snatched the General's son.

"Easy, Butterfly." Jackson laughs. "She's traveled a long way and then had to endure a few tongue lashings from Frost."

I arch a brow at the ridiculous pet name. *Who the fuck wants to be called Butterfly?* I wonder to myself until I notice the matching tattoo on her ankle. Maybe that's why?

"Thank you again for rescuing me." Lily steps back to let me breathe. "If there's anything you need, please let me know."

"Actually, she needs a place to crash for the night. Can they borrow your cave? It's cleaner than the guest houses and has more snacks."

Lily's eyes light up. "Of course they can stay there. It would be my honor."

"Mom, my controller needs new batteries." A young man with dark hair pushes his way towards Lily. His eyes land on Angel and he blinks. "Who's that?"

My daughter lifts her chin. "My name is Angel."

He wrinkles his nose. "But why?"

"Hunter," Lily chides. "Don't be rude to our guests."

Angel's lips curl into a devilish grin. "Your name is Hunter?"

"So what?" He puffs out his chest. "It's better than Angel."

"I'm named after my mom," Angel sneers.

"Hey! I'm named after my mom too." An older child rounds the corner and chimes in on the conversation. "My name is Ash."

I watch the trio and smirk. In a perfect world, these pups could be best friends. I nibble my lip. If the treaty goes into effect, maybe there's still a chance for that to happen.

"Guys, give the girl some time to chill." Jackson shoos the boys out of the room. "Hunter, I'll grab batteries so you can defeat your zombies." Once the boys relax in the living room, Jackson kisses Lily on the cheek. "Why don't you get our guests settled, then meet me in bed so we can play our own *game* together?"

She blushes and pushes him away. "Make sure they don't stay up too late. I'll be back soon."

Lily clears her throat and guides us inside a nearby cave. It doesn't escape my notice that Azure was watching our every move from where he was positioned at his own door. Lily may trust us, but her brother doesn't. *Smart man.*

"Here you go." She shows us around the cave. "Help yourself to anything. I have towels, clothes, tea… anything you want."

"Thank you for your generosity." I smile, and it's the first genuine one I've had in a long time. Lily is such a sweet soul. I'm glad I could save her.

"Mom." Angel tugs on my shirt. "Can I fight zombies too?"

It takes a minute for me to figure out what the hell she's talking about. I guess that nap really rejuvenated her. *Fuck. I wish I could be so lucky.*

"Honey, I'm ready to pass out." I stroke her hair. "And we need to head back at first light."

"But I've never killed a zombie before." Her serious tone makes me laugh but also sigh, because she has no fucking clue what a video game is.

Damn. Did I shelter her too much? Focus too long on training and not playing? The poor girl is going to be upset when she realizes what the two boys are really doing.

"I can keep an eye on her for you," Lily offers. "Then walk her back before we head to bed."

"I don't need a babysitter. It's not that hard to find." Angel pivots

322

and walks out without permission.

My brain is sluggish. How did my pup move so fast? I rub my temples. I should sleep.

"I can go with Angel if you want," my beta suggests.

"No. I trust that Angel is in good hands."

"Plus, she's a trained killer." Sylvia snorts. "*They* require the protection, not her."

I elbow her in the stomach. "Why don't you shower first?"

She nods and marches towards the bathroom. Once the door closes, I sit at the kitchen table and wonder if I'll even make it to the shower before I drift off.

"How's Jake doing?" Lily whispers, then adds, "I know his actions are unforgivable, but I knew him before he worked for his dad." She twirls her long hair. "He was a good man."

I don't mention that I met a younger Jake too or the fact that I hoped he wouldn't turn into a piece of shit. But that's not what she wants to hear. She's looking for closure and permission to write off the human she used to care for.

"Well, as always, the General fucked up another person with his madness." I shrug. "But Jake *chose* to continue down that destructive path. He had a choice. We all did. That friend of yours is long gone."

"He's *dead*?"

"Not yet," I answer honestly. "We're hoping to use him to secure the General first."

My words wash over her, and her emotions play out on her face. She doesn't like what we are planning to do, but she won't stop us.

"Is your mate gone too? I mean, after everything that he's done and still doing." Her statement cuts deep. The sad thing is, she's probably right.

"I hope not."

Warmth encompasses my hand. I lift my gaze and meet hers. "I hope not too, Angelica."

We share a moment of understanding. Lily's someone I hope to get to know better, because I know her kindness would eventually seep into my soul, reminding me that life isn't as fucked up as I think it is. I stare into her eyes and my throat closes up.

No. Fucking. Way.

"Angelica?" She pats my shoulder. "You're looking pale. Do you need something to eat?"

I stand on shaky feet and force out a laugh. "I just need some sleep." I throw a thumb behind me. "Is that the bedroom?"

"Yes, right through there."

"Thanks."

I swallow the bile rising up my esophagus. *I'm a horrible person.*

"Good night and sleep well," Lily's singsong voice answers.

I pivot to watch her exit her cave. The scars on her back scream at me. *Lily* is the female Experiment 217 was assaulting that night at the cabin. I run a sweaty palm over my face. *And I let it happen.* Her beautiful body is fucked up because of me.

"Hey, Lily," I call out to her scars.

"Yes?" She pivots to meet my searching gaze.

The children's laughter sounds from the neighboring cave and my heart squeezes. Is her son the aftermath of that sexual assault? What kind of fucked-up world are we living in?

"I'm truly sorry for all the pain you must be going through." I swallow my confession and allow her to believe the apology is directed towards the loss of Jake and her pack.

"Thank you. But don't worry. Everything always works out in the end, Angelica. You'll see."

Angelica

Family Ties

*L*ight filters in through the sheer curtains, and I jolt awake from one of the most peaceful night's sleep I've ever experienced. *Where am I?* I look around the stone walls, adorned with vividly-colored scenic landscapes.

"Mom?" Angel stretches out beside me.

"Hey, little one." I kiss her forehead. That's when it all comes back to me. We're staying with the Tala pack inside Lily's den. "How did you sleep?"

"Good, but the sun woke me up." She glares at the offending window.

One downfall to living underground is that we miss the sun's daily rotation. Our pack wakes and falls asleep to utter darkness. A chill runs up my spine. *Is that healthy for a growing pup*?

I comb a hand through my daughter's hair, and she curls up beside me with a soft hum. She's happy and safe. That's all that matters.

"Will I get to meet my grandma before they lock her up again?"

My heart stutters at the amount of love and admiration packed so tightly inside my daughter's tiny body. Her mate will be lucky to have her. I look forward to seeing who tames my wild child. Luna help them.

"If your grandmother returns to the hospital, I promise to take you to see her as often as you want." I pat Angel's leg. "She's not a bad person, honey. She just has some health issues she needs to work through with the help of professionals before she can safely be around others all the time."

"Does Daddy need help too?"

What a loaded question.

"Your father and I have been apart longer than we were together. I honestly don't know what is going on with him."

"Is he safe?"

I let out a breath. "I know he would never harm you on purpose. But that doesn't mean he's safe."

"So, when he comes back, can he stay in our room?"

I love my mate, but being a mother is my number one priority. "Why do you have so many questions?" I tickle Angel's sides until she pulls away from me, laughing. "Shouldn't we eat first?"

Once her giggles subside, she squints past our open doorway. I follow her gaze to see two sets of wolf eyes watching us. As soon as Angel spots them, their fluffy tails begin banging against the wall in excitement.

I toss off the covers and throw my legs over the side of the bed. "Good morning, boys."

Ash and Hunter's nails tap the smooth stone as they stride over.

I scratch between their ears, then brush past them. "I'm hunting for coffee." I hear two plops and know the pups have leaped onto the bed. "Fair warning, my daughter doesn't like mornings and she'll be a brute until she gets her breakfast."

They bark and I can hear loud slurps, telling me they're licking her face, begging her to play with them. Angel's laughter continues as she yelps for them to get off the bed.

I make my way to the kitchen and open the cupboards in search of caffeine.

"Sorry about them," Jackson says as he pushes through the front door. He places a grocery bag on the table. At my arched brow, he adds, "Lily wasn't sure what you guys drank so she bought a little bit of everything."

What's his tale?

I tilt my head as I assess the beta. Young. Hot. *And* a total pushover. But I don't say that aloud. Instead, I point out, "The boys act like they have been friends forever."

Jackson's husky chuckle lights up the room. I bet he breaks through Lily's darkness with that. I love that. "Don't let them fool you. There have been many growing pains between them. Ash's time is split between us and his adoptive parents, so Hunter gets bored easily when he's gone. That said, they are learning to share and confide in each other." He scratches his chin. "They'll be an unstoppable duo when they're older. At least until they start searching for their mates."

I rustle through the bag and pull out a container of dark roast coffee. "I don't look forward to *those* days."

A trio of fur balls darts past our legs, almost knocking me over. My neck snaps towards the front door, where I spot Hunter and Ash running for their lives as Angel snarls at their rears. They dive into the tall grass, and she tackles Hunter first, then uses his body as a springboard to jump on Ash. Once the boys recover from getting their asses handed to them, Ash says something and points to the lake in the center of the field. Then the group dashes forward before cannonballing into the shimmering water.

Thank Luna I taught her how to swim.

Images of baby Sammy drifting face-down in the current paralyzes me. I still can't believe I lost him. I clench my fists. Another body to add to my count when I'm sent to hell.

A chair scraping against the stone floor jostles me back to the present. Sylvia plops into the seat next to me and yawns. The beta never sleeps in. I smirk as she stretches and smacks her lips. Everyone seems to be getting along and enjoying our little impromptu vacation.

For now. I stride to the coffeepot and start a brew cycle.

"Where's Angel?" Sylvia asks.

I pour my beta the first mug and wait until she's had a sip. "She's playing with the Tala pups."

Sylvia tenses and eyes Jackson. He winks and she bristles.

"Don't worry. Angel'll be fine," I add. "Let her have some fun before we have to trek back home."

"Are you sure you want to leave today?" Jackson leans back in his seat.

"I didn't think we had a choice," Sylvia snips.

"I'm sure Frost would wait to toss you out on your asses until tomorrow."

"Why would he do that?" I arch a brow. "He seemed pretty adamant that we leave as soon as possible."

Jackson glances between us, and his jaw drops. "You're serious? You don't know what today is?" I meet my beta's confused gaze and he continues, "It's a cherished holiday among the shifters." He feeds us another hint. "And there's a huge celebration tonight at the ancestral grounds. Then everyone unwraps gifts nestled under the sacred tree."

"Is this one of your made-up pack things?" Sylvia challenges with narrowed eyes.

I smirk. "I think you're right. That has to be it."

"Have the two of you been living under a rock?" Jackson leans on his elbows and assesses us. I won't admit that we live under a forest, so technically there are a few boulders in the mix too. "It's *Lunamas*." He speaks slowly, like we're incompetent.

"Nope. I've never heard of it before." I shrug.

"Never?" he gasps. "It's tradition here in Cold Creek. Every pack observes the holiday. We honor our creator and the bounties she's provided for us."

"None of my packs ever did this," I admit.

"That's sad." His frown settles deep in his face. "I'm sorry."

"You can't miss what you've never had." I nudge Sylvia. "What about your packs?"

"I can't recall," she barks back before leaving the table to refill her mug.

Did something strike a nerve? I know she lost her mate and pups because of the General, but she doesn't talk much about her life before that.

Jackson clears his throat and changes the topic. "Well, whenever you're ready, Lily is cooking up a storm at my place. Make sure you grab some grub before your trip home." He rubs his palms together in anticipation. "I'll let you wake up and enjoy your caffeine." Then he pivots to walk out.

"Jackson." My mouth vomits his name before I can stop it.

"Yeah?"

I should sew my lips shut before I say something stupid…

"Lily isn't your mate." It wasn't a question, so I try to clarify. "Even though she's not your mate, are you able to love her?" I hate myself for asking that. "Never mind." I blow into the steam billowing from the top of my cup.

A warm hand rests on my shoulder. I lift my chin and Jackson smiles. "I love Lily," he says without hesitation. "But I also love my mate who passed away, and Lily is okay with that because she knows it doesn't mean I love her any less."

I shrug off his comforting touch. I don't deserve it. "I'll make sure to visit Lily before we leave the area," I promise before sipping from my mug.

"We'll see you soon," he says and then leaves as silently as he arrived.

"Are you thinking about David?" Sylvia whispers. "Or about dumping Freddy and finding someone else?"

I side-eye her, a silent warning to not push the subject. Just like I won't push her for information on her lost family. The memories are too painful.

"We should prepare to leave before it gets too hot outside."

We are quiet as we finish our java, each lost in our own thoughts. Me, wondering if I love Freddy after everything he's done to me and our kind, while my beta's probably thinking about her loved ones and if there's a second-chance romance somewhere for her too.

Angel stomps into the cave, mud splattering in her wake. I arch a brow at her pale skin covered in muck. Then I guide her to the shower. "Did you have fun, little one?" I ask as I twist on the water.

She slips into the warmth and grumbles. "We didn't fight actual *zombies* last night. We shot pretend ones, using imaginary guns that didn't even look real! Now they think I'm weak."

"Honey, if they think *that,* they are idiots and aren't worth your time. Now, wash up so we can eat and go back home."

"Fine. But I want to practice fighting zombies so I can beat Hunter and Ash the next time we visit."

"I'll consider purchasing a gaming system for our facility." I chuckle at her competitive spirit. "But, for now, I'll give you some privacy so you can finish up in here."

When I turn the corner, I run into a pampered, pedicured female. She leaps back and emits a soft squeak.

"Well, well. I can't believe you had the balls to face me unprotected." I look past her to the empty kitchen. "And unescorted."

She puffs out her voluminous chest. "I wanted to meet you face-to-face."

I lean against the wall and cross my arms. "We've already met, princess." My lip twitches. "Remember? When you were hog-tied and thrown into my alpha's room with the other shifters we stole from your pack."

The color drains from her face as she tries to feign nonchalance with a shrug. "That time doesn't count."

"Whatever you say." I pick at my chipped nails, then raise my gaze slowly as I add, "So you're the woman my mate was fucking on the side and impregnated." With the last word, I drop my hand and tilt my head.

She bristles and her gaze heats. "I didn't *know* Freddy was married."

Behind me, the bathroom grows silent. Angel will be out soon, and I don't want her to get upset when she realizes her father isn't the man she wants him to be.

"I'm just fucking with your head, Skylar. We were both burned by him." I glance over my shoulder as I hear the toilet flush. "So let's drop this for now and *pretend* to be friends."

The door opens, and steam fills the hallway. Angel stops in her tracks and stares at Sky. "Wow. You're beautiful." Her mouth drops into an O. "Those shoes are almost as tall as me."

Sky blinks, looking between me and Angel. *Did Azure not explain that I had a child? Or maybe Sky didn't realize Angel was Freddy's pup when we arrived?* Though I thought it was obvious. My little girl has her father's crooked nose and sizable ears.

Sky's face brightens as she kneels in front of my daughter. "These high heels are just like any other weapon at our disposal." She slips off the glimmering red stilettos and hands them to Angel. "We just have to learn how to wield them properly."

Angel glides her fingers over the shoes, then pinches the tips of the pointed ends. "Do we stab them with these?"

Sky laughs and shakes her head. "Sweetheart, we do far worse than that. And when you're older, I'll teach you all about it. But for now, you can practice with these." She flicks her gaze to mine, silently asking permission to hand my daughter the walking death traps. I roll my eyes but don't interfere. I'll let my girl decide what she wants to do.

"Thank you," Angel coos.

Sky brushes a loose strand of hair from the pup's face. Her eyes glimmer with something I can't place. Loss? Or is it more than that? A desire to raise a little girl into adulthood?

A knock catches our attention. "Everything okay in here?" Carly questions. "Jackson sent me over to see if everyone was ready to eat."

Sky grins at the blonde and approaches her with a seductive sway of her hips. Then she slams her lips against Carly's before quickly pulling away again. "I can't believe you let Jackson *use* you as his personal bitch."

Carly's eyes grow wide. "Hey. Lily was there too and it's hard to say no to her."

The pair walks out, holding hands and arguing.

Angel turns to me, seemingly bewildered, "Did they just kiss?"

"Come on, let's eat breakfast and I'll explain it to you." I guide my daughter out into the brisk morning air.

"Explain what?" Angel presses.

"That even though we're shifters with destined mates, we can still have strong feelings for other men or women." I bite my lip as memories of David wash over me. "Life is complicated. But you should love who you want. In a respectful way, of course."

"Even if it's more than one person?"

The relationship between Carly, Sky, and Azure must confuse her.

"Yes, sometimes it can be more than one person."

"Hey!" Lily sings as she waves us into the house. "I hope you're hungry!"

I spot my beta already at the table, stuffing her face with pancakes. She must have sneaked out while I was helping Angel into the shower. I settle in next to her and let Lily fill my plate to the brim. Once everyone joins us, I look around and my heartaches. Could this have been me if my situation was different? Laughter, sun shining through open windows, and friends swapping stories of their days. Instead of training, dark tunnels, and armies to lead.

I bring the fork to my mouth and chew my eggs. Maybe I can still have it. All the stuff I missed out on. Angel's laughter breaks the silence, followed by Hunter's, as milk squirts from Ash's nose.

Okay, maybe I don't want all of this. I smirk as Jackson leaps up, covered in snot and white liquid. *But something similar would be nice.*

"Happy Lunamas!" Raven calls out as she bursts into the cave.

I wrinkle my nose at her bright red-and-green outfit lined with jingling bells. Then again, maybe it's a good thing we don't celebrate this ridiculous holiday.

"Happy Lunamas to you too!" Lily ushers the alpha's wife inside. "Are you hungry? I think we have a few biscuits and a bit of the sausage gravy leftover."

"No, thank you. I spent the morning teaching Maya how to cook a feast for her budding family. Then we ate everything we baked." Raven rubs her belly before pivoting to me. "I actually was hoping to snatch Angelica for a moment." She's suspiciously cheery. She may break out in song or shove a cookie down my throat and kill me with kindness. "I promise it'll only take a moment, then you may be on your way," she adds when she senses my hesitancy.

"We can help Sylvia keep an eye on Angel," Lily chimes in as she cleans maple syrup off the kitchen table.

I shove back my chair and sigh. "Why the hell not?" I ruffle my pup's hair. "I'll be right back, little one."

The boys grin wickedly at Angel, and I know I've made a grave mistake giving them her nickname.

I wave the alpha in front of me. "Lead the way."

Raven hums a catchy tune as we stride through the grass before stopping in front of a tall tree. Its branches are glittering with tinsel and tiny twinkling lights. Shifters place wrapped gifts at its base while laughing and sipping from steaming mugs.

"I noticed your birthmark and thought you'd want to see your old pack again. Maybe even introduce Angel before you head back home."

I dig my toes into the dirt and snatch Raven's arm. "What the hell do you mean by my *old* pack?"

Is Spike alive? Fuck, I hope she's wrong because I wasn't on the best terms with my former alpha.

"The Lupe family, dear," Raven clarifies. "Your marking suggests that your parents were Lupe, were they not?"

Every shifter is born with a unique mark, symbolizing their Luna-given pack. I rub the back of my neck where mine is located. I never cared to know where my piece-of-shit parents came from. The pack I belong to is the family of *my* choosing, and it's not my blood kin.

"Raven! There you are!" A tall man strides over. "The wife insisted that I bring you this." He passes her a cup and the scent of hot chocolate surrounds us.

"Robert." Raven hugs the male. "I'm so glad you were able to come. Especially after I heard that Bridgett is still missing. Are there any leads?"

While they chat, I assess the man's complexion. Tan skin, blonde hair, blue eyes. I run my fingers through my own golden locks and swallow the lump forming in the back of my throat. *Is he the Lupe's alpha? Do I care? I have a family. I don't need another one breathing down my neck, claiming that I must adhere to rules and regulations.*

As soon as there's a lull in their conversation, I square my shoulders, step forward, and make my decision. "Thank you again, Raven, for your hospitality, but it's time for me to return to my family. I hope you have a wonderful Lunamas."

Before she can respond, I pivot and stride towards Jackson's cave without a backward glance. My head swims with all the new information I learned. I can feel Robert's gaze on the back of my head, probably zeroing in on my birthmark. Let him have a glimpse at what he's missing. I'm a kickass female, even though his pack abandoned me and my parents in our time of need. And now *my* pack is the strongest in the world.

Suck on that, Lupe pack.

"When can Angel come back to play?" Hunter asks as he picks at a scab on his elbow.

"I'm not sure, buddy. They live pretty far away." Jackson pats the pup's back before turning to us. "Are you sure you don't want someone to drive you?"

"No, thank you." I don't add that I'm not ready to show the world where we're located or take the Talas away and ruin their Lunamas celebration.

Lily hugs me and whispers, "Please consider bringing Jake to the authorities for legal action."

I sigh at her final attempt to warm my cold heart. "For *you*, I'll consider it." I pull away. "If only because our kids want to play together again soon."

"You and your pack are welcome here any time." Lily's smile touches her ears.

"Yes, but please call for approval first," Jackson is quick to add. "Frost is already in a foul mood after what we did. No need to poke the furry beast."

I stare into the distance at the alpha's cave. I agree. He's a grumpy old man. Just before I look away from his welcome mat, the front door swings open and Raven exits with a convertible K-9 backpack swinging on her fingertips.

"I would like to visit your pack as an official liaison of the Talas to learn how we can better coexist with our human neighbors." She lifts her chin. "And to build a stronger bond between our two packs."

What is up with the Talas shoving their noses in everyone's fucking business? And she's not asking to go with us; she's insisting on it. What am I going to do about that? There's a reason I remain hidden, and it's mostly because I don't want to deal with the bullshit politics of wolf protocols.

I pinch the bridge of my nose as a headache builds. Why is this pack filled with so many strong-willed women? I'm afraid if I don't let her join us, I'll be breaking a rule and in turn jeopardizing our fragile relationship. And the Tala pack can either be a formidable opponent or a great ally.

"Raven, you do realize what *we* are risking by taking you with us, don't you? You are the wife of the alpha of the Tala pack. If something happens to you, all-out war will ensue and I'm done watching those I care about bleed out at my paws."

Her back stiffens. "I don't wish to place any lives in danger." She leans forward and whispers to me, "If you're reacting this way because you're angry about me introducing you to Robert..."

I raise a hand to cut her off. "No, it's not that. It has everything to do with the welfare of the packs."

She nods. "Then I give you my word that *if* something happens to me while in your territory, it will not reflect poorly on you or your pack. Because I'm going *without* an alpha title and only as a curious shifter."

Why me?

I nibble my lip. How is that possible? How does one *get rid of their title*? Did she break things off with her husband? The tension between them yesterday was downright explosive. Is she traveling with us to injure his ego? Or can I trust that she really does want to assist our packs? I scan her face for evidence of either. Raven has displayed nothing but compassion towards our cause since we arrived. I don't see why that would change now.

"You may come, only if you allow Angel to return to visit the boys whenever she wants."

Angel jumps up and down in excitement. "Please say yes."

"Angel will always be a welcomed guest of the Tala pack. You have my word."

"Then let's go before we lose the light." I shift to fur and gallop through the dense foliage.

As we put distance between us and the Tala territory, my mind wanders. *Will Debbie be willing to assist the Talas with capturing Freddy's mom?* The two women are family. Maybe the sisters can talk things out, so no one gets hurt.

Something tugs on my tail. I peek over my shoulder in time to see Angel's wolf darting past me. I laugh, lower my head, and bullet through the valley as we race home.

It takes longer to reach our territory than I want, because we're still sore from the trek to the Tala pack. As we near our boundary, my ears twitch but the woods are noiseless. An unease settles in my gut. I signal our group to halt and peer through the brush. My wolf eyes zero in on the brigade of uniformed men closing in on our home. My heart stutters and I step closer to my pup.

Why aren't the alarms going off or the guards rushing out?

"What is our plan of action?" Sylvia questions from beside me.

I glance at my daughter. I won't risk her being captured and forced into a breeding facility. I also won't allow her to get shot.

Raven stiffens at the sight looming in front of us. Then she locks eyes with me. *"I can call the Tala pack for assistance,"* she suggests telepathically.

I consider the option and quickly dismiss it. Their help will arrive too late. I should have taken Jackson's offer to drive us closer, then we would have been more evenly matched.

An explosion sounds and the earth trembles under our claws. I jerk my attention towards the enemy. They are setting bombs off and collapsing our hideout. I'm running out of time.

"We have to fight them, Mom," Angel insists. *"We can do it."*

My head buzzes. If it were just me and my beta, I'd risk it all. But the suffocating memories of being tortured are stopping me from involving my pup too. I know she can fight off a handful of soldiers, but not after running all day. And I can't let my pack die. I'm their leader and it's my right and honor to go down with them in battle.

"Raven, take Angel as far as you can and call for aid." I swallow hard as I take in my daughter's beautiful face. *"Then return to the Tala pack until it's safe here."*

"No!" Angel whimpers. *"Please. I can help."*

I run my muzzle over her fur, hiding my glimmering eyes. *"I know you can, little one. That's why you have to protect Raven. She'll need your help. Think about Hunter and Ash. They could be hurt next. We are heroes and sometimes that means sacrificing what we want to do for what we need to do."*

"Mom." She nips my shoulder, forcing me to look at her. She searches for something, and she must have found it. She dips her head. *"I'll come back with help."*

Another explosion shakes the earth.

"Go."

Raven nudges Angel forward before offering me a parting glance. *"Stay alive. For her."* Then the pair gallops back towards the way we came, sticking to the shadows.

Once they're gone, I turn to Sylvia and growl. *"How did this happen?"*

"Maybe we trusted too many people with our location."

Over the last few months, we've let more people learn of our whereabouts than ever before. My blood boils with rage. Whoever fucked us over is dead meat.

"You run to the escape tunnels and make sure everyone has a clear path."

"But what about you?"

I crack my head from side to side. *"I'm going to take out as many soldiers as I can."*

"That's suicide!" she shouts down our telepathic line.

"No. It's an order," I press out with every ounce of my alpha tone.

I will not witness her bloody corpse anywhere near our beloved home. The same place that we built together. Sylvia is my cherished fur sister not by blood but by heart, sweat, and tears.

She runs her muzzle over my neck, and I know she's thinking the same thing. We've gambled with fate one too many times, survived hundreds of triumphant victories, and brazenly celebrated our successes only to be betrayed and end up here, saying goodbye.

"May Luna guide your path, sister." Sylvia bows her head while masking her tears.

"You too, sister."

Freddy

Vengeance

Earlier…

Fire hisses as black smoke twists into the air, and soldiers shriek in panic. Another compound is destroyed. I should be proud. I glare at the wreckage. But I'm not, because I failed my mate *again*. The General wasn't amongst this group of corrupt humans and there weren't any shifters to rescue either. Almost as if they knew we were coming and cleared out the prisoners beforehand.

Mom breathes heavily as she leans into my shoulder. Her once-powerful magic is slipping… along with her mind. As much as I hate to admit it, *Angelica was right*. Mom needs to return to her padded cell so they can stabilize her or I risk losing her forever.

My life is crumbling beneath my feet and there's not a fucking thing I can do about it.

"I'm sorry the General wasn't here, son," Mom coughs.

"Don't worry about it. We'll find him." I wrap an arm around her waist and guide her forward. Away from our destruction and towards the congested city streets filled with spectators. Sirens blare as they speed past us, their lights illuminating the drab concrete.

I tug a cigarette out of my pack and flip my lighter until the end is blazing. I breathe deep. *Damn, that tastes good.*

I ignore my mom's death glare and blow the toxic air away from her face. The map inside the facility showed another potential location. Should we attack there next or give up and run back to Angelica with our tails between our legs?

My heart squeezes in warning, reminding me that I should be with my mate. By the third drag, I make up my mind. I'll complete this final mission. My wife deserves to have her revenge on the General. We both do.

I nod towards the other side of the city. "Mom, how do you feel about making one more stop before we head home?"

A smile brightens her face as she wipes the sweat from her brow. "Lead the way."

After breaking in, and Mom crushing the welcoming committee, my heart leaps with pure dark joy. There, in a cell, is the man himself.

"Oh, how the mighty have fallen," I sneer at his orange jumpsuit. "I'm loving the new color. It really brings out the hellfire in your eyes."

The man in question slowly turns in his moldy cot, and his chapped lips twist into a smirk. "Well, if it isn't my favorite mutt. How are you doing, Freddy?"

That *voice*. It's fucking haunted my nightmares and yet he looks so tiny now. *Insignificant*. "Oh, and you even brought me another toy to play with." His gaze slides over my mom's frame. "Unfortunately, she's too old to be of any use to me."

Mom snarls, baring her fangs. "I'll show you who's old!"

"Oh, but I do love the feisty ones." His eyes flick back to me. "You should know that by now. I mean, your wife was one of my favorite *pets*."

My blood boils, adrenaline fuels my rage, and I tear off his prison door. "Leave my mate out of this."

"How could I possibly do that? She's perfect in *every* way." He grins as he drags the word out.

I toss the metal frame aside. It clangs against the silence. I fist his jumpsuit and slam him against the grimy wall. "I can't wait to watch Angelica rip you limb from limb."

"It's funny, isn't it?" The General tilts his head, seemingly unfazed.

I drag him out of his room and towards the exit. "Shut the fuck up."

"...that you think she *loves* you." He continues to prattle on. "When, in reality, she fell head over heels for my physician."

I stumble over the statement. I shake him until his head jiggles. "I said I don't want to hear another word from you!"

"You don't want to hear how she fucked David before they ran away together? Or how he broke her out of my compound and delivered your pup? Oh, and the best part, they were going to raise the child together. *You* were never part of their end game. And yet, here you are, risking everything to bring little old me... *to her*."

I drag the bastard outside. Towards the dark woods. With my free hand, I twist Angelica's ring. He's not telling me the whole truth. The General is a master manipulator.

347

"Don't make me ask my mother to melt your lips together," I snarl as I continue to drag his bare feet through the dead leaves littering the floor.

"You're both idiots if you think they don't already know where my son is. You made a grave mistake, boy. You're seeking to quench your revenge, when you should be protecting your pack."

I stop as his words sink in. *Fuck.*

"Your son has a tracker in him, doesn't he?" I glance at the scar on my arm and the words rush out as I put the puzzle pieces together. "And the pack may overlook that because he's your son, a soldier, and not a shifter."

Double fuck.

"The real question is are you too late to save them from the inevitable?"

My blood runs cold. He could be fucking with us. But why lie about this? It would mean we'd rush to the compound and that his death would be closer than if we took our time. No, this asshole is gloating over his presumed victory.

My mom rests a hand on my shoulder. "He may still be useful, son." She glances at the General. "If he is telling the truth, we can use him as a bargaining chip."

I clench my fists so I don't kill the man prematurely. "If he isn't lying, can you handle a batch of soldiers on your own?"

She nods. "If it's the last thing I do, I'll protect my grandbaby and my son."

I wish I could trust the other packs. I'd beg on my knees for their assistance. But they wouldn't lift a paw. I've fucked up in their eyes. They'll never believe a word I say. Plus, I should see if there is a threat first. Otherwise, Angelica will have my balls for bringing every shifter in Cold Creek to her hidden doorstep.

"Mom, steal a vehicle with four-wheel drive. We're going home."

It's hard to recall where exactly the compound is located. But with my good memory, great sense of smell, and the help of a GPS, I narrow it down to a clearing up ahead. I park the stolen vehicle and grab the General by the collar of his jumpsuit.

"If you're playing games, old man, I'll rip out your spine through your mouth."

"Oh, come now, Freddy. We both know you're a little pussy who—"

My fist collides with his chiseled jaw. Bones crunch under my knuckles and the blow knocks him out. I shake out my throbbing wrist. *Damn, that felt good.* "You never know when to shut. The. Fuck. Up." I drag the General through the overbearing weeds until I find an oak tree and set him against the thick trunk. "Ma, hand me that rope in the back seat. Oh, and the duct tape in the center console."

I bind the General, then rise to my feet. I double-check the distance of the clearing from where I think the hidden base is set up. I can't risk the General being too close, especially if he has a tracker on him. I'll return to him *after* I check on my wife. Then I'll use the ass for leverage or maybe as a gift for Angelica. But one thing is for sure, no matter what happens, today is the last day this piece of shit will walk this earth.

The ground beneath our feet trembles, right after an explosion sounds in the distance. Mom and I glance at each other, before shifting and taking off towards the chaos.

The General's words replay in my head: *...are you too late to save them from the inevitable?*

Before we reach our destination, a howl pierces the forest. My ears tremble and my wolf whimpers at the familiarity of the pitch. I pivot towards the sound and gallop as fast as my four legs can carry me, leaping over stumps and dodging rabbits chewing on clovers.

Please, Luna, let me get to her in time. My nose tremors before I see her furry face. *Oh no...*

Angel's wolf form is snarling at a soldier who's aiming a gun at her temple. Blood coats her beautiful pelt and her breathing is uneven. Rage blinds every single thought as I rush to save my child. A venomous snarl erupts from the back of my throat just before my fangs sink deep into my enemy's abdomen, knocking him to his knees. The gun goes off but I don't stop tearing through his flesh.

Fuck you for hurting an innocent kid!

Once he's limp and no longer a threat, I scan the horizon for more men in uniform. When I'm sure no one else is coming, I turn my attention to Angel.

Luna, help me. I've never been so scared in my life. I don't know what the fuck to do. Her wolf is heaving and tears glide through her fur. Then her eyes roll back in her head, and she crumbles into the grass, morphing to her human form as she goes down. I catch her limp frame in my arms.

"Daddy's here." I wipe away the moisture on her cheek. "I'm right here." I rub her blood-crusted limbs but find no open wounds. "Where does it hurt, Angel?" I ask but more sobs are her only response. "You need to tell Daddy where your pain is so I can help you."

"I tried to save her."

Her who?

I force my gaze away from my daughter to search for whoever's she's talking about. Until I spot the other female a few feet away. I close the distance with my daughter nestled in my arms. The shifter is whimpering and twitching in agony. *Fuck.*

The wolf turns its head at our approach, and I let out a sigh of relief. It's *not* my mate. The fur transitions to skin as blood oozes from the woman's gunshot wound. "Is she safe?" she wheezes out while reaching for Angel.

"Yes." Angel sniffles and extends her little fingers in return.

Once their hands touch, the female's arm drops to her side. "Good girl." Her eyes shutter closed. "The Tala pack is on their way." Her leg twitches towards a backpack.

I set Angel down, dig through the contents of the bags, and locate a cell phone. There are over twenty missed calls from Frost Tala. *No fucking way.* I do a double take. This is the alpha's wife, bleeding at our feet.

Another explosion sounds, and I lift my attention towards a billow of smoke.

"Dad!" Angel screams. "Mom's in there. We have to help her."

Damn it.

"You stay here. Help is coming." I kneel at my pup's side and tug her into my arms. She shouldn't have to be this strong. She shouldn't have to witness this shit so young.

"The soldier was hiding. He shot her. I'm sorry," Angel whimpers into my chest. "I was supposed to protect her."

"Shh. It's not your fault. Shitty things happen to good people. It's going to be okay."

Fuck. I hate lying to my kid. But what can I say? We're all going to fucking die, so enjoy the last few minutes of your short life? I'm not a motivational speaker.

My mother snatches up Raven's phone and speaks to an emergency dispatcher, but I know it's more for the soon-to-be wounded shifters than the one dying on the ground. Everything is going to hell. I stare up at the sky and beg Luna to watch over my daughter. She's the only innocent one in this mess. The only one who should walk away from this bullshit. Because the rest of us… we all made it to this point in our lives because of our own choices. Angel only followed us.

What great role models we turned out to be.

I kiss the top of her head. Maybe there's still a chance to redeem myself and show my little girl right from wrong. But I can't attack our enemy knowing Angel is close by, and I don't know how long it's going to take for the others to arrive.

"Do you know the way to the Tala pack?" I ask my daughter.

"I can find my way. Why?"

"They will need your help to find us," I lie, knowing they are racing here in four-by-fours just like I was moments ago. But she needs to get as far from the danger as possible. "Now go with Grandma and do your job."

"But I can *fight*," she begs.

"I know you can, but sometimes we need to learn when to fight and when to run so we can fight another day." I stare into my daughter's eyes. "We are so proud of the young woman you've grown into." I hug her again. "Your mom and I love you. Never forget that."

"I love you too, Daddy."

She sucks in a breath, and I follow her gaze. My mom's side is stained crimson. Shit. She must have been hit by a stray round.

"I'm fine," Mom pants. "But we are running out of time. We should attack while we can."

I realize what she's saying but… "Are you sure?"

"Fredrick, if I go down for anyone, it'll be for my family. Now let's go." She strides towards the smoke without a backward glance.

I return my gaze to Angel. "Please do not follow us. I'll be able to save Mommy faster if I know that you're out of harm's way.

Okay?"

She sits in the grass by the wounded shifter and rubs the woman's pale cheek. I watch my daughter's tiny lips tremble. "I want to stay with her. Just for a little bit."

I glance around and sniff the air. There are no signs of wayward soldiers. But I don't like this one bit. "Only a few more minutes, then look for the Tala pack. Do you understand me?"

Angel nods, then buries her face into the female's hair. "Please don't go to sleep, Ms. Raven. I'll be a good girl. I promise."

My heart cracks and I ache to wrap my little girl in my arms again. But I have to save my mate before she shares the same fate. I shred to fur, scan the perimeter, and take off towards my mother. I follow Angelica's scent until we push past some brush and literally run into her just outside the compound.

"Freddy?" my mate barks as her wolf looks me over.

"Frost's mate is dying," I inform her softly. *"Angel is by her side and will meet up with the Tala pack soon."*

Angelica winces. *"No, that can't be. They should have had a clear path to escape."*

"It seems a rogue soldier spotted them."

If there're more men lingering behind, the General's location won't remain a secret for long.

"Did you see the beta on your way here?"

"No." I tilt my head. *"Why?"*

"With all of these explosions, I fear the pack is trapped inside and unable to escape through the hidden passages."

Mom leans against a tree in her human form. "I can use my ability to take out the soldiers but we have to hurry."

Angelica eyes the blood dripping from Mom's side and shakes

her head. *"Why is everything falling apart?"*

"If it makes you feel any better, I did get to the General."

Her brows shoot to her hairline. *"Where is he?"*

"Tied to a tree at the moment, but maybe we could use him for leverage."

"No. They won't give a shit about him." Angelica glances at my mom and nods at the troops. Mom purses her lips and strides towards the chaos.

"Angelica. I'm sorry. I fucked up."

"We've all fucked up. But that doesn't matter. You're here now."

She blinks at me, and I add, *"Thank you."*

Heavy paws approach and our hackles rise. The group slides to a stop and narrows their eyes. I tilt my head. Wait! I know them. They're from Robert's pack.

"We are looking for my son," the female snarls. *"You've taken him prisoner."* Angelica and I share a confused look. We don't have time for this bullshit. *"Jake is my son,"* the shifter clarifies.

Angelica appears to study the female before responding. *"You're the General's wife, the one who left him for…"* Her eyes widen. *"Wow. No wonder he hates shifters."*

The female steps forward, fangs bared. *"Where is my son?"*

Angelica closes the distance with a snarl. *"Probably under all the rubble, because your ex-husband's men are bringing the place down."*

The female winces and leaps towards the chaos of soldiers.

"Wait!" Angelica calls after her. *"There's a back way. I can show you. But we are wasting time standing around here. Either help us rescue my pack or leave."* My mate doesn't wait for a response. She takes off around the corner with me at her heels.

This shitshow keeps growing. The smaller pack branches out, attacking straggling humans as they clear our path towards the escape route. Screams echo in the air as I feel my mom utilizing her powers.

Then silence. No more explosions, gunshots, or cries of agony.

There's a hole in my heart and I know she sacrificed everything to give us as much time as possible to rescue the other shifters. *Luna rest her soul.*

"I can't believe her," Angelica growls.

I follow my mate's line of sight. And sure enough, there's our daughter, leaning over a hole with a rope in her hand. *"I told her to leave. Does she ever listen?"*

"Well, she is your child," Angelica grumbles.

"You mean yours, right?"

We morph to two legs and stand behind our daughter. All three of us tug on the line until a shifter emerges, coughing and covered in black mud. I peek over the ledge. There're at least three more people waiting to be rescued. Once our arms are burning, we switch places with Robert's packmates. They help us until the small group is pulled to safety.

"I'm getting my son," Jake's mother declares, glancing around at her friends. "I don't blame you if you want to remain here where it's safe." Then she leaps into the hole.

Angelica's gaze bounces around as she takes in all the wounded. "We're missing a lot of people, including Sylvia." She bites her lip. "I need to save as many as I can."

"The ambulance should be here any minute," I remind her. "They'll be more equipped to handle the situation."

"You can't predict when they'll arrive," she snaps. "They could be on the General's payroll for all we know. And they want us dead for bringing down all those government buildings." Angelica lifts her chin. "It's because of my leadership that my pack is in this mess and I won't allow them to pay for my sins alone. They need me now more than ever."

Then I watch on helplessly as my mate jumps into the hole. *What the hell is wrong with her?*

Angel steps towards the edge. I reach out and clutch her wrist. "Fuck no. You wait here. I mean it this time. I'll put you over my knee and whoop your ass if you follow us." I tug my daughter's arm until she meets my eyes, and I let the fear of Luna blaze through my warning. "When the Tala pack arrives, direct them here."

She hesitates until her mother calls out from the hole in the ground, "Listen to your father and do as you're told." My heart bursts with pride at the title. "Freddy! Stop looking at me like that. Let's go."

With a parting glare, I release my daughter's arm and join my mate. Darkness encompasses us. The smell of mold causes me to gag. I hate being underground. I don't know how they've lived like this for so long.

"Take a left!" Angelica shouts to the group ahead of us. "The holding cells are just ahead. Last I heard, Jake was in the third one on the right."

Robert's pack rushes forward while my mate and I guide the wounded back to the opening in the ceiling.

"Who's David?" I ask once the first round of shifters is tugged to safety.

"Why do you want to know?" Angelica fires back.

"The General mentioned him."

"Of course he would," she sneers, and I can hear her feet stomping into the darkness.

A stream of light illuminates the grief and agony I see flashing in her eyes. *Oh shit. Was the fucker right?*

I snatch Angelica's wrist. "Did you *love* this David guy?"

She meets my glare. "Because of *that David guy*, Angel and I are alive right now. He gave up everything to protect us."

I swallow the bile rising in my throat. She does love him. "But you're my mate," I blurt out, trying to understand how this happened.

Angelica laughs and shakes her head. "David literally delivered Angel in the middle of the Luna-forsaken woods. He breathed life into her when she was born blue. Then he sacrificed himself so Angel and I could be together." She shoves at my chest. "He's done more than you could possibly imagine," she screams as tears wet her cheeks. "And *he* made me kill him."

I tug her into a hug and let her cry. I rub her back as I soak in her words. "David made you kill who?"

She groans. "No. The General made me kill David."

Oh, fuck. I may not like the man who stole my wife, but I didn't want him to die like that.

"I'm sorry." Because that's all I can fucking say right now. No matter how dumb it sounds.

She pushes away from me and wipes her tears. "It's in the past. Now, can we just move on and save more lives?"

The way she looks into my eyes it feels like she's asking me if we can start again and forget the horrible shit that's happened between us. I run my thumbs over her cheeks. "I'll fight for you and our daughter until my dying breath." I kiss her softly, then sigh. "I guess we should continue looking for our packmates and help them get out too."

She punches my arm. "That's really chivalrous of you."

"I try."

We return to the tunnels with lighter hearts. I know it won't be perfect, but I can't wait to prove to Angelica how much she means to me.

I swipe my brow. I never realized how many people fit into this compound. It's crazy. Soon, we locate the bitchy beta, but her leg is broken with the bone puncturing the skin. I lean down to help her but she snarls.

"Don't worry about me," she grits out as she shoves me aside. "There are children in the training room. Help them first."

My mate's eyes meet the beta's and they nod in silence. Angelica's lip quivers. "We'll come back for you, but until then, you need to crawl towards the exit. That's an order. If anyone passes you, tell them to take the first right, then a sharp left. They need to follow it until there's a hole in the ceiling. Look up and find the rope. There's a group of shifters that will help tug it to safety."

"I will."

"You better. Or it's back to toilet duty for you," Angelica declares, choking out a sob on the last word. She takes a steadying breath and squares her shoulders. "Let's find those kids, Freddy."

I straighten my back, but the beta snatches my wrist. "Don't fuck this up."

I grind my teeth and bite back the retort currently running through my head. *I'm more successful than she is at the moment.* Instead of voicing as much aloud, I nod. She releases her grip and grunts as she drags her broken body through the dirt.

"She'll make it," Angelica whispers the command before continuing towards the training room.

On our fourth trip back through the tunnels, the walls around us quake. We pause mid-step. Dirt clumps crumble before dropping into our hair. My mate coughs out the dust but struggles to catch her breath. I clutch Angelica to my chest, wishing I could protect her from all the evil in the world. Her breathing steadies as she hides her face in my shoulder and breathes in my scent. A deep rumble echoes in the gloom, and she squeezes me like I'm her fucking hero.

"It's okay, babe."

"How do you know that?"

I kiss the top of her mud-covered head. "Because when you're in my arms, everything is right in the world."

Angel

Shattered

I steady myself against a tree as the ground quakes beneath my toes.

"What's happening?" a shifter yells out.

Before anyone can answer, dust belches from the hole in a black cloud and the rescue rope is swallowed up in a cave-in.

"No!" I leap for the only exit my parents have. "Mom?" I flop onto the blocked dirt path. "Help me!" I scream over a shoulder as I viciously scratch at the rocks. "Hurry!"

Everyone surrounds the area and follows my lead. Some even shift into wolves and dig with their jagged claws. My fingers ache. Blood trickles and mixes with the grit.

How long can they last in there? My heart races, deafening everything around me.

"We found someone!" a female calls out as a wolf tugs on a hand connected to an unconscious male.

I pause in stunned silence as I watch as body after body is hauled from the wreckage. Humans and shifters jump into action, performing CPR and first aid. *But where're my mom and dad?*

"Sylvia!" I run to the next form to be tugged from the rubble and rub her cold hand. "You have to wake up!"

"We'll take it from here." A female gently guides me back to the dirt pile, so she can assess the beta's condition.

As time ticks by, I know the odds of locating my parents alive aren't good.

"Shit," another female shouts as she swipes at her brows. "I just received word that the Tala pack is under attack."

We can't catch a break. Tragedy after tragedy keeps raining down on our families. How much longer until we break under the pressure of it all?

Hunter and Ash… My heart clenches as I think about my new friends.

"Are they okay?" I squeak.

All eyes are on me but it's the female who speaks up. "They've evacuated to Willow Creek Hill," she says, without offering a definitive answer on their well-being.

"Who attacked?" a male demands.

"They didn't say who it was, only that the enemy advanced when Frost and some males left to come to our aid." The female swallows hard before continuing. "But the shifters turned around to face their adversary head-on and lost a few good men in the process."

Grief and loss weigh heavily on our hearts. Fingertips graze mine, and I look into a shifter's tear-stained face. She's the female Mommy was helping, the one with the human son. She holds my hand, then I hold her son's dirt-crusted palm next to me. After a few moments of silence, we encircle the dead in our loop of suffering.

"May our lost loved ones find peace. Luna, please help us through the next stages of our lives," the older woman beside me says. Her words echo through the beautiful clearing that I once called my home.

My packmates' bodies decay in front of me, my parents are buried below my feet, and I've never felt so lost and alone.

A helicopter flies overhead, and we all look up to see emergency services weaving through the clouds, attempting to land. My spine tingles and I focus my attention on the horizon. Towards the path to the Tala territory. There may be nothing I can do for my family, but my friends are in danger now.

"We need to help the Tala pack," I declare with clenched fists. "They were coming to us and now it's only right we help them."

"I'll drive," Brad offers. "We'll show those assholes who the fuck they messed with."

We break into three groups. One stays behind with the paramedics to continue the rescue attempts. Another jumps into a four-wheeler to warn the remaining packs of Cold Creek about the synchronized attacks. Then my group squeals out of the field to race towards Tala territory.

"Buckle up, little lady," Brad warns as he twists the steering wheel and quickly maneuvers us around a fallen tree.

I click the strap into the receptacle, fold my hands in my lap, and battle my tears. *What will I do now?*

"Angel," Brad says over the roaring engine. "We will locate your parents. I promise."

He doesn't add: *dead or alive.* But I know that's what he means.

"I know."

"We're still a family," he whispers. "We'll have each other's backs. Always."

I stare at the human sitting beside me. He's one of my greatest supporters. I won't mention the fact that most packs won't allow a nonshifter to live amongst our kind. My mom was the first one to do it successfully, and now she's...

"We're here," Brad announces as he taps his GPS. "I'm going to drop the group at the battlefield. Then you and I are going to check on the evacuees."

"But..." I protest.

"I'm not risking your safety. End of discussion."

Why does everyone always misjudge my abilities?

My fingertips crackle and electricity sizzles in my hand. I yelp and shake my wrists, throwing the ball of light onto the dashboard. The truck sputters and abruptly dies. I blink at my hands.

Did that really happen? I shake my head. *I'm hallucinating.*

"Everyone out!" Brad yells. We all scramble into the field and he kicks the tires. "I don't know what happened. It was working fine."

I bite the inside of my cheek. I guess he didn't see the light show. I peek at the others, who appear just as oblivious.

"We'll travel the rest of the way on foot." Brad rubs at his chin. I roll my eyes and shred to fur. There's no way a human can keep up without a car. "Angel, no!"

I bullet through the tall grass, letting my nose do its job. *I'm on my way, Hunter and Ash!* I send through our telepathic abilities, but only silence thrums in response.

Thunder rolls in the distance as a roar vibrates the ground. The fur on my legs stands on end. The Guardians are here to aid us. This battle will be over, and retribution will be ours.

"Hunter? Ash?" I whimper as the silence continues to weigh on

my soul. *"Please be okay."*

My nose twitches. A familiar wolf is close. I howl my greeting.

"Angel?" the female answers. *"Where are you?"*

"Celeste!" I use the rest of my strength and dart towards her welcoming scent.

Her ears poke up from a boulder, and she meets me halfway. She purrs as she rubs her nose over my shoulders and checks for injuries. *"Oh, sweetheart. It's so good to see that you're all right."* She pivots and barks twice, before shouting down the line. *"It's safe to come out."*

"Angel!" Ash howls as he turns the corner and bullets to my side with Hunter on his heels.

I collapse into the wildflowers as relief crushes me. *I made it in time. They're alive.*

"Where's Angelica?" Celeste pauses her medical assessment of me and scans the horizon.

I shift to my human form and cover my face as I sob. The boys warm my sides and hug me close.

"It's okay." Ash pats my back.

"No, it's not!" I scream at the top of my lungs, letting the anger loose. "She's dead."

Everyone tenses before sharing a look, clearly unsure as to what to do next. Celeste glances at us and whimpers her regret before licking my tears.

"I lost my mom too," Ash whispers.

"I lost my nana and papa," Hunter adds as he squeezes me into another embrace.

Their grief combines with mine, and we weep together. Our friendship melds into something stronger as it's forged in the embers of our sorrow.

Angel

Willow Creek Hill

*T*he silhouette of a black wolf blurs on the horizon. Hunter tilts his head and furrows his brows. "Mom?"

Lily shifts and trudges over, out of breath. "Maya. Baby. Coming," she pushes out. Celeste's beast's eyes grow wide before they flick to us. Lily waves the doctor towards the hills. "You go. I'll be right behind you with the pups."

Celeste hesitates, but then gives us a classic mom look that translates to: *Don't give her a hard time or else*. Then she gallops forward, her long legs eating away at the distance.

Once her form disappears in the foliage, Hunter leaves my side to hug his mother. "Is Maya going to be okay?"

Lily strokes her son's long, dark hair. "Yes, sweetie."

"Why is the baby coming *now*?" he questions her.

"Only Luna knows why." She kisses the top of his head. "Let me catch my breath and then we'll check on her and the others." The breeze tosses her mane, and she leans into it, allowing the chill to caress his sweat-covered face.

A group of thundering paws shakes the earth below us. Lily curses before she returns to her beast form and stands in front of us with her hackles risen. Tufts of red inch closer to Hunter's mom. They slide to a stop a few feet from us, coats glimmering in the sunlight. A blonde female wolf breaks off from the group and steps forward with a bow.

I share a look with Hunter. "Who's that?"

But it's Ash who rushes forward and wraps his arms around the female's neck. "Aunt B!" Tears well in his eyes. "Where've you been?"

She morphs into two legs and hugs him to her chest. "Oh, thank Luna!" She pulls back and looks him over. "Are you hurt?"

"No."

She squishes him again. "I came as soon as I could."

Hunter attempts to walk over but Lily leaps in his path with a snarl directed at the newcomers.

The woman straightens to her full height. "I know I'm not your favorite person right now, but please understand we came here to help the Tala pack." She holds up her hands when Lily doesn't back down. "If you don't believe me, call your brother and confirm that half of the Lobo pack is helping the Guardians right now. I'd be there too, but I broke off from the group to check on Ash." She places a palm to her bare chest. "Lily, I swear I'm not here to cause trouble. I needed to check on my best friend's pup."

What's the history between these two females?

A toned male wolf approaches the arguing women, his massive shoulder brushing against the blonde's waist. His eyes narrow on Lily, a silent warning that if any harm comes to the other woman, he will take it personally.

Lily nudges the boys with her snout, her eyes never leaving the male's as she puts more distance between the newcomers. She corrals us together, then urges us to shift into wolves. We follow her instructions as we continue to back away from the other shifters.

Lily snarls, her fangs bared. *"These children are under my care, and I do not trust your pack."* She nods towards the blonde. *"And the last time I saw her, she wasn't very nice to me or my friend."*

The red devil side-glances the blonde but nods. *"We will not follow you or your pups. You have my word."*

The blonde's human form glances between us, unaware of the promise her male friend just made on their behalf. When Lily herds us away, the blonde shifts to join us.

"Wait," she calls out.

"No," the red alpha booms, stopping the blonde's paw midair. *"The Tala pack needs our assistance at the sacred tree."*

Lily narrows her eyes once more, giving the other shifters her final warning before she gallops towards the setting sun.

But it's hard to look away from the visitors. Something is oddly familiar about the blonde's scent.

What pack is she from?

The red male meets my searching gaze, and his stance relaxes as he crouches in front of me. Then he taps his snout on my shoulder. *"Go to safety with your pack, pup."*

The statement hits me hard. *My pack.* I don't have a pack, a family, especially if the rest of the rebels die in battle. But I do as I'm commanded.

We swerve between the saplings and the tall, lush grasses of the valley. The day's events weighing on my heart. Green morphs into gray as we near the cliff's edge. We concentrate on the path until it becomes narrow and leads to a cavern. Two large beasts stand guard, accompanied by two seemingly human individuals. As we near, the wolves snarl a warning and energy zaps from the people next to them.

"It's okay," Lily coos to me. "Those are spellcasters and they're here to protect us, just as the Tala pack has done for them."

Another outburst of power tingles at my toes, calling out to its counterpart. I clamp it down as much as I can and avoid eye contact, because I have enough to worry about without proclaiming how dangerous I really am.

The cave is furnished with the bare necessities and simple furniture. Our ears twist as shouts echo from inside the darkness. Lily picks up the pace, her talons clicking across the stone floor. I glance towards the corner of the dwelling and spot a woman on a cot. She's the one making those ear-splintering sounds. At our approach, her screams devolve into sobs.

"Maya." Lily joins the team of women supporting the shifter as she cradles her newborn pup. "Congratulations."

"I wanted to have him in the hospital," she breathes as a welcome.

"You're doing great, dear," Celeste instructs from between Maya's legs.

"I've changed my mind." Carly swallows as she passes the doctor a towel. Her skin is an odd green color. "I don't want to be pregnant anymore."

I ignore the other shifter's response as my adrenaline drains and I can't even raise my head. I settle onto the cold stone floor, wrapping my tail over my muzzle to hide my tears. I'm not even sure why I'm crying. Is it sadness? Anger? Pain?

Ceramic bowls slide towards my cheek. I peek an eye open to see Ash offering me pieces of meat and water. When I meet his gaze, he settles at my side and sits with his legs crossed. He rubs my ears with his fingertips. I lean into his touch and drop my chin onto his lap. A fleece blanket warms my shoulders, then Hunter props himself against his self-proclaimed brother and strokes my paw.

As I release a wounded sigh, fur melts to skin. I snuggle closer to the brothers, wishing I could reverse time and recreate the events that transpired today. There's so much I would have said to my parents. I also would have insisted that we stay with the Tala pack for Lunamas instead of traveling home.

"Where is she?" a male roars from the entrance, and my whole body tenses at the rage-induced demand.

"Over here, son," Celeste calls out in response.

My neck snaps towards the noise as Sable pushes his way through. "Maya?"

His mate lifts her head. "We're fine, Sable."

His eyes scan her body, until his gaze falls on the bundle in her arms. "We?" Sable drops to his knees at her bedside. "Fuck, he's so tiny."

Maya laughs. "It's okay. He was born a little early, but he's breathing on his own and Celeste said he's healthy."

Everyone watches as she passes the pup to her husband but he backs away. "I'm dirty."

I cringe. He's not lying. He's covered in blood, dirt, and various bodily fluids.

"So is he," Maya insists. "He's a wolf. He can handle a little filth."

Sable accepts the newborn. His biceps flex as he protectively smothers his child with kisses.

My soul weeps at the lovely picture they're painting. *The perfect family*. Something I'll never have. A gust of a phantom breeze stirs their ankles and works its way up through their hair. They pause their celebratory moment and share a confused look.

Before they can speak their questions out loud, another familiar visitor hollers, "Lily? Ash? Hunter?" Then the beta stumbles into the room, out of breath.

"Jackson!" Lily rushes to his side. "You're bleeding."

"We'll be right back," Ash whispers to me before he and Hunter scramble to help Lily guide their father to a sitting position on the stone floor.

Celeste goes into physician mode again and assesses the blood oozing from several places on the man's arms and legs. "He needs stitches," she proclaims, before grasping Lily's palm. "But he'll be fine."

Lily buries her face into the male's neck and sobs. "I thought…"

"Shh." He strokes her dark hair. "I'm right here, Butterfly." He grabs his sons and hugs them with his free arm. "You won't get rid of me that easily."

Lily kisses his lips, almost like she's trying to prove him right. "Thank Luna." She wraps the group into another embrace.

"Jackson?" Maya calls from her cot.

Jackson's gaze flicks to hers. Shock racks his body before he pushes off the wall to walk towards the pup. The beta's hands shake as he runs a finger over the newborn's cheek. Then he squeezes Maya's shoulder. "Please tell me you're both okay?" Panic tinges every syllable. "I can't handle anymore loss today."

Celeste gently guides him away. "They're fine. But *you* need to sit back down, young man, and let me clean you up."

A female ruffles Ash's hair before she tucks a chair under Jackson and helps him sit. "You've done your part and have kept us safe, young warrior, and now it's our turn to take care of you."

He pats her wrist and leans against the headrest. "Thank you, Cynthia."

Celeste threads her needle, then starts locating Jackson's injuries. Silence envelops us again, except for the muffled grunts of pain when the doctor pushes the sharp tip through the beta's swollen skin. I admire the woman's tight pattern and wonder how long she's been healing shifters and if she also treats humans. Our anatomy is very similar to theirs—at least that's what Sylvia always told me. I rub a scar on my arm from when I fell out of a tree and a rock dug into my skin. Sylvia jumped in to save me that day.

"That should do for now. I'll be happier once we can get you to my office and I can properly clean and bandage you." The doctor pats Jackson's knee and stands. "I can give you a pain reliever if you want?"

"No," he pushes out, exhaustion weighing down on his shoulders. "I need to be clear-headed just in case."

"Jackson, where's mom and dad?" Maya asks from her cot.

My whole world darkens as I realize her mother is *Raven*. The woman I was tasked with protecting.

Jackson's lip trembles as he stares at his feet and shakes his head. And Maya sucks in a breath before Sable passes the newborn pup to his sister so he can comfort his mate.

"Oh no," Lily breathes out. "What happened, Jackson?"

He runs a hand through his girlfriend's hair as he gathers his thoughts. "I'm not sure. Raven called Frost and told him she needed help. So he grabbed a group, called the other packs, and took off like his tail was on fire. Since we're still in the doghouse for leaving without permission." He throws a thumb towards Sable. "We were told to stay back with the others." He swallows a lump in his throat. "But after they left the territory, a convoy of uniformed humans attacked the north quadrant." Jackson gestures to Sable again. "When he heard the vehicles approaching, he gave the warning call for the pack to evacuate, then asked Frost to return with the other warriors."

Maya's sobs echo around the cave, and Sable rubs her back before

Jackson continues.

"Frost had to make a tough call when he decided to fight by our sides, instead of rescuing his mate. And when he received the news that Raven didn't survive, he ran off the battlefield." Jackson scrubs his face with his hands. "I've never seen him like that." His eyes glaze over. "It reminded me of when I lost it after Ashley died."

Lily squeezes his thigh, pulling him from his haunting memories. "I'm sure Frost will return when he's ready. Just like you did."

They lock eyes and rest their foreheads together. "I hope so." Jackson sighs.

Maya dabs her face with a tissue. "I want to believe that too, but..." She bites her lip. "I felt the alpha's power transfer to me. It was a sudden burst, and I swear I felt mom's presence."

Sable runs his knuckle over her jawline, as if he can see her new abilities. "So did I."

Their words sink into the hearts of their packmates, and grief floods the safety of the cave like a tidal wave.

The alphas of the Tala pack are gone, and the new reign of Maya and Sable begins. One day, that same burden will fall on their newborn pup's shoulders. The great circle of life.

Then it hits me. Will *they* allow my pack to stay together? I scan the room. There're a few humans resting under the Tala's protection. One is even cradling the alpha's pup and kissing his chubby cheeks.

I rise off the stone floor on shaky limbs. I need to know what our future holds. With each step towards the alpha, it's harder to breathe. *What if they cast us out? Turn us over to the authorities?*

"What will happen to the rebel pack?" I whisper past my anxiety.

Maya ushers me closer to her. "You're Angelica's pup, right?"

"But she's gone." I push past my dry lips.

"What about Freddy?" Sable's lips curl into a snarl, which he drops when Maya smacks his chest.

"My parents were rescuing those trapped in the escape tunnels when the whole thing collapsed on them."

Sable jolts back as if he can't believe it. "Are you sure?"

"Sable!" Maya hisses. "You are being insensitive."

He shakes his head before kneeling at my filthy feet to assess my face. "I'm sorry for your loss. You don't deserve this."

"Neither did the other members of my family. So please, can the humans stay with our pack?" I beg.

Maya and Sable never lose eye contact as they communicate telepathically.

The female alpha nods before offering me a small smile. "Your family is welcome to join the Tala pack, and we'll rebuild our future one day at a time. All of us. Shifters and humans, side by side."

The burdensome weight of the unknown drops to my feet, and I lean on the cot for support.

The rebels may have lost the final battle, but we won the war on segregation. Now we'll live together with the humans *in* the light and out of the darkness.

Angel

Epilogue

Morning after morning, I dutifully assist the others as we continue our never-ending efforts to find our loved ones in the aftermath of an unforgiving war. A week trickles by and frustration continues to build and coat my cheeks.

"Angel, sweetie." Lauren settles beside me at the kitchen table.

"They found them, didn't they?"

Lauren looks to her brother, and he nods for her to continue. "Yes."

It's finally happened and all I want to do is run and cover my ears. I clench my fists to ground myself. "Tell me everything. I need to know."

Her hand rests on my shoulder, her thumb brushing my skin.

"They were crushed instantly by the weight of the cave-in, so they didn't suffer."

"What else?" I whisper. "Don't hold anything back."

Lauren shares a pained expression with Brad, who takes over. "The position of their bodies suggests that they died in each other's arms." He pauses to let everything sink in. "Angel." He encourages me to look at him. "They would want you to have this." He slides over a mud-covered ring.

The rest of their sentiments blur into the background as I rotate the dirty jewelry. This is the last thing I'll ever receive from Mom. No more hugs or kisses, not even an *I love you*. The light sparkles on a chip along the ring's surface. Its unique shape symbolizes Mom and Dad's relationship. Their love wasn't flawless, yet it broke through their dark pasts and shone brightly so our world could begin to rebuild.

Years later…

The cold touch of the gold band warms as I clutch the metal to my chest. Today's the day it all ends.

"We hereby find the plaintiff, Levi Ashford, guilty of all charges." The gavel slams into the wood, the sound echoing in the courtroom.

Great Aunt Debbie squeezes my hand and releases a breath. "Justice is finally served, and the General will pay for all those people he murdered."

"Do you think he'll get the death penalty?" Debbie's adoptive daughter, Sara, asks from beside her.

"If he doesn't, I'll be surprised. Especially with the new treaty's success hanging in the balance."

I snort my disgust. Why it took this long to go into effect is beyond me. Why did so many humans and shifters have to die before anything was done about it?

I lean back against the bench and watch as the guards escort the traitorous bastard away. His dark gaze scans the room, until it lands on me. I'm not sure what he's hoping to see when he holds my attention. Rage? Agony?

I lift my chin high and throw him my best *fuck you* glare. Let him rot behind bars while I sit pretty with my freedom. He chuckles and even has the audacity to wink before they drag him out of the room.

"The Guardians have promised to retaliate again if the treaty isn't obeyed," Sara adds, oblivious to my stare down with our enemy.

Yes, who could forget the Guardians? They saved our asses the day the government attacked the packs. They were just too late to protect my parents. I twirl Mom's ring between my fingers. I wish I could turn back time and stop her from running into those tunnels. I still have nightmares of it collapsing, of me digging for their bodies, and of when they pulled Sylvia from the wreckage. Another part of me still holds on to the hope that they made it out and are waiting for the right time to show up and whisk me away.

But the tick marks on the sacred tree marking their end and this ring say otherwise.

"I still can't believe the government reported that their attack was for the protection of the nation," Sara hisses. "And using the rebellion as an excuse, labeling it a terroristic threat is bullshit."

"Language, Sara," Debbie scolds before adding, "Well, with all the new officials replacing the corrupt ones, things are bound to get better soon." Debbie stands with the rest of the courtroom of onlookers. "Let's pray that peace is on the horizon."

I slide Mom's ring past my knuckle and follow everyone out into the crisp afternoon. As we pass a crowd of people, shifters congratulate us on the verdict and take a moment to embrace loved ones in celebration.

With true unending peace between humans and shifters comes stability and the conclusion of the rebel's reign. Making my parents selfless *heroes*. If only they could celebrate this triumph too.

I pause on the pavement and stare into the cloudless sky. I hope they know how many lives their rebellion touched. That their sacrifice will forever live on in the wolves of Cold Creek. And above all, that the rebel's revenge was achieved.

The wind strokes my cheek, and as it caresses my ear, a familiar voice whispers, "I love you, little one."

Want one more chapter?

Scan the QR code on the next page and join my newsletter to get Angelica's final chapter where she comes face to face with her creator.

About the Author

Brittany Putzer is constantly turning to books to escape her dull suburban existence. Most days, she can be found exploring new coffee houses and bookstores to pass the time. She craves caramel macchiatos, pumpkin spice goodies, and tall, dark, and fictional men (preferably in gray sweatpants). When she's writing, her scribblings are dictated by her character's persistent opinions and generous hearts (most of them anyway).

If she's not writing, she's soaring through the pages of other fictional worlds. Because of this, she's also a lady of the night court, a scribe with an alpha shadow daddy (she's afraid of heights so the other quadrant wasn't an option), and a mafia princess with a touch-her-and-die king. Additionally, Brittany loves the excitement of book conventions, both as a writer and a reader, where she loves to build everlasting friendships and eat tons of nachos and drink tons of margaritas.

Scan the QR code to chat with her on social media, review her books, get signed paperbacks, meet her at her next book signing, and join her exclusive newsletter for freebies and sneak peeks.

Thank You

Without you, amazing reader, I couldn't rally the motivation to pen my stories. You make my world a brighter place and I hope my tales offer you the same experience. Remember, you are unique. Loved. My hero.

Thank YOU!

Now adjust your cape (or wings) and continue to be a badass! I believe in you! You are capable of doing more than you know.

I also want to give a huge shout-out to my editor, Kat Pagan. She is my mighty word witch, and without her incredible techniques, this book wouldn't be as life-changing as it is.

Thank you, Frankie Page, for the incredible formatting on all my paperbacks. I hate all the technical stuff with manuscript layouts, but she makes it look so easy and beautiful.

Also, a super-sized thank you to all my beta readers: Jennifer, Heather, Alicia, Stephanie, and B.L. You guys are amazing! The fact that you took time out of your already crazy schedules to read and answer feedback blows me away! I couldn't have done it without you!

Additional Titles by the Author

Wolves of Cold Creek (18+, paranormal romance):

The Cold Creek packs are loyal—while bursting with mouthwatering, unclaimed shifters—all just waiting for their mates. Why not drop in and enjoy the picturesque views by day and scorching fires at night? Don't be shy. They don't bite… hard.

Suggested Reading Order:

Scarlett's Tail

Sky's Tail

Lily's Tail

Rebel's Revenge

Feathered Dreams, completed series (clean romance):

Join Ann and be swept into a world of swoon-worthy characters, glittering gowns, and unrelenting intrigue.

Ann is beginning to see how naïve she has been, though by no fault of her own. Farming side by side with her father, away from the drama of the outside world, is what she has always loved most. But now that she is at the Palace, she is forced to focus on other people and their daily struggles. In the midst of her personal growth, she starts to realize how cruel the world can be. Will she shy away and run back to the familiarity of her old life? Or can she share her unique sense of compassion and fierce loyalty to help those in need?

Feathered Dreams (Book 1)

Plucked (Book 2)

Molting (Book 3)

Split Feather (Book 4)

Final Flock (Book 5)

www.ingramcontent.com/pod-product-compliance
Lightning Source LLC
Chambersburg PA
CBHW071644260626
47170CB00001B/227